AFTERWAR

Also by GLORIA SKURZYNSKI

Devastation

AFTERWAR

The Revolt
The Choice

GLORIA SKURZYNSKI

Atheneum Books for Young Readers
NEW YORK   LONDON   TORONTO   SYDNEY

ATHENEUM BOOKS FOR YOUNG READERS

An imprint of Simon & Schuster Children's Publishing Division

1230 Avenue of the Americas, New York, New York 10020

ATHENEUM BOOKS FOR YOUNG READERS is a registered trademark

of Simon & Schuster, Inc.

For information about special discounts for bulk purchases, please contact Simon & Schuster Special Sales at 1-866-506-1949 or business@simonandschuster.com.

The Simon & Schuster Speakers Bureau can bring authors to your live event. For more information or to book an event, contact the Simon & Schuster Speakers Bureau at 1-866-248-3049 or visit our website at www.simonspeakers.com.

Book design by Sammy Yuen Jr.

The text for this book is set in Apollo MT.

Manufactured in the United States of America

First Atheneum Books for Young Readers paperback edition March 2011.

2 4 6 8 10 9 7 5 3 1

CIP data for this book is available from the Library of Congress.

ISBN 978-1-4424-1681-9 (bind-up paperback)

These titles were previously published individually.

The Revolt

For Tom Thliveris,
Stephanie Alm, Beau Benson,
and Alexandra Hesbrook,
also known as Corgan,
Sharla, Cyborg,
and Ananda

PROLOGUE

Time. It kept screwing him up, screwing up his whole life.
He needed more time to get what he wanted! Groaning, he
paced the room, then, grabbing an i-pen, he began to write
all the things that had happened.

YEAR 2001
THE FIRST TERRORIST ATTACKS

2012
THE FIRST PLAGUES

2012 TO 2035
ELEVEN NUCLEAR ACCIDENTS

2038
NUCLEAR WARS BEGIN

2038 TO 2058
WORLDWIDE CONTAMINATION; DEVASTATION COMPLETE.
DOMED CITIES BUILT TO PROTECT SURVIVORS

2066
CORGAN AND SHARLA ARE BORN IN THE WYOMING DOMED CITY.

2070
BRIG, THE GENIUS OF STRATEGY, IS BORN.

2080
VIRTUAL WAR FOUGHT. THE WESTERN HEMISPHERE
FEDERATION TEAM OF CORGAN, SHARLA, AND BRIG DEFEAT
THE EURASIAN ALLIANCE AND THE PAN PACIFIC COALITION
TEAMS TO WIN THE UNCONTAMINATED ISLES OF HIVA. CORGAN
AND SHARLA SPEND SIX MONTHS TOGETHER ON NUKU HIVA.

2081
BRIG DIES. SHARLA CLONES BRIGAND AND CYBORG IN HER
LABORATORY. SHE TAKES BABY CYBORG TO NUKU HIVA FOR
CORGAN TO RAISE. THE CLONE-TWINS ARE PROGRAMMED TO GROW
TWO YEARS OLDER EACH MONTH.

2081 (FOUR MONTHS LATER)
WHEN THE CLONE-TWINS ARE ABOUT EIGHT YEARS OLD, CYBORG
NEARLY DROWNS, BUT BRIGAND RESCUES HIM BY CUTTING OFF
CYBORG'S HAND THAT HAD BEEN TRAPPED BENEATH A BOULDER.

Light from the i-screen illuminated the gold braid on his sleeve as he bowed his head and held his hands over his eyes. Minutes passed before he raised his head and picked up the i-pen once again. Now he began to write more rapidly.

FEBRUARY 2082
CORGAN AND BRIGAND FLY FROM THE ISLAND OF NUKU HIVA TO THE WYOMING DOMED CITY WHERE THEY JOIN SHARLA AND CYBORG. CYBORG NOW HAS A POWERFUL, MAGNETIC ARTIFICIAL HAND. BRIGAND GOES INTO HIDING AND RECRUITS REBELS FOR THE WYO-DC REVOLT. CORGAN TRAINS VIRTUALLY WITH ANANDA, THE CHAMPION OF THE FLORIDA DOMED CITY, AND USES A SIMULATOR TO LEARN TO FLY THE HARRIER JET.

APRIL 2082
BRIGAND AND CYBORG BECOME THE SAME AGE AS CORGAN AND SHARLA—SIXTEEN. BRIGAND'S REVOLT BEGINS, AND HE TRIES TO KILL CORGAN. CORGAN ESCAPES IN THE HARRIER JET, FLIES IT TO THE FLOR-DC, AND CYBORG GOES WITH HIM—

Scowling, he stood up. Revenge. That's what he wanted. And he would get it. Soon enough.

ONE

The sky was clear, with only a few clouds sheared off at the top as though they'd been sliced by a machete.

"Are we there yet?" Cyborg asked.

Corgan didn't answer. How could he admit to Cyborg that he had no idea where they were, except somewhere in the sky? Cyborg, who'd left the security of the Wyoming domed city to flee with him, who'd caught the bullet that would have killed him, who'd betrayed his own clone-twin to save Corgan's life—he deserved more than a totally lost pilot.

Cyborg's voice crackled over the Harrier jet's communication system as he asked for the second time, "Are we there yet, Corgan?" And then after a pause, "You don't have a clue, do you?"

At ten thousand meters above ground level Corgan strained to see a landmark. Any kind of landmark. Mumbling into the communicator, he told Cyborg, "Look for something big and blue."

"Big? Blue?"

"Yeah. We need to find the Atlantic Ocean."

"The Atlan . . . !" From the second seat of the jet Cyborg leaned forward, as if that would make his voice boom louder through the headset. "You want me to look for a whole ocean? Be a little more specific, Corgan. Any particular part of the Atlantic Ocean?"

"You know what I mean. The part next to Florida." Corgan frowned, trying to think and fly the plane at the same time. Once, when he and Ananda had been training together in virtual reality—Corgan in the Wyoming domed city and Ananda in the Florida domed city—he'd asked her if there were any particular ruins around her. He knew that most of the domed cities, called DCs, had been built near the ruins of destroyed metropolises, so the Florida DC might be near one too. Ananda hadn't been certain—after all, the devastation had happened decades before either of them were born—but she'd thought maybe there'd once been a city close by called Carnival. Or something like that.

Corgan anxiously checked the fuel gauge. It showed one-eighth full, but could he trust that? The Harrier jet was forty years old, bolted together from whatever discarded parts the robotic mechanics could find. Only robots sorted through old junkyards for usable pieces, because most of the world outside the domes was too contaminated for humans to enter. During the devastation every known meter of Earth's surface had been scorched, leveled, laid barren, and poisoned by nuclear blasts, toxicity, plagues, and bioterrorism.

So the plane was old and Corgan was new to flying. This was his first actual flight, but he tried not to think about that because the fact was terrifying. The virtual simulator Corgan had trained on hadn't duplicated the feel of the Harrier in flight, the powerful forward thrust he felt beneath him now, the roar of the engine, the sense of air rushing around the wings, holding the craft aloft like powerful hands. All those dials and gauges at Corgan's fingertips demanded his immediate attention, because if he made a mistake, both he and Cyborg would die, with enough seconds before the crash that they'd know death was inevitable. Having control, being responsible for handling this roaring force, meant that all Corgan's senses had to wrap around the job of flying. He gripped the stick tighter to stop his hands from shaking.

Through the headset he heard a rattling. "I'm looking at this old map," Cyborg announced. "We're high enough that we ought to be able to make out the shape of Florida. I mean, it's got water all around it, right?"

"If you say so." Corgan dropped the jet five thousand meters to fly beneath the clouds, peering through the side window. "Ananda told me her DC is so close to the ocean she can look through the dome and see waves."

Twenty-three minutes and forty and a quarter seconds later they spotted the Florida DC, Corgan with a vast sense of relief. From the air it looked twice as large as the Wyo-DC they'd lived in, Corgan for the first fourteen years of his

life and Cyborg for the last several months. "There it is,"
he called out. Circling slowly, he tried to see the retractable
doors that should be visible in the top of the huge transparent dome—that is, if they'd been installed the way they
had been in the Wyoming dome. He'd need someone on the
ground to open those doors so he could lower the Harrier
in a vertical landing straight down onto the landing pad
inside. He wished he had radio contact to signal an opera-
tor inside the dome for guidance, because the retractable
doors seemed to be so cleverly hidden that he couldn't spot
them. But radio communication was a thing of the past.
The communication satellites had long since fallen out of
orbit and burned when they entered Earth's atmosphere.

If he flew around and around over the dome, someone
in there ought to notice him and open whatever entrance
doors there were. "Maybe they're afraid to let us in," he
told Cyborg. "Maybe they think we're an enemy."

"Well, they for sure won't be expecting a strange aircraft to pay a visit. I'm wondering . . . ," Cyborg mused.
"What if the Flor-DC doesn't own any aircraft? I mean,
almost all aircraft were destroyed in the nuclear wars.
We were lucky our Wyo-DC saved the two Harriers, even
though one of them's just a piece of junk that can't fly, but
if the Flor-DC never had any aircraft, they wouldn't have
any dome roof doors. What would be the point? Right?"

No entrance? The possibility chilled Corgan's insides.
If he couldn't bring down the Harrier through the roof
of the dome, how were they supposed to get inside, and
if they couldn't get inside, where else could they go? The
only other domed cities were thousands of miles away. He

circled once again, lower, trying to find a usable entrance somewhere . . . anywhere. At ground level maybe. Negative. Next he looked for a possible landing spot outside the dome. Nothing but ocean to the east of it; high, jagged, shell-like ruins of buildings to the south; and moldy swamps everywhere else around the periphery.

Right then the Harrier engine started to sputter. The craft bucked and bolted, almost pulling the controls out of Corgan's hands. "Fuel's almost gone!" he yelled.

Wait! Wait! This same situation had been thrown at him in the virtual simulator—if the plane runs out of fuel, what does the pilot do? *Think!* He knew that fixed-wing aircrafts need forward motion to avoid crashing, but the Harrier could change its engine thrust from horizontal to vertical, from forward motion to straight down. If there was even a little fuel left, maybe he could move the nozzles to vertical and shoot out blasts of hot air, cushioning a vertical landing into the ocean. Better that than a nosedive crash.

No go. The engine choked again. With the last drops of fuel he pulled up the nose of the aircraft and gunned her, and then the fuel was totally gone. "Eject! Eject!" he shouted, hoping Cyborg remembered where the eject handle was on his seat. Bracing himself, Corgan leaned back hard, with his head pushed against the headrest and his feet on the rudder pedals. That was the position the simulator said a pilot should take before ejecting. "Cyborg, let's go!" he yelled. Then he yanked the handle.

With a deafening explosion the canopy blew away. At the same instant the rockets beneath Corgan's seat fired, and he felt himself shoot like a cannonball out of the

Harrier. Still in the seat, he got hit so hard by wind it blew off his helmet. Had Cyborg made it out? Corgan couldn't see anything because he was tumbling head over heels in somersaults, with clouds above him and ground beneath him and then the opposite as he flipped upside down. He was still strapped into his seat.

A sudden tug told him his parachute had deployed, and at the same time the seat fell away. He tried to yell Cyborg's name, but the wind tore into his mouth like a fist, shoving his voice back into his throat. After what seemed an interminable time, although his time-splitting ability let him know it was only nine and nineteen hundredths seconds, the parachute filled with air and jerked him upright. Far beneath he saw the Harrier crash into the ocean, splashing water so high, Corgan instinctively jerked up his feet. Then the aircraft was gone, sinking into the Atlantic.

A strong wind began to blow Corgan away from the coastline and out to sea, but he managed to yank on the parachute risers to drift back toward shore. Why was he descending so fast? Did the parachute have a rip in it? And where was Cyborg? Down, down, down Corgan dropped, with the choppy whitecaps reaching up as if to grab him— and then he hit.

The water sheathed him like a shroud, swallowed him, blocked all sound. Dazed, not sure how deeply into the water he'd sunk, he gagged at the nauseating taste of rancid water on his lips. *Focus! Get rid of that parachute fast,* he told himself, *or get tangled like a fish in a net.* The murk stung his eyes, making it hard to see as he fumbled with the harness, somehow loosening it. Pushing himself upward to gasp air, he searched the sky for Cyborg's chute. Nothing. The sky was empty.

Maybe Cyborg had already fallen into the ocean. He could swim; he swam like a fish. Corgan had taught him how when Cyborg was so little he could barely toddle into the Pacific. But what if he'd been knocked unconscious when he ejected? Corgan dived deeper into the water and searched. Though the contamination burned his eyes, he forced himself to keep them open so he could peer through the murk for any sign of movement. His mind flashed back to the time on Nuku Hiva when he'd tried so hard to rescue Cyborg from the pool. But he'd been too late. Too late to save eight-year-old Cyborg from mutilation by his clone-twin.

Something floated slowly toward Corgan, half a dozen meters away. Cyborg? No, as it came closer Corgan could see what looked like an enormous, flopping mouth in an undulating body surrounded by mucuslike slime. A mutation—with a mouth big enough to swallow Corgan whole! Jerking in fright, he splashed into a fast U-turn, only to swim head-on into a long tentacle with a hook on the end. No! It wasn't a tentacle; it was some kind of enormous worm slithering out of a hole. Other creatures came wavering toward him, but it was hard to see because of the murk. He had to get away from them before they dragged him into their lairs and ate him.

He thrust up for air and again searched the surface for Cyborg. Waves still rippled outward from the impact of the crashed Harrier jet, but beyond that the waters seemed ordinary—no one would have guessed what horrifying mutations lurked underneath, spawned by the toxins in the water. The shore was nearby; it promised safety. But what about Cyborg? How could Corgan desert him and let him die in a poisoned ocean? Once again he dived underwater to search for Cyborg. Nothing! Then up for air and down again, over and over, forcing his eyes to stay open no matter how badly they stung so he could escape any grotesque terrors that lurked beneath him.

Like that one! Only this time the creature moving toward him looked less ugly, not as vile and slimy, not as fleshy. It appeared almost . . . mechanical. It had two rings of multiple fins whirling in opposite directions on its back end, or tail or whatever it was. The thing was cylinder shaped, narrower at the rear than at the front, and on its flat, round face was a . . . a . . . some kind of a beam of light! As it whirred closer it shot out a tentacle that whipped around Corgan's neck and began to pull him down. Struggling, kicking at it, knowing he would drown if he couldn't free himself, Corgan grasped his throat, trying to pull off the tight, whiplike coil that choked him, but no matter how hard he fought, he couldn't tear himself loose. Then something soft covered his head and clung, sucking at him, smothering him.

And suddenly—he could breathe! He was still underwater, but he was breathing. Whatever was stuck to his face was bringing him . . . not air, but something that smelled strange and not unpleasant. He felt himself being pulled along by the tentacle, or wire or whatever was around his neck, pulled gently as the creature moved ahead of him, churning the water with those whirring fins.

Corgan began to relax. The mask kept the stinging water out of his eyes, even as the strange creature pulled him deeper and deeper toward the ocean floor. He could feel his mind slipping into some kind of dream. *Must fight to stay alive, must find Cyborg.* But why not sleep? Sleep would feel good. In the softly churning water ahead of him he saw Ananda. "Is it you?" he tried to say, but the mask fused his lips, molding around them so he couldn't speak. It didn't matter. Even as he sank into unconsciousness he knew this was not a real Ananda, but a watery illusion, a dark-haired, dark-eyed Ananda surrounded by sea mutations. . . .

I'm dying, he thought, and it was no longer Ananda he saw. The face that swam before his eyes was Sharla's.

TWO

He must not be dead. Or maybe when a person died, he found himself in the place where he'd been happiest while he was alive, because there Corgan was, on Nuku Hiva. It was after he'd won the Virtual War and Sharla was with him for those six months and it was their fifteenth birthday and they waded into the surf holding hands. He knew he loved her even more than he loved the freedom of living in the real world, away from the virtual-reality Box that had imprisoned him for most of his life. Her wet dress clung to her and he wanted to look at her and keep looking because she was so beautiful, but he couldn't get his eyelids to open. They felt as heavy as rocks. He struggled to open his eyes, and then when he managed to, he quickly closed them again because Sharla had disappeared. No matter how tightly he squeezed them after that, it didn't matter. He couldn't bring Sharla back.

He rubbed his eyes to ease the pain, then paused, gingerly touching each lid with his fingertips. Once upon a time Corgan had possessed the most sensitive fingers of anyone in the Western Hemisphere Federation. He'd been genetically engineered that way, in order to be able to move the small digital-image soldiers in the Virtual War, move them without actually touching them, using only the electromagnetic energy that radiated from his fingertips.

He'd lost a great deal of that sensitivity during his year on Nuku Hiva, but enough of it remained that now, even though he was pretty much in a stupor, he could tell something was wrong with his eyelids. He touched them again, carefully, and then again before he realized—he had no eyelashes!

"Huh?" he muttered, still dazed. He ran his hands over his arms, his armpits, the rest of his body. Smooth as a newborn baby! Frantic, he grabbed the top of his head. All he could feel was skin. His hair was gone! His thick black hair, the one feature he was really proud of—gone! Forcing his eyes open in spite of the pain, he groaned, "What happened to me?"

He couldn't see anything because a bright light blinded him, but he clearly heard a voice, soft as dew dripping off a rose petal and yet oddly unemotional. It answered, "You were saved."

"Where am I?" he asked. "Did I die? Please turn off the light."

Immediately the lights dimmed and the voice continued, "You are in quarantine in the decontamination chamber. You have been irradiated."

Trying to raise himself on his elbows, Corgan searched
for the source of the voice. With the light less intense he
could see a little better. Above him a face with bland features appeared so close to him that he fell backward. "Who
are you?" he asked.

"I am Number Eleven from the Robotic Nurse Corps.
Because you are a patient in the decontamination chamber,
no human can attend to you. We robotic nurses carry out
instructions from human doctors, and we carry them out
perfectly, but you will never see the doctors because they
must be protected from contamination."

"What kind of doctors? What did they do to me?"

Eleven answered, "They made certain that all the toxins have been removed from your skin and from inside
you. It appeared that you swallowed a dangerous quan-
tity of ocean water."

As she—or he or it—spoke the face remained expressionless, although the lips moved. Corgan wanted to touch
Eleven to see whether the robot was an actual physical
entity occupying space or whether it was just a virtual
image, but when he reached out, Eleven slid backward so
fast Corgan's eyes couldn't follow the motion.

"No contact is allowed until you are fully decontaminated," Eleven said.

"When will that be?"

"That is unknown. It depends on your degree of contamination."

Corgan sat up on the edge of the flat table and dangled his hairless legs over the side. "Can I have something to wear?" he asked, ashamed of his glossy skin—he looked like an egg. "What happened to my clothes?"

"Vaporized." Eleven came a little nearer and said, "I will bring you sterile garments, but you must not get off this table." As the robotic nurse backed away Corgan saw that Eleven moved on wheels rather than feet.

When his head cleared, he looked around. He was in a room about the size of his virtual-reality Box back in the Wyoming domed city, but whereas his old VR Box had had images on all the walls and the floor and ceiling, this room was blindingly white. And then it hit him! He hadn't asked about Cyborg! "Eleven!" he called. "Eleven, come back!" But Eleven had vanished, apparently slipping through the walls, which made Corgan think it was a virtual image. But if that were true, why would the robot have wheels and a placid face rather than appear as a human?

Eleven did not come back, but a voice spoke from somewhere—or everywhere: it seemed to surround him.

Yes, Corgan, what is it you want?

"How do you know my name?"

Everyone in the Western Hemisphere Federation recognizes Corgan, champion of the Virtual War.

"Where is Cyborg?" he asked.

The wall to the left of Corgan lost its brilliant whiteness, slowly becoming transparent enough for Corgan to see through. There lay Cyborg, unmoving, on a table like the one Corgan was on. He appeared as hairless as Corgan, and the first thought that hit Corgan was that Cyborg had been so proud of that silly little mustache he'd grown, as red as the hair on the top of his head, and now both were gone—the mustache and the hair, too. Even worse, Cyborg's artificial hand seemed to be missing. His right arm ended at the wrist.

"Is he dead?" Corgan whispered.

No. He is alive. But his progress has been slower than yours. Sounding almost conversational, the voice said, *You may not know this, Corgan, but redheads have more sensitive skin. Your skin is darker, so neither the contamination nor the irradiation affected you as much as it did Cyborg. He also sustained more damage in the crash, hitting the water with a greater impact than you did.*

"How do you know that?" Corgan asked. "Did you see us eject? And who are you, anyway? You're not Eleven."

We are irradiation specialists. Our lookout team watched your plane crash and then sent out the Hydrobots to rescue you. You were brought in through the subsurface entrance— our only entrance, actually. Few people ever come into this domed city, and no one ever leaves.

No one left? Corgan considered that, then decided he had no other place to go anyway. The good news was that Cyborg was alive.

"Uh, one last question," Corgan said. "Will my hair grow back?"

Laughter seemed to come from all four walls—not just the laughter of the one who had been speaking to him, but laughter from other voices as well. People or robots or who knew what must be peering at him like at a bug under a microscope. Corgan became embarrassingly aware of his nakedness.

Yes, Corgan, your hair will grow back. We had to remove all of it to irradiate your skin against contaminants that might have caused you to mutate. You're safe now, and you'll have visible hair in a week or two.

"Then, why can't I get out of here? I mean, if I'm safe now."

The quarantine period is two weeks. That's the rule.

"Well, could you at least bring me some clothes?" he asked, and again the walls seemed to vibrate with laughter, yet within minutes Eleven entered the room carrying a dark blue LiteSuit. As the robot came near enough to hand it to him Corgan reached out and touched Eleven. The robot was solid, not virtual, and was made of some sort of metal or hard-surfaced composite.

With no display of emotion Eleven said, "Now see what you've done? According to the rules, I must now be sterilized with steam for one whole hour, which means that I am no longer functional until the sterilization is complete. You will be without nursing care during that hour."

"I'm sorry!" Corgan said, getting off the table to slip into the LiteSuit. "I was just curious. What am I supposed to do for the next hour? Can you let me see the city—virtually?"

No answer. As Eleven's wheels whirred Corgan watched it exit through a door he hadn't noticed earlier. He tried to run to catch the door before it closed, but his knees gave way and he fell. He might be alive, but he certainly wasn't anywhere near his normal strength. His head felt full of crawling insects. Through the buzzing he thought he heard the words *"good chance now . . . take mental . . . ,"* but they sounded so muted and distorted that he might have imagined them.

Trying to preserve his dignity by walking without stumbling—after all, who knew who was observing him—he made his way back to the flat, narrow table. As he reached it he heard the polite request, *Corgan, would you please lie down?*

"Why?"

It is medical procedure. We need your personal history for our records.

"Do I really need to lie down? It's kind of hard for me to get up and down. Can't I just sit?"

Lie down, Corgan! This time it was an order, loud and clear. *Stretch out flat, arms straight against your sides, palms down. That's the way. Good! Do not move.*

He felt too tired to argue, and there was nothing else to do or look at in this bare room. "You want my history, so here it is. My name is Corgan, I'll be sixteen tomorrow, or maybe in a couple of days . . . what day is it today? I'm not sure. Anyway, I was genetically engineered, and I was raised in a virtual-reality Box by Mendor, a computer program—"

Stop, Corgan. You don't have to say anything. Just remain completely still on the table.

Softly at first, he heard a gentle noise that turned into the crash of surf hitting shore, and he was back on Nuku Hiva. Alone. Where was Sharla? It was Seabrig running toward him out of the waves, Seabrig when he still had his real hand, before everyone called him Cyborg. "Hey, come here, little buddy," he called out to Seabrig. "Get your clothes on before the sun turns you into a lobster."

Suddenly time reversed itself, like a virtual simulation going backward. He saw another redheaded boy, but it wasn't Seabrig, it was Brig, the mutant. Corgan became fourteen again. Sharla, Brig, and Corgan were fighting the Virtual War. Brutal! Blood everywhere. Civilians blown to pieces, babies screaming, virtual soldiers dying when Corgan touched them. Poor little Brig, brilliant but weak, visibly withering under the strain of the daylong war. That's why Brig died. But no, not during the war . . . Brig didn't die till later. Time pushed forward now, so fast Corgan felt dizzy.

Sharla again. Sharla, who cloned Brig—she made two clones, but the Supreme Council wanted only one. Kill the other one! Sharla wouldn't do it. She kept one baby clone, Brigand, and brought the other, Seabrig, to Nuku Hiva for Corgan to raise. "Who, me?" Corgan had cried; "I can't take care of a baby." But Seabrig grew up fast, programmed to age two years every month. In four months both clones turned eight years old. Seabrig—pesty, funny, a nuisance, but he loved Corgan. Then Sharla brought the clone-twin Brigand to Nuku Hiva. And Brigand hated Corgan. Right from their first meeting Brigand hated him.

Corgan thrashed on the table and clutched his head to halt the memories because he knew what was coming.

No, Corgan, put your hands down, the voice from everywhere commanded him. *Do it, Corgan, or we'll have to strap you to the table. If you cooperate, this will be over soon.*

"Stop it now! Please stop!" Corgan cried, but he couldn't fight them. He felt his arms grow rigid and straighten themselves against his sides as the pictures and sounds began to churn again inside his brain:

Brigand pushing Seabrig down the waterfall, causing the rockslide. Seabrig caught in the bottom of the pool, Corgan diving over and over until his lungs almost burst trying to rescue Seabrig, but then it was the clone-twin Brigand who made the rescue by cutting off Seabrig's hand. Eight-year-old Brigand crying out, "I had to do it! He was trapped under a rock! If I hadn't cut off his hand, he would have drowned!"

"Liar! Liar!" Corgan screamed inside his head. "You didn't have to do it. I could have saved him! All my fault . . ."

Then the voices from the white walls spoke sharply, *He's becoming agitated. We should conclude the procedure before he spasms.*

Just a little longer, another voice urged. *We need to learn what happened next.*

All right. Turn it back on. But if he starts trembling too violently, turn it off.

He was in the rain forest on Nuku Hiva, where the wild boar rushed at him, attacking, its yellow eyes filled with malice. Corgan drove the spear deep into it, thrusting farther and farther until the boar's red blood spurted all over him. Brigand, twelve years old now, dropped down from the tree, and in the heat of murderous passion Corgan almost killed him, too, with the spear. Almost, but couldn't do it.

Should have. Should have killed him. Because back

in the Wyoming DC, Brigand grew older and tried to kill Corgan. But Sharla—Sharla! When Corgan fled for his life, Sharla stayed with Brigand! "Why didn't you come with me, Sharla? Why?"

That's it. Turn it off. He's getting too emotional and he's still weak.

Agreed. Shut it down. We've seen enough.

Everything turned white then. Soft, clean, white, and blessedly quiet. Exhausted, Corgan slept.

THREE

Corgan heard a soft whiff of air and, very slowly, the door began to open. It couldn't be Eleven returning, because the hour wasn't up—only thirty-nine minutes and forty and three hundredths seconds had passed since Eleven's exit.

A man came in, apparently human, not robotic, shuffling as he moved forward. Corgan stared. This man was old, the oldest human being Corgan had ever seen. The skin beneath his eyes hung down in puffy little bags, and his cheeks were sunken, not just in creases, but in deep grooves. The folds of skin beneath his chin reminded Corgan of an iguana he'd once caught on Nuku Hiva: sagging, wrinkled, spotty. With each step the wisps of thin white hair standing upright on the old man's scalp wavered in the tiny air current stirred by his forward motion.

"Greetings," the man said in a voice stronger than Corgan expected.

"Hello," Corgan answered. "Who are you?"

"The name is Thebos. I used to have two names, a first and a last, but in this new way of doing things people use only one name. Back in the old days my last name was Thebos and my first name was . . . was . . ." He scratched the top of his nearly bald head and squinted in concentration. "I don't actually remember. It might have been Paul . . . or Patrick . . . or Peter . . . mmm, I don't know. It did begin with a *P*, I believe."

Was that what happened when people got really old? Corgan wondered. Their brains failed so much they couldn't even remember their own name?

Thebos went on, "I'm ninety-one, considered too ancient to do any real work, but everyone in this domed city is supposed to have a job if they want to eat, so I was put here as a greeter. Of course, that means I'm not supposed to leave the medical center, because I might carry sickness into the city—so They say, but I think They just want to keep me out of the way." He chuckled—it sounded like a bird's squawk. "They keep hoping I'll catch a disease in here that will kill me, so They won't have to keep feeding me, but I fool Them. I stay alive."

Corgan knew who "They" were. The Supreme Councils in the domed cities of the Western Hemisphere were always referred to as They, with the word stretched out a little longer than the ordinary *they* to show its importance.

Thebos rocked backward and forward, catching one end of the table to keep his balance. "Mind if I visit with you," he asked, "so They can see that I'm working?"

When Corgan nodded, two chairs unfolded from the table, swinging around to face each other. Thebos sat on one and gestured for Corgan to take the other. "Now," he began, "you start first. Tell me who you are."

"I'm Corgan."

Thebos lowered his chin and touched his nose with his forefinger as though concentrating. Looking up, he asked, "Is that name supposed to mean something to me?"

"Corgan! I'm the champion of the Western Hemisphere Federation, or at least I was. I won the Virtual War in 2080. Well, not all by myself—I had help from Sharla and Brig. Brig's dead now, but he was cloned, and one of the two clones is Cyborg, lying in the next room. He's unconscious. Maybe you can tell me—what happened to Cyborg's hand?"

"Oh, yes!" Thebos exclaimed. "The fellow in the next room. I stopped by to greet him, but he wasn't very responsive. His hand? It looked perfectly fine, although I noticed he had only one of them. How did that happen?"

Corgan willed himself to stay patient. This muddled old man might be his only source of information. "Cyborg was drowning—well, his name wasn't Cyborg back then . . . anyway, his clone-twin, Brigand, said Cyborg got caught under a rock at the bottom of the pool and the only way to free him was to cut off the hand, but I never believed that. I think Brigand cut off the hand because he wanted to be the dominant clone. Brigand has this insane idea that he's going to rule the whole Western Hemis . . ." Why was Corgan rambling like this? He sounded as rattlebrained as the old man. "What I'd really like to find out is, what happened to Cyborg's artificial hand? He had it on when we ditched the aircraft, so where is it? Did it get lost in the ocean?" And if it did, Corgan silently wondered, could they build him another one here in this Florida DC? Or maybe the real question was, would they?

"Mmmm, that's all very interesting," Thebos murmured. "I will try to discover what has become of the artificial hand. I'm very curious to see it, to find out how it's engineered. Scientific curiosity, you know."

"You're a scientist?"

"Oh my my yes," he declared, bobbing his head up and down for emphasis. "In my day, before the devastation, I was considered quite brilliant in the field of aeronautical propulsion. A natural genius, because in those days we didn't have all that genetic engineering and genetic enhancement and genetic muckety-muck. I had two intelligent parents, so I inherited my genius biologically, as nature intended."

Thebos rose to his feet, straightening one section of himself at a time—first knees, then hips, back, shoulders—until all of him stood upright, wavering, again clutching the edge of the table for balance. "And so, I will attempt to find information about your friend's artificial hand. You and I will meet again . . . uh . . . what did you say your name is? Corgan? Ah, yes."

Thebos moved so slowly as he shuffled toward the door that Corgan considered hurrying behind him to grab the door before it could close, maybe escaping that way to get into Cyborg's room. But Thebos was so tottery, Corgan might knock him over. Better to wait and see what information Thebos could bring him. The door had almost closed when Thebos turned back to say, "Corgan, why do you believe that Brigand mutilated Cyborg on purpose? Do you feel guilty? I mean, you didn't protect Cyborg because you wanted to be alone with Sharla, and you thought she was paying too much attention to Brigand. So you left those two eight-year-old clone-twins all alone in a dangerous place. Maybe you feel responsible for the mutilation and you've transferred the guilt into hatred of Brigand."

"Wait a minute!" Corgan cried out. "How do you know all that? I never told you any of it."

"Mmmm, I may have heard it somewhere," Thebos murmured as the door closed behind him with a soft whiff.

"Corgan? Are you awake?"

It was only a whisper, but he came instantly alert. He looked up to see Ananda. She bent over him just as Nurse Eleven had, but while Eleven's face had been vacuous, Ananda's dark eyes showed real concern.

"Yes, I'm awake. Are you real, Ananda?" He already knew the answer. She was a virtual-reality image, just as she'd been so many times when they trained together virtually, he in the Wyo-DC and she in the Flor-DC. Even on the day she kissed him. He could reach up now to touch her cheek, but the touch would carry no emotion, though she would feel it slightly. Virtual touch always got diminished to a fraction of the tactile pressure at its origin.

"What happened? How did you get here?" she asked.

He swung his legs over the side of the bed and gestured for the seats to unfold. Although Ananda was a virtual image, she could sit next to him in the virtual environment—at least, it would appear that way. "An awful lot happened," he told her. "Brigand pulled together a small army of rebels and overthrew our Supreme Council. He might have killed Them, for all I know. Then he came after me, to try to kill me. Sharla and Cyborg got me out of the city."

Ananda's breath caught. "Wow! That's awful! How did you escape?"

He didn't want to answer that. It hurt too much to remember that scene in the tunnel, where he'd begged Sharla to come with him even though he knew it was no use. He'd kept on pleading like a fool while she made it perfectly clear she wanted to stay with Brigand. But why? Why would Sharla choose that vicious assassin, who might already have murdered the Wyo Supreme Council?

He stammered a little as he explained, "Sharla . . . um . . . distracted . . . Brigand, and while she did that, Cyborg led me through the tunnels to the hangar. Then we both ran like crazy to the Harrier jet, and I flew it here."

"Oh, I'm so glad you learned to fly it," Ananda cried, then sighed deeply. "It makes me ashamed to remember how I complained about all those hours you spent practicing the Harrier simulator when I wanted you to be with me virtually, training me. And it turned out to save your life. But what about Sharla? Didn't she try to escape too?"

Evasively he answered, "There was no way she could

come. The Harrier had only two seats because it was built as a trainer—one seat for the pilot and a seat behind that for the student. It was just me and Cyborg, with no room for Sharla." Why admit to Ananda that if Sharla had agreed to come, Cyborg would willingly have stayed behind? Cyborg had nothing to fear from his clone-twin. Although wildly different from each other in everything but looks, the clones possessed such a close psychic connection that neither one would ever harm the other.

Ananda sighed again. "Those times when you and I trained together, I dreamed that one day we'd be in the same place, in the same space so I could really touch you. And now you're here and we're still virtual images to each other. It's not fair!"

"I agree. This is supposed to be a two-week quarantine, and I've served only one day of it, so I figure it'll take me another one million, one hundred twenty-three thousand, and ninety-four seconds to get out of this cell."

Ananda laughed. "Quit showing off. I can do time calculations too, you know, but I don't go around bragging about it."

"I'm not bragging." Suddenly he wondered what Ananda must think of him—completely bald! No eyebrows even; his face was as bare as a baby's backside. Self-consciously he rubbed his hand over his scalp and muttered, "You didn't say anything about the way I look."

"What? You look the same as you always do."

"My hair . . ."

"What about your hair? It looks fine."

So someone had mercifully altered his virtual image! He

mentally thanked whoever did it, whoever had found his computer-generated likeness from the old files and posted it. He'd have been humiliated if Ananda had seen the way he really looked now.

It made him wonder how real her image was. Did she actually have on that pale yellow LiteSuit that contrasted so dramatically with her dark hair, with her skin the color of tea laced with milk? Was she as tall as she seemed? Even though they'd spent hours training together virtually, her appearance could have been altered or even distorted. Then as well as now.

Impulsively he asked her, "Could you do something for me? I've been trying to find out how Cyborg is coming along and what happened to his artificial hand, but I can't get any information. I asked Thebos if he'd check it out—"

"Oh, Thebos." Ananda waved her hand dismissively. "He's just a strange old man. He tells everyone he's a genius, but nobody pays much attention to him. I'll find out for you. I can ask the Supreme Council—I visit Them anytime I want to. I have privileges."

Yes, Corgan thought, he'd had privileges too, back in the Wyo-DC, when he was being trained to fight the first Virtual War. And now if the Virtual War was to be refought, Ananda would become the defending champion of the Western Hemisphere Federation, replacing Corgan.

"One more thing, Ananda," he said. "Could you . . . maybe . . . find out right now? I've been really worried about Cyborg. He needs that artificial hand. If it fell in the ocean—"

"If it did, the Hydrobot Corps will find it. They're

magnetic. They scour the ocean bottom for anything salvageable that we can use."

"I guess that included me. They salvaged me. And Cyborg."

"I am so glad about that!" Her virtual image faded just a bit and then brightened again. "I'm getting a signal—time for my training session. Once you get out of here, Corgan, we can train together. I mean—really together. Bye." And she was gone.

Really together? How different it would seem to share the same physical space with Ananda once he got out of Decontamination. She'd never made a secret of her feelings for him, so why couldn't he feel more for her? She was good at games, a superb athlete, and eager to be with him—what more could he want?

But he knew what he wanted. Sharla. And he couldn't have her.

So deal with it, he told himself.

FOUR

There were no doors to open or close in virtual reality. Ananda's image had vanished as though someone had thrown a switch, leaving no trace, no aura, no afterglow, no scent. Yet eighty-nine seconds after she disappeared, the real door opened and Thebos shuffled in, asking, "Had a nice little visit with Ananda, did you?"

"How did you know that?" Living in this room was like being in a specimen jar, Corgan realized.

Without answering, Thebos settled himself in the seat Ananda had just vacated, but unlike the virtual Ananda, Thebos had volume and mass, so the seat creaked a little. "You asked me to find out about Cyborg's titanium hand," he began, "and find out I did. I removed it from the sterilization chamber and dismantled it."

"You what?"

Thebos cocked his head. "You have a limited vocabulary, don't you, Corgan? *Dismantled* means that I took it apart because I saw that it had an inferior engineering design. I will improve it and then reassemble the hand."

All sorts of alarms went off inside Corgan's head. That weird old man had taken apart Cyborg's hand! He'd probably screw it up so it would never work again. What would Cyborg do then?

"You're very fond of Cyborg, I can tell," Thebos stated, "even though you hate his clone-twin. So you'll be happy to know that Cyborg is conscious now. But not too healthy. Three of his ribs are broken and his liver is lacerated. They'll repair it using a laparoscopic procedure." Laughing a little, Thebos said, "Laparoscopy for a lacerated liver. How alliterative!"

What the devil did that mean? Couldn't this old guy speak in plain English?

Seeing Corgan's consternation, Thebos told him, "They'll insert a thin tube through his abdomen and sew up the tear. He'll get well, but it will take some time."

Corgan jumped off the table, then stumbled. He needed to remember that his strength had not yet completely returned. The last thing he wanted was to fall flat on his face and break a bone and have to spend even more time in this confinement. "Can I see him?" he asked.

"May, may, may. You should have used *may* instead of *can*. Follow me."

The door that Corgan had so much wanted to go through now opened automatically. As he followed Thebos into a hallway Corgan noticed that the decontamination chamber occupied very little space. Cyborg's room was a duplicate of Corgan's: the same white walls, the same narrow bed, the same lack of furnishings.

And there was Cyborg, looking even paler and weaker than he had through the transparent wall. Corgan murmured, "Hey, Cyborg, we both made it, didn't we?"

Smiling up at him, Cyborg answered, "I think you're in better shape than I am, although both of us look like we got skinned. Have you seen my hand?"

That was the question Corgan didn't want to answer. He stalled for a moment, then said, "I haven't actually seen it. But it wasn't lost in the ocean, so that's good news. Thebos has it and he's going to fix it for you."

The ruse didn't work—Cyborg definitely looked alarmed. "Is that right? Uh . . . Thebos, I didn't know you could fix mechanical hands."

"I can fix anything," Thebos declared. "I am a scientist supreme and an engineer extraordinaire."

"What kind of engineer is that?" Corgan asked.

Thebos laughed in that cackle that sounded like a saw cutting steel. "Oh, Corgan, my boy, if I had a year or so, I could improve your vocabulary a hundredfold, not to mention your brain. Now, I'll leave you two to your little chat—"

The voice came from wherever, the voice of the irradiation specialists. *We've been waiting to ask Cyborg some questions.*

Cyborg tried to sit up, but when he winced in pain and fell back, Corgan raised a fist at the unseen voices in the walls and threatened, "You better not whack his brain like you did mine. He's way too weak."

Corgan, we're the trained medical personnel. You don't have to tell us how to do our job. So seal your mouth.

"Yes, sir. Sirs. Whoever," Corgan muttered. "Just don't hurt him."

We need to know Cyborg's approximate age, since we aren't mathematically certain how to calculate this rapid maturing process you talked about.

"I didn't talk about it," Corgan told them. "You siphoned it out of my head."

Corgan! Quiet!

Trying to prevent trouble, Cyborg broke in, "Sixteen! I think I'm about sixteen now. Same as Corgan. Only I got to sixteen a lot faster than he did. It took me only eight months from the day I was born."

Fine. That's all for now. There may be other questions as we assess your condition.

Corgan detected a barely audible click. Apparently the irradiologists, or whoever they were, had finished with them, but that didn't mean he and Cyborg would have any privacy. Who knew how many people and machines were observing them through the walls or ceiling? It was bad enough to be almost a prisoner, but being secretly peered at and listened to was worse.

He took Cyborg's hand, but gently because Cyborg looked so frail. "At least we survived," he said.

"Yeah. But look at us." Cyborg began to laugh, then

clutched his ribs tightly, as though laughing hurt too much. "We're as hairless as a couple of fish."

"They said it would grow back."

"Well, it better. I don't want to go through the rest of my life looking like an eel." At that both of them grew silent. Cyborg's life expectancy was grim. Two years from now he'd be the equivalent of sixty-four; a year later he'd be almost as old as Thebos; and a year after that, or sooner, he'd be dead of old age. If he'd stayed in the Wyoming domed city, Sharla might have found an antidote for the rapid aging, since she'd cloned him in the first place, but here—would anybody care?

It was then that Ananda appeared again, this time in Cyborg's cell. "Stop!" Cyborg cried. "Close your eyes! I'm naked."

The virtual Ananda looked startled, while Corgan burst out laughing. "Not to her, you're not," he said. "Ask her. Is Cyborg naked, Ananda?"

"Only where . . . where his right hand should be. Is that what he means?" she asked, hesitating. "So you're Cyborg! I thought I should come and say hello and welcome you to our Flor-DC."

"She sees you with clothes on," Corgan whispered, and then said aloud, "Cyborg, I'd like you to meet Ananda, future warrior of the Western Hemisphere Federation, if the Virtual War is ever refought. You should see how good she is at the high jump. When we trained together virtually, she could run for an hour and hardly break a sweat."

"Hello, Ananda. Corgan's told me about you," Cyborg

said. "He talked a lot about your amazing physical abilities, but he didn't mention how beautiful you are."

"Th-thank you," she stammered, reaching up to touch her cheek as though she could feel the blush that rose there. This time she wore a shimmering green LiteSuit, a perfect complement to her tawny complexion. She looked so vibrant that by contrast Cyborg appeared even more sick and pale.

"I like your sun tan," he told Ananda. "I guess that's from living here in Florida, where the sun shines all year long."

"That's only part of it," she answered. "My skin color is inherited. Two of my great-grandparents were from India. My name—Ananda—is Sanskrit for *bliss*, the harmony between mind, body, and spirit."

"A perfect name for you. So you're part Indian," Cyborg said, smiling at her. "That's kind of nice."

"Thanks. I think so." She added, "Another pair of my great-grandparents were American Indians from a tribe called Lakota. So I have Indian and Indian in my ancestry— but two different kinds. Plus some paleface ancestors too."

"How do you know all that?" Corgan asked. "Weren't you genetically engineered? What you're saying sounds like the natural selection Thebos was talking about— biological reproduction."

"I was genetically enhanced. That's different, but the results are the same. I'm supposed to be the most successful example of genetic enhancement ever created, at least in the Florida DC," she said, sounding modest in spite of the words.

"Do you mean you have biological parents?" Cyborg asked. "A real mother and father?"

Ananda looked away, looked down at the spotless white floor, then answered quietly, "Had. They're dead. They died when I was two. They were standing too close when one of the huge scrap-melting vats exploded. It killed them and six other people." With a smile that seemed a little too bright, she said, "I don't miss them because I don't remember them. The Supreme Council raised me, and They spoil me like crazy. Speaking of Them, I need to go to practice now. They like me to stay on schedule." Before she vanished, she said, "Tomorrow I'll come to see you again, Cyborg. I mean, both you and Corgan. Well, bye then!"

And the virtual Ananda disappeared.

"Corgan," Cyborg told him, "you don't know anything about talking to girls. You're supposed to say nice things to them about how they look, not tell them they're great because they don't sweat too much when they run. No wonder Sharla didn't—"

"Didn't what?" Corgan demanded. "Sharla didn't what?"

"Never mind. Forget what I said."

They heard the telltale whiff of sound that indicated the door was opening, and Nurse Eleven whirred into the room. "Visiting hours are over," Eleven said in that mild voice that sounded neither male nor female, but somewhere between. "Return to your chamber, Corgan. You're tiring Cyborg."

"But I hardly got to talk to him! What if I touch you again, Eleven, and you have to go get sterilized? Then I can stay here as long as I like."

An electric arc crossed the space between Eleven and Corgan, stinging him right in the middle of his forehead. "Ow!" he yelled, and rubbed the spot as Eleven stated in a dry voice, "One arc will not affect your hair growth. Two arcs will, leaving you bald forever."

"I'm going! I'm going!" Corgan cried.

The next day dragged as Corgan counted the seconds one by one, wanting someone to open his door to let him out, wanting to get back to Cyborg's room to make him finish what he'd started to say about Sharla. But when he finally got there, Ananda had already arrived—virtually—so he couldn't ask the questions he was burning to ask. Instead he said, "Yesterday was my birthday. I'm sixteen now."

Cyborg told him, "Happy birthday to the guy who knows exactly how old he is from a guy who's never sure."

"What does that mean?" Ananda asked.

"Doesn't she know?" Cyborg asked Corgan, who answered, "Maybe not. Tell her."

Still lying on his table, Cyborg locked his hands behind his head and said, "There's no way to be mathematically certain about my age. I'm supposed to grow two years older every month, but it's not an exact calculation. It would be nice if I could say, 'Hey, today's my birthday,' but I can't tell for sure, although I can guess it pretty closely. I figure that by the time I've finished these two weeks in Decontamination, I should be about seventeen."

"So . . . ," Ananda began, hesitating a little, "if I'm only fourteen, and you'll be seventeen, do you think that's too much age difference between a guy and a girl?" Once again she blushed, then quickly said, "Oh, forget it. I need to leave now, but I'm going to bring a surprise tomorrow, Cyborg. For both you and Corgan."

"The best surprise I could ask for is to get out of here," Corgan mumbled.

Cyborg threw Corgan a disapproving look, then told Ananda, "Don't pay any attention to that slug over there. He has no manners. Corgan may be a patient, but he doesn't know the meaning of patience. That's really nice of you, Ananda, to bring us a surprise, and I appreciate your coming to visit me."

"Tomorrow, then," Ananda said, and disappeared. One thing about virtual reality, when an encounter was over, it ended fast.

"So, about Sharla," Corgan began, but Cyborg said, "I told you to forget it. Don't bring it up again or I'll tell Eleven to zap you with the arc gun. Go away. I'm tired and I hurt. If I could get up, I'd kick you out of my room right about now."

Corgan tried not to take offense. Cyborg was usually so good natured, it just wasn't like him to act hostile. Must have been that talk about birthdays, Corgan guessed, and then he felt stupid because he'd started it all.

"Sorry. I shouldn't have said that," Cyborg muttered. He rubbed his right arm, the arm that ended so abruptly at the wrist. Only on rare occasions had Corgan seen that arm bare of the artificial hand. He marveled at how cleanly the real hand had been sliced off, especially since Brigand had been only eight years old when he made the amputation, using Corgan's machete. Corgan never could figure out how Brigand had found the strength to carve such a clean cut at the bottom of the pool, where water resistance would have slowed his motion.

That was right after the clone-twins had discovered the body of the cannibal chief. Brigand claimed he'd become filled with the power of the dead chieftain, but if Brigand had, why hadn't Cyborg? They'd been together when they found the tomb.

What would it be like to age the way Cyborg did, growing two years older every month, knowing that in three more years you'd be as old and doddery as Thebos? That had to be hard to bear. And maybe, Corgan thought, that was why the clone-twin Brigand acted so warlike, always boasting that he'd one day rule the world. His day of world domination, if it ever happened, would need to arrive pretty fast, sometime within the next thirty-six months, because after that there'd be no more days or months or years for him to conquer anything. Maybe that explained Brigand's craving, his rage, his fierce, fire-breathing conviction that had attracted so many followers in the Wyo-DC. Brigand had turned violent, but Cyborg had remained as good natured as he'd always been.

"Don't be sorry," Corgan told him now. "My fault. I shouldn't have stayed so long when you're not feeling great. I'll see you tomorrow." Worried, he went back to his room, or as he called it, his jail cell. Cyborg was his only male friend. Corgan's life had been so limited, so controlled, that he could count all his friends on three fingers—Cyborg, Sharla, and Ananda.

He began to imagine what Ananda's surprise might

be the next day. Food? The meals had been flavorless, so a piece of real fruit would be welcome, and Florida had all that sunshine coming through the dome to grow fruit, right? Or maybe she'd bring a new virtual game. He'd welcome a challenge, welcome the chance to beat Ananda at something. She was good, that was certain. When they'd trained together, she'd always surprised him with her quickness, her agility, and her strength. Oh yeah, and her looks.

The night lasted too long. After he'd counted off the appropriate number of seconds, letting them whir inside his head, the following morning arrived and so did virtual Ananda, in Cyborg's room, just as Corgan got there. "Here's the surprise. This is Demi," Ananda announced. "She's my darling dog. Isn't she beautiful?"

Corgan felt a stab of disappointment. A virtual pet? Wasn't Ananda a little old for that? When Corgan was a little boy, he'd loved his virtual pets—they were engineered to be warm and cuddly, if that's what he wanted, or fun and playful, depending on his mood. He'd had virtual kittens and dogs and a koala bear and once even a baby kangaroo. But he'd outgrown that by the time he was twelve. Well, maybe girls took a little longer to get over the fun of virtual pets. "Yeah. Beautiful," he answered.

"I heard that people who are sick can be cheered up by visits from pets. Go ahead, touch her, Cyborg. Feel how silky she is, Corgan. Demi likes to be petted."

Humor her, he thought. Even though the tactile sense wasn't all that well developed in virtual reality, the digital dog did feel silky. He stroked the black and white hair, shook the paw the dog held out to him. Demi's eyes seemed more intelligent than the eyes of the virtual pets he'd played with—maybe since Ananda was fourteen, the digital engineers had created a more complex model.

But the dog was still virtual, and Ananda was in some deep conversation with Cyborg, and since none of them even noticed Corgan, he said, "I think I'll go torment Eleven for a while, and then I'll electrocute myself."

"Yeah. You do that," Cyborg answered, paying no attention.

Only eight hundred twenty-one thousand, six hundred and twenty-nine seconds left and counting, Corgan thought. *I can't wait to get out of this quarantine.*

FIVE

"Hi, fuzzball," Corgan greeted Cyborg, coming into his cell. "That stubble on top of your head makes you look like a red caterpillar."

"The last time you said that," Cyborg answered, "you were talking about my mustache."

Corgan remembered that. It had been the morning of the day they made their escape from Wyoming. "So where is your mustache now? Doesn't look like it's growing."

"I shaved it. Ananda didn't like it."

"Didn't like the way it looked?"

"Didn't like the feel of it. She said it was scratchy."

That stopped Corgan short. It meant Ananda had kissed Cyborg, virtually, but how could she have felt that two-week growth on Cyborg's upper lip with the limited tactile sensation of virtual reality? Unless they'd really been going at it.

"What about you?" Cyborg asked. "Did you shave too, or aren't you old enough to grow a decent mustache?"

"I shaved," he muttered, and rubbed his hand over the top of his head to see whose hair was growing back thicker and faster—his or Cyborg's. "Pretty soon I'll be leaving here and I'll get to see the real Ananda, in the flesh."

He shot a look to see whether Cyborg would react to that, and Cyborg did—he looked envious. "I'm not sure how much longer they're going to keep me here," he said. "I don't mean here in Decontamination—I can leave here when you do—but in the medical wing. They say my liver got torn pretty bad when I hit the ocean." Then he brightened. "But Ananda will be able to visit me in the new place. The real Ananda. Like you said—in the flesh."

Corgan felt jealousy creeping into his insides, and he didn't know why. He liked Ananda, and he'd been flattered when she seemed to more than like him, back when they knew each other virtually across a distance of thirty-five hundred kilometers. But Sharla was the girl who filled him with longing. Sharla was the first human he'd ever touched, right after she'd freed him from his virtual-reality Box, before the two of them and Brig fought the war.

And here, sitting on the chair in front of him, was Brig's clone. And back in the Wyo-DC was Brig's other clone, Brigand. "Have you been able to connect to Brigand?" he asked Cyborg now. "Like, you know—the way you can read each other's minds?"

"No. I don't understand it. It's not because of the distance between us. When I stayed with you on Nuku Hiva and he was in our Wyo-DC, I could read his thoughts and see images from his brain. But now—nothing. It's like he's found a way to shut me out."

"Then, I wonder if he's still able to read your thoughts."

"Don't know. If he can, he knows we're here and knows the Harrier's at the bottom of the Atlantic."

Corgan heard that soft whiff as the door opened. Eleven? No, it was Thebos, carrying Cyborg's titanium hand.

"Finally!" Cyborg exclaimed.

Thebos held it out like an offering, his gnarled, knotty fingers contrasting with the smooth, shiny bands of titanium that circled each finger joint of the artificial hand with the palm-shaped stainless steel pod that could become a magnet. Then he plunked the hand down on the bed as though it were no more delicate than a brick, saying, "I totally reengineered it. Had to wait till They approved a few new parts that I needed—that's the reason for the delay. Try it. Just slip it on over your wrist, Cyborg. I based the design on quantitative biomechanical principles that will predict the pressure distribution at the stump-socket interface. Not only that, I increased the magnetic force, at the same time diminishing the energy necessary to flex the titanium joints. Go ahead, put it on and see how it works."

Cyborg picked it up with his real hand and gently fitted the prosthetic to the part of his wrist that remained. "Goes on really smooth," he murmured. Flexing the shiny fingers, he said, "I can't believe how responsive this is." When he flicked on the magnetism, the hand slammed onto the metal bed frame so fast that the impact nearly knocked Cyborg off the bed. "Yow!" he yelled.

"I had it set at the highest magnetic power," Thebos explained. "Maybe you'd better lower that. Just bend the index finger—that's the controller for the degree of magnetic force. You can reduce it as much as you want." Seeing that Cyborg was impressed, Thebos nodded and smiled. The deep lines from the sides of his nose to the sides of his chin folded in even farther as his lips parted to show yellowed teeth.

"This is incredible!" Cyborg enthused, flexing his titanium fingers so fast they blurred. "It's so much better than before!"

So the old man might really be a genius. Corgan realized he'd have to rethink his opinion of Thebos. He'd dismissed him as a rambling relic who couldn't even remember his own first name, but it looked like Thebos had proved him wrong. He held out his own strong hand to shake Thebos's thin, veined, brittle fingers, which felt as fragile as a sparrow's wing. "Congratulations, Thebos," he said. "Great job!"

"Didn't think I could do it, did you?" Thebos laughed that cackling laugh. "You'd be amazed at all the technological miracles I invented before the devastation. I try to tell Them, but They don't believe me. I could be useful here if They'd just let me."

"They must be crazy," Corgan said, remembering that not long ago he'd called *Thebos* crazy.

"I've diagramed the whole design," Thebos told Cyborg as he headed toward the door, "so when I die—I'm ninety-one, you know, and it's hard to tell how much more time I've got—when I die, someone else can rebuild your hand if it ever gets damaged again."

Smiling, Cyborg said, "You'll never die." As the door whiffed shut behind Thebos he added, "He's all right, that old guy. I can't believe how much better this hand works now. So, sit for a while, Corgan. You look like you're ready to rush off."

Corgan stayed standing. "No time to sit. I came here because I'm down to the last three minutes and fifty-seven seconds now, and before I go, I want you to tell me what you started to say that time about Sharla. You started with 'No wonder Sharla didn't.'"

"I told you to forget that."

"I can't!"

Corgan could hear the pain in his own voice, and Cyborg must have heard it too, because he lowered his eyes before he answered, "I was going to say, no wonder Sharla didn't want to go with you when you ran away from Brigand. Look, Corgan—you were the champion of the Western Hemisphere Federation, but then you just sort of . . . stopped. Stopped being anything. Stopped learning anything. On Nuku Hiva you herded cows. When you came back to the Wyo-DC, you played around virtually with Ananda and the Harrier simulator—"

"And it's a good thing I did, because it got us out of danger," Corgan said hotly. "If I hadn't trained on the Harrier simulator—"

Cyborg broke in, "For you, learning to fly the simulator was just one more game. It's like after the Virtual War you stopped growing up. What Brigand's doing is . . . uh . . . maybe not so good—"

"Not good? It's a whole lot worse than not good!"

"But at least he's *doing* something! Sharla, too. She keeps learning new things, keeps working in her laboratory. She left you behind, Corgan. She outgrew you."

Jaw clenched, Corgan muttered, "I thought you were my friend."

Cyborg smacked the side of the table. "See? You're doing it right now. You ask me to tell you the truth, and when I do, you act like a baby, whining, 'I thought you were my friend.' Grow up, Corgan! I knew you'd take it wrong. That's why I didn't want to say anything. But you made me say it, so now I'm going to ask you, what are you going to do with the rest of your life? You're sixteen, so you'll probably live another eighty years. Doing what, Corgan? Eighty years! Do you know what I'd give to have eighty years ahead of me?"

Corgan wanted to shut out the words. Forget the words, just count the numbers, those seconds ticking inside his head. *Twenty-two . . . twenty-one . . . twenty . . . nineteen . . .*

"Aw, Corgan—say something!"

Nine . . . eight . . . seven . . . six . . . His mind spun off not only the seconds, but the hundredths of seconds. "Zero!" he yelled just as the voice that came from nowhere and everywhere pronounced, *Corgan, you're free to go.*

The door stood open, and he plunged through it. Before the door shut behind him, he heard Cyborg yelling, "Corgan, come back tomorrow, will you?" but he didn't answer.

He had no need to go back to his room because there was nothing in it that he could take with him. Each day Eleven had brought him a clean LiteSuit and removed the one he'd been wearing. Each day before he put on the fresh LiteSuit, he'd stood in a corner of the room where jets of vapor shot out to cleanse his body. In the two weeks he'd been forced to stay there, he'd formed no emotional attachment to that plain white cell; all he wanted now was to exit the decontamination chamber and never return.

He found Thebos waiting for him right next to the outer door that would lead to freedom. "I know you'll be returning to visit your friend," the old man said, although he looked a bit doubtful, which meant he'd been listening to the conversation, as usual. "I'd like it if you visited me sometimes too, Corgan. I can tell you about the old days, what it was like to live outside a dome."

"I already know," Corgan answered tersely. "Remember, I spent a year and a half in the open on the island of Nuku Hiva in the Central Pacific Ocean. I breathed actual air and swam in the waves and ate real fruit from the trees. So did Cyborg."

"Oh. Yes. That's right." Hesitant, Thebos seemed to be searching for another possibility. "Well, I could explain to you about space missions. I know all about—"

"Sure. Someday." Corgan had to get out of there, had to purge Cyborg's words from his head. He shrugged off Thebos, then pushed open the door that set him free from his two-week confinement. "Wait!" Thebos cried. "See that little box outside the entrance to the medical center here? That's the DNA identification scanner. When you

51

come back here to visit Cyborg—or me—you need to touch that box. It's been imprinted with your DNA code. When you touch it, the door will open for you."

"Right. Fine." Then he was out, with the door closing behind him.

For the first fourteen years of his life Corgan had been kept inside a virtual-reality Box and hadn't known he was missing the whole world. The glorious months on Nuku Hiva had changed all that. There he could come and go as he pleased, and he'd vowed to himself that he'd never be caged again. Yet here he was, stuck inside a dome once more. Cyborg had said Corgan would live for eighty more years, and the voice that came from nowhere had said that no one ever left this domed city. Eighty years to never feel a breeze, or run on a beach, or swim in an ocean. Eighty years of being . . . a nothing!

As he'd expected, Ananda stood there waiting for him. She said, "Welcome, Corgan," and gave him a quick hug. He grabbed her hard, trying to prolong the hug, because during all those hours that they'd trained together virtually he'd wondered how her real body would feel—strong and sinewy? Soft and feminine? But she pulled back and cried out, "What happened to your hair?" That's when Corgan knew for certain that this meeting was real and not virtual, especially when Ananda pointed to the stubble on his head and started to giggle.

"It'll grow back," he told her, embarrassed.

"I sure hope so. You look like—"

"Yeah, I know. A fuzzy caterpillar."

When she had stopped laughing, she told him, "There's

someone I want to introduce you to. Demi, come here!" The black-and-white dog came bounding toward them, the most incredible example of digital imaging he'd ever seen.

"Demi, this is Corgan," she said. "Give him a kiss."

The dog leaped up, hitting Corgan's chest with her front paws—fifty pounds of unexpected force! When the wet pink tongue licked his nose, he realized that this was no virtual-reality dog. "She's real!" he exclaimed.

"Of course she's real. What did you think?"

"I . . . I've never seen a real dog before." On Nuku Hiva there'd been real birds and a live boar and a few feral cats that he hardly ever saw and a whole herd of transgenic cattle he'd had to take care of, but none of them looked up at him like Demi, with alert brown eyes that seemed to find him interesting, not just a loser who couldn't keep the girl he loved.

"She's an Australian Shepherd," Ananda told him. "Before the devastation they were bred to herd sheep and cattle. There are only a few of them left; they're all in zoos in the domed cities."

"I could have used one on Nuku Hiva to help with the cows." He knelt and held out his hand, remembering how Demi had offered him her paw when he was in the cell, when he thought she was virtual. Immediately the dog extended her snowy white paw and placed it in his open palm.

"Say hello, Demi," Ananda told her.

The dog barked once, a deep "Woof."

"Now you say hello back, Corgan."

"Hello, Demi." He felt a little silly. "Uh . . . Ananda,

where am I supposed to go now? Is there a place here for me? What am I supposed to do now that I'm out of Decontamination?" Since Cyborg believed Corgan was wasting his life, he'd better find something important to do. But what was he qualified for?

Ananda answered, "First I have to take you to meet our Supreme Council." Gesturing for him to follow her, she began walking down a corridor. "They'll give you your assignment. I don't have any idea what They think it's going to be, but I'll tell Them I want you to be my trainer. They almost always give me whatever I want. That's how I got Demi. I'm the only person in the whole domed city who has a real dog. I told Them I wanted one, so They bred one of the dogs in the petting zoo. I got to pick the one I wanted; the others stayed in the zoo. After we get through with the Supreme Council, I'll show you some of her tricks. She's so smart!"

He didn't say anything. Ananda seemed more interested in her dog than in him. *Pay some attention to me!* he wanted to tell her. After all, the past two weeks had been total boredom, and just nine and a half minutes ago he'd had a fight with his best friend. It would be nice if this pretty girl with the dark eyes and black hair that swung so rhythmically when she walked would focus on him, ask him how he wanted to spend this first day of his freedom, and maybe find him something decent to eat.

If she always got everything she asked for, and she wanted him to be her trainer, was that what he'd be assigned to do? That would put him in the background, with Ananda as the future champion while Corgan was overshadowed and overlooked. He needed something better than that, something that would make Cyborg take back what he'd said about Corgan not growing up.

For a while he forgot his aggravation as Ananda led him down a thoroughfare unlike any he'd ever seen before. Tall buildings rose on either side of him, twenty or thirty stories high, so lofty they touched the roof of the dome. The inside of the dome was blue; sun streaming through it tinted all the buildings the same cobalt blue color. "When evening comes," Ananda mentioned, "and the sun is setting, the blue in the dome makes the sunset look purple. It's pretty. Then after the sun's gone down, the blue goes away so we can get maximum illumination from the sky before it's totally dark. Both ways it saves energy."

Corgan felt unexpected motion beneath his feet and had to twist to keep his balance. "It's the people transporter, the traveling walkway," Ananda explained. "Didn't you have one in your DC?"

"No. Your city looks twice as big as ours, and a lot more technologically advanced."

They'd reached a portal where a door slid into a recessed panel to let them enter. "This is where we'll meet the Supreme Council," Ananda told him. "Let me do most of the talking."

"Go right ahead." Corgan wouldn't know what to say to a bunch of strangers anyway, especially if They were real rather than virtual. As They turned out to be. Entering the room behind Ananda, he saw that the Florida Supreme Council had eight members rather than the six in

Wyoming's council. Other than that, They looked pretty much the same.

"Well, Ananda, back again?" one of the men greeted her, fondness in his voice. "What is it you want this time?"

"Another dog?" a councilwoman asked her, smiling like the rest of Them. Ananda seemed to be a great favorite with the council.

"No, I just brought Corgan here so you could welcome him. He needs a job, so I'd like him to be my trainer. He already helped me train virtually when he was in his own Wyo-DC and I was here, but now that he's in our DC, the training can be in person, and that'll be a whole lot better for me."

A short, round councilman asked, "What do you say to that, Corgan?"

He stalled, saying, "Fine with me. Except . . ." Thinking fast, he tried to come up with something that would give him a little stature.

"Yes?"

"All this training is supposed to prepare Ananda in case the Virtual War has to be refought, since there was a question about the final score." The final score that Sharla had cheated on, she'd secretly admitted to Corgan. He would never tell anyone about her confession, even if that made him a conspirator. "But there's no way the war can be refought anytime soon," he announced, "because Brigand overthrew the Supreme Council in Wyoming."

Smiling as though Corgan's comment was past history, one of the council members answered, "We know. We receive current news through the underground fiber-optic cable network, and I happen to think *overthrew* is too strong a word, Corgan. Would you like to hear the official announcement?" The councilman reached behind him to flick a switch. After a bit of static a voice announced, "Greetings from the Wyoming domed city, headquarters for the Western Hemisphere Federation."

"That's Brigand!" Corgan exclaimed, but another council member shushed him with, "Just listen."

"The Wyoming Supreme Council," Brigand's voice continued, "recognizes that the New Rebel Troops led by Brigand have improved the welfare of every citizen in the Wyo-DC. Food production has increased. Housing has been reassigned, so that workers are enjoying larger and cleaner quarters, many with a clear dome-view of the sky. Working hours have been shortened, allowing the citizens to enjoy greater leisure. Because of these reforms the Wyoming Supreme Council has voluntarily resigned and has been replaced by Brigand and three officers of the New Rebel Troops: Brookhart, Emichore, and Danila. All glory and honor to the New Rebel Troops!"

"So you see, Corgan," the soft-spoken councilwoman told him, "Wyoming's transition has gone smoothly. Apparently that government needed some reforming— unlike ours here in Florida, where all the citizens are quite content. We have no worries about any revolt happening here."

"Well, you should! Brigand has this crazy idea that he's going to rule the whole Western Hemisphere Federation, and that would include you." Corgan hesitated. "I don't know how refighting the Virtual War fits into his plans, or if it does at all, but if the refighting team is supposed to be made up of Cyborg, Ananda, and . . . and Sharla . . ." He found it hard to speak her name. "And Sharla's in Wyoming with Brigand, while Cyborg's here in the Flor-DC . . ."

"Oh, Corgan, you're worrying far too much about things that don't concern you," a white-haired woman answered. "Of course, all plans for a Virtual War reenactment have been put on hold until the situation in Wyoming is made completely clear. Nevertheless, we would like you to train Ananda for several hours each day."

"Yes, I can do that, but maybe I could do more. I can tell you everything that happened in the Wyoming domed city leading up to the revolt, and what I know about Brigand. . . ."

The council members spoke among Themselves, and then one of Them, another woman, announced, "That would be slightly useful perhaps. We will discuss it. For now, Corgan, we have assigned a sleeping room to you. It is right next to Ananda's. Ananda, will you please show Corgan to his room? You'll find it well stocked with food, Corgan."

"Thank you." Since it sounded as though he'd been dismissed, he nodded stiffly to the council and followed Ananda—followed Demi, actually, because the dog trotted right at her heels.

"That didn't go so well," he said.

"Don't worry about it. At least I got you for a trainer. We'll go the long way now so you can get a tour of the city," she said as she led him back onto the people transporter. "Look at the sky. See how purple the sun looks?"

The blue tint in the dome not only made the sun look purple, but turned the ocean an unnaturally deep blue. Corgan shuddered as he remembered the mutations that had come at him in those toxic waters. "The last thing I knew, I was being pulled deeper and deeper into the ocean by the Hydrobots," he told Ananda. "How did I get from there to here?"

"Through the underground decompression chamber," she answered. "From there you were wheeled into an elevator and brought up to this level."

"You mean there's an underground level beneath the city?"

"Yes, but I don't know much about it. It's off-limits. It's where they bring the junk they salvage out of the ocean." When she reached out to move a lever, a section of the people transporter swung smoothly sideways, feeding them onto a moving belt that ran at a right angle to the moving walkway. "We're almost there. My room's large, and it's nice. Yours will be smaller and not as nice," she said unapologetically, "but it's right next to mine. When Cyborg is discharged, he'll have the room on the other side of mine."

Corgan wondered whether Cyborg's eventual room would be larger and nicer, or smaller and not as nice, like Corgan's. As they entered an elevator Ananda said, "Top floor, please, Demi," and the dog stood on her hind legs to push a button with her paw. "Isn't she amazing?" Ananda asked, laughing. "It took me only eight days to teach her that, and she always hits the right button." She leaned down to ruffle the dog's silky hair.

When the elevator had stopped and they were walking toward their rooms, Ananda said, "Corgan, you're in a new city and you're probably feeling a little lost, so I thought you might like some company in your room tonight."

He stammered as he answered, "Yes . . . sure." Was Ananda planning to spend the night with him? Where would that lead?

She leaned over to stroke Demi again. "Good night, baby," she cooed. "You take good care of Corgan. I already put your food dish and your water dish in Corgan's room. I'm sure he won't mind if you sleep on his bed, like you do on mine."

With a smile and a wave she said, "Bye, Corgan," and vanished into her room.

SIX

Corgan glanced down at the dog, who was looking up at him, apparently waiting for a command. "Well, let's go in, then," he said.

The door opened at his touch. Inside, the room wasn't much bigger than the cell he'd just left in the decontamination chamber, but the walls shone with undulating, brightly lit, colorful art images. A small panel beside the door held a list with the instruction:

Press button for art selection:
1. Impressionist
2. Classical
3. Modern

4. Landscape
5. Seascape
6. Off

He touched 6. The walls faded to a uniform soft peach color.

Demi trotted over to her dog dish and sniffed, then drank from her water bowl. Corgan watched, interested. How did dogs manage to get water inside their mouth when their head was bent down like that and they had to stick their tongue down into the water? You'd think gravity would work against them. On Nuku Hiva whenever he'd bent over a stream to drink, he'd sucked the water into his mouth, but this dog was lapping, not sucking. What was the mechanism? However inefficient it looked, it seemed to work. Demi raised her head, her chin dripping, then bent to drink some more.

A small table that folded down from the wall held a tray full of food, his dinner. He sat at the table, picked up a fork, and poked at the food on the plate. Fish. Not synthetic, but real—he could tell because it still had fine bones inside it.

He put down the fork. On Nuku Hiva he'd caught and eaten fish nearly every day, but that was different. When the island was declared a contamination-free zone, the surrounding Pacific waters were tested too and were pronounced pollution-free. So it was safe to fish there.

That was the Pacific. This was the Atlantic. He was pretty sure the Florida DC would never take fish from that tainted ocean and feed them to the citizens; they probably had a fish farm inside their dome. But he'd suddenly lost his appetite for fish.

"You like fish?" he asked Demi. She might be a smart dog, but she couldn't answer him in words, so he broke off a small piece of fish and held it out to her. Very daintily she reached for it with her teeth and swallowed it whole.

"Want more?" He kept feeding her little bits of fish until it was all gone. Then he started to worry. What if dogs weren't supposed to eat fish? He'd carefully removed all the bones so they wouldn't hurt her, but maybe fish just wasn't good for dogs. How would he know? This was the first real dog he'd ever seen.

"Okay, move away from the table so I can enjoy the rest of my dinner," he told her, but she just stood there. "Back up," he said, making a pushing motion with his hand. The dog moved backward. So, she reacted to hand signals. He'd remember that.

As he ate he tried to guess which foods were real and which were synthetic. Most of the synthetic stuff was made of cleverly disguised soybeans, just like back in his own Wyo-DC. It didn't matter too much because he was hungry enough to eat everything on the plate except the fish.

After he'd finished eating, he stretched out on the bed, which was wider than the table he'd slept on in Decontamination and much more comfortable. On the wall next to the bed was another list:

Press button for entertainment:
1. Action/adventure
2. Historical

3. Romance
4. Educational
5. Off

When he pressed 2, a battle erupted on the ceiling above his head, with men in military uniforms shooting one another as bombs exploded overhead and underfoot. "No thanks," he said, and pushed 5. He didn't want to watch a war enactment that reminded him of the Virtual War, the war that had made him a hero. Back then. As Cyborg had said, that was then, this was now.

He decided to close his eyes and just go to sleep, but when he did, he heard a little whimper. Raising his head, he saw Demi standing next to the bed, gazing intently at him with those warm brown eyes.

"What? You want to come up here?" he asked. That was all the invitation the dog needed. She jumped up and stretched out beside him, her head at the foot of the bed and her nearly tailless hindquarters facing him. "That's not the end I want to look at all night long," he told her. "If you plan to stay up here on the bed, you better change your direction." When he gave her a little nudge, she did exactly as he'd told her, turning around to face him, with her nose only thirty centimeters from his chin. Settling down again, she sighed contentedly.

He let his hand rest on the spot between her two ears and gave her head a little scratch. Without opening her eyes, she licked his wrist. "Don't take up too much space," he warned her, and then he closed his own eyes once more to dream of Sharla.

* * *

Three hours every day he trained with Ananda. Two hours he spent with the Supreme Council, sharing whatever information he could. One hour with Cyborg, who seemed to be a little healthier, but not a lot. The medics told him he was not healing satisfactorily, which worried Corgan.

In the hours of day that remained he explored the Florida DC. It seemed wealthier than his own Wyo-DC. The street-level chambers of all the tall buildings held entertainments, where people gathered to sit around tables and talk or play games or dance.

In his whole life Corgan had never danced. Well, almost never. There was that one warm afternoon on Nuku Hiva when Sharla had sung to him and pulled him, stumbling, into the ocean foam at the edge of the beach, his steps as awkward as hers were graceful.

"You want to dance, I'll teach you right now," Ananda told him. The training session had just ended, and surprisingly she was staying with Corgan, walking beside him. "Dancing's easy. You just kind of move around to the beat. Most of the music is electronic, but there's one place where they have musicians who play real instruments."

"Some other time," Corgan answered.

Ananda stopped and turned to face him. "You know, Corgan, you're not like I thought you'd be. You don't say much or want to have fun. I mean, Cyborg's too sick to dance or anything, but he talks to me a lot."

"And tells you you're pretty."

"Well . . . yes."

"I can say that. You're pretty, Ananda."

She lowered her eyes. "It doesn't sound the same when you say it. But never mind. I have about twenty minutes before I have to leave, so let's just play with Demi. See over there along the base of the dome? That's real grass. The Supreme Council gave me permission to take Demi there for playtime every day."

"Fine." Better than dancing. And better than trying to talk sweet to Ananda. Demi didn't care about compliments. Corgan had found himself growing fond of the dog, wishing Ananda would let Demi stay in his room every night, but she was Ananda's dog and after that first night Ananda had wanted her back.

"Watch this," she said. "I'll throw this toy up in the air and Demi will leap for it."

"That doesn't look like a toy, it looks like a dinner plate," Corgan said.

"It's called a Freeze Bee, but I don't know why they call it that, because it isn't frozen and it doesn't look like a bee. It's aerodynamically shaped to spin flat like a plate, but it's made of compacted aerogel, so it won't hurt Demi's teeth when she catches it." With a flip of her wrist Ananda tossed the Freeze Bee, which curved up and then down as it flew through the air. When it was still a full two meters off the ground, Demi leaped up and grabbed it with her teeth.

"See that?" Ananda exclaimed. "Isn't she graceful? And strong! You throw it now."

Corgan did, getting the knack of hurling the Freeze Bee so that it flew high before it curved downward. Even before he released it, Demi would begin to run, following the trajectory of the toy and then soaring into the air at the precise time and place the Freeze Bee arced down. The third time he threw it, Demi leaped even higher than two meters, her body twisting in midair as she caught it and then landed gracefully on the grass.

"That's enough for today," Ananda decided after glancing at an old-fashioned clock that hung above the grass strip. "Why don't you take Demi for a walk while I visit Cyborg? His therapy treatment ought to be over about now."

So that's why she'd stayed with him—Cyborg was busy. *Great*, he thought, *Cyborg gets the girl and Corgan gets the dog.* "Right," he answered. "Tell him I'll come by in a little while."

"Don't hurry," she called back.

Kicking a loose stone as he went, he strode along the sidewalk at the edge of the grassy strip, feeling sorry for himself. Sharla preferred Brigand. Ananda preferred Cyborg. Who did Corgan have? Demi. And unlike a virtual dog, this one left mementos on the grass that Corgan had to clean up into little bags he dumped at the nearest trash compactor.

"Don't hurry," Ananda had said. Counting off the seconds in his head, he gave them half an hour—that ought to be enough. With Demi at his heels he walked to the medical center and touched the DNA identification scanner, which allowed the door to open for him. Inside, the corridor led past the decontamination chamber to the medical wing, to Cyborg's room.

There they were, Cyborg and Ananda, sitting together on

the edge of the bed, their arms wrapped around each other, their lips locked together. "Hey!" Cyborg yelled when he saw Corgan. "Either come in or go out. Preferably go out."

Ananda pulled back from Cyborg, but not very far. She seemed totally unembarrassed. "I told you not to hurry," she said.

"Go on, Corgan, lose yourself," Cyborg said. "And take the dog with you."

Corgan was about to argue, when Nurse Eleven entered the room and insisted, "No dogs are allowed in the medical wing. You must leave, Corgan."

"Well thanks, guys, I'm glad to see all of you, too," he fired back.

"Here!" Cyborg threw a ball at him—Corgan caught it just before it would have sailed through the door. "Go play with Demi."

Steaming, Corgan left, and Eleven did too, right behind him. Evidently the robot had come into the room for the sole purpose of telling him that no dogs were allowed.

Outside he sat on the ground with his back against the wall, right beneath the sign that said CENTER FOR DECONTAMINATION AND MEDICAL TREATMENT. *Whatever happened to loyalty?* he asked himself. Corgan had raised Cyborg on Nuku Hiva from the time he was an infant until he was eight years old. True, it had taken only four months for Cyborg to grow from babyhood to pesty-little-kidhood, but still! And now he'd started to lord it over Corgan because more weeks had passed and he was nearly eighteen. And it felt funny. Not ha-ha funny, but strange. What would it be like in another month, when Cyborg reached twenty? And the month after that?

Demi leaned her head on Corgan's knee. He knew what that meant—she wanted him to scratch her neck behind her ears. He threw the ball and said halfheartedly, "Go get it."

Demi bounded after the ball, caught it on the bounce, brought it back, and dropped it into his hand. "It's all spitty!" he complained, but he tossed the ball again. And again. Over and over because Demi never seemed to get tired of the game.

After twenty throws of the drooled-on ball a door opened and Thebos peered around the doorframe. "You look as sour as a pickle," he told Corgan.

"What's a pickle?"

"It's a delicacy we used to eat in the old days. Come visit me in my quarters while you're waiting for those two make-out artists to finish."

Make-out artists? Thebos sure used strange words. "Can't," Corgan said. "The dog's not allowed in there."

"She's not allowed in the medical wing," Thebos corrected him. "She is allowed in my quarters."

Why not? It would be better than sitting here getting his hand all sticky from Demi's drooled-on ball. He stood up and followed Thebos past the decontamination chamber, past the medical wing, past several other doors that didn't have names on them.

"Here we are. This is my dungeon," Thebos said at last. He was joking, Corgan hoped.

They entered the room and Demi flopped down on the floor, tired from all that ball chasing, while Corgan stood in the middle of the room, not sure what he was looking at.

The walls displayed virtual programs, much like the walls in Corgan's own room, but these virtual walls were covered with some strange kind of writing he couldn't interpret.

"What is that stuff?" Corgan asked, pointing.

"Oh, just my scribblings. They're equations about advanced propulsion systems."

That's when the idea hit Corgan, swept over him like one of the big waves that crashed on the beach at Nuku Hiva when a storm raged. Hit him in the head like a falling tree. Lit up his brain like lightning. "Thebos, can you teach me?" he asked. "All those numbers, those equations—can you teach me about that? Once before you said that if you had enough time, you could educate me, and I could really use some educating. It would help me figure out what to do with the rest of my life."

"Hmmmm," Thebos murmured, rubbing his nose. "Perhaps I could turn you into an engineer." Looking skeptical, he said, "I suspect it will be an uphill task, because you don't have an excess of mental equipment to begin with. But if you're willing to work hard—"

"I would. I mean, I am. I'd really like to be an engineer." Corgan didn't know what an engineer actually did, but whatever it was, it had to be better than what he was doing now, which was nothing.

"It would take me years to teach you enough. Years and years. You would need to dedicate yourself to learning." Thebos touched a button and all the equations began to rotate, whirling around the walls and around Corgan.

"Being able to acquire knowledge is the most valuable tool a human being possesses. One never knows when a

70

particular bit of learning will become useful, or will even save one's life. Every time you add data to your memory center, Corgan, you increase your worth as a human being."

"That's what I want to do," Corgan told him. "Improve my worth." He added, "I learn fast. I learned to fly the Harrier simulator in a couple of weeks."

"Learning to fly a simulator, that's easy," Thebos scoffed. "Learning to build a spacecraft—that's infinitely harder. I can teach you how to build an advanced propulsion system far greater than any ever launched on this planet. That was my job, and I was the best. Sadly, I was never able to complete the spacecraft I created, so I never got to fly it. But perhaps you could. Eventually."

"How? How could I fly something that doesn't exist?" Corgan sat down on a wooden stool in the corner of the room because the whirling, rotating equations were making his head spin. Those white marks on the black background kept going around and around.

Looking sly, Thebos again touched the side of his nose with his forefinger. "Are you so sure that it doesn't exist?" He pulled up a chair and sat facing Corgan. "Let me tell you something," he began. "You and I are alike. You were once the hero of the Western world. You could ask for anything you wanted, and you got it. People admired you, revered you. You were important."

Thebos leaned closer to murmur, "You know, Corgan, it was the same with me. In my field I was the best on Earth. I was famous. People respected me." His eyes watered, and for a moment Corgan worried that the old man might break

71

down and cry, but he shook his head and went on, "Now look at us, you and me. Our fame is gone. We are reduced to uselessness—you training a younger, better champion, me greeting patients in the medical wing. But inside"—he poked his bony finger into Corgan's chest—"inside us we're still as good as we ever were. Maybe better."

Rocking backward, Thebos declared, "There's nothing sadder than yesterday's hero, Corgan. But I can teach you the secrets of space travel, secrets no one else knows, and perhaps one day you'll become a hero again. But our main goal, the most important job for the two of us, Corgan, will be your education. We'll have lessons every day, and as I instruct you about propulsion I'll turn you into an aeronautical engineer, as I once was."

"Right. Good. That's wonderful. But first please make the walls stop spinning around. They're getting me dizzy."

Thebos waved his hands and the walls grew still. "So we'll start tomorrow. Come at about ten o'clock."

What was Corgan getting himself into? It sounded overwhelming—lessons every day with this strange old man. Did he really want to do this? But if not this, then what else? It would be better than spending every empty daylight moment brooding over Sharla, every nighttime dreaming about her, always wondering why he lost her. Anyway, if he became an aeronautical engineer, Cyborg could no longer say that Corgan was wasting his life. Anxious to tell him, he stood up to leave, saying, "I think I'll stop in to see Cyborg."

"I'll go with you," Thebos said. "I want to talk to him about his clone-twin."

Corgan frowned. He'd rather not have Thebos tagging along when he impressed Cyborg with his new plans. "I was hoping Demi could stay here with you for a few minutes, since she isn't allowed in Cyborg's room."

"She can stay here without me," Thebos said. "I trust her not to chew up any of my belongings." Thebos had already opened the door, leaving Corgan no choice except to follow.

They found Cyborg alone in his room. He sat up and said, "Hey, Corgan, good to see you," as though half an hour earlier he hadn't told Corgan to get lost. "You too, Thebos. To what do I owe the honor?"

"Honor? Perhaps not. I thought we needed a little information exchange," Thebos answered. "I suppose both you and Corgan are aware that an underground fiber-optic cable runs between your Wyoming DC and our Florida DC."

"We know that," Corgan told him. "That's how Ananda and I could train together in virtual reality, even though we lived thirty-five hundred kilometers apart. Signals traveled through the cable."

"Precisely. Until recently there hasn't been much communication across the cable, but during the past couple of weeks we've received continuous reports from Wyoming. Propaganda, actually, saying that Brigand's revolt was a huge success, that the Wyo citizens have never been happier."

"Yeah, as if I believe it," Corgan scoffed. "I heard the broadcast when I met the Florida Supreme Council. It was Brigand's voice. I already told Cyborg."

"Let me continue, please, Corgan," Thebos said. "The propaganda arrives over the main frequency that's always been in use. But no one in the Florida Supreme Council—because They're a complacent bunch of dolts—ever bothers to test other frequencies, which is something I always do, since I have access to the cable. This morning when I checked the frequency at the farthest end of the spectrum, I discovered a coded message from Brigand himself to a core group of rebels located right here in our Flor-DC. These rebels seem to be recruiting others for Brigand's revolution."

"Using code?" Cyborg asked. "Sharla is the supreme code breaker, so she could easily make a code. Or a dozen codes for a dozen different domed cities, if she wanted to."

"This one's very simple," Thebos went on. "Mathematical. I had no trouble deciphering it. Would you like to hear the message?"

"Sure." Corgan and Cyborg both nodded.

"Here it is, and I'm quoting: 'All six members of the Wyoming Supreme Council were captured, imprisoned, and tortured. Two of the six died because They were old and Their hearts gave out under torture. Brigand, the commander of the rebels, extracted confessions from the council about how They oppressed and stole from the citizens—'"

"That isn't true!" Corgan cried out. "Well, maybe the council controlled the way people lived, but the people weren't oppressed and the council didn't steal."

"I believe you, Corgan, but under torture people admit to untruths. There's much more in this message," Thebos went on, pointing to lines of code on the paper he held. "These are instructions for the small but growing rebel group here in Florida, telling them how to create torture devices—electric prods, deafening sound chambers, branding irons, thumb screws. Nothing very imaginative, actually; most of it is almost medieval, including the directions for making a guillotine."

"What's a guillotine?" Corgan asked.

Turning so pale that he almost matched the white walls, Cyborg answered, "It's a device to cut off people's heads. I can't believe this, Thebos. If this came from Brigand, it makes him sound like a maniac."

"See for yourself, Cyborg. I've printed it out. Do you think you can interpret the code?"

"Maybe. Sharla taught me a little about coding." Cyborg's hand shook as he reached for the paper. After a quick glance he said, "You're right; this one's very basic, just a logical sequence of numbers. Very easy to read. But . . ."

"But what?" Corgan asked.

"Give me a minute. I think there's a code within the code. Another message. A subset."

"Mm-hmm. That's why I wanted to show this to you, Cyborg," Thebos said. "I sensed there might be something more, but I couldn't make it out. Can you?"

"I'm trying. It could be patterned geometrically." Cyborg lifted the page close to his eyes, as if that would help reveal any hidden message. Next he laid it on his hospital bed and began moving his index finger in diamond patterns across the page. He rubbed his forehead, concentrating, before he finally announced, "I think I've found it."

"What does it say?" Corgan demanded.

"It says, 'Cyborg Cyborg Cyborg it's getting worse.'" He looked up. "I think it's from Sharla."

seven

Arriving again at Thebos's quarters, Corgan asked, "Any new coded messages?"

"You've asked me that every day for a week. I told you I'd let you know if any more came. And let me remind you, I don't want you mentioning any of this to the Florida Supreme Council when you talk to Them."

"*I'm* not meeting Them anymore," Corgan said. "I've told Them everything I know about Brigand except for that coded message that you won't let me bring up. Why not, Thebos? Shouldn't They know about this?"

"*I'm* the one to tell Them," Thebos insisted. "I requested a meeting, but They said They were too busy to see me. They think I'm senile and useless—well, let Them think that. Until They begin treating me with respect, I'll provide no information."

"But this is so important. . . ."

"You are not to inform the Supreme Council or Ananda. Understood?"

Sighing, Corgan nodded. "Okay, let's make a bargain. I'll keep that secret if you tell me what you hinted at the first day I came here to your chamber, something about an advanced propulsion system that really exists but no one knows about. You said maybe I could fly it. Is that true?"

Thebos looked away, looked back, drummed his fingers. "You must keep this absolutely confidential, then. I don't want anyone to find out."

"I won't tell anyone." Thebos and his secrets! How many more secrets would Corgan have to promise to keep?

Bending even closer, Thebos whispered, "Beneath us there is an underground area where useful salvage from the ocean is decontaminated and stored."

That wasn't any news. Ananda had already told Corgan that. "So?"

"At the far end of the salvage area is a heavy locked gate. Behind the gate is a tunnel that leads to a space facility. This Florida domed city that we're in was built adjacent to the site where the United States used to launch its space missions. Everything aboveground at Cape Canaveral was destroyed in the devastation, but there are laboratories beneath the ground that were not destroyed. One of them was mine."

Cape Canaveral. Carnival! That was the name Ananda had remembered of the city that had once existed nearby, only she didn't get it quite right.

"Yes, my laboratory and my project survived, for all the good it's ever done anyone," Thebos said, looking sad. "The spacecraft was—is—not quite complete, but I haven't dared to go through the tunnel to get the missing parts because the tunnel has become polluted, or at least I think it has."

Corgan considered that, then said, "You mean you're not *sure* whether the tunnel is polluted or not? Maybe I could check it out."

"How?"

"With Demi. I've been finding out more about dogs, reading things about them. Dogs have about two hundred million smell receptors in their noses, compared with five million in human noses. They can detect one drop of blood in almost five liters of water. Demi could sniff the tunnel—"

"And then what?"

"I dunno. I'd see how she reacts. I mean, I wouldn't want to hurt her or anything, but if she acted like something smelled dangerous, I'd get her out of there fast."

"You know, that's not such an outlandish idea," Thebos told him. "In the old days they used dogs to sniff and search for illegal substances in airports. However, you and the dog wouldn't be allowed down into the underground chamber. It's off-limits."

"Not a problem," Corgan answered. "Ananda gets to do anything she wants—the Supreme Council lets her. And she owes me for all the dogsitting I do for her. I'll tell her I want to see the underground chamber, and when she takes me down, I'll check out the tunnel. That means she'll find out about it. Is that okay with you?"

"As long as she keeps it secret." Now it was Thebos who became excited. "I will give you the code that unlocks the door to the tunnel. The door is hard to find, but I can describe its exact location."

"Then what?" Corgan asked, repeating Thebos's question.

"Then—whatever happens next will depend on what you find, whether the tunnel is contaminated, whether it's possible to travel through it to my laboratory. Who knows, the tunnel may have collapsed, too, in all the years I've been afraid to go there."

Corgan stood up to leave and Demi rose to follow him. "I'll talk to Ananda," he said. "*If* I can pry her away from Cyborg."

"Good luck," Thebos answered. "Then come back here to finish your lesson."

The next day a reluctant Ananda complained, "I don't know why we have to do this right now. I'm on my way to see Cyborg."

"Look, how long can it take?" Corgan asked her. "An hour maximum. We'll go down there, we'll check out the tunnel if there is one, and we'll come right back."

"Oh, all right, if it matters so much to you," Ananda told him. "Let's hurry up, though."

She clearly didn't want to do this, Corgan realized. And why was he doing it? To humor an old man? No, it was because Thebos had understood Corgan's feeling of discontent, pointing out that both of them had once been heroes but were now forgotten. Since Thebos was right about that, he might be right about what would restore Corgan's spirit—the chance to master something new. Space flight sounded interesting, not that he believed it could ever happen for him, but learning about it would be worth the study hours.

Ananda pointed and said, "It's over there." Although the door to the elevator that led to the underground level was hidden behind a shimmering virtual wall, Ananda knew exactly where to step through. "But keep a good hold on Demi's leash," she told Corgan. "Illusion camouflage like this always confuses her."

The size of the elevator startled Corgan. "Why is it so big?" he asked. "You could fit a hundred people in here all at once!"

"It isn't used to transport people," she told him, "it's for bringing up decontaminated, reconditioned metal and motors and things like that to be rebuilt into new machinery. The machine shops and factories are on the main level."

"You mean people never ride in this thing?"

"The workers do, when they change shifts. Come on, get in."

The elevator worked silently, considering its size, but the silence ended with a blast of sound when its doors opened underground. Ananda and Corgan stepped into a vast, astonishingly noisy cavern. Dozens of robots were smashing rusted machinery, then dumping the pieces into huge vats that bubbled loudly. Swirls of orange and green vapor rose to the high ceiling.

"Stop! What do you want?" a human guard demanded.

"I'm Ananda," she said, "and I'm showing Corgan around our Flor-DC. I'm giving him the full tour."

"Corgan?" The guard suddenly acted friendly. "Are you Corgan who won the Virtual War?"

So at least someone remembered him. "Yeah, that's me," Corgan answered.

"Well sure, show him around, Ananda. If you have any questions, Corgan, I'll be glad to answer them for you."

Corgan pointed to the bubbling vats. "What's in those things?"

"It's an acid solution to neutralize the toxins on the scrap metal. From there the scrap gets taken to the furnaces to be melted down. You'd be surprised how much metal our Hydrobots find in the ocean, even after all these years. During the devastation every seagoing vessel in the Atlantic was sunk, not to mention the old cars and junk that people used to dump in the ocean when the landfills overflowed. Half our city is built from salvaged metal. . . ."

The guard stopped suddenly. Concerned, he placed a hand on Ananda's shoulder and said, "Sorry, Ananda. It must be hard on you to see those vats, knowing that . . ."

"It's all right," she told him. "I'm fine."

Then Corgan remembered. Ananda's parents had been killed by exploding vats. It must have happened right here. No wonder she'd argued about bringing Corgan to the underground chamber—she didn't want to be reminded. But he'd insisted because he didn't catch on to that. Still, since they were already here, he should do what he came for and then get her out.

"Thanks for the explanation," he told the guard. "Can we just wander around and look?"

"Help yourself. But don't touch anything that hasn't been processed, and make sure the dog doesn't either."

As they left him Corgan tried to think of something to take Ananda's mind off the tragedy. "It's no wonder your DC is so much bigger than the Wyo one," he said. "We didn't have a cache of material to salvage like you do. No oceans in Wyoming."

"Is that right?" she answered without interest. "Now, tell me again what we're supposed to be looking for."

"A tunnel. Behind a wall."

Corgan scouted the cavern. Immense as it was, he could see that it had been dug into a rectangular shape, so when Thebos had said "at the far end of the salvage area," he probably meant one of the walls at either end of the long rectangle. The two end walls were about four hundred meters apart from each other. *Choose one*, he told himself, and pointed. "That way."

"All the way over there? Do we really need to—"

"I'll race you," he said, knowing that would get a response. Ananda had never been able to beat Corgan at running, and he knew it bothered her. "You'll lose," he predicted, and that got her moving! The two of them started out evenly, but before they'd gone a hundred meters, Corgan pulled ahead, even while holding Demi's leash. And the way Demi ran! Before that he'd only seen her gallop short distances to fetch the ball. Now she raced so fast her long, silky hair streamed behind her, and with her mouth open and her teeth showing it looked as though

she was grinning because she knew she could easily out-
run the two humans, even if they were champions.

Corgan and Demi finished a full three meters ahead of
Ananda, who panted as she joined them, saying, "I guess
you're up to speed—the irradiation didn't slow you down
any. But one of these days I'm going to beat you. That's
my goal."

"You can already beat me at the high jump and the
broad jump, so let me have at least one thing I'm better
at." Actually, he was better at time splitting, too, in spite of
what Ananda had told the Supreme Council, but he didn't
want to mention that right then. Winning the race was
enough satisfaction for the moment.

He touched the far wall, which seemed to be of solid
earth, scooped out but never finished with any surface
material. Next he began walking along the width of it,
stopping to tap it every meter or so. When the thump
sounded a little different, he speculated, "This might be
the spot. Thebos told me if I scraped away some of the dirt,
I'd find metal behind it."

As Corgan removed a small patch of soil with his fingers Ananda asked, "Did he tell you to scrape the layer
off the whole door? If you do, everyone will notice it. I
thought this was supposed to be secret."

"He said first I'm supposed to expose a circle of metal
about eight centimeters in diameter, then tap a code onto
the metal with a nail."

"You mean a fingernail or a nail nail?" she asked.

"A building nail. I brought one with me. The code
will release the lock, and then the whole door will push

itself open." He looked around to make sure no one was observing him. The nearest worker stood at least fifty meters away and was busy with the vats, so Corgan told Ananda, "Hold Demi's leash while I tap the code." He had no trouble remembering the string of numbers Thebos had instructed him to use. Four taps, nine taps, two, seven, six, and on and on through twenty single-digit numbers. When he finished, he waited, but nothing happened.

"So it was just another one of Thebos's made-up stories," Ananda said.

Corgan felt a little disappointed, and that surprised him because he hadn't really expected a different outcome. Still, he'd found metal behind the dirt, so that much was true. He crossed his arms and thought about what to do. Should he try the other end of the cavern? It seemed unlikely that there would be a second metal door hidden behind a dirt wall there. Maybe he'd remembered the code wrong or, more likely, Thebos had given him incorrect numbers, not because he meant to, but because he was a very old man who couldn't even remember his own first name.

As Ananda fidgeted impatiently and Corgan stood there thinking, cracks began to appear in the dirt wall. Little bits of dirt flaked off, revealing the outline of a rectangular door. "There it is," Corgan murmured, trying to hold down the excitement in his voice. "It just took a long time." Still covered with dirt, the door swung open very slowly.

"Should we go inside?" Ananda asked, peering into the darkness.

"No. Thebos just wants to prove to me that the tunnel exists. Here, let me hold Demi's leash."

"Why?"

How could he tell her he wanted Demi to test the tunnel for contamination? "I . . . uh . . . just like to hold her," he answered lamely. Shrugging, Ananda handed over the leash.

Using a slight head motion, Corgan indicated the open door, hoping the dog would react to that signal the way she did to hand signals. Demi looked up at him as if asking just what it was he really wanted, and he made the same motion, again very slightly. Demi turned toward the door. Cautiously extending one paw and then another, she stepped forward, sniffing constantly, until she'd gone all the way past the entrance. Suddenly she began to sneeze.

"Pull her back!" Ananda ordered, and Corgan yanked hard on the leash. Demi sneezed a few more times while Ananda quickly grabbed the leash and led the dog away. "Can we leave now?" she demanded. "I don't like what just happened. You shouldn't have let Demi go in there—what if it's contaminated?"

"Sorry!" He tried to apologize, but Ananda had already started back toward the elevator. "Wait for me," he called. He couldn't follow her because he had to enter the code again so the door would close. He held his breath as he took two cautious steps into the tunnel, reaching for the exposed circle. Once again he tapped the numerical sequence, causing the door to close much more quickly than it had opened. Next he had to patch the exposed circle of metal. Scraping a handful of dirt from the unpaved floor, he spit into it a couple of times and kneaded it into mud, which he pushed against the bare metal.

After he satisfied himself that no one would notice that part of the patch job, he made more mud to fill the cracks around the doorframe. Then he hurried to catch up to Ananda, who was kneeling in front of the elevator, her arms around Demi.

The dog seemed fine.

EIGHT

Because of his daily lessons with Thebos, Corgan spent less time visiting Cyborg. And often when he arrived at Cyborg's room, Ananda was there, so they couldn't talk about the coded message from Sharla because Thebos insisted it be kept secret. Corgan knew how much Cyborg worried about the message, and about Sharla, and even more about his clone-twin, Brigand. Maybe all that worrying slowed his recovery, because he wasn't improving as much as he should have.

On one occasion when Thebos and Corgan happened to meet in Cyborg's room, Cyborg asked, "Can we talk? I mean, without everyone hearing." He gestured toward the walls.

"No one will hear," Thebos answered. "I took care of that, the same as I did on the evening we spoke about Brigand's message."

"Really? So tell me how I can turn off the snoops myself," Cyborg begged, but Thebos just smiled and said, "It's a secret."

"Thebos is full of secrets," Corgan added.

"Have you heard anything new on the cable?" Cyborg asked.

"No, I came here to report that no additional coded messages have arrived. Nothing but the usual propaganda about what a great leader Brigand is and how all the citizens love and support him, blah, blah, blah. Do you believe that, Cyborg?"

"I . . . don't know. He does have . . . I think it's called magnetism. Back in Wyoming when he spoke, guys paid attention. He made promises to all the workers that they'd share in everything they produced. He told them the Supreme Council had cheated them of what rightfully belonged to them and that certain people got too much—"

"Like me," Corgan broke in. "Before we left, he told his rebels that I was spoiled all my life and got everything I asked for, while the workers had barely enough to stay alive. Lies! All lies!"

"But the rebels wanted to believe him. He told them they'd been exploited," Cyborg explained, "and that if they followed him, he would punish the council, and then he would become the new leader of a better world and he'd make things perfect for every citizen in the Wyo-DC."

"Well, at least Brigand has done a part of what he

promised," Thebos commented wryly. "He got rid of the Wyo Supreme Council."

Cyborg looked away unhappily.

"Ask *me* if I believe Brigand's a great leader," Corgan spit out. "He's not only a liar, he's crazy. Did I tell you that after he cut off Cyborg's hand, he *ate* it? He said he had to, to get the power of the cannibal kings inside him. I think he really believed that."

"No doubt he did," Thebos stated. "The most dangerous kind of tyrant is one who believes he's been chosen to rule the world, appointed by the gods or, in this case, by the cannibal kings. If the tyrant is totally convinced that he is divinely inspired, others become convinced too. That's how tyrants win followers, no matter how cruel or barbaric they act. Back before the devastation the world was full of brutal dictators, all of them claiming that they, and they alone, knew what their gods wanted. Anyone who didn't follow them became their enemy."

"Well, Brigand just better stay away from Florida," Corgan declared.

"Or what?" Cyborg asked.

"Or I'll beat him in a fair fight."

"Oh, Corgan," Thebos murmured, sighing. "Sometimes you talk like a stupid little boy. You have so much to learn." Shaking his head, Thebos left the room.

"More lectures? I thought you just got finished lecturing," Corgan told him. But he followed.

"He's right," Cyborg agreed. "Verbally, you're a case of arrested development."

"Yeah, well, I'd rather talk like me than like you," Corgan

shot back. "You blabber like a professor. Like Thebos."

"Hey, I was programmed to sound smart and you were programmed to win virtual games. You want to talk like some numb-nuts guy? Take a listen." Cyborg screwed up his lips and squinted his eyes. "Hey, dude, let's blow this here joint and see what—or who—we can score."

His sneer matching Cyborg's, Corgan corrected, "*Whom*. Say *whom* we can score. Dude, your grammar's not all that great. But yeah, you're right. We are who we were programmed to be, and I'm finished with that. I can do anything I want."

"And that is?" Cyborg asked. "What do you want? I don't hear an answer. You need to educate yourself, Corgan. Your ignorance is scary."

The door slammed behind Corgan and he slumped into the hall, rage seething through his veins like the vile, polluted waters of the Atlantic. Just because he was programmed for a certain skill didn't mean he had to stay stuck in that hole for the rest of his life. He could be whatever he wanted to be.

Only he didn't know what that was.

Every day Thebos would instruct or ramble or question Corgan, sometimes doing all three at once. Thebos loved the sessions. Corgan found them difficult, tedious, baffling, and frustrating. So why was he doing this? There ought to be an easier way to decide what direction his life should take.

"I was the young hotshot design engineer," Thebos said during their first week of classes. "When I started, I was just in my midtwenties. Others before me had talked of antigravity propulsion, but no one had ever been able to figure it out completely—until I came along. I had to fight to get funding. NASA didn't want to give me any money."

"Who is NASA?" Corgan asked.

"It was the space agency of the United States, when there was a United States. So then, using my own money, I produced the first successful antigravity prototype. After that, NASA practically threw money at me. I'll show you the diagram of the prototype I designed back then," Thebos announced, pointing at the black virtual walls, holding a white stick.

"Why do you write white on black instead of black on white?" Corgan wanted to know. "Black on white would be easier to read."

Thebos chuckled in that cackling way. "Because it reminds me of my very early childhood. In the old school buildings the walls were covered with blackboards, and we wrote on them with chalk."

"Chalk? Was it like laser pens?"

"No, my undereducated young friend, chalk is calcium carbonate, $CaCO_3$. Now, pay attention. I'm drawing a diagram of the antigravity spacecraft."

The drawing took shape clearly enough—a large sphere flattened at the top and bottom. "Aerodynamically this shape is the most reliable in a spinning craft—" and then Thebos took off on an explanation of the physics of high-spin nuclei and superconductivity at close to absolute zero, while Corgan tried not to tune him out. But all this was so far over his head that he had trouble focusing.

"I knew that kinetic gravitational force exists in conjunction with static gravitational force," Thebos went on. "I'd proved it in my underground laboratory at Cape Canaveral. I knew that if I could control interaction, I could control gravity. And that would let spacecraft to achieve flight without propellant and fly at the speed of light. The speed of light! In a vacuumlike emptiness of outer space, light travels at seven hundred million miles per hour."

Trying to look interested, Corgan asked, "What's the speed of dark?"

Thebos burst out laughing, almost doubling over with hoots of hilarity. "Oh that is so comical, Corgan. The speed of dark! That's the first time I've ever heard you make a joke. You have a sense of humor after all."

What was so funny? If there was a speed of light, wouldn't there be a speed of dark? Maybe not since Thebos was almost falling down laughing. Corgan grinned, as if he'd really meant it to be joke. Thebos, still snorting with mirth, blew his nose with a loud honk, and chuckled. "So amusing. Now let's get back to the monatomic temperature-independent superconductors."

By the middle of the second week Corgan was searching for ways to find out more about the spacecraft, because although Thebos was easy to distract, he never strayed off target for very long. "I want to know what happened when you were ready for the test flight," Corgan finally asked flat out.

Wearily Thebos leaned back on the tall wooden chair he said was good for his back. "I was all alone in my laboratory that night," he began slowly, "checking every-thing, because we planned to launch the vehicle the next day. My entire group of scientists and engineers had gone into town to celebrate the coming launch . . . so . . . so . . . I was alone. . . ."

"You said that."

"Yes, well, that happened to be the night of the first nuclear bombardment. All the other scientists were killed. I survived because I happened to be underground. Only people who had been in basements or vaults or caves—only those survived that first nuclear holocaust."

Corgan tried to picture the horror. He couldn't. "What happened to the spacecraft?" he asked.

Thebos became evasive again. "We'll talk about that another day. Now, let's return to resonance coupling and two-dimensional quantum oscillators. You know, Corgan, you're doing better than I expected. I think there might be a brain under that brush of black hair."

For the next few days no matter how many questions Corgan tried to ask, Thebos shrugged them off—unless the questions happened to be about science or engineering—until the day when Corgan said, "So I guess when you came from your underground lab to the domed city, you came through the tunnel, right?"

"No, no, there was no tunnel then. I built it myself, later. No one knows the tunnel exists—no one but you and Ananda. You did swear her to secrecy, didn't you?"

"Yeah, sure. But wait a minute, back up. You say you built it yourself? How far does it go?"

"Two and a quarter miles. It took me seven years."

"Seven!" Corgan got up as if to leave. "I'm not going to listen to any more talk about quantum physics until you explain to me how you built a three-and-a-half-kilometer tunnel all by yourself."

"Sit down! I am the teacher and you are the student, so I make the rules!" Thebos declared, color rising in his face. But then he relented. "I will explain. Back then, when the Florida domed city was new, workers were needed so badly that they could decide when they would work and for how long. The ones who dug the underground cavern quit work each day at exactly five P.M. That's when I would go down there, all alone, to dig."

Corgan pictured Thebos with a bucket and shovel, but even though he'd been maybe forty years younger back then, he couldn't have managed all that by himself. "No way!" Corgan said. "That's impossible."

In a huff Thebos explained, "I am not only a scientist, I'm an engineer. Pieces of scrap metal and old motors were lying all over the place down there. I built an efficient digging machine, but still it took me seven years to finish the tunnel."

"What did you do with all the dirt?" Corgan asked. "I mean, you had to put the dirt somewhere."

Thebos allowed himself a small smile of satisfaction. "I plastered it onto the floor, layer over layer. The cavern had been dug so large that no one noticed sixty-four hundred cubic meters of dirt spread evenly over the floor, little by little, over the course of seven years." He chuckled and began pointing again to the equations on the virtual walls.

"Don't stop now!" Corgan demanded. "Finish the story."

"You're a persistent pest," Thebos groused, but he continued, sighing. "All right, I will tell you the whole story, but you must swear on every bit of honor you possess that you will never speak of this to anyone else. Do you swear?"

"I swear," Corgan said, raising his right hand, once again promising to keep a secret, glad Thebos trusted him.

Closing his eyes and shaking his head as though it hurt to remember, Thebos began to explain, "After seven years of effort I broke through to my laboratory. My spacecraft was still there, undamaged. I started to dismantle it, piece by piece, and night after night for the next year, between midnight and five A.M., I brought the structural pieces back through the tunnel into the domed city."

"The pieces are here?" Corgan asked, excited. "Where?"

"Not the pieces, the whole craft. As I returned each piece I rebuilt the spacecraft, until it was nearly completed. In just one more trip I could have transferred all the parts here, and it would have been finished, but then . . ."

"What happened?"

Thebos shuddered, remembering. "I'd gone through the tunnel to retrieve the last two flight panel instruments when the ceiling collapsed. The laboratory ceiling. All the outside pollution rained down on me. The rubble was not only toxic, it was radioactive, and I knew it, I could almost feel it burrowing through my skin. I managed to crawl out of the laboratory into the tunnel, slamming the door behind me. I staggered, I fell, I fainted, but many hours later I reached the domed city. I never went back."

Corgan stared, trying to absorb it all. "You mean you brought back all the pieces except for the two missing parts and put everything together, so the spacecraft is almost finished? Is it hidden somewhere around here?"

"Some other time." Thebos spoke each word so deliberately that Corgan knew it would be useless to argue. "For now we will return to our topic of macroscopic spin alignment."

By the third week Corgan had begun to understand a little bit about quantum physics, and marveled at the enormous range of Thebos's knowledge. "The first time I met you," he said, "you said you couldn't remember your first name. That was just an act, wasn't it?" If Thebos could remember vast stores of information about nuclear physics, he certainly knew his own name.

"An act," Thebos admitted, "yes, it was an act. For two reasons. In Greek mythology gods sometimes disguise themselves as beggars to see how mortals will treat them. Shallow souls will bow before kings but kick and starve beggars. I wanted to find out what kind of soul you were, Corgan—one who would show pity to a demented old goat, or one who would ridicule him. Turned out you were neither. You withheld judgment. Very wise. That's why I trust you, Corgan."

Corgan reflected on that, trying to remember how he'd behaved toward Thebos in the beginning. He was glad he'd passed the test. "What's the second reason?" he asked.

"It's that I never tell anyone my real name. I never have, not since I started kindergarten."

"You can tell me. I won't say anything to anyone." He'd lost count of how many secrets he was keeping for Thebos.

"Hmmm." Thebos rubbed his chin. "We'll strike a bargain. You learn these equations, and I will reveal my secret name."

"Ha-ha, joke's on you," Corgan cried. "I already learned them last night."

"Prove it."

Corgan took the pretend chalk and wrote each equation on the fake blackboard:

$$T = \frac{\dot{m}}{q} V_e + (P_e - P_a) A_e$$

$$V_{orb} = \sqrt{\frac{Gm}{r}}$$

"Now it's your turn," he told Thebos. "What's your first name?"

Thebos mumbled, "Prometheus."

"What? I didn't quite hear it. Prom—"

"Prometheus!" Thebos said louder.

Corgan considered that for three and seven-tenths seconds, then said, "What's wrong with that? It's long, but . . ."

"Picture a five-year-old boy in kindergarten. None of the kids could pronounce Prometheus, so I told everyone my first name was P. T." Frowning, he added, "I always blamed my parents for naming me after that particular Greek god. He was a good god, but he came to a bad end." Thebos began to quote,

"All arts to mortals from Prometheus came.
Yet, hapless, for myself find no device
To free me from this present agony."

Tears filled the old man's eyes, then rolled down his cheeks. He wiped them away with a shaking hand.

Corgan wanted to reach out or to say something that

would show he cared, but he didn't know how. Awkwardly he took a step forward and then stopped, asking quietly, "What is the agony that you can't be freed from, Thebos?"

"Why, my imprisonment in this frail old body. I suppose death will free me from it soon enough. If only I can pass along some of my knowledge to you, Corgan, death won't be so hard to bear. So, back to our lesson."

Afterward Corgan felt unsettled. He was becoming fond of the old man, and Thebos's tears disturbed him. Corgan now had two friends who were hurting, both Thebos and Cyborg, because they were approaching death. He wanted to help them, but didn't know how. On his way back he stopped to see Cyborg, who still looked too pale and drawn. "How much longer do you think you'll be here in the medical wing?" Corgan asked him. "It's been almost a month now. Plus those two weeks before that when you were in Decontamination."

"They say my liver was hurt worse than they thought at first," Cyborg answered, clenching and straightening the fingers of his artificial hand. "But everything's healing, sort of, so maybe in another week or two I can get out of here. What's it like living next to Ananda?"

"Huh," Corgan grunted, "I may as well be living underground, for all she cares. We train together, but we don't really connect. You're the one she likes, not me. I'm not so great at getting girls to like me."

Gesturing for Corgan to take the folding seat, Cyborg said, "I've been wanting to talk you about that. I was pretty rough on you when you asked me about Sharla. There's a lot more to it."

"There is?" Corgan forgot his worry about Thebos, forgot everything except that Cyborg was going to explain Sharla. "You mean it isn't only that she outgrew me, like you said?"

Cyborg tried to make himself comfortable, using his artificial hand to pull on the bedpost and straighten his body, as he began, "I'm a strategist. That's what I was cloned to be, so I look at all the angles in a situation. There are a lot of hours when I just lie here on this bed and don't have anything to do but think, and lately I've been thinking about you and Sharla and Brigand. In this situation all the angles form a *triangle*."

Intent on every word, Corgan waited for what was coming.

"Consider all of us," Cyborg went on. "The Supreme Council had us created for specific jobs. They didn't care about our feelings, just our functions. They didn't even know I existed, and that worked great for me. But Sharla raised Brigand herself. He was her baby, her little boy, and she loved him the way a mother loves a child."

"Right." Corgan had seen that during the week they were together on Nuku Hiva—had seen Sharla's pride in Brigand's cleverness, and the way she indulged his bratty behavior.

"But then what? He grows up. She can't turn off the love, but she can turn it into a different direction. He's still her creation—"

"Yeah, but—"

"Let me finish, Corgan. Added to her love for him is her guilt because she's the one who designed him to age fast, and she knows he can't live more than three or four more years. She's frantic to save him, so she works like crazy in her lab trying to find a way to reverse the rapid aging, which of course would help me, too. But she fails. So does she abandon Brigand because he turns into a power-crazed fanatic?"

"No," Corgan answered. "It's pretty clear she's staying with him."

"Do you understand why? It's a mixture of all those different kinds of love and pride and guilt and fear and responsibility, and besides that, Brigand loves Sharla fiercely, and he tells her that all the time and shows it." Cyborg lay back down on the bed and covered his eyes with his arm. "Okay, that's it. My analysis, for whatever good it is."

"There's one thing you left out in your analysis. What about the message in code: 'Cyborg Cyborg Cyborg it's getting worse'?"

"I don't even know if it was from Sharla. Maybe it was from Brigand. Maybe it meant that time keeps running out for him."

How hard that must be for Cyborg to say, knowing that Brigand's aging and approaching death applied equally to him. Corgan went to him, gripped his good hand, and whispered, "Thank you. I mean about Sharla." He wished he could find better words to say it, but he'd been engineered for fast reflexes, not for fancy speech. "I'll leave you now," he said. "Ananda ought to be here soon. You deserve her."

nine

In the fourth week of his lessons with Thebos, Corgan told the old man, "You keep teaching me the science of anti-gravity flight, but what I really want is to fly the simulator. You haven't let me do that."

"Because you are not ready! You need to study the technology and master every single part of every physical principle before you can fly the spacecraft."

"Fly the . . . ! What do you mean, 'fly the spacecraft'? Do you think I . . ." Corgan stopped, stunned.

Thebos looked down, then pressed his fingertips together like someone about to pray or doze or perhaps figure out the best way to answer. After a pause he said,

"Actually, I was referring to the simulator. I get confused sometimes, you know."

Corgan didn't believe that for a minute. He knew by now that Thebos put on his confused-old-man act when he wanted to hide something.

"At any rate," Thebos added, "my expectation is that you'll be ready for the simulator in another six months or so, after you've mastered a rudimentary knowledge of zero-gravity propulsion principles."

"Six more months! I can't wait that long."

"Such impatience!" Thebos grumbled. "The impatience of youth. All right. We will take a short hiatus from the lessons on the physics of antigravity to teach you what you'll probably think of as the fun part, as soon as we finish this section on upper-atmospheric pressure."

Hiatus? What was a hiatus? Thebos kept throwing out those strange words as though Corgan should know what they meant.

Thebos went right back into lecture mode, but as he droned on and on Corgan's thoughts were on the simulator. How different would it be from the Harrier? A lot more complicated, he supposed. His fingers itched to get started on it. Finally Thebos halted his discourse to exclaim, "All right, I can see you're not paying attention, so I'll give in and turn on the antigravity spacecraft simulator."

"Fun part" was exactly what it turned out to be. If learning to fly the Harrier simulator had been exciting, this space simulation was ten times better, even though all of it was virtual and Corgan had no real stick, no real steering column, no rudder pedals, nothing physical to grab on to. To illustrate distance, Thebos produced a cache of fiftyyear-old images taken from space by the crew of something called the International Space Station.

"And I *think* it may still be up there, the ISS," he said, "even though we've had no communication with the crew since the devastation." Then, downcast, he added, "Although all of them are most likely dead by now. They'd be my age or older."

"Uh-huh." Corgan was hardly paying attention because he was so intrigued by the controls. Even though both the Harrier and the antigravity spacecraft had vertical take-off and landing capabilities, flying the spacecraft would be totally different. The Harrier was tough, built to fight, to maneuver fast and take a beating, while the spacecraft prototype that Thebos had designed—eight meters wide and four and a half meters high—had a thinner shell molded of a single piece of superconducting material. Inside, to counter gravity, all the parts were aluminum or titanium. Its flight simulator had been so cleverly engineered that Corgan could actually feel the differences in the metals when he touched them virtually. Holographic 3D screens operated the flight control hardware. A supercomputer managed the navigation, as well as the propulsion, power, and life support systems, so there wasn't a lot for the pilot to do except sit back, check the holograms, and enjoy the ride. It felt like being inside an actual physical space that he could reach out to handle, far superior to the old Harrier simulator. Yet all of it was virtual, a convincing illusion.

For four days in a row Corgan did nothing but practice on the sim. Thebos didn't say much about Corgan's progress, but Corgan could tell that the old man was impressed—he'd never before seen Corgan's superfast reflexes in action. *Maybe I'm not so smart about all those math and physics equations*, Corgan thought, *but this I can do. I can fly.* And then he realized he'd said it out loud: "I can fly!"

"Yes, I believe you could." Thebos stared hard at Corgan for half a dozen seconds before he continued, "The real spacecraft has never been flown, but it would have been flightworthy, I'm sure of it. I was going to fly it myself, you know. I'd programmed everything for that first test flight. I'd stake my life that the craft would still fly, if I only could finish it."

"Is there a chance that I could go through the tunnel to your old lab and get the missing parts?" Corgan asked.

"Not bloody likely," Thebos answered. "I told you the contamination in the tunnel nearly killed me. And you said Demi reacted badly to it."

Corgan argued, "But you managed to get back all the way through the tunnel. It didn't kill you. So the tunnel air might still be breathable." He paused, then offered, "I'd be willing to take the chance to find out."

"No. Absolutely not. It's much too dangerous." Thebos stood up to turn off the simulator, saying, "Let's get back to basics. You've been neglecting your studies ever since you started playing with this simulator. You need to learn more about the zero-point field, which provides the gravity-control force for moving the vessel."

Corgan walked up to Thebos, put his hands on the old man's shoulders, and pushed him gently onto his high-backed stool. "I want to know the truth, Thebos. You said the spacecraft is here somewhere in the domed city. Every time I ask about it, you talk about something else. If you want me to keep coming back to study with you—and I think you really do—then it's time for you to trust me with the truth. Where is the spacecraft?"

Thebos peeled Corgan's hands off his shoulders and slowly rose to his feet. For eleven and twenty-three hundredths seconds he said nothing, just stared steadily into Corgan's eyes as though evaluating what he saw in them. Then he nodded and ordered, "Follow me. But leave the dog here."

Staying close behind him, wishing the old man would move faster, Corgan trailed Thebos through the corridor. They were not moving toward the outer door, but in the opposite direction, quite a long way, eventually reaching the far wall, which was totally blank. "Here?" Corgan asked. "But there's nothing here. It's a dead end."

Not answering, Thebos waved his hand across a pinpoint of light in the wall, and a panel slid sideways, revealing a large room beyond it. "What you see before you is the power and heating system for the entire decontamination chamber and medical wing," he said. Pointing to two large tanks in the center of the floor, he told Corgan, "These are the boilers that hold hot water and steam for the showers, the sterilizers, and the subfloor heating system."

Corgan wondered what all this had to do with the spacecraft, but he'd learned to keep quiet. Thebos disclosed whatever he wanted to whenever he wanted to.

"The system is connected through a series of pipes

to solar panels on the roof. We had to use ninety square meters of solar panels, which is a lot, because the sunlight gets diluted as it comes through the dome. I designed and built this whole thermic unit thirty years ago, in the days when the Supreme Council didn't think of me as just a doddering old fool. I had complete autonomy back then—that means, Corgan, that They let me issue all the orders and do anything I wanted."

Thebos paused and gave a little laugh that sounded like a snort. "And no one ever knew, because I never told them, that above this ceiling"—he pointed upward—"is another room."

Corgan felt a stir of excitement. That must be where the zero-gravity spacecraft was stored.

"Shall we climb?" Thebos asked, bowing slightly toward Corgan. "If you will press your palm against that wall over there, a narrow opening will appear. Behind it is a flight of stairs. You go first, Corgan. It will take me much longer than you to climb those stairs."

Corgan bounded up the steps in four and fourteen-hundredths seconds. He didn't need Thebos to explain that though the roof overhead held dozens of solar panels, it also held fake panels that were nothing more than windows. Enough light streamed through them that Corgan stopped short, his breath catching in awe at his first sight of the spacecraft.

Although he'd studied the diagrams and flown the craft on the simulator, this was different—reality was always orders of magnitude superior to virtuality. Here it stood, the real thing, as if it had come to life. It was shaped like two of Demi's Freeze Bees placed one atop the other with the rims meeting. The top fourth of the craft had been made of clear polycarbonate so that everyone on the command deck would have a 360-degree view of the universe. Like a mirror, the wraparound window reflected the Florida sky outside. The rest of the shell was built of the same smooth, tough composite, but solid, not transparent—a dark blue gray. It looked powerful, perfectly molded, and at the same time sleek and beautiful, like a hawk ready to soar.

Corgan wanted to touch it, to explore it outside and in. As he ran his fingertips over the outer shell he noticed the name painted across the bow: PROMETHEUS.

Thebos had finally reached the top of the stairs. Panting, he said, "You noticed the name. This is my spacecraft, so I named it after myself, *Prometheus*. I had hoped to see the day the *Prometheus* would rise, unbound, from Earth. . . ." He stood very still, breathing rapidly, then outstretched his hands toward the spacecraft without touching it, as if paying homage. "This was my life," he murmured. "The irony of it—do you understand the word *irony*, Corgan? It's the difference between what you expect to happen and what actually happens. A cruel joke of fate."

Now Thebos leaned against the *Prometheus*, his palms flat against the smooth side. "The irony is that if I'd allowed the spacecraft to remain in my laboratory, I would have been able to fly it straight up through the hole in the roof when the laboratory ceiling collapsed. Fly it right into the sky. But by then I'd already brought all the components here into the domed city and reassembled them. And here, because we're completely covered by a dome, there's no way the craft can be flown up and out, even if I did have the two missing parts. There's simply no opening."

Corgan knew that. He hadn't been able to land the Harrier because the Florida DC had no retractable partitions. Even if the *Prometheus* spacecraft fit through the underground entrance the Hydrobots used to get into and out of the ocean, there was no way to get it down there. The elevator was large enough, but the *Prometheus*, as it stood, couldn't be moved from here to the main level to the elevator, unless Thebos took it apart again and then rebuilt it. . . .

As if he'd read Corgan's thoughts, Thebos told him, "No, it's hopeless. Years ago I suggested to the Supreme Council that we should build retractable openings in the top of the dome. They kept asking me why, but I wouldn't tell Them, because if They'd found out I had the *Prometheus* here, They would have claimed it for Themselves. The *Prometheus* is mine! Mine alone! No one else can know about it! Except you, Corgan. And . . ."

"And I will keep your secret," Corgan finished for him. But he wanted to know more. "So which parts are missing?"

"Two monitors for the holographic three-dimensional view screens. They were made by a process I can't duplicate here because I can't get the right materials. But it doesn't matter. Even if the *Prometheus* could fly, it's trapped here like a moth in a jar. There's no way out."

"Yes. I understand." Still, even if it could never be flown, the *Prometheus* was an astonishing piece of work.

"I'm really glad you're showing it to me," Corgan said. "It's . . . it's amazing. Can I see all of it? Can I get inside?"

"You can, but I can't. The entrance hatch is on top of the craft. To climb up there would be beyond my strength. Go ahead, although you already know how the inside will look—you've seen it in the simulation."

The smooth hull had no foothold, but Corgan dragged a wooden box from near the wall and climbed on it. From there he could grasp the top of the spacecraft and hoist himself up. Right where it should have been, the hatch door appeared, the same as in the simulation. Corgan twisted the handle, wondering if it would open after all these years, and it did. He lowered himself inside.

As realistic as the simulator had felt, this was infinitely more exciting. The command-control deck had four seats of molded composite arranged in a semicircle in front of the window portal, enough for a pilot and a crew of three. Corgan sat in the pilot's seat, cautiously touching the flight controls, knowing exactly where the missing panel screens should go. How he'd love to fly this thing! Corgan, the time splitter, forgot about time as he imagined rising from Earth in the *Prometheus*. He'd fly much higher than in the Harrier jet, up to where Earth looked like a blue sphere streaked with clouds, just as he'd seen in those images taken from the space station. What a ride it would be!

After he'd absorbed the feel of it, his fingers twitching as though working the controls, Corgan exited the hatch and slid down to the floor. "It was great," he told Thebos. "In perfect shape."

"Yes, well, I have something else to show you," Thebos said, moving to a cabinet built into the wall. "Look inside," he said after he'd pulled open the doors. "Those shelves hold samples of specially processed dried food that's been double-sealed so tightly that I doubt it's deteriorated, even after four decades. All that's needed to reconstitute it is water. There's a year's supply of food here. I brought it here thinking that one day the Supreme Council might give in and build retractable doors at the top of the dome. But like everything else, it sits here useless."

"Thebos, tell me, where would you have gone if you could have flown the *Prometheus* out of here? Did you have a plan? What destination?"

Thebos had begun to look weary and his hands shook slightly. "Up," he said. "To a star in the night sky that isn't really a star. Where there was someone . . ." He stopped and seemed unable to say more.

I'd better get him back to his quarters, Corgan thought. "Let me go down the stairs first," he offered. That way if Thebos fell, he'd fall on Corgan, who could catch him.

"I'll use your shoulders for support. Make sure you take the stairs nice and slow, easy does it."

As they descended, one cautious step after another, the lament of Prometheus played in Corgan's mind: *"Such cunning works for mortals I contrived,/Yet, hapless, for myself find no device/To free me from this present agony."*

"I'm a bit tired," Thebos said when they reached his quarters. "Class is dismissed, Corgan. Come back tomorrow."

That was the first time Thebos had sent him away early.

May as well check in on Cyborg, Corgan thought as he left. He pushed open the door to Cyborg's room and found Ananda there, but she wasn't sitting close to Cyborg, wasn't kissing him or doing any of their usual huggy stuff. She looked tense and unhappy.

"Am I interrupting anything?" Corgan asked.

"No more than usual," Cyborg answered. "Come on in. We were just calculating how long I've been here in the medical center."

Right away Corgan understood what was wrong. They'd been counting the passing of time, and it was taking an emotional toll. Every day Ananda became one day older. Every day Cyborg became about twenty-four and a third days older. Cyborg kept maturing. Ananda didn't. The gap between them kept widening, and there was no way she could catch up.

As Corgan thought back over the past few times he and Ananda had trained together, he realized she'd become increasingly moody. During their sessions he'd found himself doing most of the talking, telling her about the simulator, about Thebos's quirks, but never trying to explain the difficult math and physics he was studying—after all, Ananda was only fourteen.

"So!" he exclaimed, trying to pretend he didn't notice their gloom. "My school let out early today. Got any good games around here that three people can play? No? Well, maybe I should just go back and get Demi out of Thebos's quarters. I was so glad to escape from class that I almost forgot about her." Even to himself he sounded falsely cheerful.

"You don't need to bother," Ananda told him. "I'll go and get her. I need some Demi kisses."

Cyborg raised his eyebrows at that, but as soon as Ananda had left, he said, "And I need some quiet time, if you don't mind. Sorry! See you later, Corgan."

TEN

The next day Corgan stopped in the doorway to Cyborg's room, hoping to cheer him up a little. But the look on Cyborg's face brought him up short. Cyborg was standing at the foot of the bed, clutching the railing as if to keep from falling over. "Brigand!" he cried. "I just clued in to Brigand! I can see his thoughts again. He's on his way here! In the Harrier jet, the one that wasn't working. He got it fixed and he's flying here—with Sharla!"

Corgan gasped as Cyborg's words fought their way into his consciousness, swirling around the one word that had exploded in his ears so much louder than the others. Sharla! "Are you sure?"

"Yes, I'm sure," Cyborg answered, staring wide-eyed at

Corgan. "I'm so sure, I think I need to get out of here and get to an observation point in the dome. He might be really close, and he won't know there isn't any entrance. Or maybe he does!" Cyborg rubbed his head, where the new growth of hair looked redder than ever against his pale skin. "Maybe he's been reading my thoughts the whole time we've been in this place."

Electrified, Corgan shouted, "Come on!" When he reached for Cyborg's arm to support him, Cyborg brushed him off. "I can keep up if you don't go too fast," he said.

Just as they approached the outside door Eleven appeared to bar the way. "You are not permitted to leave the center, Cyborg," Eleven intoned.

"Oh, go recharge yourself or something, Eleven." Cyborg pushed the robot aside and muttered, "We're out of here." Immediately an alarm bell began to ring.

"Move it!" Corgan yelled as they bolted through the outer door. At least, Corgan bolted; Cyborg came more slowly, so Corgan had to make himself slow down. He wanted to run! All he could think of was Sharla. Part of him doubted she could really be headed toward them; part of him desperately wanted it to be true.

He'd spent enough time exploring the Flor-DC that he knew the observation platform's location on the topmost level. After steering Cyborg through the illusion curtain to the elevator that had taken him to the salvage cavern, Corgan pushed the button for up instead of down.

"Brigand's coming and it's going to be bad," Cyborg agonized as they exited onto the observation platform, where an area of the thermoformed, high-molecular-weight

114

polycarbonate of the dome had been left clear rather than tinted blue.

"I see it! Over there!" Pointing to the west, Corgan located the speck in the distance that had to be the Harrier heading toward the dome, growing larger by the second. "He'll have the same problem we had," he cried, "not finding an entrance. What if he runs out of fuel and crashes just like we did?"

"No, he won't run out of fuel. You just won't admit how smart Brigand is, Corgan—he'd have thought of everything." Cyborg's voice shook. "I'd say he already knows there's no opening in the dome."

"So what's he going to do? Land outside? Swim down to the underwater entrance? What about Sharla? Is she really with him?"

Cyborg pressed his fingers against his temples, crying, "I can't read him now. He's turning me on and off like a computer. Right now all that's coming through is his hatred—he wants you, Corgan!"

"Let him come!" Corgan cried, his own hatred seething like the acid in the corrupted ocean below.

The Harrier had flown close enough now that they could hear the drone of the engine even through the dome. It was flying straight toward them. From the pilot's seat Brigand might even be able to see Corgan and Cyborg standing on the observation platform. The jet kept coming and coming—it was going to hit! Corgan threw Cyborg down onto the platform and fell on him to protect him, but at the last possible second the jet swerved into an upward spiral, following the curve of the dome.

"He's playing games with us," Corgan cried, standing up and helping Cyborg to his feet. "The filthy slime, he thinks this is funny." Why was Sharla letting him do this? Was she actually inside the jet?

"No, he's not trying to scare us and he's not playing games," Cyborg decided. "He wants to set the plane down on the roof of the dome, but he's not a good enough pilot to do it. He's going to try again."

Brigand circled the jet slowly, hovering—because the Harrier was a hovercraft—directly above the dome, then just as slowly he changed direction and headed out to sea. Did he plan to ditch in the water? If he'd been reading Cyborg's thoughts, he'd know where the underwater entrance was. But no, the jet turned back, flying straight toward the dome once again. It hovered above the dome as the thrusters got lowered, pointing downward.

"He needs to rev up the engine," Corgan cried. "If he doesn't, he'll stall."

Far below, on the ground level of the Flor-DC, people had been watching and pointing as though the whole episode were nothing more than an exciting air show put on for their entertainment. Corgan realized that they probably believed it was virtual. Again Brigand pulled up, spiraled into a loop, headed out to sea, and then turned back.

"He doesn't have a clue what he's doing," Corgan ranted. "If he wants to land on the dome, he's got to go high enough to get thrust and set the jet down slowly." For the third time the aircraft headed straight toward them. Corgan cried, "Pull up! Pull up!" not because he wanted to save Brigand's life—he'd be just as happy if Brigand crashed and killed himself—but because Sharla might be in the jet with him.

"He's losing it!" Corgan shouted as the Harrier stalled twenty meters above the dome. And then it was plunging toward them. Seconds later it crashed through the dome with a thunderous explosion. Shards of dome glass flew everywhere, falling like sharp blue icicles as the people on the streets screamed and ducked in their attempt to find shelter. The impact knocked Corgan and Cyborg flat, but Corgan scrambled up fast enough to see one seat ejecting from the Harrier. Only one. It flew higher and higher, its jets shooting flame for thrust, going up to gain enough altitude that the parachute would probably open. Who was in that ejection seat—Brigand or Sharla?

The Harrier's left wing caught on the ragged edge of the dome, slowing its fall through the splintering dome glass. The impact as it smashed on the street shook the whole city. Panicked, people began to run, doubling back and hurtling into one another, knocking one another down, not knowing where to go.

All Corgan could think about was Sharla. Leaving Cyborg, he rushed to the elevator and banged on the door. Miraculously it opened. It was still working, even after the impact, but it seemed to take an eternity to descend to ground level.

In a state of pandemonium, the crowds raced to get out of the polluted air, mothers screaming to their children, "Don't breathe!" as fathers tried to grab toddlers who wailed in fright. People ran in every direction. Corgan fought his way through the throngs, the only person heading toward the downed Harrier, while everyone else tried to get away from it.

When he was still thirty meters away from the jet, he saw her hanging halfway out of the cockpit, her arm dangling lifelessly, her golden hair dripping with blood. "Sharla!" he yelled, his voice hoarse with fear. "Sharla!" But she didn't move.

Small flames had begun to lick upward toward the cockpit, and Corgan had a horrifying thought—the plane might explode with Sharla still in it! Knocking people out of the way, he reached the Harrier and hauled himself up to yank on the straps of the harness, trying to free Sharla from the seat. Why hadn't she been ejected? The crash's impact had knocked off her helmet, if she'd worn one—her head looked battered.

Corgan could feel the heat from the flames as he finally freed her from the straps. He lifted her into his arms and leaped away from the jet just as flames curled up around the cockpit. He began to run, this time in the same direction as everyone else.

"Get out of my way!" he kept yelling, but no one paid attention. The citizens were wrapped in their own fear, dragging their children by the hand, holding sleeves and handkerchiefs across noses to avoid breathing the pollutants that were pouring into the city. "Move!" he screamed at them. "I need to get to the medical wing."

Blood from Sharla's head wound spread over his LiteSuit. If she was bleeding that much, it must mean her blood was still circulating, so she was at least alive. Suddenly a few people stopped and began pointing to the sky. When Corgan glanced up, he saw that a para-chute had caught the wind and was being blown side-ways. Brigand! As the parachute floated down through the ruptured dome Corgan hoped Brigand would be impaled on one of the sharp shards sticking up, but he couldn't wait around to see.

Frantic, he reached the medical center, finding Thebos standing just inside the door. "Where's Cyborg?" Thebos demanded before he even inquired about the girl in Corgan's arms.

"I don't know where he is. Sharla's hurt."

Immediately Eleven appeared out of nowhere, all busi-ness and bustle. "Both of you must go into the decontami-nation chamber. You've been breathing polluted air."

"So has everyone else in the whole city," Corgan yelled. "She needs medical help right away! I'm taking her to the medical wing."

"Stop or I will arc you," Eleven said in the same even voice the robot always used, but the threat was real. Eleven looked just about to loose another of those high-voltage electric arcs right into the middle of Corgan's forehead when Thebos pulled a lever on the robot's arm, stopping it in midmotion. "Go ahead, Corgan," he said. "Take her to Cyborg's room—it's open. I've got to wait here for Cyborg so I can let him in. He's in no shape to be out in the middle of that chaos."

Corgan rushed into Cyborg's room and placed Sharla on the bed, shouting up at the ceiling, "Get someone in here fast! We need help!" Her blood looked shockingly red as it dripped onto the stark whiteness of the floor.

Kneeling beside her, he touched her face. It felt so cold it frightened him. "Hurry!" he yelled.

The door opened and someone came in, but when Corgan whirled around, he saw only another robot. Saying nothing, it placed its metal hand on Sharla's head. Instantly an image of the inside of her head appeared on a screen in the ceiling. The voice that came from the walls, or the ceiling or wherever it originated, boomed forth then.

Yes, that's a good scan, Nurse Sixteen. Now move around to the back of the patient's head.

When Sixteen changed the position of its hand, the picture on the ceiling changed too.

The voice declared, *The patient will live*, and Corgan's heart flooded with joy and relief. Sharla would live! She'd become well again, and she'd be here, with him.

But she is brain damaged. She will be mentally disabled.

"Brain damaged! You're wrong! You're crazy! Get down here and make her well!" Corgan bellowed, but the voice had stopped speaking. "Do you hear me?" He pounded on the walls until his fists bruised, but it was useless.

Thebos appeared at the door then, saying, "It's pandemonium out there. The population of the whole city is being evacuated to the underground cavern. And Cyborg has not yet returned. I'm worried he might have gotten trampled in the crowd."

"Worry about Sharla!" Corgan yelled, almost crying. "I can't get her to wake up. The voice said she has brain damage, but they won't come to help her."

Thebos didn't answer. He just stood there looking sad.

"Thebos, do something! You're a scientist!"

"I'm not a doctor." He hesitated, then said, "I have to get back to the door. This is the only contamination-free area, and it's in lockdown mode now, so the DNA identification scanner has been shut off. Cyborg can't enter unless I smuggle him in. I'm sorry, Corgan." And then Thebos turned and left the room.

Helpless, agonized, Corgan knelt beside Sharla, his forehead against her arm, his fingers on her wrist, feeling the thin pulse that proved she was alive. *Make them be wrong*, he begged silently. *What they said—they have to be wrong, Sharla. Wake up and talk to me, show me that you're the same as you always were. Say something to me.*

Leaning back, he studied her face, watching for any sign, any movement of her eyes or her lips. Her features looked made of wax—smooth, pale, and lifeless. "Oh, Sharla," he moaned, "I wanted you to be with me, but if you'll just *live*, I'll never ask for anything again!"

Nurse Eleven came in then—Thebos must have turned it back on—and told him to move away so that Sharla's bleeding could be stopped. Corgan moved, but not far. He stayed right next to the bed, wincing when he saw how deep the gash was in the back of her skull.

"Will she really be . . . ," he whispered to Eleven.

"Mentally impaired? Yes."

Corgan groaned. Sharla—that fine, quick mind. "How bad?"

"That is to be determined," Eleven answered, beginning to clean the blood.

The room suddenly turned dark. "Power is out," Eleven announced, glowing with a weird bluish light—

had the robot always had that glow emanating from it? It must not have been visible when the room was lighted, because Corgan hadn't noticed it before. "Go somewhere else, Corgan. You're in the way here," Eleven said.

He shook his head, not knowing whether Eleven could see that in the dark, but it didn't matter. Nothing could make him leave. "I'm staying with her," he insisted.

His despair ran so deep that he couldn't tell how much time had passed when Eleven finally left. He sat on the floor next to Sharla's bed, holding her hand. Maybe it would help if he talked to her. "Remember," he asked, "the first time we met? On that virtual beach. Both of us were fourteen. You came right up to me and challenged me to a game of GoBall." Even though he was a superb athlete and the whole game was played in virtual reality, he'd been so flustered by her beauty that he'd lost. "And you laughed at me," he said now. "That was the first time you laughed at me, but there were lots of other times because you were always about three steps ahead of me. In everything. You called me Corgan the Obedient. But you said it was boring never to question anything, and maybe you were right. I guess I *was* boring. You never were."

He touched her hair, still damp from the cleansing. That golden hair. . . . Soon after that game on the beach he'd seen the real Sharla, in the corridor outside his virtual-reality Box, which she'd unlocked for him. Genetically engineered like Corgan, she was the unexcelled code breaker. She could unlock anything.

That night in the corridor he'd touched her, his first real physical contact, and he'd loved her from that moment on.

Sometime later, perhaps two or three hours afterward, Cyborg returned to the room. "Where have you been?" Corgan asked him dully. "Are you all right? Thebos was worried about you."

Cyborg ignored the second question to answer the first. "I've been with Brigand," he said. "How is Sharla?"

"Brain damaged, the doctor said, or whoever that invisible voice belongs to, but I don't know how they could tell." Corgan got to his feet, fury rising in him. "Brigand did this to her! If I had him here right now, I'd kill him."

"*He* wants to kill *you*," Cyborg said, "but that's only his secondary objective in coming here, so he's in no big hurry. The revolt in the Wyo-DC was a complete success, he tells me. More and more rebels joined him after the Supreme Council was kicked out. Now he plans to start a revolt here in the Flor-DC."

"He'll fail."

"If you'd just stop hating him long enough, Corgan, you'd realize how powerful he is. And smart. Men and women—they're pulled in by his words and his promises. The rebels here have been waiting for him. They think he's a messiah. 'Destroy the council and set yourself free'— that's his message."

"Messiah!" Corgan scoffed. "Some messiah! He's more like the devil."

"Maybe. But if I remember right, the devil was often successful. After the revolt here Brigand wants to control all the other cities in the Western Hemisphere Federation. He's got this tremendous need for power—it energizes him so much he practically throbs with it. He doesn't really care what happens to people, he just wants to be the absolute ruler of the world before he dies."

"He's deranged," Corgan insisted.

"I understand him. It's because he has only a few years left."

Just like you, Corgan thought, *but you don't want to kill people*. They sat in silence for a while, then Corgan asked, "What's happening outside?"

"Well, a good chunk of the dome collapsed, and with the seal broken open like that, atmospheric contamination is getting pretty bad. We're lucky that the decontamination and medical areas are shut off from the rest of the city. Everyone else is being evacuated underground."

"Everyone?"

"Yes. A hundred eighteen thousand people. No, correction—two thousand will stay in the city to repair the dome as fast as possible. That's how many air-filtration masks there are. Everyone else is being sent into the underground cavern. The evacuation started right away, but getting them down there is a big problem because the elevator can hold only a hundred at a time, or a hundred and twenty if there are a lot of little kids in the load. Everybody's jammed up trying to get in it—they're all pushing and yelling. . . . I tried . . . ," he stammered, "I tried so hard to find Ananda, but I couldn't. I thought maybe she'd be here looking for me. That's why I came back."

Corgan assured him, "You don't need to worry about Ananda. She's strong, she's quick, and she's smart—she'll be okay. So when will Brigand come after me?"

"Not right away, I don't think. Like I said, you're only his second target. He's gone into hiding underground. With all those people being taken down there, and all the confusion, he can lose himself in the crowd for as long as he wants to. The Flor-DC Supreme Council will be down there too. They're his first target. You're safe for a while."

Corgan didn't feel fear; he felt rage. "You're just going to sit there and let him do this? Why didn't you try to stop him? You're the only person he might listen to."

"What do you think I've been doing?" Cyborg answered wearily. "I talked and talked, but he doesn't hear. I can't reach him. I think . . ." Cyborg's voice sounded muffled as he admitted, "I think he really has gone insane."

ELEVEN

Corgan must have slept, because when he opened his eyes, the lights were on. Sharla's eyes were open too. She looked at him in puzzlement.

"You're awake," he whispered. "Do you know where you are?"

Her expression didn't change—she kept the same bewildered look and didn't answer. Her pale blue eyes, which had once been so vibrant, now held no luster, no life.

They were alone together. Thebos had arranged for Cyborg to move to an adjoining room. Corgan reached to take Sharla's hand and held it tightly, but there was no answering pressure. Her fingers lay limp in his.

During the time Corgan had slept, the robots must have

been in the room attending to Sharla. All the spilled blood had been cleaned away, and the gash in the back of her head was covered with some sort of mesh. Except for that, her hair looked the way it always had—shimmering gold in the light.

Eleven came in then, carrying a tray of food, not for Sharla, but for Corgan. "As long as you're here, Corgan, you need to eat," Eleven said. Did he imagine it, or had he heard a slight note of sympathy in the robot's normally expressionless voice?

"What about Sharla?" he asked.

"She will be unable to feed herself. Her nourishment will need to be inserted by osmotic delivery."

Corgan didn't ask what that meant, but it sounded awful. "Let me try to feed her," he said.

"As you wish." Eleven produced a bowl of something unrecognizable that had been blended into slush, and handed him a spoon. "It's very nutritious," the robot added as it exited the room.

When he bent over Sharla, her blue eyes fastened on him as though waiting for a signal. "Are you hungry?" he asked. No answer. "Can you sit up?" Again silence.

He changed the position of the bed to prop her upright, then held a spoonful of the unappetizing mush near her mouth. "Will you . . . uh . . . open please?" he asked, not sure how to make this work. When she didn't respond, he touched her lower lip with the tip of his finger, then pressed down on her chin. Her mouth opened, and he placed the stuff on her tongue, waited for a few seconds, then realized he would have to lift her chin to close her mouth, which he did. *Swallow, please swallow*, he prayed silently, and she did.

Starting to sweat, he wondered if he could manage this. In his whole life he'd never had to feed another human—on Nuku Hiva when Cyborg was a baby, the computer caretaker named Mendor had fed him and kept him clean. Getting that first spoonful into Sharla had taken four minutes and seventeen and a quarter seconds, and he had a whole bowlful to go. Maybe this was a mistake, maybe he shouldn't try to do this, but he couldn't quit now. *She needs me to help her, and I can*, he assured himself, *because no one else cares as much about her as I do*. Concentrating, he kept at it until the bowl was empty.

Just as he put the bowl back on the tray Cyborg, Thebos, Sixteen, and Eleven all entered the room at the same time. "Let the robots take care of Sharla," Cyborg told Corgan. "You and I have to talk. Thebos will stay here with her. He can find extra help if anything goes wrong."

"Where are we going?" Corgan asked as he followed Cyborg through the door.

"Right here, in the hall," he answered. "We can't talk in my new room because the walls and ceilings hear everything. I wish I could get a look at those guys so I could see who they are, the invisible ones who suck in all our talk and then spit back orders." Looking exhausted, Cyborg leaned against the wall near the outside door. The redness of his newgrown hair now seemed muted—worry had dampened its fire. "I saw Brigand again," he whispered.

"You did? Where?"

"Down in the salvage cavern. Thebos sneaked me out

and then let me back in later because Brigand sent me a mental picture of where he was. He does that sort of like a command—you know, like, 'Here's my location, I want you to come to it right now.' So I went. I tried to reason with him again, but it didn't do any good." He paused, then added grimly, "He has Ananda."

"What do you mean he has her?"

"He's holding her. Brigand and his rebels."

Corgan's jaw clenched. "He better not hurt her!"

"He won't. But he's keeping her until you bring Sharla to him. It's supposed to be a trade. A barter."

"No!" Corgan cried, and Cyborg hissed at him to keep his voice down. "How could I take Sharla to him even if I wanted to?" Corgan asked in a guttural whisper. "She's barely alive. She's . . . she's . . ." His voice rose in anger as he cried, "And Brigand's the one who did this to her!"

Cyborg clapped a hand over Corgan's mouth. "I told you to keep it down! Anyway, you've said that before. Don't waste your time repeating what we already know."

Corgan shook the hand away and said, "Wait a minute! Is Brigand cluing into you again? Is he hearing what we're saying? If he is . . ." This time he yelled it: "Come and fight me fair. You want to kill me? Then, come and get me!"

"You idiot!" Cyborg flared. "You're going to alert Thebos and the robots, and you'll get us locked in here so tight I won't ever get out. I'm trying to negotiate things. You care about Sharla, but I care about Ananda! So shut up and let me plan." He shoved Corgan hard against the wall, and Corgan was about to shove back but stopped himself because Cyborg was still so weak.

Covering his eyes with his hand, Cyborg suggested, "Let's go down to the cavern together. Brigand can't do anything to you down there. People are packed so tight there's no room for a one-on-one fight. Anyway, it would attract attention, and Brigand's trying to keep undercover for a while. If the citizens—the ones who aren't in the rebellion with him—realized he was the guy who'd wrecked their city, they'd throw him to the sea mutations and he'd be fish food."

"Great idea," Corgan said. "Let's tell them."

Cyborg frowned at Corgan, saying, "I don't want him killed. He's my clone-twin. No matter what he's turned into, we're attached in a way nobody else understands. I have to try to change him, if I can, and remake him into a reasonable human being."

"Impossible! He'll never be reasonable and I don't think he's even human."

"He's as human as I am. And don't forget, I'm also trying to protect you, Corgan. Right now Brigand's pretty mad—yeah, mad in both ways, angry mad and a little bit insane—but he's not stupid, and he probably won't start a personal brawl with you as long as all those witnesses are around down there. He's a strategist, and he needs to build support for his revolt, so he wants people to think of him as a leader, not a thug. Come on, let's get Thebos to open the door and let us out of here."

Corgan wasn't sure what good it would do to confront Brigand, but since Cyborg was a strategist too, he followed him out of the center. Outside the city looked shattered. Crews wearing air filters swept up broken dome glass, while others built scaffolds so they could repair the massive hole in the dome. "Breathe as shallowly as you can and move fast," Cyborg told Corgan. "Once we get into the elevator, we'll be safe."

The virtual illusion curtain no longer hid the elevator door. Corgan was amazed that in spite of all the destruction the elevator still worked flawlessly, even filled with heavy cartons of food, tubs of water intended for the citizens in the cavern, and at least fifty people being lowered during this particular descent. He heard a man say, "It's a good thing it goes this fast. Twenty seconds down and twenty seconds back up. The loading is what takes the most time."

Another man answered, "I heard they're opening up a staircase they used a long time ago, before the elevator was built. It got sealed off when it was no longer needed, but now they're trying to restore it to help with the evacuation."

"That's good news," Cyborg muttered to Corgan.

When the doors opened at the bottom of the shaft, Corgan was shocked by the scene—it literally crawled with humanity. Tens of thousands of people were already jammed into the salvage cavern, and more arrived every two minutes or so. He knew the area was immense—at least 48,000 square meters in size, he'd figured when he went into the cavern that day with Ananda. But with the multitudinous crush of Flor-DC citizens crowded into it, the cavern seemed to have shrunk. And though this was only the second day of the influx, it smelled and folks looked grimy.

"The walls and ceiling were never really finished,"

Cyborg explained, "so the surface dirt keeps filtering down on everyone. There's no water for washing, and all the drinking water has to be brought down tub by tub in the elevator, along with all the food. If that elevator ever stops working, this whole population will be in real trouble."

"How long before the dome gets fixed?" Corgan asked.

"Who knows? They have to manufacture more dome glass from scratch, then mold it to fill the hole."

The noise was just as startling. People shouted to be heard, their shouts echoing off the high ceiling. Few of them had anything to do—they milled around, mothers pushing through crowds to grab their children by the arms, screaming at them not to play on the piles of contaminated salvage; men holding boards level, waist high, while other men dealt cards or threw dice onto the boards because there was no room to sit down to gamble. "A family of three gets only one and a quarter square meters of living space," Cyborg said.

"How do you know all this stuff?"

"How else? Thebos told me. Thebos always knows everything about everything. Who can say where he gets his information?" Signaling for Corgan to follow him, Cyborg wove through the throngs toward the far wall, the one where Corgan and Ananda had found Thebos's door. *Don't look toward that door*, Corgan told himself, *not even in the direction of it. Don't give Cyborg any clue about where it is.* He was glad he'd never told Thebos's secret to Cyborg, because if he had, Brigand could have milked that information right out of Cyborg's brain.

"Where is Brigand?" Corgan murmured.

"About a dozen meters ahead of us."

"I can't see him."

"That's because he's surrounded by a ring of guards, handpicked from the New Rebel Troops. No one can get through to him unless he gives the signal."

As they drew closer Corgan could recognize the pattern. In that mass of ordinary people, all those men, women, and children trying to shove past one another in random directions, he noticed a circle of men standing still, side by side, all of them about the same height (tall), the same age (young), and the same physical build (muscular), wearing the same bland expression, as though they'd been programmed. If a little kid came too close, they'd grab him—not roughly—and, smiling, hand him over to his mother. Though they appeared pleasant enough, they gave off an air of menace unmistakable beneath the smiles.

One of them saw Cyborg and bent his head as a signal for him to come forward. The man next to the first one moved aside to let Cyborg and Corgan pass through, and after they did, the circle closed again behind them.

In a cavern filled with people almost on top of one another, Brigand was surrounded by space, an empty circle more than three meters in diameter. He wore a robe with a hood that shadowed his face, but Corgan would have known him instinctively—one glance and he felt the heat rising in his blood. "Come forward," Brigand ordered, sounding like an emperor ready to sentence a prisoner.

"Meaning me?" Corgan asked. "Quit hiding behind that hood. Show me your ugly face."

Brigand yanked the hood back hard, then threw off the robe, so that he stood before them naked to the waist.

If once the clone-twins had been hard to tell apart, they weren't any longer. Ever since Brigand had gotten the notion that his powers came from the cannibal chiefs on Nuku Hiva, he'd been tattooing himself with native symbols, the same ones he'd found on the preserved body of the long-dead cannibal chief. The last time Corgan had seen Brigand's thickly muscled torso, it had already been covered with tattoos of swirls, sunbursts, and triangles connected to look like the teeth of sharks, and of turtles, fish, and some shapes that didn't resemble anything in particular.

But his face—this was something new! The left side had been tattooed from the middle of his forehead in a straight line down the middle of his nose to the bottom of his chin, with dark colors that might have pictured leaves or birds' wings or beaks or other patterns whose meaning only Brigand knew. But only on the left side! The right side of his face was clear and pale. With that flaming red hair sticking straight up on his head in spikes, he looked like a nightmare. How could Sharla love this monstrosity?

Corgan forced himself to keep his expression impassive as he asked, "Where's Ananda?"

"Where's Sharla?" Brigand countered.

"In the medical wing upstairs, locked up nice and safe so you can't get at her."

"I want her back," Brigand said in that imperious tone.

"You do, huh? Well, she can't walk, she can't talk, and she can't eat, all because you ejected yourself safely and left her to die in the Harrier. She isn't dead, but she's close to it."

"You're lying!" Brigand pointed a tattooed finger and ordered, "If you want Ananda, bring me Sharla."

"Wait a minute," Cyborg said as he stepped between the two of them. "It isn't Corgan who wants Ananda. It's me."

"And why is that?" Brigand demanded.

"Because . . . I love her." He hesitated, as if it was the first time he'd said it out loud, maybe even the first time he'd realized it was true. "If you feel any loyalty to me, Brigand, you'll let her go."

Brigand let his eyes run over Cyborg from the top of his cropped red hair to his feet, in medical-wing sandals that were never meant to be walked in outside the center. "You look like crap," he said. "Even if I gave you the girl, you're in no shape to do much with her, baby brother."

"I'm not your baby brother. I'm not even your brother. We're clone-twins."

"Well, you act like a big baby. And look at you. You're puny!"

"I've been sick."

"If you'd stayed with me, you would never have been injured, but you deserted me. You left me! And you went with . . . him!" Although he pointed angrily at Corgan, blaming Corgan, the hurt in Brigand's voice was all about Cyborg; that seemed clear enough. "You abandoned me," he said again, more in sadness now than in anger. "But we'll forget all that if you come back to join my revolt."

"I don't want to revolt," Cyborg said.

"Why don't you? You *should,"* Brigand cried. "For the same reason I want to. The Supreme Council created me to do what They needed, knowing that then I'd die! I've already destroyed the council in Wyoming, and I'm going to terminate every other Supreme Council in every domed city on the planet."

Cyborg argued, "Why? It was the Wyoming council that had you created. Not the council here in Florida or anywhere else."

"What does it matter? My mission is to destroy all authority everywhere."

"Then, someone will surely destroy you."

Brigand laughed in a sinister, mocking burst that sent chills through Corgan. "No one will need to destroy me. Time is going to do that." Pointing to his clone-twin, he said, "Time will destroy you, too, the same as me!"

Wearily Cyborg answered, "Everyone dies, Brigand."

"But not after only four years! Everyone else gets to *live* first. Everyone except you and me, brother." His voice rose with emotion as he raged, "Death to the Supreme Council! Death to all the Supreme Councils everywhere. They created me to die, but I'll make sure *They* die first."

Cyborg took a step backward, as if Brigand's rage might infect him. "I heard what you did to the Wyoming Supreme Council. You tortured Them with thumb screws and branding irons and electric prods—that's inhuman cruelty."

"Is that right?" Brigand asked with fake innocence. "Inhuman cruelty? Well, did you know that Corgan zapped me with an electric cattle prod when I was just a little kid on Nuku Hiva?"

"What?" Cyborg looked astonished. "No way!"

Corgan flushed. It had happened, all right, a part of his past that he was ashamed of, an incident he thought no one would ever hear about. Before he could answer, Brigand added, "Talk about torture! First Corgan tied me up. Then he shot the electric cattle prod right at me. How old was I back then? About eight, Corgan?"

Trying to defend himself, Corgan cried, "The electric charge never hit you! I just wanted to scare you with it." To Cyborg he said, "It was right after he cut off your hand. I was freaked out."

Brigand goaded him, "So it's fine to use torture when you're freaked out—is that what you're saying, Corgan?"

"I'm sorry!"

"You're a little late with your sorries. It was probably that cruel act during my childhood that turned me into the monster I am today."

Filled with shame at being exposed like that in front of Cyborg and the guards, Corgan realized that Brigand, the strategist, was playing with him. Hotly he claimed, "I didn't make you a monster. You were already a monster, even back then. You'd just cut off your clone-twin's hand."

"To save him!" Brigand hissed. *"Save him. SAVE HIM!* That's why you have to join me in this revolt, Cyborg," he pleaded. "You owe that to me because I saved your life—I saved it for at least a few more years, until both of us die because the Supreme Council programmed us that way. But I'm going to make all of Them die first, and nobody will ever remember Them. But everybody will remember *me*, forever! I'll be the hero of all the rebels. The king. The emperor."

"The joke," Corgan declared.

All sound seemed to stop, as if the whole cavern had been muted. In the shocked silence Corgan heard Cyborg try to deflect disaster, stammering, "H-how about letting me see Ananda right now, Brigand, okay? Where is she?"

"She's around. But later, bro." Brigand's voice was venomous. "Right now I'm going to take care of your friend Corgan. Watch this. This'll be the *real* joke." He reached behind him, and when he pulled his hand forward, it held a gun. *The* gun. The same one Brigand's female rebel had used to shoot at Corgan in the Wyo-DC, the only gun still in existence.

Corgan felt no fear, only cold fury, as he said, "If you kill me now, you'll never get Sharla. You can't go into where she's kept. If you tried to, the robots would zap you with an arc that could fry your brain . . . if it isn't fried already, which I think maybe it is, since you—"

He didn't see it coming, the fist that smashed into his mouth. It wouldn't have hurt so much if Brigand hadn't been holding the gun in that fist. The blow knocked Corgan to his knees and stunned him enough that his head became filled with a roar that sounded like surf crashing on rocks. He felt hands under his arms, dragging him, pulling him to his feet—whose hands? Next he heard Ananda's voice cry, "Cyborg, get in front of Corgan." He saw both her elbows lash out and hit two of Brigand's guards in the throat, knocking them down to create an opening in the circle, and then he felt her hands against his back, pushing him forward through the break in the guards' circle while she shouted, "People, it's me, Ananda. Move aside. Let us through."

They burst into the mob of startled citizens, Cyborg first, Corgan next, with Ananda both shoving and dragging them as she shouted, "Move, people! Give us room! Make a passage."

"It's Ananda!" the crowd exclaimed. "Look, it's our Ananda." For the first time Corgan realized Ananda's celebrity in the Flor-DC, and he was grateful. The people seemed to revere her. They tried to huddle around her, reaching out to touch her as she instructed Corgan and Cyborg to keep moving. In spite of the crush she managed to clear a path for them, while the citizens closed in behind her, effectively blocking any pursuit by Brigand's guards.

Corgan knew Brigand couldn't take the chance of shooting into that crowd, not if he wanted them to support his revolt. It took seven minutes and thirty and three-quarters seconds for the three of them to break through to the elevator, just as two men were about to unload big tubs of water. Ananda shouted to them, "Leave them! Get out!" And they listened to her.

Once inside the elevator, they were safe. No one could follow them, since there was no other way as yet to get to the upper level. Panting, Cyborg sank back against the elevator wall, and Ananda put her arms around him and leaned against him, whispering, "Are you all right?"

"I'm fine," Cyborg answered, resting his chin on the top of Ananda's head. "From now on we're both going to stay inside the medical center, where you'll be safe."

Still a little groggy from being hit so hard, Corgan asked Ananda, "What happened back there? Where did you come from all of a sudden?"

She laughed and answered, "Well, they had four guards around me who were supposed to hide me and hold me back. But when you guys got there, the whole scene turned pretty dramatic. The guards wanted to hear everything, and I . . . well, I wanted to hear what Cyborg would say . . ."

"About you," Cyborg finished for her.

"Yes. I'm so glad I heard it. I love you too, Cyborg. But we have problems, don't we?"

"Big time," Cyborg agreed. He looked grim, and no wonder, Corgan thought. Their problems had no solutions.

"Keep talking," Corgan told Ananda. "Finish your story about how you got us out of there."

She went on, "They were pretty dumb guards—if all Brigand's rebels are that useless, his revolt won't go far. 'Cause when things got a whole lot more intense, after Brigand said that about the cattle prod, the guards were paying more attention to you guys than to me. That gave me the chance to kick some butt. After all, I'm Ananda! Training with Corgan turned me into a champion butt kicker. Corgan, did you really arc Brigand with a cattle prod when he was little?"

Ashamed, Corgan answered slowly, "I just wanted to scare him. The electric shock never really hit him. It only scorched the tree I tied him to."

"You tied him to a tree? When he was how old? Eight?"

Corgan leaned his head on his arm against the elevator wall. He'd never expected anyone to find out what he did that day, and now the humiliating story would spread through the whole Flor-DC. And as stories always did, it would grow each time it got repeated, until Corgan became the monster, not Brigand. It might even win sympathy for Brigand, the last thing Corgan wanted.

The elevator door opened then and Ananda pulled Cyborg forward, saying, "Come on, we have to get out."

They could barely squeeze through the crowd of people who strained to get in. Corgan wondered how much longer the total evacuation would take and how these people had survived the pollution so far. Most of them held a cloth against their mouth and nose, so he supposed that helped. And mostly they were men, which meant that the women and children had been evacuated first.

As they got close to the medical center, before they could even touch the DNA identification scanner, Thebos swung open the door to hurry them inside.

"How's Sharla?" was the first thing Corgan asked, needing some good news to help him forget his public humiliation.

"They gave her a powerful injection of dexamethasone steroid and got her walking," Thebos answered.

"That's good, isn't it?" Corgan exclaimed.

"It was a mere physical reaction, so don't get your hopes up. Mentally . . . well . . . nothing's happening. She still can't talk, and she doesn't understand a word spoken to her. It looks irreversible."

"Don't say that," Corgan begged as he went straight to her room. He'd never give up hope.

TWELVE

Morning. The third day after the dome crash. Sharla stared at Corgan, once more without a hint of recognition, but this time she was eating the bowl of unappetizing mush all by herself. So that was an improvement.

"Hello, Sharla," he said. "Do you know who I am?"

No answer.

"I'm Corgan. We fought the Virtual War together. With Brig." Why was he bothering with this again? If she didn't even know who she was, how would she know him? Maybe if . . .

As much as he didn't want to, he tried another name. "Brigand," he said, his lip curling around the bad taste of it in his mouth. "Do you remember Brigand?"

Did he see a flicker of response in her eyes? He said it again. "Brigand."

Her lips moved, but she made no sound. Her eyes, though, stayed fastened to his.

"And I'm Corgan," he told her. "Can you say 'Corgan'?"

She lowered her eyes to focus on the bowl, beginning to scrape it with the spoon. He gave up.

During the next seven minutes and thirty-two and nineteen-hundredths seconds he paced the small room nineteen times—forward, angle to the right, backward, angle to the left—trying to turn his mind as numb as Sharla's so all this wouldn't hurt so much. Then Ananda entered.

"I made Cyborg stay in his room to rest some more," she said. "He's pretty beat up physically and emotionally. I think you and I need to figure out what we're going to do."

"I'd rather wait for Cyborg," Corgan said. "Or Thebos."

"Why? You think I'm not smart enough to plan anything?" Ananda flared. "You think all I can do is run and beat up guards? Or 'soar like a bird'—I remember you said that about me when we trained virtually, each in our own DC. Back then I thought you were a kind of god."

"And you don't think so now?"

"Aw . . . Corgan." She sank to the floor, her legs criss-crossed in front of her. "You never give me credit for having brains, but I do. I'm at least as smart as you are. Neither one of us is as smart as Cyborg, that's true, but we're not total idiots, either. So let's have a little two-person conference and see if we've got any good ideas."

Corgan sat on the floor near her, his back against the wall. "What kind of ideas?"

"First, how do we fight Brigand when we're locked up here in the medical center? If I try to go down into the cavern, he'll know I'm there, because everyone recognizes me. He'll have his punks grab me again."

"And you can't fight them off?"

She looked at him scornfully. "Four at a time, yes, but a dozen or more? Come on, Corgan. You couldn't do it either."

"But we're faster than they are," he said, getting a little excited. "If we worked as a team, the two of us together might be able to take them."

"And then what?"

"Then . . . I don't know. Go after Brigand?"

"Who has a gun and who'd like to shoot you dead. Great plan, Corgan. Can't you come up with something a little more . . . intellectual?"

From behind the door that led to the hall a voice said, "No, you can't. Neither of you. That's why you have me." The door swung open then and Cyborg came into the room, hanging on to the doorframe for support.

"I told you to rest," Ananda cried, jumping up and running to him. "You're making yourself sicker."

"I'm fine," he said. As he slumped into the chair at the foot of Sharla's bed he didn't look fine at all. His skin had that gray pallor, and he rubbed his side as though trying to soothe the pain. "Listen, guys," he said, "maybe I'm not in the best physical shape right now, but my brain is working perfectly. Look at the two of you—you're like the empress and emperor of perfect bodies. Me, I'm weaker, but I'm older, which maybe makes me . . . uh . . . a little smarter?"

"For sure," Ananda agreed.

Age. It factored into everything. Cyborg was now three-plus years older than Corgan, which bothered him because those extra years meant superiority—at least up to a point. Too much age and you lost advantage, like Thebos, who couldn't stand up without creaking. When did it turn around? Corgan wondered. At what point did the arc start to curve, so that age made a once superior person spiral downward into deterioration? He'd have to sort it out later because Cyborg was telling him, "Pay attention. We only have a little time to figure this out before Brigand tunes in to me again. Right now he's . . . involved."

"Involved?" Corgan echoed. "Like planning the Flor-DC revolt?"

"No, involved, like with a woman."

"You mean he's having . . . ?" When Cyborg nodded, Corgan yelled, "That dirty slime, that scum, that filth—he's with *another* woman now, after what he did to Sharla?" All three of them glanced toward Sharla, but she seemed oblivious, staring into her empty bowl.

"Yeah, well, what can I say? It happens frequently." Cyborg spoke mostly to Ananda. "Brigand and I may be genetically identical, but we think and act differently. Very differently. The point is, while he's busy, we can talk and he won't telepath into my brain. But let's focus before he . . . uh . . ."

Corgan reached to take the bowl from Sharla's unresisting hands, then lowered the bed so she could rest. If only she knew! Or maybe she did. Maybe Brigand had been just as obscene in Wyoming.

"This is what we need to do," Cyborg was saying. "Ananda can't go into the cavern because everyone knows her. I can't go because Brigand would read my thoughts. That leaves you, Corgan, but I don't want you to go alone."

"You don't want? Who appointed you commander?"

"Shut up! Shut up and listen! You need to go down there with Thebos. The two of you can warn the Supreme Council. Brigand won't recognize Thebos."

Corgan considered that. It sounded reasonable. "Okay," he said. "When?"

"Now," Cyborg answered. "You have to find Thebos and explain this to him. I can't talk about it anymore. Brigand is through with his . . . woman . . . and he'll start tuning in to me pretty soon. You and Ananda get Thebos. I'll stay here with Sharla."

"You should rest in your own room . . . ," Ananda began, but stopped when she saw the look on Cyborg's face. "All right, I'm going. Come on, Corgan."

When they knocked on the door of Thebos's quarters, they heard a bark. "Demi is staying with him," Ananda explained. "So am I. Ever since I got away from Brigand, Thebos has been letting us share his room, which is fine with me, since it means I'm living closer to Cyborg." As Ananda opened the door the dog leaped at her, covering her face and hands with wet licks. "Enough kisses!" Ananda said. "Yes, I missed you too, baby." She scratched the dog vigorously around the neck and ears. "You're the prettiest thing that ever lived. Isn't she, Corgan? Isn't she pretty?"

"Yeah, sure, Ananda." He turned to Thebos and said, "Cyborg made this plan—"

"I know. I was listening."

"So you're the one!" Corgan cried. "We've been trying to figure out who listens through the walls and ceilings to everything we say. You spook!" That explained how Thebos always knew when help was needed, when to open the door, when to send in the robots.

"It's not just me," Thebos answered. "There's a whole team of us. I wouldn't say we're sneaks; we're just doing our job overseeing the well-being of the patients. And when I don't think the others should hear something, I just shut them out, because I'm the tech wizard."

"Plus scientist supreme and engineer extraordinaire," Corgan added.

"But enough talk. If you and I are supposed to go to the Supreme Council, Corgan, let's get to it. Ananda, there's food on the table. I've already fed Demi."

"What about me?" Corgan asked, feeling his own hunger now that food was mentioned.

"You can wait to eat until we come back."

"Unless I'm dead by then."

"If you're dead, you won't be hungry." Rubbing his shaky hand across Corgan's hair, which was softer now and no longer as prickly as when it first started to grow out, Thebos gave Corgan's head a fond pat. "Don't worry. You're not going to be dead. You're going to carry Eleven's arc gun just in case there's trouble."

"I don't want to," Corgan protested.

"Well, I want you to carry it. It will be a psychological

tool," Thebos said with a grin. "Your own symbol. Corgan the Arc Man, good with cattle prods and arc guns."

Slamming his fist against the wall, Corgan felt himself go rigid with anger. "Never call me that again! Do you get that, Thebos? Never again!"

Thebos's voice quavered just a little. "Yes, I got it. I won't. I'm sorry."

Corgan's willingness to tackle this dangerous mission took a sudden dive. Had the cattle prod story already spread through the whole underground cavern? Would people point at him? If he attracted attention, how was he supposed to protect this old man whose hands shook, whose steps faltered, whose fragile body was held up by bones so weak they might crack if one of Brigand's thugs so much as pushed him? It suddenly seemed like a very bad idea, but Thebos appeared unworried. He held out a threadbare garment. "Put on this old sweater of mine. Your LiteSuit is too bright and clean. It will stand out and attract attention. We don't want that." As Corgan shrugged into the dingy sweater (was that what Thebos had called it?) Thebos was already at the door, gesturing for him to follow. "Here. Hide this under the sweater, if you don't mind," he said cautiously, holding out the arc gun to Corgan.

They shared the elevator with about seventy men and three large containers of food. While the men were unloading the tall boxes, Corgan and Thebos slipped behind them, exiting unnoticed into the congested cavern. In the single day since Corgan had last seen them, the people looked even grubbier. Corgan didn't know whether to walk in front of Thebos to clear a path for him or to stay behind him so he could make sure Thebos didn't trip and fall down. He compromised by walking beside him. "Hold on to me," he told Thebos, extending his arm.

"Gladly. Now we have to find the Supreme Council. I beg your pardon," he said to a woman braiding the hair of a young girl. "Do you know where, in all this"—he waved his hand—"I might find the Supreme Council?"

"No, I don't," the woman answered curtly, but the child said, "I do. I'll show you."

"I'm not finished braiding," her mother scolded, but the girl had already started to push through the crowd. Corgan had a hard time propelling Thebos fast enough so that they wouldn't lose sight of the child. No one paid attention to them, not to Thebos and fortunately not to Corgan.

"Over there," the girl said, pointing. "Now you have to give me something because I helped you."

"Give you what?" Corgan had nothing with him that any kid might want.

"Look in the left pocket of the sweater," Thebos murmured. When Corgan did, his fingers closed around a flat, round disk with a cord looped between the holes in whatever the thing was. "Give it to her," Thebos instructed.

Puzzled, the girl asked, "What is this?"

Thebos answered, "It's very old, and it's called a button. See this garment my young friend is wearing? Watch."

Corgan hadn't even noticed when he put on the sweater that three of the round, flat disks Thebos called buttons were lined up on the front of it. Thebos took one of them in his fingers and pushed it through a hole in the left side of the sweater. "See?" Thebos said. "This is how we used to fasten the clothes we wore."

Corgan figured that must have been long before Magnasnaps, the magnetic fasteners everyone used to hold edges together.

"And now," Thebos told the little girl, "look what you can do with the button I'm giving you."

He grasped both ends of the loop of cord that ran through the button and began to twirl the cord until it twisted tightly around itself. Then he pulled the ends and the button spun, making a buzzing sound as it did.

The little girl clapped her hands. "Can I do it?" she cried.

This whole thing was taking too much time, Corgan thought. People were beginning to look curiously at the twirling, buzzing button toy, and soon they might notice Corgan. "Let's move," he whispered, pulling Thebos's elbow.

"I like little children," Thebos whispered back. "I'm sorry I never married and had any."

They slipped easily through the bystanders who were now engrossed in the little girl's toy. Just two meters ahead a pole had been stuck in the ground with a sign on top reading FLORIDA DOMED CITY TEMPORARY GOVERNMENT HEADQUARTERS. Other poles supported cloth draped into a makeshift tent. Corgan tried to find an opening to the tent but was stopped by a middle-aged man who was evidently a guard.

"Who are you and what do you want?" the man demanded.

Thebos stepped forward to say, "You should ask who *I*

am. This boy is my personal assistant, and I am Thebos. I'm here to see the council."

The man looked unimpressed. "Wait here," he said, and pushed through the cloth to go inside.

"Let me do all the talking," Thebos told Corgan. Funny, that was exactly what Ananda had said when she introduced Corgan to the council weeks ago. Did everyone think he couldn't string words together into useful thoughts? Before he had a chance to object, the man returned and told them they could enter.

"Well, if it isn't old Thebos," a councilman drawled. It sounded so disrespectful that Corgan stiffened in surprise. "What does he want?" the councilman asked Corgan.

"He'll tell you," Corgan answered, moving back to let Thebos stand in front of all eight members of the council. What was the matter with these people? Didn't They understand how valuable Thebos was, with all his knowledge? Or maybe because Thebos had faked his dim-witted act for the past few years, They didn't know any better.

"First," Thebos began, "do you realize who crashed the aircraft through the dome?"

"We do," answered a councilwoman, the older one who spoke slowly. "It was Brigand, the rebel you told us about, Corgan."

"Do you know why Brigand is here?" Thebos asked Them.

"We hear he plans to lead a revolt in our own DC," the short, round councilman answered. "We're not worried. We have patrols out searching for him, but even if we don't find him anytime soon, he's no threat to us."

Corgan declared, "That's what the council in Wyoming thought too, but Brigand overthrew Them pretty fast. I don't even know if any of Them are still alive."

"That has nothing to do with us," the councilman said.

"But it could! It could happen here, too. Brigand is no doubt spreading the very same propaganda right here, right now," Thebos told them. "Spreading the infection of rebellion. He's a charismatic leader preaching anarchy, mutiny, and insurrection, gathering followers to himself like ripe fruit gathers insects—"

One of the councilmen, who was sprawled in his chair, not bothering to sit upright, interrupted, "Thebos, Thebos, just listen to yourself! You certainly must realize that our citizens are content here in the Florida domed city. They would never want to overthrow us, because we have governed well and fairly, with the citizens' welfare always in our hearts."

Why doesn't Thebos tell Them about the coded message? Corgan wondered. Maybe that would alarm these stubborn, unheeding people and convince Them that They were in danger. But Thebos, just as stubborn, seemed determined to keep his own secrets. Corgan could almost feel the resentment radiating from Thebos at the way They were treating him.

Corgan tried again. "That's what the council in Wyoming—"

"No. Stop!" The councilman held up his hand. "We don't need to hear any more of this. Eventually we will capture Brigand and incarcerate him. Once the dome is restored, our city will go back to normal, and for all of us normal means contentment. Our people are loyal to us.

There will be no upheavals in the Florida domed city."

"You just had an upheaval!" Corgan blurted out.

"That was an anomaly."

Another councilwoman leaned forward and pointed at Corgan. "You've visited many parts of our city. You must have seen that we're more advanced in every way than your Wyoming domed city. I've heard that yours was, in fact, rather backward. Why would our citizens follow this renegade Brigand to rise up against us? Our workers live comfortable lives, with nightly entertainment."

The other seven council members murmured in agreement until Thebos announced, "You said your deputies are searching for Brigand. We know where Brigand is—Corgan and I do. We can lead you to him."

That should make Them sit up and take notice, Corgan thought, but They didn't look too concerned. "We'll send a deputy to check your story," the round councilman said.

"A deputy? You'll need more than one. Brigand is already gathering troops," Thebos told Them.

"Unlikely," one of Them murmured, and the others echoed, "Yes, unlikely," until one said, "All right, three deputies. That should be enough to capture one renegade."

They just don't get it, Corgan thought. What was the matter with these people? His own Wyo Supreme Council had been just as complacent, but They'd had no warning about the insurrection, so he couldn't blame Them as much as this council. These people were being warned, and yet They tossed if off as if it were some unreliable fantasy from Thebos's imagination. They must not have any intelligence-gathering system here, since They seemed to know nothing about Brigand's plans.

The three deputies who came with Corgan and Thebos looked as though they couldn't manage to arrest anyone. They seemed out of shape, bored, and incompetent, and they carried nothing with them that could be used as a weapon. Corgan tightened his arm against his side to feel the reassuring presence of the arc gun. In a battle between Brigand's gun and the arc gun Brigand's would certainly be more deadly, but maybe the arc gun could fake him out. The way the cattle prod had, once.

"The council—They're not prepared for insurrection," Thebos panted as once again they pushed through the crowds. "Nothing like that has ever happened here. The city pretty much runs itself—people are content, just as They said. So content that . . . ," he wheezed, "the whole population will most likely keep sitting on their fat duffs and let a handful of maladjusted agitators wreck things. Stop a minute till I catch my breath!"

Corgan held up his hand to signal the deputies to halt.

"War," Thebos mused. "They don't understand it. They've never known it. They're too young to remember the wars that caused the devastation. So are you, for that matter. The difference between you and Them is that you've already seen what Brigand can do. And you fought the Virtual War, while They only watched. To Them it was nothing more than one of Their entertainments."

As they moved forward again, the three deputies lagged behind. Finally they came close to where Brigand and his guards had stood yesterday, but Corgan felt pretty sure they wouldn't be in the same place. To avoid suspicion,

Brigand would certainly keep moving around the cavern.

Thebos asked, "You're sure this is where he was?"

"Positive."

The deputies shrugged as though they hadn't expected to arrest anyone anyway. "No sense us staying here," they said. "We'll look around on our way back."

"You do that. Do you know what you're looking for?" Corgan asked.

They didn't answer, and soon they were swallowed in the crowd.

"What a bunch of idiots," Thebos muttered. Then he pulled Corgan aside to ask, "Did you ever say anything to Cyborg about my tunnel?"

"You ought to know I didn't, since you listen in on our conversations." When Thebos looked a little embarrassed, Corgan told him, "Cyborg doesn't have a clue, so he can't thought-transfer it to Brigand, if that's worrying you."

"Good. Good." Then Thebos declared, "I want to check the tunnel. A little while ago, Corgan, I heard you saying that Cyborg had been cloned from Brig, a genius, so that made Cyborg a genius too. But Brigand possesses those identical genius genes. How else could he have led the revolt in Wyoming with no resources except his evil mind and his clever strategies? Never underestimate him. He might have discovered my tunnel, which would be a perfect place for him to hide—if he could in some way protect himself from the pollution." Thebos grabbed Corgan's arm again. "We'll go and see."

THIRTEEN

As he and Thebos edged closer to the hidden door Corgan wondered how they could open it without attracting attention. Anyway, would Brigand be in there if the tunnel was full of polluted air? So why should they even bother going in to look for him if they'd have to breathe the same contamination themselves? While he was debating this, a scream pierced the air. A mother had spotted her three-year-old perched precariously on a high pile of scrap metal, and she was yelling at the top of her lungs, "Get him down, get him down! Someone help me. He'll get hurt!"

Several men rushed forward to rescue the little boy. As they pushed people aside to get to him those people knocked into others, who bumped into others, and soon dozens of people were shouting at one another. During the confusion Thebos keyed the code that opened the tunnel door. "Quick! Get inside!" he urged Corgan.

In the seconds before the door closed, Corgan realized that the two of them would make perfect targets, outlined as they were against the light of the cavern behind them. Anyone in the tunnel would have a great shot at them. He ducked, pulling Thebos forward, half expecting a bullet from Brigand's gun. But nothing happened, and the door shut quietly.

After more seconds passed in total silence, Corgan said, "I don't think Brigand's here, and it's too dark to see anything anyway, and you said this air might be bad, so let's go back."

There was no answer from Thebos.

Scared, Corgan asked, "Thebos? Are you all right?" If the air really was poisoned enough to choke them, Thebos would react to it faster than Corgan. Maybe he was already unconscious.

Thebos answered with a snort, "I feel as well as I ever do, which isn't saying a lot. This air seems breathable. Perhaps after all these years whatever noxious elements might have been here have dissipated. Let's hope so."

"But Demi . . . ," Corgan began.

"She sneezed. Perhaps she was just sneezing from the dust in here. As you said, dogs have very sensitive noses."

"Maybe. But why should we take a chance? Let's get out of here. Brigand's not in here or I would have been shot by now." Corgan reached for Thebos's arm, but the tunnel was so totally dark that he grasped thin air.

"Yes, you might have been. So we shall depart the tunnel. But this has put an entirely new light on every- thing." Corgan could hear Thebos shuffling toward the door, groping for the handle that would open it.

Corgan kept his hand on the arc gun while they made their way through the throng in the underground cavern, half wishing that Brigand would appear out of the crowd so he could zap Brigand's ugly, tattooed face with the electric arc. This time he wouldn't deliberately miss. But neither Brigand nor any of his thugs were visible, even though Corgan kept scanning the area while he waited for the elevator to come.

On the ride up Thebos seemed energized, even hum- ming a little tune. Corgan didn't know why the old man should feel particularly happy about anything, since the meeting with the Supreme Council had been a disaster, but his steps even had a little bounce to them as he and Corgan made their way to the medical building.

Ananda opened the door for them and asked, "How did it go?" but Corgan was already rushing down the corridor, calling back to her, "Thebos will tell you." He'd been gone much too long from Sharla.

"Any change?" he asked Cyborg when he got to Sharla's room.

"No change. They gave her more of that steroid stuff to decrease the inflammation in her brain, and she's asleep now. What happened with the Supreme Council?"

"Nothing. They're a bunch of gonks." Starving, Corgan had just reached for a handful of soy biscuits when the voice boomed, *"CORGAN, THIS IS THEBOS. COME TO MY QUARTERS. WE HAVE TO TALK."*

"So, it's been him all along," Cyborg said. "I should have figured."

"Thebos is just one of the voices. There are lots more, mostly med techs, he told me. I wish he'd leave me alone," Corgan grumbled. "Can you stay here with Sharla a little longer?"

"Sure. I'll stay."

Demi greeted Corgan with her usual enthusiastic wiggle as he entered the quarters. He ignored her, asking Thebos, "What?"

Thebos, who was seated on his high stool, smiled in a superior, maddening way and said, "Corgan, do you know what it means to be obsessed? You are so obsessed by your love of Sharla and your hatred of Brigand that you can't see what's right before you, as clear as the nose on your face."

"What are you talking about?"

"Think, Corgan, *think*!" Thebos placed his fingertips together, tent fashion, and peered at Corgan like a wise old owl. "Are you thinking yet? I'll give you a clue. How did Sharla and Brigand get here?"

"In the Harrier."

Thebos shook his head impatiently. "Yes, in the Harrier. Did he land the Harrier?"

"No! He crashed it through the dome."

"Uh-huh." Thebos started making motions with his hands that looked like, *Come on! Come on! Keep thinking!*

"Through the dome, and he broke a big . . . ," Corgan stammered. "I mean, now there's a big . . ." His breath caught. "A big hole in the dome!"

"Through which . . . ," Thebos prompted him.

"The *Prometheus* could fly!"

"You got it!" Thebos exclaimed. "And the tunnel to my old laboratory doesn't seem to be particularly toxic. And at the end of the tunnel is a box with two monitors that you could bring back here, where I could install them into the *Prometheus* and you, Corgan, could fly it out right through that great big hole."

It was as if the whole room began to quiver around Corgan. Fly the *Prometheus*! But then he said, "No, I couldn't do that."

"Wait, my boy, you have not thought clearly enough. I'll give you a number of good reasons why you *should* do precisely that." Raising his hand, Thebos began counting them off on his fingers. "First, you need to get out of here, out of the Florida domed city. Now, don't interrupt me. This is what you must understand: You aren't safe here. The Supreme Council is going to fall in defeat. They're too stupid to even know They're at risk. Brigand, as I said before, is brilliant, even if his mind is twisted. As I told you, before the devastation there were many tyrants like Brigand in the world, all of them filled with hate, all of them able to manipulate their followers to cause chaos and death and destruction."

"But—"

"Don't interrupt! You are one person against a scourge. Brigand will kill you. That's an excellent reason for you to escape, and I'll give you another. The second big reason is Sharla."

This time Corgan didn't even try to interrupt.

"Sharla," Thebos continued, "will be recaptured by

Brigand, but when he sees her condition, he'll abandon her. You can save her from that. Bring her into the *Prometheus* and fly her to the space station. The station is still in orbit—I see it passing through the night sky."

"Space station!" Corgan sputtered. "Why?" All he knew about the space station had come from the images Thebos had shown him.

"I'll tell you why. The last crew to be launched to the space station consisted of a husband-and-wife astronaut team plus the world's greatest neuroscientist, Hong Ly. Hong was brilliant. He invented incredible new methods of electroencephalography—well, no matter, I see you looking at me with that uncomprehending expression again. Suffice it to say Hong Ly is—was—a century ahead of his time. He flew into space to do cerebrovascular experimentation, to devise ways to allow astronauts to stay in space for long periods without losing physical or mental agility."

"What does this have to do with—"

"*Think*, Corgan! If Hong's still alive up there, he could repair Sharla's brain. Not only Sharla, he could probably fix Cyborg, too. The so-called doctors in our medical wing are nothing more than useless med techs who stay in a little room playing cards and letting computers diagnose the patients. They avoid hands-on contact because they're afraid they'll catch something. They've done nothing to help Sharla or Cyborg, but Hong Ly could. He's a genius!"

Corgan jumped to his feet. "This is all impossible. There may be a hole in the dome, but there's a ceiling above the *Prometheus*—remember, the ceiling with all the solar panels?"

"Oh, ye of little faith," Thebos answered. "That ceiling is made of thin metal plates bolted together. You and Ananda could take them apart."

"Ananda? You didn't say anything about Ananda!"

"If Cyborg goes, I imagine Ananda will too," Thebos said drily. "As for food—there's a year's supply. I showed it to you. You can carry water up the stairs in tanks, you and Ananda, enough water to reconstitute the food and get you to the space station. Once there, you'd use the station's recirculating system."

Corgan sank back down on the chair, clenching his fists. "I'd be running away from Brigand. That means he'd win. I need to stay here and fight him."

"Would you really kill him if you had the chance?"

"Yes!"

"Aha! You answered that too fast, Corgan. You answered from your gut, not your head. Not your heart. I've learned to know you, Corgan, and you're not a killer."

Maybe that was true. On Nuku Hiva he'd had the chance, had held the spear in his hands, raised it high, ready to thrust it down at Brigand, twelve-year-old Brigand lying helpless on the ground. And he didn't do it. He'd hated Brigand, but not enough to kill. And he loved Sharla, but did he love her enough to follow this wild plan Thebos was urging on him?

"Someone's got to stop Brigand," he told Thebos.

"No one can stop him," Thebos answered. "Brigand's going to win, Corgan, at least until his followers realize they're worse off than before, but that could take years. We used to say, 'Those who fight and run away live to fight another day.' If you stay on the space station for a couple of years and then come back here, Brigand will be an easier target for you to overthrow. By then he'll be old like me."

"So will Cyborg."

That stopped Thebos. "Hmmm. That's true," he mused. "I hadn't given that much thought. But it's a better alternative for Cyborg than having him remain here under the destructive control of his clone-twin. I tell you, Brigand is going to win this revolt. It's just a matter of time, and not too much time at that."

Corgan started to pace around the room in short, jerky steps. "It just sounds too crazy. Not long ago you told me I'd have to study for six months before I could even learn the simulator."

"And you defied me. And proved me wrong. Now I'm saying that you can fly the real thing, can take the *Prometheus* into space."

"I don't think so," Corgan decided.

"As you wish. Stay here and die. Sharla will remain an invalid. Ananda may be captured by Brigand and become his new toy. Cyborg will—"

"Stop! You're twisting everything! You don't know what's going to happen. Sharla . . ." Corgan's voice cracked as he thought of Sharla's empty eyes, which might stay empty forever.

"You love her, don't you?" Thebos asked more gently.

"Yes."

Thebos rose from his chair, placed his trembling hands on the top of it, and leaned forward, staring into Corgan's face. "I loved a woman once too," he said. "And I lost her. Another man took her away from me because I was too proud to go after her. Maybe too scared. I've regretted that every day for the last sixty years of my life. Every day—do you hear? You've already let Brigand take Sharla away from you. Now you have a chance not only to bring her back, but to save her."

"I don't . . . I'm not . . ." Corgan couldn't think straight now—he felt tired and hungry and confused. "We're not really sure the tunnel air is breathable. What if I die in the tunnel? Who will take care of Sharla then?"

"Who will take care of her if Brigand kills you? Don't take too long to think about this, Corgan, or it may be too late."

Corgan stood up to leave, but as he reached the door Thebos called out, "Come back, Corgan! Don't go yet. I've been unfair to try to push you into a mission that could be dangerous."

When Corgan hesitated, Thebos said, "Honesty compels me to admit that there may be a good deal of risk. There's the threat that the tunnel is polluted. There are perils with space flight, and there may be other factors we're not even aware of—no one can foresee every hazard. You must carefully consider all these potential dangers when you're trying to decide. If anything bad should happen to you, Corgan, I could never . . . ever . . ." Stumbling over his words, he said, "I think of you as a son. Or grandson. Or more accurately, I suppose, my great-grandson, considering the age difference between us. I'm saying this all wrong. It's just, I never had a child of my own, and you've been . . ."

A little embarrassed, Corgan answered, "And I've never had a father. It's nice, having you act like one. But don't worry. If I decide to go through the tunnel, I'll get there fast, find the monitors, and get out of there fast." He reached to take Thebos's hand. "I promise you."

FOURTEEN

The underground cavern was dark, at least part of it. Lacking space for all the people to lie down and sleep at the same time, the area had been divided in two. Half the citizens got packed into the far end of the cavern for eight hours so the other half could have room to lie on the floor in the near end. Later the other half would lie down for their own eight-hour stretch. Luckily for Corgan, in the section between the elevator he'd just exited and the hidden tunnel, the overhead lights had been dimmed to near darkness. It was nighttime for that half of the cavern.

People lay stretched out on the floor, sleeping fitfully; mothers with their arms around children, protective fathers lying close to them, lovers entwined. Corgan had to find a path between outstretched arms and legs because if he stepped on a single finger, the victim's yelp would waken everyone. Darkness was a two-edged sword: It hid him but made his passage more difficult. Although Thebos had given him a monochromatic light-emitting diode flashlight that projected a pale blue beam, Corgan was afraid to turn it on. Someone might notice. The last thing he wanted was to alert Brigand's New Rebel Troops.

Cautiously, staying as close to the dirt wall as he could, he made his way to the tunnel and dug away the small circle of dirt to tap the code. At the entrance, he took a deep breath before he pulled on the air filtration mask Thebos had made him take, then he shook the flashlight to make sure it didn't go out. "It works on Faraday's principle of electromagnetic energy," Thebos had told him, "which states that when an electric conductor, like a copper wire, is moved through a magnetic field, electric current will flow in the wire. Oh well, never mind the principle, Corgan, just remember to jiggle the flashlight vigorously for thirty seconds every so often, or it won't stay lit."

In the dim blue light Corgan couldn't see more than twenty feet ahead of him, and the floor of the tunnel was uneven, strewn with clods of earth. He'd have to move fast to reach Thebos's laboratory, find the box with the monitors, and get back to the underground cavern before the sleepers woke up and the lights were turned on again. He should have time to spare, but Thebos had warned him to leave extra time for the unexpected.

Flexing his leg muscles, bouncing a little to build momentum, he took off. If the path had been smooth, he could have made the three-and-a-half-kilometer run in twelve minutes easy, but the path was bumpy and he couldn't see well. Halfway there something slapped him in the face, scaring him so much he yelled out. He whipped up the flashlight beam to discover that roots had grown through the tunnel's roof; thin, stringy roots from a tree, maybe, way aboveground or from weeds that had mutated abnormally large because of nuclear radiation.

When he reached the door to Thebos's lab, he yanked hard on its handle but couldn't get it open; perhaps the door had warped after the ceiling collapsed in the lab. Searching the tunnel with the flashlight, he spotted a metal pole narrow enough at one end to be used as a crowbar, and with it he forced open the door.

Inside he found a chaos of rubble, dirt, broken beams, and twisted metal, all of it visible in the daylight that streamed through the collapsed ceiling. That daylight would make it easy to search, but Corgan's skin crawled at the thought of sifting through radiation-contaminated debris. *Why am I doing this?* he asked himself for the tenth time. He knew the answer: When he brought back the monitor panels, Thebos would finish the spacecraft, and that would give Corgan a choice. He could choose to escape in the *Prometheus*, taking Sharla with him, or he could choose to stay and fight Brigand. Without the monitors there would be no alternative, no option, and he wanted one. He wanted to decide for himself. It meant he'd be in control for the first time since he arrived in this Florida domed city.

"I can tell you precisely where you'll find the monitor

panels," Thebos had said. "They're in a wooden box with the name SPATIAL 3-D SYSTEMS etched on the side. Locate them as fast as you can and then leave. I'll reactivate the DNA identification scanner, so that when you come back here, you can get into the medical center immediately, without waiting for someone to let you in. Good luck, dear boy. Move quickly."

Quick is good, but smart is better, Corgan told himself now. Before burrowing through the rubble, he walked around it, checking for any shape suggesting that a box might be buried beneath. A box about sixty-one centimeters square, Thebos had said. Corgan kicked at the dirt, dislodging bits of wood and metal discolored by decades of rain coming through the collapsed roof. He knocked over several mounds of wreckage before his foot hit something solid. Using a broken beam, he scraped away the dirt and found what he was looking for—a wooden box of the right size. Whatever lettering might have been on its side was long gone.

Better make sure, he thought. After he'd scraped the dirt from the top of the box, he used the pole to pry up the lid. "Gotcha!" he yelled. Inside lay the two flat-panel holographic monitor screens.

Carefully, making sure no dirt fell inside, he replaced the top of the box, then lifted it. Not too heavy, but heavy enough that he wouldn't be able to run back through the tunnel as fast as he'd made it there on the way over.

No sense wasting time resealing the door to the laboratory. With the flashlight in one hand, he sprinted as steadily as he could so the monitors wouldn't bounce around too much inside the box. He reached the cavern a good hour before the lights would be turned on, slipped into the elevator, and closed the doors behind him.

On the main level he hurried to the medical center, placed the tip of his index finger into the DNA identification scanner, and as the door opened called out, "I'm back. I got them. How's Sharla?"

To flee? Or fight?

Corgan couldn't sleep, and in spite of not wanting to, he began to plan. How could he get Sharla up the stairs to the *Prometheus*? How much water would they need, both for drinking and to reconstitute the dried food? How long would it take him and Ananda to remove the roof panels?

Crazy! Stop this! He covered his ears with his arms, as if that would keep him from hearing his own thoughts. Why stew over this when he hadn't decided anything yet?

Lying on a blanket on the floor of Sharla's room, he listened to her breathe. Earlier, when he'd asked Nurse Eleven whether Sharla had made any progress while he was gone, Eleven had said no. Next he'd asked Cyborg whether anything new had happened with Brigand, and Cyborg had said, "Plenty. More and more people are joining up with him. Pretty soon he'll have a whole army."

With those words repeating too many times in his mind, Corgan tossed and turned on the floor all night. Toward morning, when he finally fell asleep, he dreamed of soaring in the *Prometheus*, with Sharla beside him, touching him, kissing him. . . .

"Wake up!" It was Cyborg, nudging him with a toe.

"Eleven wants to bathe Sharla and wants you out of here. Come over to my room. Ananda's there."

Groggy, Corgan stood up and started to fold the blanket. "I'll attend to that," Eleven said in its level voice. "Please leave, Corgan."

He followed Cyborg into the next room, where Ananda sat cross-legged on the bed. "Have you been here all night?" he asked her. "I thought you were staying in Thebos's quarters."

Ananda blushed hotly and pointed to the ceiling. Corgan got the message. "She's blushing, Thebos," he yelled up to the ceiling.

"Thanks a lot," Cyborg muttered. "First I get my mind read by my clone-twin, then we get spied on by the eavesdropping police. What ever happened to privacy?"

Again shouting toward the ceiling, Corgan said, "Hey, Thebos, I'm hungry. You got anything to eat in this place?" He grinned at Cyborg and Ananda and told them, "As long as we're being listened to, we may as well order breakfast."

"Will you shut up and sit down?" Cyborg grumbled. "We have serious stuff to talk about. Thebos told us about the *Prometheus*. He thinks we should all fly out of here."

"When did he tell you that? Doesn't that old man ever sleep?" Corgan asked. "I'm starting to think he's a clone too, 'cause he's everywhere all the time. Did they make human clones back before the devastation?"

"Irrelevant!" Cyborg snapped. "We need to talk now while we can. Brigand is having a meeting with his lieutenants, so he won't clue in to me for a while. I don't know how much time I have. First, we need to hear your

171

thoughts, Corgan. Ananda and I have already gone over this."

"Oh, you have? Without me? Since I'm the one who'd have to pilot the *Prometheus*, didn't you think my input would matter?"

"Corgan, that's why you're here now," Ananda broke in. "We want to hear what you think."

"I think the whole idea is insane," he answered. "Why should I sneak away from a fight with Brigand? I can take him in a fair fight."

"Which it *won't* be," Cyborg pointed out. "It can't be a fair fight if Brigand has the only gun."

"That's something I just don't understand," Ananda broke in. "Guns would be so easy to manufacture. Our technicians here in the Flor-DC could do it, and hey, if the guys in your Wyo-DC were smart enough to make your artificial hand, Cyborg, why wouldn't they make a whole pile of guns for Brigand's revolt?"

Cyborg answered, "Brigand wouldn't let them. It's all strategy. I can tell you how his mind works on this. He's the only person in the entire Western Hemisphere Federation who owns a gun. It makes him feel unbeatable, like he has the *potential* to hurt anyone who defies him. I don't think he'd ever actually use it, because he'd lose popular support, since the last two generations have been raised to believe that all weapons are evil. But he likes to wave it around as a symbol of supreme power, like a king's scepter or Zeus's lightning bolts. It's his insignia."

"That doesn't make a whole lot of sense," Ananda said uncertainly. "I'd never trust him. Anyway, we need to talk about the spaceship 'cause that's what's important. If this Hong guy will make Cyborg get well, then I'm all in favor of flying out of here."

"Yes, if Hong happens to be alive," Corgan answered. "He'd be as old as Thebos."

The door opened with its little *whoosh* sound and Eleven entered, bearing food. "Room service," Eleven said. Corgan detected a note of sarcasm in the droning voice, just as once before he'd thought he heard sympathy. Eleven told them, "Food may become scarce here in the medical center. There are guards outside the door, and they're not allowing our supplies to be delivered."

"Brigand's thugs!" Corgan muttered. "So now he thinks he can starve us out."

Ananda picked up a bowl of the same unpleasant mush they'd been feeding Sharla. She sniffed it, turned up her nose, and handed it to Corgan. "Here. You're the one who's hungry."

"Not that hungry," he answered, but then he changed his mind. If food was going to be scarce, he'd better take what he could get while he could get it. Grimacing, he swallowed some of the stuff while Cyborg and Ananda watched. Through the mouthful he said, "Okay, I've heard what Ananda thinks, so what do you think, Cyborg?"

Cyborg answered, "I figure the plan will work and I'm ready to go. Do you think I like being here and watching my clone-twin turn into a tyrant, a criminal? You know how that makes me feel? Like there might be something wrong with me, too, since the two of us have the same genes, the same DNA. Maybe something in me will suddenly snap and I'll turn into a menace like him."

"Never!" Ananda declared, touching his arm. "You're too good inside."

Cyborg smiled at her, but the smile didn't look convincing. "How can you know that, Ananda? What makes me any different from my clone-twin?"

"Humph, that's easy. I can give you the answer," Corgan announced. "When you were a baby and Sharla brought you to me on Nuku Hiva, she said that you and Brigand were in different surroundings before you were born. Brigand was gestated in an artificial womb in Sharla's lab. You were . . ." He hesitated, then said, "You were placed into the womb of a mutant, a girl with no mental capacity, but a usable body. I don't know much about gestation, but—"

Ananda broke in, "It means that prebirth, Brigand was in a machine, while Cyborg grew inside a real mother, in a warm womb, hearing her heartbeat. And I bet when you were born, Cyborg, that mutant girl held you and loved you in the time before Sharla took you away from her. That's the difference between you and Brigand."

"You think so?" Cyborg looked troubled as he said, "I'd like to know what happened to her. That girl, I mean. Maybe someday I could go back and find her."

"Probably not. The mutants never lived very long," Corgan explained quietly. "They weren't treated too well— they were crowded into a small space, and people gawked at them through the glass. Brig tried to make things better for the mutants, but he couldn't do much before he died. I imagine Brigand got rid of them. Terminated them."

Downcast, Cyborg said, "No. He wouldn't do that. There's got to be some decency left in him." Then he raised his head. "For now, though, we're wasting time talking. Let's get back to business while we can. The answer is yes, I'm willing to go in the spacecraft. So is Ananda. But you're the one who has to decide, Corgan. You're the only one who can pilot the *Prometheus*."

Corgan didn't answer right away. The one factor in all this that they hadn't discussed was Sharla, and he was half afraid to bring it up. Tersely he said, "*If* we do this—and right now it's a very big *if*—we have to decide on the best time to leave here. The *Prometheus* is ready. Last night I installed the two holographic control panels myself. Thebos went over the diagrams to show me what to do, and after I put them in, I tested them, so I know they work. He said I did great. Right, Thebos? Hey, Thebos!" he called out to the ceiling. "If you can hear me, knock three times."

Silence.

"What about the other listeners?" Ananda asked. "Do you think they're hearing us talk about this?"

Cyborg shook his head. "I think Thebos is the main snoop. Probably the med techs are too busy playing cards to bother listening to us, and the robots don't care what we say. So let's plan." He turned toward Ananda, who whispered, "Go ahead. You have to say it."

Reluctantly Cyborg began, "There's one huge hole in what you just mentioned, Corgan, and I'm not talking about the hole in the dome. It's just—you didn't say anything about Sharla. Thebos told us she'd be your real reason for going."

"That's right. My only reason."

An uncomfortable silence followed. Cyborg and Ananda again glanced at each other. After a moment Ananda put her hand over Cyborg's and said, "Go on. Tell him."

"Tell me what?"

When Cyborg didn't answer right away, Ananda said, "All right, then, I'll go first. Corgan, Cyborg and I want to go, but we don't think we should take Sharla with us. Not the way she is now."

Once the words were out, Cyborg took over. "She'd be a liability, Corgan. She couldn't contribute anything to the mission, and she'd use up food and water and oxygen—"

"Do you really want to attempt this mission with someone in Sharla's condition?" Ananda broke in again. "It doesn't make sense."

"You have got to be joking!" Corgan stood up, kicking the bowl against the wall so hard the mush spilled over the sides. Angry, he declared, "This is not negotiable. If I go, Sharla goes. If she stays here, so do I. Which means," he said, his voice rising, "that you two will be stuck here too to face all the bad things Thebos tells us are going to happen. But hey—I haven't even made up my mind yet. I'm just laying down the rules for *if* I go."

"Don't freak out," Cyborg told him. "We're trying to think of the angles. Thebos fed you this one possibility about Brigand and Sharla, that when Brigand sees she's in such bad shape, he'll dump her. How do we know that's what will actually happen? We don't know that any more than we know whether Hong Ly is still alive."

As if on cue, Thebos was standing at the door. "I didn't

knock three times, I just came. And I happened to turn off the sound so the med techs wouldn't hear you. Do you want answers to your questions, or do you just want to sit there like cows, chewing the same complexities over and over? Look at you!" he announced. "Two supreme physical specimens and one extraordinary mental giant, tangling yourselves into knots over problems that can be solved so simply."

All three of them stared at Thebos, Cyborg a little embarrassed, Ananda interested, Corgan disturbed. "So I guess you mean you have the answers," Corgan said.

"Wrong, Corgan." Thebos shook his head. "The answers are up to you. I'm only trying to save your lives. What I proposed should help both Cyborg and Sharla to recover, but as you keep saying, the whole thing is your choice, and yours alone. Right now I've come to give you a warning. I've been eavesdropping, as you like to call it, on the guards at the door. I heard them say that the actual revolt will begin tomorrow."

"So soon!" Ananda cried, looking a little frightened. "Will that give us enough time?"

Thebos answered, "If you decide to flee in the *Prometheus*, I'll have the water containers ready for you to load." He turned to go but stopped at the door to say, "You're good at calculating time, Corgan, so you know how fast tomorrow is going to arrive."

After he'd gone, Ananda breathed, "Yes! Tomorrow is . . . pretty soon!"

The three of them looked anxiously at one another before Corgan broke the silence, saying, "I don't know yet what I'll decide. But like I said, if I go, Sharla goes, and the two of you can come if you want to. If I don't go, you're stuck here, and when I fight Brigand, you can be with me or not with me. That's the part of it *you* get to decide."

Cyborg scowled as he said, "You've got us in a bind, don't you, Corgan? Since the revolt starts tomorrow, we'll have to get out of here tonight, no more than fourteen hours from now. So make up your mind fast! Are you going or not?"

"Only if Sharla—," Corgan began.

"Yes, Sharla. You keep saying 'Sharla.' Okay, I withdraw my objections and Ananda does too—correct, Ananda? So let's start moving! Or at least tell us if we're going to do this. You're the one in charge now."

"Right. I'll let you know." He left the room quickly and stood in the hall with his back against the wall. He was in charge, but he didn't really want to be. His decision wouldn't affect just his own life, he'd be responsible for three other lives. Still, Corgan was the only one threatened with death. Brigand wouldn't kill his clone-twin or Ananda—what reason would he have to kill her? Or Sharla. Sure, he might abandon Sharla, but abandonment didn't mean death.

Yet Brigand wouldn't have a way to cure her, and Corgan might. Or might not. To make it happen, he'd have to fly the *Prometheus* without crashing it, find the space station, and hope that Hong Ly was still alive. A lot of ifs.

And if he chose to run away, Brigand would brand him a coward. Did that matter? Why should he care what that insane revolutionary called him? He did care, though. But he cared more about Sharla.

When he entered Sharla's room, he was aghast to see that Eleven, or one of the other robots, had cut Sharla's hair. "It was a matter of cleanliness," Eleven reported. "With all the troubles going on in the city, the robotic nurses could not take the time to care for that long hair."

"You shouldn't have done that!" Corgan stormed.

Eleven intoned, "It is hospital procedure for long-term female patients. She should have been shaved bald, like you were, but she was too weak to undergo decontamination. Like you had to do."

"Long-term patient?" he cried. "You think so? Well, you're in for a surprise. She's not going to be a long-term patient."

And just like that he made up his mind. He knew what he was going to do. "Go away, Eleven," he said. "Leave us alone."

"As you wish." With the usual puff of air at the door Eleven exited the room.

Sharla sat at the foot of the bed, staring blankly at Corgan. He walked to her and touched the edge of her hair, still golden and beautiful, but cut so short now that it barely brushed her chin. "It'll grow back," he told her, as if she cared. As if she even knew.

FIFTEEN

"You can't loosen that bolt with your fingers, Ananda. Here, use this," Corgan said, handing her a wrench.

"Yeah, you're right. Thanks."

Corgan and Ananda had already hoisted water vats into the ship's cargo bay, along with the entire supply of dried food. Now they were working on the ceiling panels. "Turn the bolts enough that they're almost all the way off, just hanging by a few threads. Once we get Cyborg and Sharla inside," he told Ananda, "we can unfasten the roof panels altogether, shove them out of the way, and take off."

"Cyborg, Sharla, and Demi."

"Huh? What did you say?"

"Once we get Cyborg, Sharla, and Demi inside. I'm

taking Demi. She's my dog and I'm not flying off into space without her. Remember what you said about Sharla? You said, 'If I go, Sharla goes.' Well, I'm saying the same thing about Demi. If I go, she goes."

"That's totally impossible," Corgan sputtered. "What about food?"

"Demi will eat the same food we eat," Ananda told him.

"You can't take a dog in a zero-gravity spaceship. She'd float all over the inside."

"I'll hold her."

"There are only four seats on the control deck," he argued.

"She doesn't need a chair of her own. I said I'd hold her."

"For the whole trip? It'll take days, at least, to get to the space station, if we can find it at all."

"Corgan! Give it up! It's a done deal and you're wasting time fighting me." For emphasis Ananda smacked a panel with the wrench.

He would have fought longer if they hadn't been running out of minutes. The escape didn't have to be precisely timed to the split second—a few minutes either way wouldn't wreck anything—but there was still a lot more to do. Cyborg and Sharla were waiting for them in the corridor downstairs. Sharla would need to be led up the narrow stairs, and that might be tricky—if she didn't respond, one person would have to pull her while another pushed from behind. And then there was Thebos. Corgan couldn't just rush off without saying a decent good-bye to Thebos.

Only an hour earlier Thebos had handed Corgan a

letter, saying, "This is for Jane Driscoll, the astronaut who has been in the space station since before the devastation. I've told her all about you and asked her to do everything she can to help you. That is, if Jane is still alive."

Something about the way Thebos said the name *Jane*, with a little catch in his voice, made Corgan wonder. "Is Jane the woman?" he asked. "The one you loved, but another man took her away from you?"

Thebos nodded in short, jerky little nods.

"Sure, I'll deliver the letter," Corgan said. "Is there any other message you want me to give her?"

"Tell her . . . tell her . . . I think of her always. Tell her that the years we worked together were the happiest I ever knew. Tell her . . . no, never mind. There's nothing more to say." Thebos had turned away then, his lips trembling.

Corgan had said, "I'll tell her that you're still a scientist supreme and an engineer extraordinaire." He tucked the letter in the inside pocket of his LiteSuit, hoping he would actually be able to deliver it, if they ever found the space station in that great vastness of sky, and if this woman Jane Driscoll was still alive.

"Don't make that last bolt too loose," he told Ananda now. "We don't want it to fall off before it should. Anyway, I think we're finished with this, so let's go back to the med center and bring up Sharla and Cyborg."

"Yes, boss," Ananda said agreeably, now that she'd won her battle over Demi.

The two of them slid down the side of the *Prometheus* to the floor. Corgan looked around for one last inspection, then followed Ananda down the stairs. His mind was so preoccupied with a checklist of what still needed to be done that he didn't immediately grasp what he saw when they entered the long corridor. Sharla, Cyborg, and Thebos, with Demi right behind them, stood close together, very tense and erect. And holding all of them at gunpoint . . . was Brigand.

So shocked he dropped the wrench, Corgan demanded, "How did you get in here?"

"It was easy," Brigand answered with his usual insolent grin. "The door opens for all of you when the DNA identification scanner releases the lock. I touched it with my finger and it opened right up. Didn't any of you smart people realize that Cyborg and I have the same identical DNA? We're clones, remember?"

Cyborg looked disgusted with himself, probably because he should have thought of that and he hadn't.

"I know all about your plans because I siphoned them out of Cyborg's mind," Brigand went on. "You think I can't pull in your thoughts, Cyborg, when I'm doing other things? Hey, I can do lots of things at the same time—talk to my troops, make a plan—"

"Cheat on Sharla by sleeping with other women," Corgan put in.

Brigand had the decency to look flustered. "Who says I cheated on Sharla?" he demanded. "I don't call it cheating. I'm using these women to create a future dynasty, so that when I rule the entire world, each of my sons will command a domed city of his own."

Incredulous, Cyborg asked, "You mean you're trying to get these women pregnant? Sharla too?"

Brigand answered, "Sharla and I have not yet mated. I'm saving her to be the empress of my worldwide domain."

For almost a full minute Corgan's hatred of Brigand vanished, replaced by wild elation. As Brigand had put it so curiously, Sharla and Brigand had never mated! Would it matter to Corgan if they had? He loved her no matter what, but to know that she'd never given in to Brigand . . . could that mean she really loved Corgan? He felt so buoyed up that he almost missed what came next.

"Very amusing, Brigand," Thebos was saying, "that you expect to create all these sons. Hasn't anyone ever told you that clones are sterile? You'll never father anyone, which is a good thing because the world will be a better place if your malevolent qualities do not get passed along."

Furious, Brigand had raised his arm to strike Thebos, but Cyborg was faster—he clamped his powerful artificial hand around his clone-twin's wrist and hung on. With his eyes boring into Brigand's, he said, "If you touch this old man, you will lose me forever. It'll be over between us."

Anger, hurt, regret, cunning, and contempt swept over Brigand's face so rapidly they were hard to read. "It'll never be over between us," he muttered.

Feeling invincible, Corgan shouted, "If you want to hit someone, try me!"

"Glad to," Brigand sneered. "First I'm going to beat you dead, then I'm taking Sharla, and who knows what I'll do to her now that she's in no shape to refuse me. Notice I said 'beat you,' Corgan, not 'shoot you.'"

"Yeah. Well, I'm waiting."

As Brigand stepped to the center of the corridor his

naked torso gleamed in the light. With the convoluted tattoos covering his skin like mold, and his ugly, half-tattooed face, he looked utterly repulsive. In spite of what he'd just said about not shooting Corgan, Brigand held the gun in his hand and waved it around as he spoke. "Bring Sharla over here," he ordered Ananda.

Not taking her eyes off Brigand, Ananda moved toward Sharla and grasped her arm. But instead of bringing her to where Brigand waited, she dragged the unresisting Sharla to stand in front of Corgan as a shield, saying, "Cyborg says your gun is just a symbol, but if he's wrong and you decide to shoot Corgan, you'll hit Sharla instead."

"Don't!" Corgan ordered. No way was he going to hide behind Sharla or anyone else. Gently he moved her out of the way. "Brigand is saying that we'll have a fair fight. Or am I getting it wrong, Brigand? Is your idea of a fair fight that you'll beat me with the gun again? Maybe I should go back and pick up the wrench."

"No, that is not my idea," Brigand taunted. "I don't need a weapon in my hand to whip you stupid."

"Then, let me hold the gun," Thebos suggested, stretching out his trembling hand.

"Forget that!" Brigand swung around to face Thebos. "You're so old you're senile. Old people like you are a waste of resources, the same as that dog behind you. You take up space and food that a worker could use. After the revolutions, when I'm running things in this DC and all the rest of them, I'll eliminate old bags of bones like you, Thebos, and I'll eliminate the dog, too."

Thebos's hand may have been shaky, but his voice rang

out loud and strong. "The dog's intelligence and character are far superior to yours, Brigand. And you'd better hope your revolt works fast, because in three years, with your rapid aging, you'll be just as old as I am right now."

His eyes flashing, Brigand glanced from one to the other of them. Apparently realizing that he had no allies in this face-off, he said, "No, the only person who can hold this weapon to keep it neutral is . . ." He paused, and with a mocking smile he turned and pointed to Sharla. "That's fitting, isn't it, since she's the trophy we're fighting over? If she's as out of it as you say she is, she'll just stand there with the gun in her hand until our fight to the death is finished."

"Forget that," Corgan commanded.

"You're detestable," Ananda told Brigand.

Cyborg, the strategist, said, "It's not a totally insane idea. We'll keep Sharla over here. Ananda, bring her over to me." But Brigand, also a strategist, answered, "No you won't. She'll stand right there." He pointed to a spot in the exact center of the corridor. "She'll be close to us two combatants, but not too close. Count off four meters from where Sharla is, Corgan, and that's the spot where you and I will stand together to fight our death match. The winner gets the gun and the girl."

"Sounds good to me." Corgan wanted nothing more than to fight and win and take Sharla out of there. He went to her, turned, and paced off the four meters. As Brigand approached Sharla, Corgan tensed, ready to leap forward in her defense. Not for a split second did he trust Brigand, who might grab Sharla and hold off the rest of them with the gun. But Brigand did exactly what he'd promised, placing the gun in Sharla's unresponsive hand, molding her fingers around it. Then, to infuriate Corgan, Brigand kissed Sharla long and hard, spiking Corgan's rage so high he tasted it in his throat. Smirking, Brigand swaggered toward Corgan and stopped to face him. "Ready?" he asked.

Before Corgan could answer, the first punch staggered him, knocking him off guard. He tried to grab Brigand, but his hands slipped off. Instantly he realized that Brigand had oiled his bare torso. Foul! But he couldn't cry foul because there were no rules in this contest, no referee. Then a blow to the side of his head knocked him to the floor.

He grabbed Brigand around the legs and pulled him down, managing to grip him in a headlock until Brigand burst loose. Brigand was strong, slippery, and vicious. Both of them clambered to their feet, but Brigand got there faster and punched Corgan in the stomach, knocking him down again. Corgan shot up like a geyser, butting his head under Brigand's chin. This time Brigand fell, and from the floor he kicked Corgan in the gut.

"Let me loose!" he heard Ananda yelling to Cyborg. "Let me help Corgan!" but Cyborg held her fast. Her yell distracted Corgan enough that Brigand was able to scramble up and land another punch on Corgan's face. Once more Corgan found himself on the floor, only this time Brigand's foot was on his neck.

Corgan tried to gasp for air, but his throat was blocked. He grabbed Brigand's ankle, struggling to move it as the increasing weight of Brigand's body pressed harder and harder against Corgan's throat. Flecks of gold shot behind his eyes, exploding like fireworks in his brain as his hands fell back against the floor. Through the pounding in his ears, he heard Brigand say, "This is called revenge, Arc Man. Sweet revenge."

He would never know how it happened or why it happened, but suddenly he heard Sharla shriek. Both Corgan and Brigand whirled to look at her just as she threw the gun in a high arc, not toward either of them, but in the opposite direction down the long corridor.

Demi must have thought it was the game she always played—running after the Freeze Bee. She tore off in the direction of the soaring gun and leaped up, managing to catch it in her mouth. As she landed on the floor the gun went off with a deafening explosion. Ananda screamed. The dog dropped like a stone and lay unmoving. At the same second Brigand yelled, "Damn you! Damn you all! I'm hit! I'm bleeding!" He lay writhing, blood streaming from his knee.

Sobbing, "Demi!" Ananda rushed to her dog, while Cyborg went to help his clone-twin. Sharla, passive again, expressionless, stood with her hands hanging at her sides.

Quickly Thebos snatched the gun and handed it to Corgan, saying, "It looks as though you've won both the gun and the girl. Now, you'd better get out of here fast, before Brigand's New Rebel Troops come looking for him."

"Right." Gulping deep breaths to fill his lungs again,

Corgan rose on shaky legs to get to Ananda. She stayed crouched on the floor, weeping, cradling Demi in her arms. "Come on, Ananda," he urged. "Demi's just stunned. She'll be all right, but you gotta help me now."

"She might die!" Ananda cried.

"She won't die! Listen to me, Ananda. It's just you and me who can do this. Nobody else can."

Cyborg had propped Brigand against a wall and was telling him, "You're not bleeding to death or anything— you'll survive till your troops get here. Your kneecap's shot to pieces and that's bad, but maybe it makes us even. Both of us are maimed now, Brigand. Think about that, twin."

Brigand reached up to hook a hand around Cyborg's neck, saying, "Whatever Corgan told you, it's a lie. I only did it to save your life."

Cyborg hesitated, but Corgan yelled, "No, Cyborg! Don't listen to him. What *he* says is lies. Come here and talk some sense into Ananda. Tell her she has to help me."

Reluctantly Cyborg left Brigand leaning against the wall, where he clutched his knee while blood spilled down his leg. Reaching Ananda, Cyborg told her, "Come on, we've got to get out of here. You and Corgan take Sharla up the stairs. I'll bring Demi. If you don't help us now, the whole plan will fall apart. You're that important. Okay? You ready? Come on, let me help you up."

As she got to her feet Ananda cried out to Corgan, "Are you just going to leave Brigand lying there? Shoot him, Corgan! You have the gun!"

Should he? He felt the gun, cold and hard, in his hand. If he killed Brigand, he might save the world from unbearable tyranny. He'd never fired a gun before, but it couldn't be too hard; you just squeezed the trigger. It felt firm but responsive behind his index finger, as though it wouldn't take much pressure to pull. Then he remembered what Thebos had said to him not long before: *I've learned to know you, Corgan, and you're not a killer.*

"What good would it do to shoot him?" he asked Ananda. "Leave him bleeding there on the floor. Maybe the robots will haul him out with the garbage."

Ananda came to help then, but just as she and Corgan began to lead Sharla toward the stairs he turned back, shouting, "Wait a minute! What am I thinking of? What about Thebos?"

"Go ahead," Ananda told him. "I can manage Sharla by myself."

Corgan dashed over to Thebos, crying, "Thebos, you have to come with us. Doesn't matter that there are only four seats, we'll work something out. You're not safe here."

He couldn't believe it—Thebos smiled! "Oh, I'm very safe," Thebos answered. "Brigand is going to need an artificial knee, and I'm the only person in the whole Flor-DC who can build one for him. He won't do anything to hurt me."

"Are you sure?" Corgan asked urgently. "Are you positive you'll be safe?" Then he realized that Thebos was making sense. Brigand may be a tyrant, but as everyone kept saying, he wasn't stupid. He'd keep Thebos alive and well at least until the artificial knee got engineered.

"It's what I choose to do," Thebos insisted. "I'll be fine, Corgan. Go now and prepare the *Prometheus* for liftoff. Don't forget to give my love to Jane."

"You're coming upstairs, aren't you, Thebos, so you can see the *Prometheus* fly?"

"I wouldn't miss that sight for the world!" His voice shook as he said, "It will be the consummation of my lifelong dream, the vision I've waited for that I thought I would never see. And it's you who will make it all come true, Corgan. I'm truly grateful, and I'm so proud of you."

A handshake wouldn't be nearly good enough; Corgan gave Thebos a warm hug and told him, "I'll never forget you. I hope we meet again."

"So do I, dear boy. Go now. I'll be upstairs as soon as I've called the med techs to take care of Brigand."

From the wall where he lay bleeding, Brigand hollered, "That thing won't fly. You're gonna crash and you'll all be killed. If you stay here, only Corgan will die."

"Wrong again, Brigand!" Corgan yelled as he ran up the stairs. "It'll fly. Thebos stakes his life on it."

Cyborg and Ananda had managed to get Sharla into the *Prometheus*, along with Demi. Now Ananda, wearing an air filtration mask, was unbolting the first roof panel. As she peeled it back Corgan looked up at raw, unfiltered sky, at bright blue natural daylight visible through the jagged-edged hole high in the dome.

"Put this on," she told Corgan, handing him a mask. After he'd snapped it over his face, he helped her lift away the second roof panel. Then they were good to go.

"Okay, you get on board now," he told Ananda.

Everyone had stowed inside the *Prometheus* except Corgan. After taking one last look around, he realized he felt not the least bit of regret about fleeing this place, except . . . the biting sorrow of leaving Thebos. And where was Thebos? Corgan couldn't go until Thebos came to witness the takeoff.

And then he saw him. Panting from the climb, Thebos reached the top of the stairs. He stood there clutching the doorframe, catching his breath before he waved. Tears stung Corgan's eyes as he waved back at that amazing, brilliant, quirky, honorable human being. How he wished Thebos would come with them!

Smiling, Thebos pointed at the ship and gave Corgan a thumbs-up, meaning, *Time to go*. After one more wave Corgan slid down through the hatch, ripped off his mask, and started the engines, never doubting that the craft would fly—after all, it had been designed by an engineer extraordinaire. He heard a slight whine as the fuel cells began to generate operational power. Then he could feel the *Prometheus* lift off from the floor. It rose slowly and evenly as it propelled itself through the stripped-away roof. He had to veer it sharply to the left to line it up beneath the hole in the dome. From there the *Prometheus* climbed into the blue sky, which looked so welcoming and harmless, even though it was neither.

"We're airborne!" he cried to the others, his voice cracking with excitement. All of them moved to the window that wound all the way around the top of the craft. They grabbed handholds when the antigravity propulsion kicked in. "Whoooo!" Ananda squealed as their bodies became weightless.

"Yeah! Wow! The simulator never felt like this!" Corgan

exulted. Even Sharla held on and peered through the window with the rest.

"Look at the ocean," Cyborg called out. "This time I want to stay out of it."

"We will." The ocean wouldn't swallow them, and a brief exposure to the polluted outside air shouldn't hurt anyone too much, Corgan figured. He had one more thing he wanted to do.

"Hold your breath," he told all of them as he opened the hatch a few centimeters and pitched the gun into the Atlantic. Then he pulled the switch that sealed the hatch, and gave one last wave toward Thebos, even though he could no longer see him.

SIXTEEN

Weightless, Demi floated inside the cabin, looking dazed but alive—much the same as Sharla. Ananda squealed and Cyborg grinned as they turned somersaults in midair. "It's like swimming in the ocean at Nuku Hiva," Cyborg exclaimed, "without the water."

Corgan had set the controls to let the ship drift straight up slowly for five kilometers, and until it reached that point, he could indulge himself by free-floating with the others. After that he'd need to get serious about steering.

The slightest touch on the ship's walls sent him soaring in the opposite direction. Though it was tricky to maneuver a path without bumping into things, he wanted to get near Sharla. He floated next to her, caught her hand, swung her around to face him, and stared into her eyes. "Sharla," he asked, "do you like this? It's like dancing, isn't it? Remember that time we danced on the beach?"

Her eyes, as usual, were vacant.

Ananda held Demi in her arms and whirled with the dog, saying, "Look! She's licking my face! She has a little burn on her tongue from when the gun fired, but that'll heal fast. We're so lucky!" she cried, spinning in the center of the cabin. "You're not hurt, Demi, and we're flying!"

The way she carried on over that dog! But Ananda was younger than the rest of them, so maybe he ought to go easy on her; after all, they were all acting pretty giddy right then. And that was okay, Corgan decided. They'd escaped Brigand, and now they were literally bouncing off the walls in triumph as they hurtled through space, flying past one another, flying toward one another, touching hands to whirl one another around, and giggling like a bunch of little kids.

If it weren't for the changing view outside the windows, Corgan wouldn't have realized the ship was moving, because the *Prometheus* felt as stable as a big, safe bubble surrounding them. Each time he glanced through the window, though, Florida got smaller, a handle he could grasp with one hand on the edge of the receding continent.

Too soon it was time to settle down and get everyone grounded. Corgan didn't want them bumping into any flight controls on their wild loops through the cabin. "Okay, guys, I'm going to generate the gravitational field in about thirty seconds," he told them, "so you better float over to one of the seats and strap yourself in. The ship's artificial gravity will hit us all at once and hit us hard, Thebos told me. Cyborg, get Sharla fastened into a seat. Ananda, hang on to Demi."

Ananda hovered just above one of the chairs, but she stayed there, calling, "Do I have to sit down? I just love floating around and looking out the window!"

"Port," Cyborg corrected her. "It's called a port even though it wraps all the way around the ship. And you can see just fine when you're sitting, so get down here."

"Whatever. Columbus sure was right about the earth being round—look at that curvature—*ooof!* Hey! Ouch!" At that moment artificial gravity had set in forcefully, dropping Ananda into her seat with a thud that made her yelp, then laugh. "You could have waited," she told Corgan. "Anyway, I liked it better before. Can we float some more later?"

He nodded, concentrating now on the control settings. If the space station was still in its old orbit, 384 kilometers above Earth, he would navigate the *Prometheus* to intersect that trajectory—no problem. If the station was not in the predicted orbit, he had no idea how he'd ever find it. He'd just have to go and look for it, but traveling across the sky would consume time, fuel, and food and would probably end in failure—it was a big sky out there. Although the temperature in the *Prometheus* stayed at a comfortable seventy degrees, Corgan broke out in a sweat.

"A day and a half," Corgan told them. "That's how long Thebos said it would take us if the space station is where it's supposed to be. We have to go around and around, chasing after it."

"Why can't we just fly straight up to meet it?" Ananda asked.

"Because, do you realize how fast we'll be going? If we tried to intersect it, we'd crash into it," Corgan explained. "We have to put the *Prometheus* into the identical orbital path as the space station, which means orbiting Earth at exactly the right speed. Too fast and centrifugal force would push us into a wider orbit. Too slow and we'd be flying too low, too close to Earth. It's all about balance, being at the right altitude and the right speed to let us creep up on the station and then—"

Ananda had stopped paying attention long before that. "Look, look, look!" she cried now. "It's a sunset. How did we get a sunset?"

"We've circled around to the dark side of the earth," Cyborg explained. "Forty-five minutes from now you'll see a sunrise, when we get back to the light side of the earth."

"Really! You are so smart, Cyborg!" Ananda enthused.

"Yeah, sure, Cyborg's smart," Corgan muttered, annoyed. "Ananda," he suggested, "why don't you go explore the cargo bay and find something for us to eat? Thebos said the stuff is all sealed in packages, so just unseal them and add water." It would probably taste like that awful mush from the medical center, but it would keep Ananda occupied for a while and give her something useful to do.

The controls worked by touch on the two transparent, vertical holographic screens—there were no levers or buttons or handles. Pleased that he remembered every operational instruction he'd learned in Thebos's quarters, Corgan decided that flying the *Prometheus* wouldn't take much effort. Finding the space station was the big worry. He was about to tell Cyborg that, but when he glanced over, he saw Cyborg slumped in his chair, looking somber.

"What's wrong?" Corgan asked him.

"Brigand. The med techs are going over him."

"You mean you can telepath him from all the way up here?"

"For now. His kneecap is gone. It's really a mess. Like we thought, he'll have to get an artificial knee," Cyborg said.

"That's good, isn't it?" When Cyborg gave him a puzzled look, Corgan explained, "First, it makes Thebos too valuable for Brigand to terminate, like he threatened, 'cause no one else can make the knee for him. Second, he's too wounded to start the revolt, and maybe by the time he gets fixed, the dome will be repaired and the people will get back into the Flor-DC. Then they'll be happy and won't want to revolt. Maybe they'll stick Brigand into prison for wrecking the dome in the first place."

"You are such a dreamer." Cyborg shook his head. "You just don't get it. Brigand could lead a revolt locked up in a closet and on his deathbed. He could get mindless robots to revolt, or three-year-old kids or digital images. He's got a power that even I don't understand. No, what's worrying me is what you just said about Thebos. Brigand's New Rebel Troops will force him to build the artificial knee so fast they'll probably work him into the ground. He's so old he might not be able to handle the pressure."

Leaning back in his chair, Corgan smiled as he answered, "You don't need to worry about Thebos. Brigand only

knows him from telepathing thoughts out of your head—
he doesn't know the real Thebos. That is one clever old
guy. He'll find ways to slow things down."

"Not the way they're treating him right now. Brigand's
naming Thebos a prisoner of the revolt. Either he cooperates,
or they kill him."

"How? The gun is at the bottom of the Atlantic." As
soon as he said it, Corgan realized how stupid it sounded.
There were many ways to kill a person. Hang him, stab
him, choke him, suffocate him, starve him—or with someone as old as Thebos, work him to death. Corgan pressed
his fingers against his forehead to get those images out
of his mind. There was nothing he could do now to help
Thebos. He had to focus on finding the space station.

Ananda came back then, clutching five metallic bags
by the tops. "One for each of us and one for Demi," she
said. "It's not bad. At least, it doesn't look too bad. I put
the water into the stuff and squished it around in the bags
to mix it, but I haven't tasted it. I couldn't find any bowls.
You have to kind of squeeze the stuff from the top of the
bags into your mouth. I brought all of us the same meal—
reconstituted chicken and noodles."

Corgan set the controls on automatic and held out his
hands. "Give me two of them. After I eat, I'll try to get
Sharla to eat. She just relearned how to handle a spoon
and a bowl a couple of days ago. I don't know how she'll
manage without a spoon."

Getting up, Cyborg said, "I can't believe there are no
eating utensils in this craft. Thebos said it had everything
we'd need. I'll go look."

"Let me go," Ananda told him. "You should rest—you look pale."

"I'm fine," he told her. "Well, maybe not fine, but I want to explore a little bit and see the rest of the ship, see what's down there."

Ananda looked worried, following him with her eyes until he was out of sight. Then she dropped back into her seat and started sucking the food out of the top of her bag, announcing, "It's almost good. A lot better than that awful mush in the medical center." Licking her lips, she said, "It's kind of amazing, though. Can you believe anything could last forty-some years and still be edible?"

"As long as it was completely dried out and then sealed tight," Corgan said. Squirting some of it into his mouth, he had to agree with Ananda—the stuff was almost good. Almost.

After a few minutes Cyborg came back carrying a bowl and a spoon for Sharla. "And look what else I found," he said, holding out a framed picture. "It was back there in a drawer in the cargo bay."

The photograph had been made into a hologram; it changed as Corgan turned the frame from side to side. It showed a pretty woman, brown hair, blue eyes, looking serious and then breaking into a smile as the hologram rotated. Scrawled across the bottom of the picture were the words, "To P. T., with XXXOOO, Jane."

"Who's P. T.?" Ananda asked. "And what does 'XXXOOO' mean?"

"Some kind of code, I guess, and P. T. is Thebos," Corgan answered. "That's what they used to call him when people went by two names—P. T. Thebos. So this is Jane!

The Jane! The woman Thebos was in love with."

"She's pretty," Cyborg said. "How old do you think Jane is in this picture? Thirty? Thirty-five?"

"I can't tell women's ages," Corgan answered. "Most of my life I've only seen women in virtual reality, where they can make themselves look any age they want. Anyway, if she was thirty-something when she went up to the space station, she's got to be eighty-plus now."

"If she's alive," Ananda said.

"The big if," Corgan agreed. "If everyone on the space station has died, it could have drifted way out of orbit and we'll never find it."

"And if we don't find it?" Cyborg asked.

Corgan grimaced. He didn't answer because he didn't know the answer. Instead he propped the hologram of Jane—*the* Jane—in front of his seat and studied it as he finished his meal. Cyborg reached for the other food packet and poured it into the bowl for Sharla.

"And when Sharla's finished, I can use the same bowl for Demi," Ananda said. "I have to take care of her. She's my baby."

A little irritated, Corgan asked, "Why do you keep saying that, Ananda? Demi isn't your baby. She's just a dog."

"Just? *Just* a dog? You don't understand. She's my family." Ananda swung around in her chair to face Corgan, but she was speaking to all of them. "You people never had parents, so you don't know what it's like. But I remember my mother and father before they were killed. I remember how it felt when my mother held me, when my father carried me. It felt so . . . comforting. So *safe*. I know I was only two, but after they were gone, there was an emptiness inside me that never went away. Until I got Demi." She stroked the silky white hair around the dog's neck, saying, "She *was* a baby when I got her. She was just five weeks old, and I was ten years old. We . . . I think the word is *bonded*. Right from the beginning."

They'd risen high enough out of Earth's atmosphere to enter the blackness of outer space. Beneath them Earth lay dark and silent, with no lights from cities showing because there were no cities left, other than the domed ones in Wyoming, Chile, Japan, Singapore, Australia, Poland, England, and Florida. At least, those used to be the names of those places before the devastation. Far apart from one another, the domed cities were hard to spot from orbit because they didn't emit much light. For them to be visible from orbit, a spacecraft would have to pass right above them.

As the *Prometheus* circled the globe the sun began to rise over the edge of the earth, first as a thin blue line. The line thickened, with red and orange creeping into it, followed by a dazzling, gleaming golden circle in the center of a thin band of brilliant white.

"It's so beautiful!" Ananda breathed. "Just a little while ago we saw the sun set, and now we're seeing it rise." She paused, then told them, "When I was really little, after my parents died, my grandmother sang a song to me." She began to sing, "Sunrise, sunset, sunrise, sunset, swiftly fly the days . . ."

Corgan had never heard her sing before. Or anyone sing, for that matter. Whatever music he'd heard had been funneled digitally into his virtual-reality Box when he was a boy or had been played electronically in the Flor-DC's bistros. Ananda's voice sounded high and pure and sweet, a perfect accompaniment to the magnificence of their first sunrise in space.

He didn't notice it right away, but Sharla had unstrapped herself from her seat and begun to walk toward Ananda, like a sleepwalker drawn into a dream. As she came closer she gently placed two fingers on Ananda's moving lips.

Quietly Cyborg told Ananda, "Keep on singing," and Ananda did, while Corgan sat perfectly still, barely breathing. Sharla was staring as though puzzled by Ananda's song, her fingers unmoving on Ananda's lips.

Was this a sign that Sharla was getting better? It was the first time she'd walked anywhere without being led, the first time she'd shown interest in anything. But after Ananda had sung the song over and over, until dawn spread all the way across the rim of the earth, Sharla removed her fingers and stood quietly, the blankness returning to her eyes. So it had meant nothing. "I'll strap her back into her seat," Corgan said, but as he did he suddenly realized that Ananda's eyes had filled with tears that ran down her cheeks.

"What's wrong?" he asked her.

"Everything!" she sobbed. "The song makes me hurt inside. I lost my parents and my grandparents, and I'm going to lose Cyborg, too."

"Not for a while," Cyborg said weakly.

"I've lost you already," she cried. "I try to act older and

think older, but I don't know how! You've outgrown me!"

Cyborg came toward her, his hand outstretched, but when he reached her, his hand dropped to his side. "I know," he said, looking miserable. "I've loved you since the first time I saw you, Ananda, when there were just two years between us. Now there's six years, and you're right, it feels different, and I'm all confused about it. I'm half afraid to touch you anymore because you're still a young girl and I'm pretty much a grown man. We just . . . have to figure it out. Have to make it work some way."

How? Corgan wondered. How could they make it work when Cyborg kept getting older almost by the minute? Why did people's ages have to complicate things? But it did matter. It made a big difference in how they connected.

Cyborg put his arms around Ananda, but carefully, gently. She leaned against his chest and wept as the earth rotated into blackness. Four people were flying on board the *Prometheus,* and in spite of the beauty they'd seen outside, not one of the four could feel truly happy. All their burdens weighed on them more heavily than gravity, Corgan realized. "You may as well get some sleep," he told them. "There should be sleeping bags somewhere behind us. Check that cabinet back there."

"What about you?" Cyborg asked.

"I'll stay here and watch the controls." That was just an excuse, because the *Prometheus* had been programmed to fly automatically once its course was set. But after what had just happened, he wanted to be alone.

Ananda had heard the song from her grandmother, she'd said. What would it be like to have had a grandmother, or parents? Real people of flesh and blood you could talk to and learn from and be touched by? Thebos was the closest Corgan had ever come to having a kinship like that.

Corgan knew a little about his genetic background because Sharla had looked up their records. His biological parents, if he could call them that—the sperm and egg that were taken out of the frozen-tissue bank and combined in a test tube—had been selected for the qualities the Supreme Council wanted him to have. He'd seen no pictures of those long-ago donors, nor had he ever heard their voices; that kind of information didn't get preserved in the files. But whoever they were, they hadn't been the only contributors. He'd received bits of DNA from other anonymous donors, none of them alive, all of their DNA revived from tissue that had been frozen for who knew how long. Sharla was the same, a genetic design that had worked perfectly. Brigand and Cyborg had been cloned. Only Ananda had been born of the union of two real people. And had had a grandmother who sang to her.

Sunrise, sunset, swiftly fly the days. How could he decide when morning really arrived if the sun either rose or set every forty-five minutes? As the *Prometheus* flew over the bright side of the earth Corgan looked down to see where the devastated metropolises had once been, although from that high he couldn't see much detail. Half closing his eyes, he imagined what it would have been like to live in those huge cities, with their populations of millions, without any domes covering them to keep out the poisoned air. Back then did the people have governing bodies like the Supreme Council? He'd heard people could travel from city to city on roads, in something called automobiles, but he'd also been taught that the pollution from all those automobiles had poisoned the air, made people sick, and caused temperatures to rise, ice to melt, cities to get flooded, and all kinds of other bad things to happen, even before the nuclear wars finished the job of wiping out most places on Earth.

What if he'd lived back then and had had a real mother and father? What if he'd been just an ordinary kid, not someone expected to win a Virtual War? What if Sharla . . .

He stopped there. No more what-ifs. Maybe he should sleep, cover his eyes with something so he wouldn't keep seeing daylight every three quarters of an hour. One more twenty-four-hour day needed to go by before he could hope to catch up to the space station; that was, if he was guiding the *Prometheus* toward the correct trajectory.

Although he'd been engineered as a supreme time counter, whenever he slept, that ability left him. So he had no idea how long he'd been asleep when Cyborg shook his shoulder and told him, "Wake up! You're missing this and it's incredible!"

"What?" Corgan asked, groggy.

"Everything's green outside," Ananda exclaimed, her voice filled with awe. "There's huge patches of green and they're swirling everywhere. Wait, now it's got some red in it too and green underneath, and we're flying right into it! What is it?"

Nervously Corgan stared at the rivers of green beneath

them and ahead of them. In the midst of it he saw spheres of brighter green light, sheets and beams of green, horizontal smears of yellowish green crossing vertical green lines tinged with red. Should he try to fly above this stuff, whatever it was? The gauges of the *Prometheus* remained steady, not showing any changes that would warn of bombardment by dangerous cosmic rays. After several minutes the green curtain started to thin, as though they were flying out of it. And then the *Prometheus* broke through into the ordinary blackness of space.

"That was scary, but beautiful," Ananda breathed. "What do you think it was?"

"What's beneath us?" Cyborg asked. "What continent are we flying over?"

"North America. I mean northern North America. The part they called Canada," Corgan answered.

"Yes! I thought so! Then, I know what it was," Cyborg said. "We just flew through the aurora borealis. It's what happens when protons and electrons carried by solar winds hit the upper parts of the earth's atmosphere. I saw it once through the dome of the Wyo-DC, but not like this! Nothing like this! Amazing! We got to be right in it because we're pretty much beyond the thickest part of Earth's atmosphere now. That's why the stars aren't twinkling. See? They're shining nice and steady, with no twinkle, because there's no atmosphere to interfere with their light."

"Cyborg, I can't believe how you know all these things!" Ananda said softly.

Corgan answered, "If Cyborg knew *everything*, he'd find the space station for us."

"I just might be able to do that," Cyborg murmured. "Look over there." As Corgan stared out the port to see what he'd pointed to, Cyborg asked, "See that star? Look at it move. Only, I don't think it is a star, because it's a little brighter and it's going in a different direction. It's pretty far away from us, but it might be what we're looking for."

Corgan peered ahead until he saw the bright star—no, not a star. It couldn't be a meteor, either, because a meteor would move much faster. It looked like one of the other stars, but since it was moving across a field of unmoving stars, it had to be . . . "You're right! That's it!" he cried. Smacking Cyborg's hand in congratulation, he shouted, "Great! We'll just follow that star, one that's not a real star. That's what Thebos called it once."

SEVENTEEN

It was their second day in orbit. The *Prometheus* had tailed the space station at a speed twenty-five times faster than the speed of sound, yet inside the spacecraft its four passengers had no sense of hurtling through a void. There were no wind sounds because there was no wind. No wrenching flattening of bodies from the pull of gravity because there was no gravity, except the artificial gravity Thebos had built into the ship for comfort.

Ahead of them the station continued to orbit the earth just slightly more slowly than the *Prometheus*. It looked like a bright but distant star, but with every ninety-minute spin the *Prometheus* made around Earth, the light from the station grew brighter and bigger. With each of those circles around Earth the *Prometheus* closed the gap by 1,120 kilometers. Still, they needed two real-time days to play catch-up.

"It doesn't look like a star anymore," Ananda announced as they got a little closer. "I can see a shape now, but I can't make out what kind it is."

"Look at the hologram of Jane," Corgan told her, handing it to her. "See the object in the background? That's the space station."

Ananda glanced at the picture, stared through the port, then looked back at the picture, saying, "It's not the same."

That made Corgan sit up straight! "You mean what we're chasing isn't the space station?"

"Don't panic. We're still too far away to get a good view of it," Cyborg told him. "It will be clearer when we get closer."

But the closer they came, the less it resembled the picture. "It's so much smaller," Ananda said. "There are only two long tubes—"

"Modules," Corgan corrected her.

"And a crosspiece connecting them, but in this picture there are a whole lot more of the big tubes. I mean, modules."

"I think it must be the space station, though. It's still got those big, wide wings," Corgan said. "Those are the solar panels—they convert sunlight into electricity. But what could have happened to all the rest of the units? I guess we'll find out when we get there, if there's anyone on board to tell us."

If there really happened to be a live human on the station, by now he or she would have seen the *Prometheus* approaching. Corgan felt an urge to wave, but that would be pretty silly. Stick a sign in the window saying WE COME AS FRIENDS?

After the distance had closed to within 180 meters, he took manual control of the *Prometheus* to make sure they crept up slowly on the station, although 28,000 kilometers per hour could hardly be called slow.

And then they reached it. Almost close enough to touch. Trying to align the *Prometheus* with the station's docking target, Corgan had to make three small course corrections. "There's the docking collar," he told Cyborg. "We gotta glide right up to it and connect. If anyone's inside, they should attach our ship to the station and then open their hatch to let us in. Get up there and look through the small port in our hatch. Let me know the second we touch."

"We're almost there," Cyborg announced. "Only centimeters away."

After a gentle nudge Cyborg yelled, "We're locked! Hooks came out from the station and grabbed our hatch. Someone must be in there docking us together!"

"Or it could be automatic," Corgan suggested. "If the hatch stays shut, it was automatic. If it opens, someone's there."

They waited anxiously. Sensing the tension, Demi barked twice. Suddenly the hatch swung open and a hand reached down to them. Corgan stared at the hand, then let his eyes rise to a face, the wide-eyed, grinning face of

211

a man. "How the devil did you get here?" the man asked. "Grab my hand and let me pull you up."

Ananda was the first to go. As she raised herself through the opening Corgan heard her exclaim, "I'm floating again! More zero gravity. Now lift up Demi, Corgan."

As he did Corgan heard the man exclaim, "A dog? A real dog? I can't believe it. I haven't seen a real live dog in forty-five years."

"Sharla next," Corgan told Cyborg, and the two of them lifted her toward the man, who was laughing now. "Who else?" the man asked. "How many people do you have down there? Any more dogs?"

"No more dogs," Cyborg said, boosting himself through the hatch. "Just me and my buddy—we're all that's left."

After turning off the controls as Thebos had instructed, Corgan exited the *Prometheus* and closed the hatch behind him. He found himself inside a connector tunnel to the space station where he stared into the happy, excited eyes of the man who'd helped them up. Something was wrong, though. This man looked to be in his midthirties. How could he have seen his last dog forty-five years ago?

"Wow! This is just unbelievable! Let's get inside the station, and then we'll have the introductions," the man was saying. "I can't wait till Jane sees you. I gotta know who you all are and how you got here. I'm David Driscoll."

Corgan's head spun, and not just because he was free-floating in weightlessness again. Jane Driscoll was the name of Thebos's old girlfriend, who'd supposedly gone off with a man named David Driscoll. Had he been an astronaut too, and was this David Driscoll their son? Corgan tried to figure out the math. If this David Driscoll was thirty-five, he'd have been born in space in the year 2047, and if the Jane Driscoll in the picture had been, say, thirty-five when she took off for the space station in 2037, she'd have been forty-five when this guy was born! Was that possible? He supposed so. What did Corgan know about female reproduction?

David unlocked the door to the module and there she was, the Jane Driscoll of the picture, looking exactly the same as she did in the hologram, giving them the same wide smile. And next to her was another man, not much older than Cyborg.

"Come in, come in," Jane was saying. "This is like a miracle! Welcome! Is that a dog? Oh, let me touch it. I haven't seen a dog in forty-five years."

"That's exactly what I said," David told her. "And Nate—you've never seen one at all!"

The woman caught Demi, who was floating in the cabin, whimpering a little because weightlessness confused her. "Here, Nate, hold the dog. She's frightened. Hold her gently. Oh, I'm sorry—I need to bring you people in here and get you secured so you'll stop floating. Grab these handles on the walls one after the other, all the way over to the table. You can strap yourselves into the chairs. I don't even know who you are! Forgive me if I sound like I'm babbling. This is the most astonishing thing, because we've been up here for forty-five years and you're the first visitors from Earth we've had in all that time! It's incredible, just incredible!"

Corgan took one of Sharla's arms and Cyborg the other

as they drifted across the module to the table. When everyone got arranged in as much order as they could manage in zero gravity, the woman said, "I'm Jane Driscoll, this is my husband, David, and that's our son, Nate. Tell us who you are and how you happened to be in the *Prometheus*. I recognized it when you were still kilometers away."

Bewildered, Cyborg and Corgan stared at each other. "I'm . . . I'm Cyborg," he stammered, "this is Corgan, that's Ananda, and the other girl is Sharla. You already met Demi, the dog."

"I flew the *Prometheus* here," Corgan added. "Thebos taught me how."

"You mean P. T.?" Jane asked. "P. T. Thebos? He's still alive?" She squealed and clapped her hands like a little girl. "But . . . he must be so old now."

"Ninety-one," Corgan told her, completely baffled, as Ananda blurted out, "And why aren't *you* old if you're Thebos's Jane?"

The Driscolls smiled at one another. "It's a long story," David began.

Corgan didn't care how long the story would be, he needed to know how this woman and her husband could look so young if they were almost the same age as Thebos. Thebos couldn't have suspected anything like this because he'd kept saying things like, "They'd be as old as I am . . . ," and, "If anyone up there is still alive . . ."

"I'll try to explain," Jane said. "I'll give you the short version. We know about the devastation on Earth; actually, we could see it happening from here in orbit, but after that all our communication with Earth broke off. There was no way for us to return to Earth because Cape Canaveral had been destroyed, along with all the rescue ships. So we were stuck here. We had a third astronaut with us—"

"Yes, Hong Ly," Corgan said eagerly. "Thebos told us about him. Where is he?"

Jane's face clouded. "It was terribly sad. A tragedy. Hong happened to be working outside, doing a space walk, when his tether broke and he went drifting off. . . ."

"And we weren't able to save him because the station was so big back then that it couldn't be maneuvered," David finished. "We watched him go, but we were helpless to go after him."

Had there been any gravity in space, Corgan would have sunk to the depths. His whole purpose in coming on this quest had just been shattered. No Hong Ly! Cyborg reached out to grab Corgan's arm, while Ananda murmured, "We knew maybe it wouldn't come true, Corgan. But we were . . . we were hoping . . . so much. . . ."

"Hoping what?" David asked. "Did you know Hong? No, you couldn't have. You're much too young."

Shaking his head slightly, Corgan signaled Cyborg and Ananda to stay silent about their reason for being there. He didn't want to reveal anything until he had a chance to figure out what was happening. Had Hong really drifted away or had these people done something to him? How could this be Thebos's Jane? What kind of magic could make these people look the way they did, if they were really who they said they were? "You were starting to tell us why you're so young," he said, his voice hoarse. "Would you please continue?"

"Well, yes," Jane said. "I certainly understand why you're puzzled about us. It's all because of Hong. He was a neuroscientist famous for human physiology experiments. Absolutely brilliant. He came on this mission to devise ways to keep astronauts mentally and physically capable during the long periods that might be needed for future flights—you know, to the edge of the solar system and beyond."

David broke in, "And he succeeded! He created an immortality machine. We call it the Locker because it will lock you into a particular age."

"Like it did me," Nate said. "Mom had me in 2039."

"Wait!" Ananda cried. "Slow down. If Nate was born in 2039 and it's now 2082, how can he look . . ."

"I'm twenty years old," Nate answered, chuckling. "Permanently. Amazing, huh? It's because of the Locker."

Any words Corgan might have uttered got stuck in his throat, but Cyborg, just as astounded, managed to gasp, "An . . . *immortality* machine? You mean you're going to live forever and stay the way you are now?"

Nate nodded, grinning. Jane smiled too, as though they'd just announced something as ordinary as the sunset outside.

"Before Hong got lost in space," Jane explained, "he'd almost completed work on the Locker. Nate had always been fascinated by Hong's project. Ever since he was a little kid, he used to hang over Hong while he worked— literally, because in zero gravity you really can hang over someone—and he'd watch Hong programming the machine. So after Hong was . . . gone . . . Nate finished the device. And it worked! We've used it three times, once on each of us."

Corgan's lips formed the word *How?* but before he had a chance to say it, David enthused, "A real, honest-to-God time-stopping machine. Or I guess I could call it an age-stopping machine. First Nate used it on his mother and me, then we used it on him. Since then we've had hardly any muscle atrophy and not too much additional loss of bone mass—all thanks to the remarkable work of Hong Ly. As a scientist, he was right up there with Einstein and Newton."

Jane added sadly, "And no one will ever know that, because we lost all communication with Earth before Hong created his miracle machine." When she glanced from one to the other and saw their confusion, she said, "Oh, where are my manners? Are you kids hungry? I could fix you something."

In a small voice Ananda answered, "Demi could use a drink of water."

Then all of them were drinking something sweet out of beakers because, as Jane explained, they had only enough cups for their family of three. The Driscolls' stories tumbled out and intertwined, revealing that since no orbital retrieval vessels could return them to Earth, they'd agonized about growing older and dying, which would leave Nate all alone in space. Then Nate—bless him, he was incredibly brilliant, and please excuse Jane for bragging about him like a proud mother, because that's what proud mothers did and this was her first-ever chance to brag about him to someone new—finished the Locker, which Hong had nearly completed. David explained that the Locker could be set to let a person go back to any age he or she wanted. And here they were, young again and perfectly adapted to living in space forever.

"Now tell us about you!" Jane asked eagerly. Corgan and Cyborg and Ananda started to stammer about the domed cities and the revolts, and about Brigand and Thebos and what had happened to Sharla.

In the midst of the talk the idea that had been simmering in Corgan's brain from the very first mention of the Locker refused to stay contained any longer. Whether or not it was the strategic time to bring it up, he had to ask the Driscolls whether they'd allow Sharla to be treated in the machine. If they would, and if the Locker worked the way they said it did, they could set the time to the day before Sharla crashed through the dome and got injured. Would that bring Sharla back to normal, back to health, back to being the person he'd once known? Would the Driscolls agree to let them try? He nearly burst with the need to ask them, but the whole concept was still so hard to believe that he didn't know how to begin.

Maybe Cyborg was thinking along the same lines, because he was saying to the Driscolls, "The *Prometheus* could hold all of us. I mean, the four of us plus you three. It would be crowded, but we could make it work. We could take you back to Earth and bring the Locker with you."

"To where?" Ananda asked. "The Flor-DC? There's a revolt going on there, remember?"

Jane reached to touch Cyborg's hand, the real one, saying, "That's awfully nice of you, but you know, we like it here. When the devastation happened, from up here in space we could see the mushroom clouds rising over city after city. One nuclear holocaust after another. Right then we knew we'd never want to go back because there's no one left on Earth that we care about. This station has become our home."

"It looks so much smaller than in the pictures," Ananda said weakly.

"We jettisoned every part we didn't need," David explained. "What we have here now is a closed biosphere, self-sustaining for the three of us. Everything gets recycled and reused, since there's no way for us to bring in any replacements. In fact . . ." He paused.

"In fact," Nate took over, "what my dad's trying to say is that you can't stay here. Our resources are limited. There's only enough to support the three of us. You'd use them up."

Corgan felt like he'd been bludgeoned! Two critical setbacks in an hour! First Hong Ly was dead, and now the Driscolls were going to kick them off the space station. He couldn't let that happen, couldn't lose a chance to make Sharla normal again. There had to be a way to convince the Driscolls.

"Please stay a day or two, though," Jane invited. "It's such a thrill to have visitors. Forty-five years!"

He could see Ananda fairly quivering with the same wild hope that was swelling in all of them—the Locker could save Cyborg, too! Stop him from ever growing older! *Don't say anything, don't blow our chances*, he wanted to yell at her, but all he could do was grab her hand and press it hard, signaling her to keep quiet until they could get a better grasp of these people.

Ananda got the message. In a voice as unruffled as Jane's she asked, "If we can't stay here, where else can we go?"

"Have you thought about Mars?" Jane asked as if she were suggesting a trip to the adjoining module.

David said, "A group of space pioneers took off for Mars in 2018. They planned to start a colony and to terraform the planet. You know, make it green."

"We're not sure what happened to them," Nate said. "They might all be dead."

"But if the terraforming experiment worked," Jane broke in, "Mars may be livable by now. I'm completely familiar with the *Prometheus*—I was there when P. T. designed and engineered it. It could reach Mars in a third as much time as the traditional space vehicles did. I also know P. T. planned to stock it with enough preserved food for a trip to Mars, because that's one of the voyages he had in mind when he built the *Prometheus*."

They went on to talk about Mars and Hong and Thebos and weightlessness and a lot of other subjects that swirled around, barely penetrating Corgan's hearing. The only things he could think about were Sharla and the Locker, the machine that could take her back and make her the person she'd been. He wished he'd been engineered as a strategist so he'd know how to bring up the subject without cooking his chances. He wished he could talk to Cyborg about it, since Cyborg *was* a strategist. Finally, unable to wait any longer, he blurted out, "I need to ask this. Could you—is it possible—can Sharla enter the Locker and be taken back to a week ago?"

Silence. Then Jane began, "I suppose so . . . ," but Nate held up his hand, saying, "Wait a minute. This requires some thought. Maybe a little negotiation."

Leaning forward, Corgan felt himself held by the restraining straps that kept him from floating all over the module, or maybe the restraint was inside him, in his chest. He didn't like what Nate had just said, didn't like the sound of Nate's voice when he'd said it. Didn't like the look of Nate, with his dark, curly hair, his hooded eyes in a too-narrow face, his thin, athletic body, his restless hands, which kept tapping the tabletop.

Jane glanced at Nate, then said, "Yes, we're all pretty tired after so much excitement. Why don't we get some sleep now, and then we can talk again after our usual eight-hour rest."

"Sleep? Now? Eight hours?" Ananda protested. "We've only been here for about two hours. I mean, if we're not allowed to stay more than a day or two, should we waste the time sleeping?"

David had already reached to unstrap Sharla from her seat. "Oh, we always stick to our schedule," he said. "We find that works best for us. We'll put all of you into the Destiny module. It's a laboratory, so there are no beds, but you'll be perfectly comfortable sleeping while you're suspended in midair. I always joke with Jane that zero gravity is the best mattress you can buy."

"Oh, and can we keep the dog out here with us?" Jane begged. "She's so sweet. . . ."

"I suppose so," Ananda agreed, but even as she spoke

they were being hustled through a second tunnel into the adjoining Destiny module, which was where Nate still did all his engineering and scientific work, David told them. Once they were inside, David sealed the hatch behind them.

"I have a feeling we can't open it from in here," Corgan predicted. He was right; when he tried it, the door wouldn't budge.

"We don't even have anything to eat," Ananda said. "All our food's in the *Prometheus*, and now we can't get out to get it."

"Forget food," Cyborg said. "This whole thing is very strange. If they haven't seen anybody new for forty-five years, you'd think they'd keep us talking for two straight days without any sleep at all, but instead they've practically shoved us in here and locked us inside. There was a lot said out there, but I think there's a whole lot more that didn't get said."

Still keyed up over the possibilities, Corgan told them, "That Locker is what we need, for Sharla and for you, too, Cyborg. If I got what they were saying about it, you can set it to any date in a person's past life and it will pull them back to that age. Think what that would do for both of you! I mean, it might heal Sharla, but it could heal you, too, Cyborg! If we put you back to the day before our plane went down, not only would you be healthy again, it would stop your premature aging."

"Like I haven't thought about that?" Cyborg grabbed his head, shoving his fingers through his red hair till it stood up in spikes. "I've been just about exploding with it every second since we heard it! If it really worked, I wouldn't have to get old and die in three years!"

"I know, I know, I know!" Ananda cried, reaching to touch him but floating right past. "It could be our salvation."

"It has to work," Cyborg said. "Think for a minute. Be logical. There's no way anyone could have gotten on or off this space station after the devastation. So we get here and we find Jane the same age as before she left forty-five years ago, not to mention David and Nate. How else could that have happened?"

"Are they aliens that took over their bodies?" Ananda asked.

"Ananda, sometimes you're unreal. Forget that fairy-tale stuff!" Corgan told her. "The Driscolls figured out how to subtract years from their lives. If it worked for them, it could work for Sharla and Cyborg."

So agitated that he moved too fast and ricocheted off a wall, Cyborg cried, "I'd have to go back to being sixteen again. Permanently! They said that once you let the Locker take you to a certain age, you're locked into that forever."

"Sixteen will be great for you, Cyborg. That'll bring you back closer to my age," Ananda cried excitedly.

"And you'll keep on getting older," Cyborg reminded her. "I'll be permanently sixteen, while you grow old enough to be my mother."

Ananda frowned. "We'll work something out," she murmured. "It won't be as bad as it is now because I'll only age a day at a time."

Corgan hadn't figured out that part, that if Sharla

stayed sixteen forever, the way Cyborg would, Corgan and Ananda would just keep on aging. What would that do to the way they related to one another? But who cared? Right now the main worry was Nate and his idea about negotiating. Just what did he think required negotiation?

Cyborg kept floating around, examining everything. "You know, they were smart to jettison whatever they didn't need in order to trim down this station and make it smaller. They've jammed a lot of stuff into this Destiny module. I wonder if the Locker is in here?"

Corgan shrugged, or he meant to, but the motion propelled him backward. "Look out, I might run into you, Ananda," he called out. Or run into Sharla, but she'd floated to one side of the module, where she seemed to be sleeping peacefully.

"Ooof!" Ananda had bumped into a wall, which meant she bounced in the opposite direction. "This free-floating isn't fun anymore. I'll be glad to get back to the artificial gravity in the *Prometheus*. Right now I feel like a prisoner in this place. A flipping, flopping prisoner."

"Yeah, because that's what we are with the door locked," Corgan realized. "But once we get out of here, where do we go? Back to Earth? To Mars? To an asteroid? Thebos told me a space probe once landed on an asteroid. I don't think we'd want to go there."

Not answering that, Cyborg said, "It sure is hard to snoop around here. Every time I see something I want to check out, I go to grab it and end up flying in the opposite direction." He switched on the magnetism in his hand to attach himself to a wall, saying, "I've looked all over this

Destiny module, and I can't find anything that might be the Locker they're talking about, but I did find a diagram of the original station. I can't believe how many parts of it they jettisoned."

Ananda floated over to Cyborg and examined the diagram. "That looks like the picture we saw with all those modules. If they disconnected stuff, wouldn't it hang around in space?"

"It probably dropped out of orbit and burned up when it fell back through Earth's atmosphere," Corgan said. "Does the diagram show if there's a bathroom here in the Destiny?"

"Over there," Cyborg answered, pointing to a closet-like stall attached to the wall. "I think it works like the Clean Rooms back in the virtual-reality Boxes in Wyoming. It recycles everything that comes out of you. Don't take too long. All of us will be waiting in line, if we could figure out how to form a line without flying all over the place."

"Demi will need to go too," Ananda said.

"I am so glad that is not our problem right now, Ananda. It's the Driscolls' problem," Corgan told her. "They've probably forgotten that dogs don't know how to use Clean Rooms. It should be real interesting." He laughed a little at that, finally finding something to be amused about in this disturbing place.

"Hey, wait!" Cyborg said, staring at the diagram. "I think I've found what I'm looking for. Might be a communications hookup." He released himself from the wall and floated across the module to a box attached next to the doorframe. Very gently he reached out to rotate its dial.

The voice they heard coming from the adjoining module belonged to Nate. "Mom, I never saw a dog before."

"Sure you have, Nate. You've seen dogs in those old movies we play over and over."

"I mean a real one. Hi, Demi. You're so cool!"

Corgan wondered why Nate had called Demi cool—if anything, the dog's temperature was higher than humans'.

"What about the blond girl?" they heard David ask. "If what they say is true, she could possibly be restored if we hooked her up to the Locker."

"I like the dark-haired one too," Nate said. "Ananda. Funny name. Cool girl."

What was it with Nate and *cool*? Was it just an odd expression his parents brought up from Earth all those years ago? Nate went on, "We can keep all of them here for a few days, can't we, Dad? After we fix Sharla, I'd like to talk to both of them, get to know them better."

"Both of them" must mean Sharla and Ananda. Nate didn't seem much interested in Corgan or Cyborg.

It was Jane who answered, "You know how delicately balanced our existence is, Nate. It's going to take a lot of reworking—"

There were no more words, just a buzz. "They found out we turned on the speaker," Cyborg said, "and they disconnected it. They don't want us to hear what they're saying." He raised his titanium hand, once again turned on the magnetism, and moved it toward the communications box until sparks flew between them. "That ought to fix it," he said. "Now they can't hear us, either. So let's talk."

While Sharla hung motionless in the corner, Corgan, Cyborg, and Ananda hovered close to one another, trying not to move hands or feet or heads, because any motion caused them to float in another direction. "Something is very, very weird here," Corgan began.

"We've already established that," Cyborg said.

"Those people, the Driscolls—they seem nice enough," Ananda added, "but you're right, they practically herded us in here with that lame excuse about their sleep schedule."

"They were excited to see us, but not excited *enough*," Cyborg said. "They should have been jumping up and down and flipping off the walls to see their first human beings after forty-five years of isolation."

Corgan frowned. He'd been so preoccupied wondering if the Locker would make Sharla normal again that he hadn't thought too much at first about the Driscolls' lack of reaction. "Maybe they're just not very enthusiastic people."

"Or maybe," Ananda suggested again, "they're not the real Driscolls."

"Would you just quit with that alien theory, Ananda," Cyborg scoffed. After a pause he said, "I think they've got some plan for us."

"To use us for body parts?"

"Ananda! Stop!"

Corgan thought about it. "Here's what I don't understand," he said. "We offered to take them with us in the

Prometheus. But they said no. Why wouldn't they want to get out of here?"

"That is tremendously odd," Ananda agreed. "Staying in this station forever, the same three people going around and around, nothing ever changing—to me it would be a living hell."

"For sure," Cyborg said. "So we need to be very cautious until we find out more about them."

"I don't care what they're like. I don't care if they have two heads or they're harboring aliens or they're really ghosts, just as long as they let us use the Locker," Corgan insisted. "That's all that matters."

Cyborg warned, "Don't let your hopes blind you. Let's get some sleep. From what they said, I think something's going to happen in eight hours. We should be ready to deal with it."

Corgan tried to stretch himself horizontally in midair, far enough away from the others that he wouldn't drift into anyone and wake them. Holding his arm above his eyes to block the light, which flooded through a big, round porthole in the module right on schedule, every forty-five minutes, he was surprised that his arm never felt heavy. Well, why should it? he asked himself. After all, it was weightless, just like the rest of him.

He couldn't sleep, though. Excitement over whether Sharla could be cured, concern over Cyborg's suspicions about the Driscolls, and the strange feel of weightlessness all conspired to keep him awake. He'd just begun to doze when a whimper woke him. Then a cry. Corgan jerked up so fast he spun as he tried to see who had cried out like that. It wasn't Sharla—both Ananda and Sharla were sleeping. But Cyborg was clutching his head as if trying to squeeze something painful out of his brain.

"What's the matter?" Corgan demanded, lashing around until he somehow managed to reach Cyborg.

"It's Brigand! He's in here!"

"In where? What do you mean?"

"Inside my mind. He's invading my skull. He's punishing me! It's like a drumbeat and it won't stop. Now it's a screech. Don't, Brigand! Turn it off! It hurts!" Groaning, Cyborg swung his head back and forth, pounding his forehead with his good hand, pressing against it with the titanium one.

"Why's he doing this? What does he want?" Corgan asked in alarm.

"I don't know! Please, Brigand, leave me alone. No, I can't come back to you. I don't know how to fly the *Prometheus*. I'm sorry you got hurt. It was an accident!" Desperate, Cyborg attempted to bang his head against the wall of the module, but the impact drove him backward until he crashed into the opposite wall and then rebounded, twisting and turning.

"Don't! Wait! You'll hurt yourself!" Flailing after him, Corgan managed to catch Cyborg and hold him. As the two of them floated together in weightlessness, with their arms and legs tangled and awkward, Sharla and Ananda amazingly stayed asleep.

"Help me, Corgan. Make him go away," Cyborg begged. Cyborg, normally so calm and self-controlled, was whimpering like a baby.

Unsure what to do, Corgan placed his hands on either side of Cyborg's head and held tight at least to keep him from writhing around and hitting himself. As he stared into Cyborg's eyes Corgan drew back in shock. Instead of a reflection of his own face in the enlarged black pupils, he saw Brigand! Two tiny images of Brigand, with his tattooed forehead and cheek and chin, a phantom Brigand who mocked and laughed in triumph because he'd captured his clone-twin's brain.

"He's using your eyes. The slime!" Corgan hissed while Cyborg kept sobbing, "Make him stop. It hurts too much! My head's going to explode!"

What to do? Corgan grabbed Cyborg's artificial arm, pulled it up to Cyborg's forehead, and turned on the magnetism. It was a crazy thing to try, but he had no other ideas. He'd seen Cyborg turn on the magnetism in that artificial hand lots of times, twice within the past hour, so it should be safe, even though it was just a wild guess on Corgan's part that it might free him from Brigand. Cyborg's body arced as the magnetic charge coursed though him, and then he slumped into Corgan's arms, unconscious but no longer writhing.

"Is he gone? Is Brigand gone?" Corgan murmured. "Talk to me, Cyborg!" Cyborg didn't respond. His eyes were closed. Gently Corgan raised one of the lids, but the pupil showed only darkness. "If you were in there when I turned on the current, Brigand, I hope I fried you," Corgan whispered fiercely. Worried, he held Cyborg for more than an hour, checking his pulse every few minutes, relieved that his heartbeat stayed steady. Finally he released him to the gentleness of zero gravity. Pale and drawn, Cyborg slept fitfully, tossing, sometimes moaning softly, "I didn't . . . I'm sorry. . . ."

After six hours, thirty-two minutes, and forty-seven and three-tenths seconds, during which Cyborg never woke and Corgan never slept, Corgan heard the module door opening from the other side.

EIGHTEEN

From the doorway David Driscoll held a finger against his lips to request silence, then, curling his fingers, he signaled Corgan to follow him. Corgan hated to leave Cyborg, but he had to find out what the Driscolls were up to. Both Sharla and Cyborg were his responsibility, Cyborg more now than ever before. But he'd be cautious.

When Demi heard the hatch door opening, she tried to reach Corgan to greet him. Not knowing up from down, she moved her paws in a swimming motion that kept her flopping sideways. But even without gravity she managed to move forward, looking so awkward that Corgan might have laughed if he hadn't been so tense.

After the hatch door closed, David said, "Nate is really

taken with that dog. Back in the good old days boys always owned dogs. I had one; his name was Chili. They used to say dogs were man's best friends, but I think they were really boys' best friends."

Why did David smile so much? He continued, "I hadn't thought about it much before this, but Nate has never had a live pet, poor kid. We have laboratory rats that breed and reproduce pretty well, but we don't get attached to them because we eat them."

If Corgan could have stopped free-floating, those words would have brought him up short. Eating rats? He hoped the Driscolls wouldn't serve any for breakfast.

Seeing Corgan's expression, David said, "People have such strong prejudices about what they will eat and what they won't eat. They should be willing to experiment."

"Come over here and I'll feed you," Jane said in her pleasant voice, "but don't worry, I won't give you any rats. I'm fixing boiled wheat for you. Did you see it growing in the back part of the Destiny lab?" She went on to explain that both the rats and the wheat were part of their bioregenerative life-support system, that plants recycle human wastes and provide human nutrients, while humans recycle plant wastes—oxygen—and provide plant nutrients, carbon dioxide.

"Nate figured out how to improve the system," David said. "Nate is great at engineering concepts. Nate the Great, that's what I call him."

Nate paid no attention. He was totally absorbed in playing with Demi. He rotated her, head over tail—except that Demi didn't have a tail because it had been cropped—and

Demi seemed to like it. Then he examined her as if she were a lab specimen, checking her eyes, her ears, her teeth, and running his hand across her silky black hair and white ruff.

Continuing to praise Nate, Jane said, "He figured out how to enhance the light coming through the optical glass port in the Destiny lab, and that increased our crop yield, which meant we had more to feed the rats, which meant more and bigger rats. . . ."

"And that's what we want to talk to you about," David said.

Rats? They wanted to talk about rats?

"That is, I suppose you're the right person to talk to, Corgan. As pilot of the *Prometheus*, you're the leader of your group, I imagine. Is that correct?"

"I guess so," Corgan answered. "I mean, yes, I am."

"So here's the deal——," David began.

"Wait, let the boy eat," Jane interrupted. "He'll be more focused if his stomach isn't growling."

"I'm focused!" Corgan insisted. Focused and cautious. "Go ahead, David." Was it okay to call this man David? When a person had two names, you used the first one to talk to him, didn't you? But protocol didn't matter now because it seemed David was getting ready to make some kind of offer.

"All right, then. First let me give you a little background. The three of us had to decide what age we wanted to be. Permanently. Because when you enter the Locker and get zapped, there's no going back. More important, there's no going forward. You stay whatever age you set the program to," David said.

"I understand that," Corgan replied.

"Let me explain a little more," Jane broke in. "David and I wanted to be adult, but young enough to remain healthy up here so Nate would never have to take care of us. But Nate was our son, so we thought he should be younger than we were, but old enough to have reached the peak of his mental abilities, because we knew he was a genius. Since most scientists do their most brilliant work in their midtwenties, that's what all of us chose for him—Nate! Will you stop playing with that dog and join this discussion? It concerns you, you know."

Concerned Nate? Corgan eyed him warily as Nate reluctantly left Demi to propel himself nearer to his parents. He ran his long, thin fingers through his curly hair but kept his gaze lowered, not looking directly at Corgan.

"Now, we want to lay all our cards on the table," David said. "We want to be totally honest with you. The Locker worked fine on Jane and me, but after Nate—well, I mean, we'd programmed it to have Nate become twenty-five again, but there was some minor malfunction that took him back to twenty years old instead of twenty-five."

"Which was perfectly fine," Jane said. "I mean, he's twenty, but he's still a genius."

"Ah, Mom," Nate grumbled, "forget all that stuff and just get to the point."

Jane and David exchanged glances. "Are you sure you wouldn't like something to eat?" Jane asked Corgan.

Where is this going? Corgan wondered, feeling more and more uneasy.

"All right, here's the deal," David said. "You want Sharla

to be re-aged to back before her accident. We can do that. We're just not sure how precise we can be. I mean, the Locker runs extremely fast, which means the person operating it has to have enormous powers of concentration and be able to compute time in seconds."

"That's not a problem," Corgan answered. Back in the domed cities everyone knew about Corgan's time-splitting ability and superfast reflexes. Up here, of course, Jane and David would never have heard of any of this. "I can handle it." Was that all they wanted to talk about? All this preliminary chatter dealt only with the Locker program not working exactly right?

David cleared his throat. "Remember, I said we need to negotiate. That means we let you use the program, but we need something in return from you."

So Cyborg had been right. They wanted to barter. Well, thanks to Cyborg's warning, Corgan had already figured out what he could offer them. He'd come prepared. "I have something here I know you'll want," he said, taking out Thebos's letter.

David had already begun to shake his head, but Jane asked, "What is it?"

"It's for you. A letter from Thebos. I mean, P. T."

With a little cry Jane reached for the letter and opened it. She seemed to forget that the three of them were there as she pored over the letter, focusing her entire attention on the pages, moving her lips a little as she read. There were four pages, and they must have been densely written, because it took her a long time to read them. When she finished, she clutched the letter to her chest and looked up, not at them, but at the sunrise shining through the port.

"Can we get on with it?" Nate asked. David shushed him, saying, "Let her have her moment."

And it was only a moment, seventy-three and a quarter seconds, before she looked at Corgan and said, "He's very fond of you. Did you know he saved your life?"

Corgan shook his head. "No, the Hydrobots saved me."

"Yes, but when the Hydrobots dragged you in, the med techs thought you had drowned, and they wouldn't even try to resuscitate you. It was P. T. who insisted that you could be saved. He worked over you until your heart started beating again. P. T. saved your life."

"I—I didn't know that." So that's why Thebos thought of him as a son, because he'd given Corgan his life back. And then he'd gone on to conceive a way to save Sharla, and Cyborg, too, even though things had turned out totally different from what he expected, because there was no Hong Ly anymore. Instead there was the immortality machine— the Locker—and everything might turn out right after all. Cyborg might be a strategist, but Corgan had negotiated this deal pretty well all by himself. "So now," he asked, "can this be considered an even trade? I brought you the letter, and you'll let Sharla be healed in the Locker."

"Nice try," Nate said, his lip curling a little. "But we're talking about bigger stakes."

Food, Corgan guessed. Probably after years of eating rats and wheat the Driscolls would want some nice forty-year-old dehydrated chicken and noodles. "Like our food supplies?" he asked.

"Bigger yet."

"Like . . . one of the girls," David answered, but he'd turned his head away, so that Corgan wasn't sure he'd heard it correctly. "As you requested, we will use the Locker to take Sharla back to when she was healthy. In return we ask you to leave one of the girls here with us. Nate needs a companion."

This time Corgan heard it loud and clear. "Impossible!" he sputtered.

Jane and David literally fell over each other in their haste to explain. "If Nate works on our bioregenerative system, he can make it capable of supporting one more occupant here in the station. But only one. And Nate needs a companion. It would enhance our lives so much for Nate to have either Sharla—after she gets healed, of course—or Ananda stay here with us."

"Why would you even ask that?" Corgan demanded. "We already offered to take you with us. If we go back to Earth, Nate could find plenty of girls."

Jane closed her eyes, breathing deeply and crossing her arms as if in meditation. "You don't understand," she said.

"Then, explain it to me!"

David, speaking softly, said, "We can't go back to Earth."

"Why not?"

"Because gravity would kill us," he answered. "After forty-five years of weightlessness we've lost too much bone mass. Our bodies can survive only here. On Earth or even on Mars gravity would crush us the way your fist can squash a spider."

Jane smiled—how could she smile? "But it's fine," she told Corgan. "We're perfectly happy here. It's what we have, what we've grown used to. . . ." Her face clouded. "Or at least what we'd grown used to until you arrived. Now we've seen another possibility, that we might be able to have a companion for Nate, and that would make all of us even happier."

No, no, no, Corgan shouted silently. He bit his lip with his teeth to keep from shouting it out. Give up one of the girls? Preposterous! But the Driscolls had something he wanted so badly he could taste it like he tasted the blood on his lip. Give up one of the girls to make Sharla whole again? His mind froze and the words *No way* got stuck in his throat.

"I guess you need time to think about it," Jane said. "We understand that."

Corgan licked his lip and leaned back, not realizing that leaning back would curl him into a backflip in zero gravity. Too appalled to be embarrassed, he was shocked further when David joked, "Look, Mother, we surprised him so much he fell over backward." Neither of them laughed or acted like that was funny; instead they looked worried and anxious, as though they knew what they'd just asked for was earthshaking, if they'd been on Earth to shake it.

Righting himself, Corgan said, "Wait, you said we were supposed to negotiate. Well, I'm negotiating now. You have to let not just Sharla, but Cyborg, too, use the Locker. He needs to go back in time too."

Jane and David seemed about to agree, but Nate stopped

them, saying, "If you get two shots at the Locker, then I get to pick which girl I want. I won't pick until I see how Sharla turns out."

Corgan wanted to hit him, wanted it so much his fists clenched. What happened if you punched someone in zero gravity? Did both of you fly in opposite directions? He managed to control himself, but his voice was gravelly when he asked, "When do we get to do this? When can we use the Locker for Sharla and Cyborg?"

Again David and Jane were about to answer when Nate said, "Anytime. The sooner we get it done, the sooner we can get the rest of you off the station. You're using up our oxygen and our water, and we don't have much to spare."

"Give us a few minutes to dust off the Locker," David said. "That's just an expression, of course. We don't have ordinary dust up here, just little flakes of skin and rat hair, and the Locker is always covered to keep it clean. After we uncover it, you can bring Sharla over."

It looked like this was really going to happen! "I'd rather we did Cyborg first," Corgan said shakily. Cyborg's condition was even more complicated now than Sharla's. And maybe if the machine didn't work on him, there'd be no point in putting Sharla through the process. He wished so much that Thebos could be here to help him with these crucial, lifesaving decisions.

"No. Sharla goes first," Nate insisted.

Corgan had no choice but to agree. David said then, "I'm assuming that you are an honorable young man, Corgan, but perhaps we'd better spell out the terms of our commitment. In return for the use of our Locker program by your two teammates, Sharla and Cyborg, you agree to leave one of the girls behind with us when you leave. Which girl it will be is to be determined later."

"By me," Nate said.

Corgan clutched a handle on the wall to keep himself steady.

"There's no point in writing out a legal contract," David went on. "If one of us defaults, there are no courts or lawyers here in space. But I'm trusting you to keep your word. A handshake will seal our bargain."

Keeping his hand at his side, Corgan told them, "You need to promise me one thing. Don't tell anyone—not Cyborg or Ananda or Sharla, if she gets her senses back—about the conversation we just had in this room. I'll shake on the bargain and I'll keep my word, but you have to trust me to do it my way."

"Agreed," David said, and held out his hand. "You shake on it too, Nate."

"What about me?" Jane asked. "I'm part of this, a big part of it, since you're bringing another female into our family." She rested her hand on the hands of the other three. "And who do we have to thank for all this?" she asked. "Why, P. T. Thebos. If he hadn't built the *Prometheus*—"

"Enough talk, Mom," Nate told her sharply. "Let's do this thing. Corgan, give us ten minutes and then bring Sharla here."

"Right. I'll be back in ten." If Corgan could have dragged his feet reluctantly, he would have, but there could be no foot dragging in zero gravity. He moved smoothly and fluidly toward the door of the Destiny lab. *Perfect name*, he thought. Sharla's destiny lay behind that door. Cyborg's, too.

They were all awake, Ananda hovering worriedly over Cyborg, asking him, "Is it your liver that's hurting you? Why did it get so much worse?"

"Never mind . . . never mind," Cyborg stammered, motioning Ananda to move away. "I need to talk to Corgan."

He looked awful, his skin gray, his eyes circled by dark shadows. When Corgan reached him, he whispered, "I didn't tell Ananda what's happening. She'd just worry."

"What *is* happening? I mean right now," Corgan asked softly.

"Brigand's not squeezing my head anymore, he's just talking. And talking and talking and talking—he won't stop."

"What's he saying?" Corgan grasped Cyborg's real hand because it trembled so much.

"He says that we're the same person. That we belong together. That he would never blame me, never hurt me, if I came back. He says he can get instructions from Thebos about how to fly the *Prometheus*, and he'll thought-transfer them to me. Once we get in the ship, I'm supposed to throw you out into space. He says he hopes you'll burn up during reentry into Earth's atmosphere."

None of that frightened Corgan, it just made him mad. "What about Sharla?" he asked.

"He says I'm supposed to bring her back with me. He

says I can keep Ananda. His words won't stop, Corgan. They just keep clicking through my ears over and over like a broken flywheel on a speeding motor. It's . . . it's so . . ."

Corgan nodded. "Stay strong. I have a plan." To Ananda he instructed, "We're all going out to the main module. Bring Sharla. The Driscolls are getting the Locker ready for her. They'll try to take her back to the day before the crash, but it's dicey because the program has been a little unreliable."

"You mean you're going to let them put her into a faulty program?" Ananda asked.

"You have any other suggestions? Remember, we're getting kicked out of here pretty soon—like in a couple of hours, if it's up to Nate. By the way, I found out why the Driscolls can't go back to Earth with us, or to Mars, either. A return to gravity would crush them, destroy their bodies. But they said it's all right. They like it up here. They're happy."

"Now I understand!" Cyborg exclaimed. "Now I know why they're so calm—they had to create some kind of self-imposed mind control to be able to stand this without going crazy. It's a delusion that they like it here; it's the only way they can deal with life in this purgatory." He paused for a moment. "I feel really sorry for them. If any of us were forced to stay here forever, we'd end up killing ourselves."

"The poor things," Ananda said. "It would be so awful to be trapped here forever."

Corgan nearly lost it. His hands began to shake and his heart felt sheathed in ice. He couldn't speak, could only gesture to Ananda to bring Sharla into the main module. She took Sharla's hand and pulled her toward the doorway as Cyborg drifted after them.

Nate was waiting, looking excited, his eyes fastening first on Ananda and then on Sharla. "The Locker's as ready as I can make it," he said. "But I'm not taking responsibility for running it. First we have to plug in the date we're shooting for, but I warn you, the program's got this quirk now and I don't know how to fix it. The dates are gonna rotate so fast through the program window that you have to hit the key at the exact tenth of a second, or you'll end up as much as a month off target."

"Or a few years off target," Jane said seriously. "We tried to stop it at Nate's twenty-fifth birthday, but we missed it by five years—we just weren't quick enough. It's fine, though," she added brightly. "He's lovely this way." *One more Driscoll delusion*, Corgan thought. If Jane believed that, she must keep herself in even tighter control than her husband or her son.

"You mean if you're off by three years, Sharla could end up being thirteen?" Ananda asked. "Forever?"

"Trust me," Corgan said. He steeled himself, forced his hands to stop trembling, and said, "Plug it in at June eighth, 2082. Then show me the window where the dates spin through."

The Locker looked like a vertical coffin, tall enough and wide enough to hold one human and the electronic gear that would be fastened to him or her. It had been patched together with oddly shaped bits of metal, probably pieces cut from the parts of the space station that had been jettisoned. Thebos would have been appalled at the sloppiness of the construction, and Corgan felt pretty apprehensive about whether anything so slipshod could work. But what was the alternative? He guided Sharla into the box, staring into her eyes one last time for any sign of understanding. There was nothing.

Nate fitted a thin metal helmet onto Sharla's head and metal cuffs around her upper and lower arms. Once when Corgan was a boy, his tutor program, Mendor, had shown him a virtual image of an electric chair, a device where murderers were murdered themselves, with the same kind of wired devices fastened to their heads and arms. Cyborg and Ananda looked worried, but Corgan couldn't allow himself to feel fear or any other emotion. He just wished he'd slept a little so that his reflexes would be at the top of their performance arc. *Don't mess up*, he repeated to himself.

"When the exact date shows, you have to hit the red button," Nate told him. "But those dates are gonna spin past so fast you'll hardly be able to see them, so get ready."

"I'm ready."

Nate closed and sealed the door to the Locker.

Let it work, Corgan prayed. He was not prepared for the shriek of the machinery as Nate turned the switch. It threw him off for a second, but he recovered fast, his eyes boring into the dates that spun backward, second by second, toward June 8, the day before Brigand crashed the Harrier into the dome. A hundred hundredths in a second, 86,400 seconds in a day, the numbers hurtling backward, backward, toward what hour of June 8? He chose 2 P.M.

Sun time, and when that exact split second appeared, he hit the red button.

This time the scream wasn't from the machine, but from Sharla. And then he heard her cry out, "Where am I? Get me out of here!"

His heart nearly stopped as Nate pulled opened the door and unfastened Sharla from the machinery, but it began to race when she leaped out of the box yelling to Nate, "Who the hell are you?" Not thirteen, not fourteen or fifteen, it was sixteen-year-old Sharla, looking just as she had the last time he'd seen her in the Wyo-DC, when she'd thrown herself against the rebel who'd pointed the gun at Corgan. Unable to help himself, he began to shake again.

Behind him he heard Nate and Jane and David congratulating one another. In front of him Cyborg and Ananda were talking bewilderingly fast, trying to explain to Sharla everything that had happened since the time of her injury, because Sharla couldn't remember anything from after the crash. "You mean I was brain-damaged?" she asked them, incredulous. "I couldn't talk or anything?"

Corgan attempted to lean against the Locker until he could control his emotions, but one touch and he sailed forward, the curse of zero gravity. As soon as he could right himself, he floated back to Sharla, in time to hear her say, "Brigand is hurt? How badly?"

He clenched his teeth. Brigand! The first name she mentioned had to be Brigand's. He wished he'd shot Brigand when he had the chance.

David was saying, "Well, we have one more to go, and the Locker worked so well for Sharla that I think we can trust it for Cyborg."

"Cyborg, this will save your life!" Ananda exclaimed.

Cyborg looked as though he needed saving. Pale and gaunt, he hung on to Ananda for support. Revolving to face the Driscolls, she cried, "It will keep him from growing old, it will keep him from dying in just two or three years. How can we ever thank you?"

Jane looked down, David looked sideways, and Nate grinned. As Nate's gaze slid from Ananda to Sharla and back he answered, "We'll find a way. So, what date do you want to set for Cyborg?"

Corgan said, "The day before we left Wyoming. Right, Cyborg?"

Ananda literally danced in space, crying, "That'll make you sixteen!"

"Perpetually," he answered.

"We'll be only two years apart! And you'll be healthy again, and that's the best part, because right now, Cyborg, you don't look so good."

Cyborg smiled weakly.

Focus, Corgan told himself after Cyborg had been wired into the Locker. *Forget how Sharla feels about Brigand. Forget that there's no way to know what's going to happen inside Cyborg's unstable head. Forget your bargain with the Driscolls.* "Wait a minute," he said. "Take off your artificial hand, Cyborg. It's metal and magnetic, so it might short-circuit the program."

Nodding in agreement, Cyborg removed the hand and

gave it to Ananda. "Hold it tight," he told her. "I don't want it to float all over the module."

Once more the machinery shrieked; once more Corgan froze his attention on the whirling seconds in the program window. April 18, 2082, at noon in Wyoming—the split seconds spun backward until Corgan pushed the red button and another yell rang out from the Locker, this time in the deep voice that belonged to Cyborg.

Nate and Ananda unfastened Cyborg, who was laughing and chattering and saying that he'd never felt better in his life, and wasn't it amazing, because even though his body had been restored to what it was back on April 18, he hadn't lost a single memory from that day forward until right now. Unlike Sharla, who couldn't remember a thing from when she was mentally injured, Cyborg had total recall.

Interrupting him, Corgan gave him his artificial arm and whispered, "What about Brigand?"

"What about him?"

"Is he—you know?"

As Corgan tapped his own forehead Cyborg told him, "Nope! All gone. It's like last night never happened. Everything's great."

That filled Corgan with relief that lasted about two and a half seconds, until Jane drifted close to him to murmur, "We're giving Nate three hours to choose."

"Choose what?" Sharla asked. Neither of them realized she'd floated close enough to hear them. "What is Nate going to choose?"

Thinking fast, Corgan said, "He's going to suggest the

best place for us to go when we leave here. Maybe Mars, but we have to figure out where to land on Mars. It's a big planet."

"No! I want to go back to the Flor-DC."

Sure you do, Corgan thought. *But from now on I'm the one who makes the decisions. I've saved you and Cyborg, and now it's time to do something that I want.*

nineteen

Sharla must have felt the need to make up for all her days of silence, because she wouldn't stop talking. "I can't stand these drab hospital clothes I'm in," she complained. "I like color! Does anyone have an extra LiteSuit I can borrow?"

"I do," Corgan said, "but it will be too big for you, and it's in the spacecraft."

"In the *Prometheus*? Corgan, you can't be serious about going to Mars in that thing," she declared, switching topics so fast he could hardly keep up with her. As usual.

"I'm serious."

"It's totally illogical. We need to go back to Florida."

Corgan changed the subject. "Sharla, there's something I wanted to ask you. Thebos—you don't know him, but he's this really smart old guy—he brought us a coded message that said, 'Cyborg Cyborg Cyborg it's getting worse.' Did you send that?"

"No. I clearly remember everything that happened in the weeks before the Harrier crash, and I never sent you any coded message."

Cyborg said, "It had to be from Brigand, then. It just proves how much he's suffering. If we had something to bargain with—I mean, that we could barter, that the Driscolls might want in exchange—then maybe they'd let us take the Locker to Florida with us and let Brigand use it. If he knew he didn't have to die in a couple of years, it would turn him around and curb his craving for power. I know there's good in him somewhere. It's up to me to save him."

"No, it's up to *me* to save him," Sharla said. "I'm the one who made him."

Corgan cried, "Save him from what? From killing people? Maybe you should try saving the people he's planning to kill!"

Ignoring Corgan, Cyborg said, "If only he didn't have to die, all the fury might drain out of him. It sure has made a huge difference to me! I feel like I'm floating all over the place, not just from weightlessness, but because I'm so happy. It's like I've been set free. I have something I've never had before. A future!"

"And that's what Brigand needs," Sharla told him.

"You're so right," Cyborg agreed. "But you know what, Sharla? I know Brigand is happy for me. During the night he bombarded me so bad it nearly wrecked my brain, but then he stopped."

"Is he in thought-contact with you?" she asked.

"Not in words. It's as though he's sending me *good feelings*."

"Good feelings?"

"Yes, like he's really glad about what happened to me. He really does care about me."

Sharla tilted her head and swept her fingers through her short hair, twirling a strand as she drifted deep into thought. Ignoring Corgan, she began to study Cyborg through narrowed eyes.

They were inside the Destiny module, and in all likelihood the Driscolls had fixed the intercom and were listening to everything that was said. So far the family had kept quiet about the bargain they'd struck with Corgan, but if they ever decided to spill it out, there'd be one more revolt, right there in the Destiny.

"Since four of us are involved," Cyborg said, "I think we should put it to a vote. Where we're gonna go, I mean. I vote for Earth."

"I vote with Cyborg," Ananda announced, twining her arms through his as both of them hovered in midair, circling each other in a strange weightless dance. "Whatever he wants is fine with me. And I think it's a great idea for us to take the Locker, if we can get it. That way when I get too old for Cyborg, I can return to the age of sixteen, just like he did."

"Forget voting!" Corgan barked. Lack of sleep, all the talk about Brigand, and worry about what would soon happen were draining his patience. "Remember, I'm the only one who can pilot the *Prometheus*. Wherever I point it, we go. And I like the idea of Mars."

"That's not really fair," Ananda protested.

"Let's go talk this over with Jane and David and Nate and hear what they have to say," Cyborg suggested. "They might tell us more about the Mars colony, but it would be good if we could get them to bargain with us about the Locker. We could trade them all the food that's in the *Prometheus* for the Locker, because if we go back to the Flor-DC, we're not going to need the food, and they don't need the Locker anymore anyway."

"*No!* Not a good idea to talk with the Driscolls," Corgan insisted.

"Why not? You can stay here in the Destiny if you want," Cyborg said. "I'll go out and speak to them. Negotiate something."

The word *negotiate* sent chills through Corgan's spine. "I'll go with you," he said quickly.

"We'll all go," Sharla said. "This is about all of us."

When they floated through the door into the main module, they found the Driscolls waiting as if expecting them. Trying to catch David's attention, Corgan shook his head slightly, silently begging David to keep their secret.

Cyborg, always a strategist, made a few bland comments about how strange it was to live without gravity, how amazing the views were through the port in the Destiny, how clever the Driscolls had been to create their perfectly balanced biosphere, and how grateful he felt for the session in the Locker. "It saved my life," he said. "I was facing death from old age in a few years, and now I think I'll live forever. I'll always be sixteen—which I sure hope turns out to be a good year." He laughed a little at that, and so did Jane and David. Politely. "I guess you folks won't ever need the Locker again," Cyborg continued. "I mean, all three of you will stay locked into the ages you are now."

"Whether we'll need it depends on . . . ," Nate began, and then he paused. Corgan froze. He knew what Nate meant, that if he chose Ananda, he'd want to stop her age at some future time so she wouldn't outpace him.

Before Nate could finish, though, Cyborg continued, "Well, we wondered if you'd consider trading the Locker for our food in the *Prometheus*."

"I didn't okay that," Corgan protested, but it didn't matter because Jane quickly said, "You'll need the food if you go to Mars. In the *Prometheus*, if I remember the way P. T. designed it, you can make it to Mars in just two months. How much food did you say is stored in the cargo bay?"

"Irrelevant," Corgan answered. "We don't need to trade."

"I can think of one huge reason why we should—," Sharla began, but Cyborg cut her off with, "Consider this, Corgan. If we flew the Locker back to Florida, we could make Thebos young again. Right now he's grown so old that he can't live too many more years. The Locker would let him choose any age he wanted to be. Return him to his youth."

Cyborg, the strategist, had hit on the single argument that sliced Corgan to the core. Thebos could be restored to youth and health. Thebos, who thought of Corgan as a son. A younger Thebos might become a real father to Corgan. He remembered Jane's words: "P. T. saved your life." Shouldn't Corgan pay him back? He felt like he was drowning in conflict. But the biggest calamity loomed ahead of him.

Whether or not they got the Locker, he still owed Nate one of the girls. He'd promised that. Jane and David had turned out to be decent, honest people who'd found a way to survive by pretending they liked their lives. Although Corgan didn't think much of Nate, he'd made a deal to leave him a companion. Space might be a weightless medium where a body had no mass, but once again Corgan felt his soul dragged down by burdens he shouldn't have to handle, burdens too heavy for him. And no one could help him.

"Know what I think?" Jane asked. "I think we need some rest."

"Again?" Ananda exclaimed.

"Yes, a little downtime. We Driscolls haven't had this much excitement in our lives in forty years, and you kids must be exhausted."

"Not really—," Ananda began, but Nate cut her off with, "There's a problem. I've checked our oxygen levels and they're getting lower than they should be. The system isn't set up for this many people, so you guys should go into the *Prometheus*. For a while. But Sharla can stay here. She's the only one I haven't had a chance to talk to."

Awkwardly David tried to explain, "Nate would like to know Sharla a little better. After all, if it hadn't been for Nate, Sharla would still be mentally incapacitated."

Sharla raised her eyebrows but shrugged and said, "I guess I do owe you, Nate. I'll stay in here if you want me to."

No, not that, Corgan wanted to yell. What if Nate liked Sharla so much that he tried to keep her? Ready to protest, Corgan got stopped by the looks Jane and David threw him. Threatening looks that meant, *You object, and we'll tell them everything.*

"Right," he agreed. "We'll see you later."

Reentering the *Prometheus* meant a return to artificial gravity. Demi certainly seemed to like it—at first she stood with her feet splayed apart on the floor as if she needed to get used to her own weight again. Then she began to dance around Ananda, giving little yips that sounded like happiness.

"Dance, Demi, dance. Look how cute she is," Ananda said.

"Yeah. Cute," Cyborg agreed, then he began, "I wish I understood how the Locker works. It's some complex interaction between mental and physical. I've been pressing my fist hard on my chest, and nothing hurts inside me, so I know my injury got completely healed from being Lockered."

"Is *Lockered* a word?" Ananda asked.

"It is now. And did you notice, Corgan, I don't have a mustache like I did before, back when I was the age I'm supposed to be now?"

"And Sharla's hair is still short," Ananda pointed out.

Cyborg said, "It's like the Locker's selective. It saves some things and doesn't save others."

Selective in a good way, Corgan thought. It had cured Cyborg's wound and made Brigand stop bombarding him. Or maybe not. "Has Brigand tried to thought-transfer you yet?" he asked.

Cyborg hesitated. "Again, not in the usual way. But like I told you before—I keep getting this sense that he's really happy about something. About me, I guess."

Maybe. Or maybe—a different possibility filled Corgan with sudden horror. What if the Locker's intensity had traveled all the way through Cyborg into Brigand? In the mysterious way the two of them were connected, that might have happened. What if Brigand had been cured too, had gone back to the time before his knee was shattered, had stopped rapid-aging the way Cyborg had? What if Brigand was going to stay sixteen forever, just like Sharla? The possibility staggered Corgan, but Ananda and Cyborg didn't notice.

"I admire the Driscolls," Cyborg was telling her. "They've convinced themselves that they're content, even though it's all an illusion. Maybe that's all happiness is— just making yourself believe that it's real."

Ananda laughed and said, "I'm very, very happy now and it's absolutely real, because I know you're going to be healthy and live forever. When they call us back, we'll figure out something to trade the Driscolls for the Locker so that I can stay young with you too."

"We really ought to talk about that, Corgan," Cyborg said. "You know, go over some strategies to convince them to bargain for the Locker."

"You and Ananda can talk it over all you want," Corgan told them, his throat tight with foreboding. *What if Brigand was sixteen again!* "I need some sleep. I haven't slept in one hundred sixty-seven thousand, three hundred and twenty-nine seconds."

"Quit showing off with that seconds stuff," Ananda joked. "Seriously, you need to stay awake and sort this out with us."

"Sorry." Corgan clomped down the stairs to the cargo bay, half afraid they'd try to follow him. But they didn't. He fell to the floor, burying his head in his hands. What if Brigand had become whole now, with a normal life span? That would change everything. The plan to travel to Mars, to stay there for three years until Brigand died, wouldn't be worth it if Brigand wasn't going to die. And in three years Thebos probably *would* die.

Corgan paced the cargo bay, taking care to move quietly, the hundredths of seconds running relentlessly through his brain until they turned into hours. He wanted to shout for them to stop. But he should eat—he'd need energy for what he was planning. As quietly as he could he rooted through the dehydrated-food containers and found something called crème brûlée, whatever that was. It tasted all right when he mixed it with water.

If his strategy worked, he'd wait at least another hour, until Ananda and Cyborg talked themselves out and fell asleep—in each other's arms, no doubt. That meant he had to stay alert. Having Sharla in the station module was a huge complication because he had no way of knowing whether she and the Driscolls would go to sleep or when, or if they'd just stay up talking.

After the hour had passed, with his pulse pounding in his ears, he crept up to the navigation deck. Just as he'd hoped, Cyborg and Ananda were sleeping, and as he'd predicted, their arms were around each other.

Couldn't be better, because Demi lay on the floor next to them.

Hoping she wouldn't make a sound, he gently lifted the dog, and then, holding her in one arm, he unlocked the hatch that led to the main module of the station. When Demi licked his face, he was almost undone, but he steeled himself to guide her through the tunnel. As quietly as he could he released Demi, who began floating through the module, making the swimming motions again.

Everything now depended on whether the Driscolls and Sharla had gone to sleep, and whether he could keep Sharla from blurting out something when he wakened her. Once he got inside the module and saw that all of them were sound asleep, stealing the Locker was easy. Even though it felt weightless, maneuvering it toward the hatch was trickier, but he moved it without waking anyone, very silently carrying it all the way back into the *Prometheus*, where it suddenly became heavy. But he handled it without making any noise, setting it at the edge of the command-control deck.

Then back to the module. Since each touch caused a reaction in the opposite direction, he placed one hand under Sharla's head at the same instant he placed the other hand over her mouth. She woke up, her eyes wide, but when she saw it was Corgan, she didn't struggle, and she let him pull her toward the short tunnel. Once inside it, Corgan quietly closed the door behind them.

Motioning her to stay silent and follow him, he guided her toward the *Prometheus*. She came, frowning, but apparently willing to humor him.

"How strong do you feel?" he asked her in a whisper.

"Why?"

"I need help releasing the hooks that connect the *Prometheus* to the docking station."

Sharla shrugged. "I'm strong enough, I guess." She knelt where he pointed, to where the large metal hooks clasped the ring around the hatch of the *Prometheus*. Corgan hoped to find some sort of release mechanism so they wouldn't have to jerk each hook loose by brute strength.

"Try that," he told her, pointing to a handle opposite the one he'd just found. "When I say 'One, two, three,' pull it toward you."

"Why?"

"Please, just do it."

To his relief, for once she obeyed him without arguing. The hooks released so quickly that Corgan barely had time to grab her by the hand and pull her into the *Prometheus* before the hatch door sprang shut. "What are you doing?" she cried, and that woke Cyborg and Ananda.

Leaping to the control panel, Corgan fired the engines and sent the *Prometheus* hurtling into space at top speed.

"Hey, what the . . . ," Cyborg cried, leaping up.

"Just shut up," Corgan commanded. "We're getting out of here. Everybody strap into a seat."

"Where are we going?" Ananda asked.

"Like I told you—out of here."

"How about back to Earth?" Sharla said, but Corgan didn't answer. Behind them the space station grew smaller and smaller. *They can't chase us*, Corgan knew, *because they don't have enough fuel or maneuverability.*

260

"Are you trying to run away?" Cyborg asked. "Why? Did you steal the Locker?" Again Corgan didn't answer.

"Where's Demi?" Ananda asked, looking around worriedly.

Sharla asked, "What's happening, Corgan?"

"Wait and see," he said as Ananda left to look for Demi. He felt horrible. He could picture her searching all the compartments in the cargo bay. After what he'd done, he didn't have the strength or the courage to face her. Not yet.

It didn't take long. In minutes she was back, saying, "I've been all over the ship and I can't find Demi. Where could she hide? We couldn't have left her back in the space station, could we?"

Again Corgan remained silent.

"Could we have, Corgan?"

"Yes," he whispered.

"You didn't. *You didn't!* Turn this damn crate around and go back for her," Ananda screamed.

"No. I'm not going to do that." Corgan secured the controls on automatic, which didn't matter because he hadn't set a course for any particular destination. All he wanted was to get far away from the space station as fast as possible. "Hey, stop it!" he yelled as Ananda began wildly hitting him with all her strength, which was considerable. It was almost a relief to have her strike him because it helped him with his guilt, but only a little. "Ananda, don't!" he pleaded, grasping her arms. "Quit screaming and listen to what I have to say. I had to make a bargain with the Driscolls—otherwise they wouldn't have let us use the Locker. They wanted either you or Sharla to stay behind to be a companion for Nate."

"You're lying! They never said anything like that!" Ananda shrieked.

"Yes they did. They said they wanted 'one of the girls' for a companion for Nate. That was the bargain. Either I agreed, or no Locker. I had to give my word. So I let them have one of the girls—Demi. I'm sure they're furious, but I kept my promise. Sort of."

"You gave away my dog!" Ananda was becoming hysterical. "She was my baby!"

Cyborg grabbed Ananda's shoulders and said, "She's a dog, Ananda, not a baby."

"She's the only family I have!"

"You have me now. And we can have Demi cloned. I'm sure her hair is all over the inside of this ship, enough so they could clone ten of her."

But nothing could comfort Ananda. "I hate you, Corgan," she screamed, tears smearing her cheeks.

"I had no choice!"

"Stop it, Ananda! Grow up!" Sharla told her. "Corgan did what he had to do. Would you want to stay on the space station? You'd be trapped like the Driscolls, with no hope of ever living anywhere else. And Nate's a slime. I saw that as soon as I met him—I mean, as soon as my head started working."

Ananda crouched on the deck, sobbing as though her heart had broken. To comfort her, Corgan said, "But there's one decent thing to remember about Nate: He likes Demi a lot. He'll be good to her. I did it because it was the only way I could save two lives—Cyborg's and Sharla's. You lost Demi, but you gained a healthy Cyborg. And if you want to stay young with him forever, you can, because I stole the Locker."

Her dark eyes flashing, Ananda accused him, "You're giving us all this 'I had to be honorable' crap, but your honor only extended as far as my poor dog. You think it was fine to steal and lie and cheat about everything else."

"Enough!" Corgan cried, standing up. "I did the best I could. And I don't even know why I bothered," he said, turning toward Sharla. "All you care about is Brigand."

Sharla took a long while to answer, "I told you, half my guilt has been lifted from me now because Cyborg's life is saved. If Brigand gets cured too, I can stop blaming myself. Then we'll decide how you and I fit together, Corgan."

"Sure! You're just saying that so I'll take you back to Brigand," he accused her.

"Don't you trust me?"

He hesitated. "No." Not since her revelation that she'd cheated in the Virtual War.

"Then, consider this, Corgan. I'm willing to go wherever you choose to go. If we take a vote, I'll give you mine."

"You will?" He couldn't believe it. *But wait a minute*, he thought. *This is Sharla. Nothing is ever straight and honest with Sharla.* "What's the reason?" he asked.

She smiled in that provocative way and said, "There are several. First, you saved me from being brain-dead. And second, you're not that innocent, obedient boy I first met. We're the same age, but you always seemed so much younger than me. But now I'll stay sixteen forever while you get older. That should make some interesting changes in how we connect."

Corgan had already thought of that. "And? What's the rest?"

"And—I overheard Cyborg say that Brigand was sending him feelings of well-being. I'd already thought about the possibility that the Locker cure might travel through Cyborg straight into Brigand. If it's true, and Cyborg's words gave me a pretty good clue that it is, then Brigand's death sentence may already have been lifted. So I'm willing to stay with you, Corgan. For a while. Like I said, I owe you."

Corgan's breath stopped.

"I mean stay with you as a friend," she added. "Can you be happy with that?"

He didn't have to think about the answer. "No, I can't. It's not enough."

Sharla murmured, "It's all I can offer you. At least for now. But you might be able to change my mind."

Holding Ananda, Cyborg said, "We should go back to Florida. Maybe Brigand's all right, maybe he isn't. But one thing's for sure—the Locker can save Thebos. What do you say, Corgan? Where do we go from here?"

"That's for me to decide," Corgan answered.

Let them question him all they wanted. He had the advantage, the leverage, the whip hand, the trump card. Only he could pilot the *Prometheus*. And that gave him the power.

The power to choose.

The Choice

For my five fabulous daughters—
Serena, Jan, Joni, Lanie, and Lauren

one

The sky was vast. Forty-five minutes of darkness followed forty-five minutes of light as Corgan circled Earth one more time. Before the next orbit, and while the others were still asleep, he needed to make his decision.

The choice was his—they knew that, he'd told them that. Cyborg's silence didn't matter, Sharla's wishes didn't matter, and neither did Ananda's tears.

Flying the spacecraft was easy for Corgan. Choosing *where* to go was infinitely harder. The *Prometheus* could make it all the way to Mars, if he chose Mars, but it would take two months to get there and would use up a huge amount of fuel. Why waste time and energy to arrive on a planet that might be as dead as the colonists who'd once tried to settle it? Those colonists had flown on a rocket ship to Mars in 2018, sixty-four years ago, but no one on Earth had heard from them since their landing. *If* they ever landed.

Corgan touched the controls to set the numbers that would keep the *Prometheus* circumnavigating Earth. Then, cautiously, he turned to look at his three passengers: Cyborg, the closest friend he'd ever had; Ananda, whose heart he'd just broken; and Sharla, who kept on breaking Corgan's heart. They stayed asleep, all three of them. Ananda and Cyborg lay together on the flight deck, her tearstained face pressed against his shoulder. Sharla slumped forward in one of the deck seats, her head resting on her arms as though she'd grown tired looking through the window—or port, as Cyborg kept reminding them to call the wraparound pane that circled the top deck of the *Prometheus*.

Corgan turned his back on them because he had to decide, and if he didn't look at them, deciding would be easier. He knew well enough what each of them wanted. Ananda was desperate to return to the space station, but Corgan couldn't go back there because he'd stolen something valuable from the three people who lived on the station. Sharla and Cyborg wanted to go back to the Florida domed city, where Brigand ruled—Brigand, Cyborg's clone-twin and Corgan's worst enemy, who would happily destroy Corgan as soon as he saw him.

He'd grown weary of all the battles and fears and controversy he'd lived through in the past year. He felt tired, disillusioned, used by everyone and without ever getting much back. He wanted to feel good again, to be happy once more, like he'd been those six great months after he won the Virtual War. Remembering, letting his mind fill with scenes of the island, Corgan could almost feel the clean air and the surf and the growing trees that gave fruit as well as shade. The islands were the one and only place on Earth where a person could live in complete freedom from contamination. Far outside the domed cities, the Isles of Hiva were a world where sun warmed your skin and moonlight shone pure into your eyes, instead of being filtered to dullness through domeglass. On Nuku Hiva he used to run on the beach with Sharla, watching her golden hair turn even brighter gold in the sunlight. Once, he danced with her on the beach—but only that one time—when he thought she might love him. Maybe Sharla remembered it too, and all those memories would bring them closer once again, if they returned to the island.

He studied the holographic control panels, the ones he'd installed by himself back in the Florida domed city. Where did the *Prometheus* happen to be flying right then, right that split second? He wasn't sure because navigation was his weakest skill, but it seemed that they were high above the South American continent.

Okay, he said to himself, *you know where you want to go, so do it—lift up your hand and change direction.* According to the holographic sphere of Earth, he was in the southern hemisphere. Focusing intently, he reached for the transparent touch screen. He would need to pilot the ship from a latitude of 26° south to 9° south, from a longitude of 48° west to 139° west.

Stay asleep, he silently urged the other three. *Don't wake up and find out what I'm doing.* The change of course as the *Prometheus* turned in the sky was so gentle that they slept undisturbed. Heading in its new direction, softly, quietly, the *Prometheus* felt almost becalmed—Corgan had to fight to keep *himself* awake. He hadn't slept for nearly two days, or to be exact, for forty-two hours, thirty-seven minutes, and seventeen and a quarter seconds. Funny how his time-splitting ability kept on functioning even when he felt groggy.

Wake up! he commanded himself. *Stay alert!* He didn't worry about the *Prometheus* crashing—Thebos had designed it to avoid sudden, dangerous impacts—but if Corgan dozed off, the spaceship could go wandering all over the Pacific Ocean far beneath them. He bit the back of his hand, not hard enough to draw blood, but with just enough pain to keep himself sharp.

After two hours of biting his knuckles he noticed Sharla lift her head slowly, raising her hand to push her hair away from her cheek. Once, that hair had been long and flowing, but now it was cropped shorter than she liked it, barely brushing her neck. What a contrast the two girls were: Sharla all ivory and gold, with wide blue eyes; Ananda a jewel of dark amber with eyes coffee brown, her hair black and shiny. Both were beautiful, Corgan thought.

As Sharla peered sleepily through the port, she caught sight of Corgan's reflection in its pane. He put a finger to his lips to signal her to stay silent. Would she? Sharla didn't react too well to orders from anyone.

"Where are we?" she mouthed.

Silently he pointed to the Earth hologram, his hand hovering over the emptiness of the ocean.

This time she whispered her question. "Where are we going?"

To the place where we were happy. He didn't say anything out loud; he just shook his head a little, gesturing toward Cyborg and Ananda.

They woke up anyway. Like Sharla, they stared through the port, curious about where Corgan had brought them. Just as Cyborg was about to speak, Corgan held up his hand and said, "Before you ask me anything, I want to say something to Ananda. I know how awful you feel about the dog, Ananda, and I want to say I'm really sorry. *Really* sorry. I'm telling you the truth when I say that I had to leave Demi up there on the space station to honor the deal I made with the Driscolls. For 'one of the girls' to stay with them."

"You already told us that, Corgan," Cyborg said.

"But I have to say it again until Ananda finally understands. It was the only way they'd let us use the Locker, and we *had* to use the Locker. So I dealt with it. In my mind I classified Demi as 'one of the girls.'"

"She *is* a girl!" Ananda cried, those dark eyes glistening with tears again. "To you she's just a dog, but to me she's my beloved friend that I was closer to than any human in the world after I lost my parents and grandparents. She was my *family*. I love her as much as I love Cyborg."

"Thanks a lot," Cyborg muttered.

Ananda whirled on him. "I know you don't understand it. No one understands. Now that I'll never see Demi again, it'll take me a while to get over the hurt."

"Hey, listen!" Corgan cried. "I did the best I could in a bad situation. I gave them my pledge, and that's got to count for something." The words came rushing out of his mouth as he tried to justify his actions, to himself as much as to Ananda. "I did what I promised, and maybe it wasn't the solution you wanted, but it saved you or Sharla from a pretty bad life, Ananda. If you want to stay mad at me, that's your choice."

"*You're* the one who's making all the choices, Corgan," Cyborg broke in. "We don't even know where you're taking us."

"You'll figure it out in a few minutes," Corgan replied tensely. At least he wasn't fatigued anymore—defending himself had fired him up. Now he felt alert and in command.

Just before they broke through the cloud cover, Corgan set the *Prometheus* to hover slowly at five kilometers altitude, and soon afterward at four, because that's where the clouds began to thin and they could see small patches of ocean. Curious like the others, Corgan peered through the port to discover what lay beneath them. He saw that he was right where he wanted to be. "Strap yourselves in," he told them. "We'll be landing soon."

As the *Prometheus* descended slowly, they could see the whole chain of islands stretched across the ocean, looking like a handful of rocks thrown randomly onto a blue carpet. The spaceship dropped lower in altitude, making the islands appear larger.

"Nuku Hiva," Cyborg said.

"Nuku Hiva," Sharla agreed.

"What's Nuku Hiva?" Ananda asked, peering through the port.

Not answering, Corgan glanced at Sharla and Cyborg to check their reactions, but they looked neither surprised nor particularly pleased.

"Is this the island where . . . ?" Ananda began.

"The island Corgan chose as his reward after winning the Virtual War," Cyborg answered.

"Well, if you won't go back to the space station, Corgan, why can't we just fly back to Florida?" Ananda demanded.

Corgan was about to tell her where she could go, but he cut it off in time. *Do not start out with conflict,* he cautioned himself. Instead he would work toward what was calm and good, and maybe create a whole new life where all of them could bury their hurts and blame and jealousies and bond into tight friendship once again.

"The Isles of Hiva are the only uncontaminated place on Earth," Sharla told Ananda. "Good choice, Corgan."

"Thanks." He hadn't expected approval from anyone, especially Sharla, but he couldn't soak it up right then because he had to land the spacecraft. At one kilometer above Earth the whole island had become visible, a lush, tropical paradise with waves rushing the shores and then sweeping back as though gathering energy for another dash forward. Corgan maneuvered the *Prometheus* toward the concrete landing pad, then suddenly slammed the controls into hover as two figures ran out from beneath the trees. Staring up in amazement, the two people shaded their eyes and bent back to get a better look. Corgan could imagine their bewilderment, since they'd be the first beings on the entire planet Earth ever to see this particular spacecraft land on solid ground.

"That's Delphine down there," Corgan said.

"Who's that with her?" Cyborg asked.

A husky boy, or man, or something in between, was running fast across the sand toward the landing pad. His skin was brown, and his hair looked black and very thick, even from forty meters up. "I guess he's the guy who came to herd the cows after I left," Corgan answered.

"He's kind of cute," Sharla murmured.

On the ground Delphine hurried to catch up to the boy, who'd reached the landing area before she did.

"Hey, he's right in the middle of the pad," Corgan cried. "He needs to move, or we'll land on top of his head."

Delphine must have realized that—she yanked the boy backward. Both of them looked worried, unsure who might be in this strange, saucer-shaped vehicle touching down on their island, but when Sharla pressed her face against the port and waved, Delphine recognized her and began to jump up and down eagerly, her face lighting with pleasure.

Cyborg waved too, with his good hand, and so did Corgan, but then he warned his passengers, "This is the first time I've ever brought down this baby. I hope it won't bounce or—"

"Or crash," Cyborg said.

"Yeah, so you better hang on to something."

The landing couldn't have been smoother. Maybe a soft landing was a good omen, Corgan hoped. Maybe life would be a little smoother too, here on Nuku Hiva.

T W O

Corgan slid down the side of the *Prometheus* and landed in the welcoming arms of Delphine. It was okay to be smothered by her hugs, but he squeezed his eyes tight when she kissed his cheek once, twice, three times. From him she moved to Cyborg, crying, "I can't believe it! You're all grown up, and it was just a few months ago that you were a little boy!" Cyborg got even more kisses than Corgan had, and then it was Sharla's turn for hugs. When Delphine reached Ananda, she asked, "Who's this?"

"That's Ananda," Corgan answered. "Who's that?"

"This is Royal," Delphine answered, smiling widely. "Royal is descended from a Polynesian prince."

Royal bent his head a little in acknowledgment. Corgan

didn't know what a Polynesian prince was, but it sounded impressive. And Royal was impressive—husky and muscular, he looked like he could wrestle a wild boar to the ground and spear it with its own tusks. "My great-grandfather was a prince," Royal said. "I'm just a cowherd."

Surprised, Ananda told him, "But you look really brave."

"*Cowherd!* Not coward," Corgan corrected her. "Meaning he takes care of cows, like I did when I lived here. I guess you took over my job, Royal," Corgan said. "And Ananda got my other job—if the Virtual War gets fought again, she'll do the fighting." *Which means, face it, I'm out of work,* Corgan thought.

Still delighted, Delphine said, "It'll take hours for all of us to learn everything about one another, and I can't wait to begin, but right now I want to know about this amazing . . . *thing* . . . you just flew in to land on our island. Whose is it? Where did it come from? How does it work?" She ran the palms of her hands over the smooth sides of the spaceship, which were just as shiny and clean as they'd been at the beginning of their voyage from the Flor-DC. No space debris had scarred the hull or pitted the smooth outside of the wraparound panes. Instead of looking like it had just landed, the *Prometheus* looked ready to take off.

"This is a zero-gravity control spacecraft," Corgan began.

Cyborg broke in with, "Designed by an old man who's the last living genius rocket scientist."

Sharla joined with, "You really need to see the inside, Delphine. It's incredible. . . ." Then she paused to take a closer look at Delphine, who'd grown noticeably heavier since they'd last seen her. "Uh . . . or maybe not. The entry is way up there on top."

"Do it this way," Royal instructed. "Sharla—that's your name, right? You climb up, then reach down to grab Delphine's hand when we boost her." Royal knelt, lowering his hands and lacing his fingers together. "Stick your left foot in here, Delphine, and Corgan, do this with your hands and lift up her right foot."

Corgan did what Royal told him to, the two of them heaving in unison to hoist Delphine toward the top of the ship, where Sharla pulled her into the *Prometheus*. The others followed.

Inside, Delphine turned around in wonderment. This woman was a biologist and a geneticist, Corgan knew, but he was surprised at how many intelligent questions she asked about the mechanics of zero-gravity flight. She peered at the holographic control panels, wanting Corgan to demonstrate them. She studied the Earth hologram, touching the position of Nuku Hiva in the central Pacific. She walked all the way around the circular control deck to examine everything. Even though she acted a little . . . *gushy* sometimes, Delphine was one smart lady, the smartest woman Corgan had ever met. And Thebos was the smartest man. What a pair they'd make! Except that Thebos was ninety-one and Delphine was . . . maybe half that? Corgan didn't know.

Royal, who followed Delphine, paused longest in front

of the Locker. Touching it cautiously as Cyborg told how it had stopped his aging, he seemed surprised that such a makeshift piece of equipment would be standing inside the sleek, technically complex spaceship.

At last Delphine said, "Let's go, then. Getting out of the *Prometheus* ought to be easier for me than getting in, since gravity will be on my side this time. I want to come back sometime real soon, Corgan, and check the programming of the flight patterns more systematically, and I'd particularly like to hear about the Locker's electronics. But now I'm going back to the lab to cook up a feast. Okay with you guys?"

Even before they answered, she went on, "What a celebration we'll have! Royal, will you slay a fatted calf? The rest of you gather lots of firewood, and we'll build a big barbecue pit."

After they'd slid back onto the ground, they rushed to do what Delphine wanted. Corgan was starved!

Beef! Real beef! Corgan stuffed himself with it. Beef and shellfish and pineapple and mango, stacked up in trays. When he couldn't hold any more, he leaned back to ask Delphine, "So how much do you know about what happened after I left Nuku Hiva last February?"

"Well," she answered, "after you left with Brigand, the Harrier jet made two more trips from the Wyo-DC to deliver supplies. And to deliver Royal—he arrived on the second trip. After that we never saw the Harrier again."

"That's because Corgan and I escaped in it when Brigand started the revolt in Wyoming," Cyborg reported. "Since we didn't know anywhere else to go, we flew to Florida."

"And I'm so, so glad you did!" Ananda said, clutching Cyborg's real hand. "Because, Delphine, Cyborg and I are . . . well, we're soul mates."

Delphine smiled indulgently. "How old did you say you are?"

"I'm fifteen," Ananda told her, "and Cyborg's sixteen, but he'll never grow any older because he's been Lockered." At the mention of the Locker, Ananda looked down at her plate, avoiding Corgan's eyes.

"I'm fifteen too," Royal said.

"Really? You look older," Sharla exclaimed. "I'd have figured you for about eighteen."

Since Sharla seemed a little too impressed by Royal, Corgan moved—casually, he hoped—to sit between them. Later, at Delphine's suggestion, they began to clear the plates from the table, a table that Royal had built, Delphine proudly told them.

"What do we do with the scraps?" Corgan asked.

"I wish we had some dogs around here to feed them to," Delphine said innocently, unaware of Ananda's stricken look. "There are a few feral cats on this island, but I don't like to encourage them because they go after baby birds." As she stacked the plates, she chattered on. "Did you kids know that dogs are descended from wolves? Genetics studies have proved that. I did my undergraduate work on dog genetics. That was a few years after they'd first been cloned successfully."

Trying to head her off from the topic, Corgan said, "That mango juice you gave us was really good, Delphine."

"Thanks." She smiled at him. "Royal made it. But what

I was saying—maybe fifteen thousand years ago the wild wolves that hung around to pick up the cavemen's scraps were the ones that became domesticated. When those wolves had pups, the cavemen took care of the pups and fed them, and that's how dogs and humans bonded. We used to say, 'A man's best friend is his dog.'"

In a halting voice Ananda asked, "Then . . . there aren't any dogs here on Nuku Hiva?"

"None that I've ever seen. None that Royal's ever seen. How about you, Corgan and Cyborg? Did you see any evidence of dogs when you lived here on our island?"

Both of them shook their heads. Corgan wished Delphine would stop talking about dogs. It was Royal who seemed to clue in to Ananda's unhappiness, because he jumped up and said, "Let's take all this leftover firewood and build a big fire on the beach."

"Great idea!" Cyborg exclaimed. "Hey, Royal, want me to show you how much weight my artificial hand can carry? A lot more than you can, I bet."

"You think so? What is this—a challenge?"

"If you want it to be."

Royal would lose, Corgan knew. After Corgan and Cyborg were rescued from the toxic Atlantic, Thebos had completely disassembled Cyborg's titanium hand and put it back together twice as strong, three times as magnetic, and ten times easier to operate. "Mind if I borrow this metal tray?" Cyborg asked Delphine. Without waiting for an answer, he magnetized and stabilized the tray into perfect balance on his outstretched artificial hand. Royal was fast, but he had to pile the wood crookedly into one arm while grabbing other pieces. Cyborg had a steady platform that let him pile his stack higher and higher. Ananda, of course, was cheering for Cyborg, while Sharla rooted for Royal.

After they had built the fire, feeding it driftwood a stick at a time, it shot sparks into the darkening sky. The sky answered, one star at a time. Corgan moved away from the heat and then moved even farther away from the others to lie on his back, staring at the constellation he recognized most easily—Orion. Inside the domed cities the skies never looked this pure and clear.

"Hello, old buddy Orion," he murmured softly. "I remember the first time I saw you, back in the Wyo-DC, when I rode in the hover car with Sharla and Brig. But here you look a lot better."

From the shadows a voice said, "So do you, Corgan. You look a lot better than you did back then."

Sharla. She came toward him and dropped next to him in the sand. "I remember thinking you were too skinny then, and you had those big, strong, powerful hands that didn't seem to match the rest of your arms. But now everything about you sort of fits together. I wonder how much bigger and taller you're going to get. As big as Royal?"

"I guess I'll grow for a couple more years," he answered. "But you'll stay just the way you are for the rest of your life. Sixteen. Do you feel good about that?"

When Sharla waved her hand in the darkness, Corgan could barely see the motion. "Can we not talk about that right now?" she asked. "This is our first night on Nuku Hiva."

"Yeah. Nuku Hiva." A beat later he murmured, "Where I was happy, and you were too, weren't you? Sharla, let me ask you something." He hesitated, leaning toward her, then said, "If you had to choose between me and Brigand right now, which one would you choose?"

He could sense the indignation rising in her like heat from the sand. "Choose for what?" she flared. "To dance with? To fight a battle with? To save one of you if you both were drowning? That's a totally stupid question, and I won't even try to answer it."

She was right; it really *was* stupid! Why had he asked it—why had he spoiled the mood? Here they were, their first night on the island, when they should be trying to discover if they could ever fit together again, and he'd messed up. "I apologize," he told her. "Could we maybe take a step back and just talk about Nuku Hiva?"

"Fine with me." But she still sounded huffy and her posture was stiff. Then slowly, as a few more waves washed toward them and receded, she began to relax— Corgan knew Sharla well enough that he could tell the shifts in her moods even when she was silent. She moved closer, scooping a handful of sand and pouring it slowly onto his bare feet as she said, "I like being back here. I love listening to the waves. I really missed the ocean after we left here."

"Yes. Me too."

"Delphine seems so happy to have us here. She's gained weight since the last time I saw her, and I think I know why—there are no more flights here, so since she can't get lab supplies to work with, she cooks instead. There's plenty of food on the island," Sharla added. "Fruit, fish, fresh milk . . . all of it healthy."

"Uh-huh. Healthy." Corgan closed his eyes, picturing the delicious feast Delphine had made that evening. Slowly the picture faded, and his eyes stayed closed as Sharla went on, "It's funny, but I almost forgot how pretty it is here on Nuku Hiva. Tonight I saw one of those frigate birds, just before sunset. They look so prehistoric." She continued talking . . . and talking . . . about the moon's reflection, splintered into bright shards by the ocean waves, about how Royal seemed older than he really was, and other things . . . flowers? No, it probably wasn't flowers she'd mentioned, it was something else maybe, but Corgan hadn't caught it. He only answered "Uh-huh" every now and then as Sharla's voice grew fainter and fainter, until . . .

"You're asleep," she said.

"No, no, I'm awake, you were saying . . . uh . . . about . . ."

Brushing his lips lightly with her fingers, she told him, "It's fine. You had to stay awake way too long when you were flying us here."

Fifty-one hours and . . . he couldn't remember the minutes or seconds.

"You need the sleep," she told him. "I'll see you in the morning."

Sleep. It felt so good. For the first time in more than four months he could actually breathe pure, clean night air, not the artificially controlled air inside a domed city. His mind drifted at first into dreams of skimming over the ocean, then he fell into a sleep so deep that he was aware of nothing—not the gritty sand beneath him or the heat of the night, neither the sound of the waves nor the calls of the night birds.

He had no idea how much time had passed when he felt a nudge against his ribs. Still deep in slumber, he tried to brush it away, but it came again, sharper this time. His eyelids raised slowly, then flew open in horror as he saw a dark shape looming above him, bending close. Brigand! How could Brigand be here? But he was, and he hung over Corgan, laughing cruelly, the knife in his hand ready to stab Corgan through the heart!

Corgan rolled over and scrambled like a crab across the sand until his hand touched a piece of driftwood. Clutching the wood, he leaped to his feet and swung it in an arc at Brigand's head. *Go for the eyes!* Corgan's instincts shrieked. *Take out his face!* The words rang inside his brain until actual shouts penetrated his ears. "Corgan, stop! What's wrong with you? It's me! Cyborg."

Panting, crouched forward, the wood still in his hand, Corgan stared at Cyborg, who'd backed off, with his arms still raised to protect his face. Bright moonlight reflected on the metal of his artificial hand—a gleam Corgan had mistaken for a knife. "I thought you were Brigand," he gasped.

"Well, yeah, we're clone-twins, so we look alike, but I'm the one here on the island, right? You must have had a nightmare."

The adrenaline rush caused by panic cleared Corgan's head, yet he could still feel his heart battering his rib cage. Cyborg said, "I'm sorry I scared you. Delphine sent me to tell you that Royal and you and me are supposed to sleep in the barn. She thought you wouldn't want to be out here on the sand all night."

That was right. He didn't want to stay there. The night that had seemed so peaceful not so long ago now felt full of menace, with danger lurking in the shadows of the palm fronds. Still breathing hard, he asked, "What about Sharla? Where's she sleeping?"

"First . . . put down that hunk of wood, will you? Were you really gonna hit me with that?" As Corgan let the driftwood slip slowly out of his fingers onto the sand, Cyborg said, "That's better. The girls will sleep in the laboratory with Delphine. So are you all right? Do you want to walk up to the barn with me?"

Corgan shook his head. "Go without me. I'll come up in a minute." He sank back onto the sand with his head in his hands, trying to squeeze the last threads of the dream out of his brain. The nightmare! About Brigand, his enemy.

THREE

When Corgan reached the barn, Royal was already lying in one bunk, and Cyborg had just crawled into the other one. "This brings back memories," Cyborg said.

"Good or bad?" Royal asked.

"Bad. The last time I slept in this bunk, I was an eight-year-old with only one hand and a bleeding stump on the other arm."

"Yeah?" Royal raised up on an elbow. "How did that happen?"

"Later." Cyborg rolled up his LiteSuit and put it under his head for a pillow, but Royal was still curious.

"Do you take off that artificial hand when you go to bed at night?" he asked.

"Don't have to. It's comfortable and I'm used to it. Hey, Corgan, since you're the last man here, you don't get a bunk, but I piled some straw over in the corner and put a blanket on top of it. The blanket's there so if there's any creepy kind of wildlife in the straw, they won't crawl up and eat you." Cyborg and Royal both laughed like that was funny.

"Thanks. If anything tries to eat me, I'll send it your way, okay?"

"*Manuia le po,*" Royal said.

What kind of answer was that? "Huh?" Corgan grunted.

"It means 'good night.' In Samoan."

Lying on a blanket on top of straw was more comfortable than lying on sand, but after his scare on the beach Corgan had trouble getting back to sleep. Brigand's image had been so real, so threatening, looming over him in the dark! A whole hour passed before Corgan's fears disappeared along with everything else in his restless mind.

In the depths of his sleep he felt nothing until sun blazed through the barn door. Its rays baked his head, making sweat creep up into his hair. "Ooh! Hot!" he exclaimed, looking around.

He was alone. Both Royal and Cyborg had gone. Corgan stretched his arms, checking them for bug bites, then examined his chest. There were no signs of stings, but he frowned at his chest's paleness. He needed to get tan, and Nuku Hiva was the right place for it. On a hunch he crossed to the shelf where Royal's possessions lay—a razor, two shirts, a pair of shorts, and a comb. And there at the edge of the shelf, neatly folded and clean, sat Corgan's old jeans.

"Yes!" he hissed as he climbed into them. They still fit just fine, although they were a bit shorter than the last time he'd worn them.

In the other corner a few square meters of LiteCloth blocked off a small portion of the room. Corgan wondered whether Royal's curiosity had taken him in there, although he wouldn't have seen anything. Corgan pushed through the cloth, stood in front of another square of the same material, and said, "Mendor, turn on." He had to wait for only a fraction of a second before the luminous LiteCloth filled with an image.

"Corgan! How long has it been?" The shimmering pale green of the face in front of him changed to golden and then grew rosy with welcome.

"Four months, eight days, thirteen hours, nine minutes, and three and seventeen-hundredths seconds," he answered.

"Well! I see you've been keeping up your time skills." Now the face grew rounder and younger, a sign of approval.

"Yes, Mendor, I don't even try. It's just there, inside me. Did you miss me?"

"Corgan, I'm a computer program. You turned me off the day you left Nuku Hiva, and I ceased to exist until now, when you restored me." Computer program or not, Mendor looked delighted to see Corgan again.

"Mendor, a whole lot has happened, but I don't want to give you a quick report just yet. I want to wait till I can really fill you in, 'cause I have a lot of questions to ask you. But—"

"Just tell me how you got here, Corgan. When you

closed me down, you told me you'd be leaving in the Harrier jet with Brigand and Pilot. Did they return with you?"

"No, I came back in a zero-gravity control spaceship. Without Brigand." Just saying that name made Corgan's voice drop several tones lower from pure loathing.

"Zero-gravity control?" Mendor's face slid toward the father figure image, a darker gold, verging on bronze. "How does that work, Corgan? I'd really like to know."

"It's about controlled interactions between atoms and the zero-point field. It was Thebos who figured it all out. Look, the design specifications are in the spacecraft. I'll go there later today and copy them onto a portable beam scanner so you can store the specs in your database, then I'll give the scanner to Delphine, because she's interested too. But for now I want to get your opinion on something."

"Please proceed."

Corgan hesitated. "You know how Brigand and Cyborg have this psychic connection? I mean, I know you know that, because you saw both of them together when they were little. But do you think Brigand could send his whole spirit, or phantom, or whatever, all the way through Cyborg so it would come out of him and I could see it?"

"You mean like a ghostly transmogrification?"

"Yes, I guess so. Whatever that means."

"I am a program, Corgan, and I therefore cannot confirm the presence of something as ethereal as ghosts. Projected images, yes, but that requires certain digital equipment—"

"All right, forget that question, Mendor." Corgan squirmed on the child-size stool, the one he'd built for

Cyborg when he was a tiny kid, before he'd grown at that dizzying rate of two years every month. "Here's another question that's sort of on the same idea: Is it possible for an electrical process—it's called Lockering—to pass through Cyborg's brain into Brigand's when they're thousands of kilometers apart?"

"Explain Lockering."

"It's a procedure that reverses time in a person. They can go back and be younger, but then they stay that age forever. We used it on Cyborg to stop his rapid aging—and not only for that reason, but to take him back to before he got hurt in the Harrier crash . . . excuse me, Mendor, but I'd rather not explain the details right now. Too much has happened since the last time we talked, and it's hot here in the barn and I want to get into the ocean." Corgan leaned forward on the little stool. "Just tell me this, Mendor. If Lockering stopped Cyborg from premature aging, could it have gone through him and stopped Brigand's rapid aging too?"

Mendor's color changed to gray as his face altered its shape: narrower cheeks, larger forehead. "It would be easy enough to find out."

"How?"

"Just wait a little while, approach Brigand, and take a look at him. If he looks several years older than Cyborg, then it didn't happen."

"Oh, great, thanks a lot!" Corgan stood up so quickly he almost knocked over the stool. "I could have figured out that much for myself."

"Then, why didn't you?"

"Because Brigand isn't *here*. He's back in the Flor-DC, leading a revolt! Good-bye, Mendor. I'll see you later." Sometimes Mendor was no help at all.

As Corgan hustled down the hill, not quite running but going faster than walking, he took deep breaths of the humid air and rubbed his sweaty chest with his fists. He couldn't wait to get into the surf and feel those waves against his skin. Delphine would probably want him to eat something first if she saw him anywhere near the lab. What was it with grown women? It had been like that with Jane Driscoll on the space station too—when things got tense, she'd ask, "Is anyone hungry?"

To avoid Delphine, he skirted through the thick growth of trees, grabbing two bananas, which he gulped before he headed for his favorite daytime spot along the shore. When he got close, he heard shouts and laughter, and as he broke through the growth, Cyborg yelled, "Well, look who's here. It's lazy boy. You finally got up."

Ananda and Sharla still had on their LiteSuits. Soaked, the material clung to them. Cyborg was wearing some bizarre kind of greenery hat with fronds that stuck out farther than his shoulders.

"You look like a palm tree," Corgan told him.

"Don't laugh, man. Royal informed me that the art of palm weaving originated in Polynesia over five hundred years ago."

"You mean Royal made that crazy-looking hat thing for you?" Corgan questioned.

"Yes he did, man. To keep my delicate white skin from turning red as a lobster."

Redheads like Cyborg tended to fry in the sun, something Corgan had learned the hard way when he'd tended the very young Cyborg on Nuku Hiva. He'd had to stay up nights putting cool cloths on Cyborg's skin and trying to stop his howling.

"The hat isn't working," Ananda giggled. "He's already burned." She was right; Cyborg looked like he'd been scalded in a boiling pot.

"How long have you guys been out here?" Corgan asked.

"We got up to watch the sunrise," Sharla answered.

"All of you? Where was Delphine?"

"Asleep, just like you were, Corgan. Royal came with us, but then he went up to let the cattle out of the pen."

Waving toward the surf, Cyborg told him, "Come on and get your toes wet. It feels great."

"In a minute." A sense of unease washed over Corgan again—not as bad as the dread from last night, but a tightening in his chest. Cyborg had just waved, not with his good arm, but with the other. The bare, naked stump.

"Where's your artificial hand?" Corgan demanded.

"I took it off. I didn't want to get salt water on it. Salt corrodes."

The sunburn on Cyborg's right arm stretched all the way to where the wrist would have been. But then it stopped. The skin that covered the end of the stump was still pale, almost white—and dead looking. Corgan turned his eyes away to block that image.

Then Cyborg, laughing, waved his good arm and fluttered his fingers, saying, "But on the other hand . . ."

Sharla and Ananda laughed too, but Corgan muttered, "Not funny."

"Yes it is. That was a joke, Corgan," Cyborg told him. "Lighten up."

"Yeah, come on, Corgan." Sharla ran to him and grabbed his elbow, dragging him into the waves. "I want to show you a sea turtle I saw a little while ago, if it's still out there. I made Royal promise not to spear it for turtle soup."

"You mean Royal cooks, too?"

"He says Delphine's teaching him." She dived underwater and grabbed Corgan around the knees, toppling him into the surf and then swimming away before he could catch her. Corgan gave chase. When they reached still water, both of them plunged deep, reaching for each other and holding tight as they circled and spun, until they had to rise for air, with Sharla still in his arms, their faces close together. Corgan felt his pulse quicken.

"In the *Prometheus*," she began, "I said that you made a good choice coming here. It's even better than I thought. I forgot how wonderful this place is."

"So did I." As the waves rocked them gently, Sharla didn't try to pull away.

"Even Ananda's mellowing out," she told him. "It figures. Since she spent her whole life underneath a dome, this feels like heaven to her. She said she could never swim in the Atlantic because of the pollution."

Shuddering, Corgan remembered. Horrible mutations had come at him in that ocean, wanting him for dinner. Just like Royal wanted the turtle for dinner.

After they'd drifted to a place where they could stand,

Sharla rubbed the palms of her hands across his shoulders. "They're starting to turn pink," she said. "We need Royal to weave you a palm-frond hat like Cyborg's."

"There's no way I'd ever wear a freaky thing like that."

"No, I don't think you ever would. Not even to be silly, not even for fun. You're so serious, Corgan. Too serious. Have you ever acted silly?" When he frowned, trying to remember, she said, "Don't bother. I can answer that. No, you've never done anything just to be silly."

"Besides, I don't burn, I tan."

Sharla just looked at him, shaking her head. Then she shook it harder and swung her wet hair smack against Corgan's cheek.

"You'll pay for that," he sputtered, plunging after her. Escape was not possible. He caught her by the ankles and pulled her beneath the surface, holding her underwater for a brief kiss.

When they lurched up into the air, she gasped, "Well, *that* was serious. But you didn't ask permission."

"If I'd asked, would you have let me?"

"NNTK, Corgan."

He stiffened. He hated it when she said "NNTK"—it stood for "no need to know." Usually Sharla used the term to hide something from him, like the possibility that she'd cheated to win the Virtual War. "Your shoulders are turning red," he muttered, downcast. "We better go back."

"Back to the beach, yes. But back to the way we used to be . . . just take it slower, Corgan. I don't know if it can happen."

Corgan didn't follow her out of the water.

FOUR

Two days later Corgan, Sharla, Cyborg, and Ananda gathered around the table to watch Royal scoop oil from a big bowl into a smaller one. "Nothing magic about it," Royal was saying. "After Cyborg got so sun-boiled, I broke open four coconuts and put the coconut milk into this bowl. I let it sit for thirty-six hours so the oil would rise to the top. It's an old Polynesian trick."

"Polynesian or Samoan? Which one are you?" Corgan asked.

"Both. Samoans are Polynesians like Frenchmen are Europeans. Or used to be, before the devastation. Okay now, Ananda, stick your fingers in here and rub the oil on Cyborg's blisters."

"Ow, ow, ow," Cyborg moaned, sounding like he had when he was a sunburned six-year-old. "But it feels better."

"From now on put it on you before you go out in the sun," Royal instructed him. "You too, Sharla. Ananda, you probably don't need it."

She nodded. "It's my Indian-Indian ancestry. But your skin's even darker than mine, Royal, so why should Polynesians—or Samoans—need the oil?"

Skimming the last drops from the top of the liquid, he answered, "You're right, it's not for sunburn. Samoan men coat themselves with oil because it makes their muscles look bigger. Watch." Royal dipped his whole hand into the coconut oil and began to rub it over his shoulders, arms, and chest. When he'd finished, he puffed out his chest and struck a pose, standing sideways, his left fist raised, his right fist on his hip.

"Oh, wow! It really works," Ananda exclaimed. "Look at those biceps!"

"Impressive." Sharla nodded, her eyes wide. "Very impressive!"

Clearing his throat, Cyborg said, "Ananda, come with me, okay? I need to talk to you about something important. Like, right away." He took her hand and pulled her toward the trees.

"Hey, yeah, me too," Corgan said. "There was something I wanted to show Sharla down by the shore. See ya later, Royal." Corgan would have grabbed Sharla's hand, but she pulled away.

"What are all these somethings that are suddenly so

important to you and Cyborg?" she demanded as she followed Corgan, but she glanced back toward Royal, who stood alone at the table, grinning a little as he poured the coconut oil into a bottle. "I wanted to stay and get some of that sun lotion."

"You can get it later. From Delphine."

The breeze was balmy, the clouds white, the ocean gentle as Corgan motioned Sharla to come sit beside him on a fallen log at the high end of the beach. There really was something he wanted to ask her, although it wasn't especially urgent.

"So, I'm here. What?" she prompted him.

How to say it? How to talk about his anxieties when this whole island looked like it had been created as a cradle of happiness? "Do you ever get a feeling of . . ." He hesitated. "Of . . . I don't know, like this place is haunted or something?"

"*What?*"

"You know. Ghosts or—"

"You brought me down here to ask me *that*? You've got to be joking." Indignant, she looked ready to get up and leave.

He backtracked quickly. "Okay, okay, but the truth is, I didn't like the way you were looking at Royal." At least that much was true, and it made her smile. Nothing like a little male jealousy to feed a girl's self-esteem, not that Sharla's needed much feeding.

"Well, you're being honest about it, and that's nice. Not to worry, Corgan. Royal's hot, but Delphine's got him locked up."

Now it was Corgan's turn to be unbelieving. "Delphine? She's . . . she's old!"

"Not quite fifty. But I didn't mean she thinks of him as a boyfriend—no, nothing like that. Delphine's not creepy-weird or anything. I mean she feels like she's his mother."

"I don't know where you get these ideas, Sharla."

"Female intuition. Men just don't clue in to relationships."

They were interrupted by the sound of footsteps and Ananda calling out, "There you are. We've been trying to find you."

"Find who?" Corgan asked. "Sharla or me or both of us?"

"You, Corgan," Cyborg said. "Ananda wants to talk to you."

"She does?"

"Yeah. Privately."

"So I'll leave," Sharla said, standing up, looking a little puzzled. "Come on, Cyborg, I guess we're getting tossed out."

As the two of them moved off, Ananda didn't sit down next to Corgan. She stood in front of him, seeming uncomfortable. It was the first time she and Corgan had been alone since . . . since the Flor-DC. He waited while she glanced at him, glanced away, glanced down at her fingernails, and finally said, "I'm supposed to apologize."

That was unexpected. "Why? Because Cyborg told you to?"

"Yes. And he was right." Getting those words out seemed to relax her a bit, and she sank cross-legged onto the sand in front of him. "I know I've tried to explain it to you before, Corgan, that when you grow up lonely, a dog can fill a big space in your heart. I'm not going to talk about that again, but . . . Cyborg had an idea."

"I'm listening," Corgan told her.

She dug her fingers into the sand as she said, "He was telling me how you used to work in the lab with Delphine and Grimber at night, after the cows were taken care of. And that you did this really meticulous work, something about separating zygotes implanted with genetic something or other. . . ."

"Right. Transgenic implantation. I didn't really understand the science, I just did what Delphine and Grimber told me to do, because they needed my time-splitting ability." *Where is this going?* he wondered.

"Well, Cyborg's idea is . . . Delphine still has some of the lab equipment, even though she doesn't do any of that transgenic stuff anymore. Then the other night she told us she completed her undergraduate work in *dog genetics*! And Sharla has already done cloning—she cloned Cyborg and Brigand from Brig's cells. So . . ."

"So?" Corgan repeated.

"So we have some of Demi's cells in that food dish she used in the *Prometheus*. Cyborg thinks they'll still be viable. What if we try to clone Demi?"

Corgan was a little taken aback, but as he thought about it, the idea didn't sound too unreasonable. He scrambled the various elements in his head, letting possibilities merge and then emerge into probabilities. And while he was thinking, Ananda murmured, "Cyborg says maybe that would help settle the hard feelings between you and me." Corgan was about to answer that most of the hard feelings were on Ananda's side, but she added, "He says we'll have to ask the experts, Delphine and Sharla, if it can be done."

Cyborg, Cyborg—was any of this Ananda's plan? But she was the one who'd actually come to him, so Corgan agreed, "Okay, let's go." He jumped up and started off for the lab, then halted to wait for Ananda, remembering that he was supposed to be more . . . what was it Cyborg always accused him of *not* being? Sensitive! Aware of other people's feelings. "We can walk up there together," he told Ananda.

Apparently Cyborg hadn't mentioned any of this to Sharla, because she was not in the lab when they arrived. Corgan stopped just inside the door, surprised at how different the place looked now. Flowers radiated their tropical colors everywhere, their stalks thrust into laboratory beakers because Delphine had no vases.

"We came to talk to you about something, Delphine," Ananda announced hesitantly.

"Well, come right in. I welcome the company. Have a seat." Delphine arranged herself on her own chair, pulling her skirt over her knees.

"That dress is really pretty," Ananda began.

"I made it myself, out of tapa cloth. I made the tapa cloth too, out of breadfruit bark. If you like, I can show you how to do that, but I suspect that isn't the reason for this visit."

"No, it isn't," Corgan answered. Ananda found a chair while Corgan sat down on a rough-hewn bench, which was probably another of Royal's handcrafts. "We were wondering if it's possible for you and Sharla to make a clone of

Demi," he announced. "There might be some viable cells in a bowl she ate from."

Delphine had been wrapping a headband around her thick, wild hair, but she stopped suddenly. The abundant hair swirled as she shook her head no. "Can't be done. Here's the problem, kids. I'll try to keep it simple so you can understand. When you worked here with the cattle, Corgan, we implanted genetically altered cows' eggs—where? Into other cattle. Where they would gestate. And when Sharla created the two clones from Brig's cells, she gestated one in an artificial womb and the other inside a mutant girl, a human. Well, I don't have an artificial womb here in the laboratory . . ."

"Couldn't you just put the cloned cells into one of the cows?" Ananda asked, still hopeful.

"Won't work. Implanting into different species is next to impossible. I need a dog. A female dog. And we don't have any of those here on the island."

Corgan frowned, trying to come up with a solution. One seemed fairly obvious. "Would a cat work? There are a couple of feral cats here on Nuku Hiva, and I could trap them."

"Nope. I just told you—I'd need a female dog. Let me explain a little. The basic method involves placing an adult animal's DNA, extracted from, say, a skin cell, which you said you have, into an egg cell *from the same species* after the egg cell has had its DNA removed. It's then implanted into a surrogate mother, *again of the same species*. Cows to cows, sheep to sheep, dogs to dogs."

In the silence Corgan could hear water dripping, one

drop at a time, from Delphine's distillation unit. "What if I could find a dog?" he suggested, thinking out loud. "The Isles of Hiva are a chain of islands, Mendor told me—ten islands. Only one other one's as big as Nuku Hiva. I'm thinking that since wild boars and feral cats have managed to survive here on Nuku Hiva, other animals might have made it on other islands in the chain, especially the bigger one, Hiva Oa. Maybe there are feral dogs there. I could go and look for them."

Ananda brightened, but Delphine appeared skeptical, asking, "You mean, fly the *Prometheus* from here to Hiva Oa, and if there are no dogs there, then fly to all the smaller islands?"

Corgan shook his head. "I wouldn't want to use up fuel in a wild-goose chase—or a wild-dog chase. I need to keep enough fuel to . . ." To keep his options open. "I'm thinking of another way," he told Delphine. "I could build a boat."

"A boat! You don't have the slightest idea how to build a boat," Delphine objected.

"Mendor could help me. And so could Royal."

"And so could I!" Ananda chimed in. "I don't know whether Corgan has told you, but I've been genetically enhanced to be the strongest female on the planet."

"Think sensibly!" Delphine cried. "Neither you nor Corgan nor Royal would have the slightest idea how to build a boat. Even if you did make one, you'd get out in the waves and capsize and drown."

Corgan leaned forward on the bench, his hands on his knees. "Hey, Delphine, I'm not trying to be disrespectful, because you're a good person and I like you a lot," he told her. "But you're not our mother. You act like a mother and that's nice, in a way, because we don't have any actual mothers. But Delphine, you can't tell us what to do. We're in—"

"—dependent," Ananda finished. "Independent means we don't have to take orders, Delphine. I don't think it's such a terrible idea to build a boat and go looking for wild dogs."

"That's completely crazy." Delphine's eyes began to widen in alarm. "You're just kids!"

"We're not 'just kids,'" Ananda answered softly. "None of us is ordinary. We're all products of laboratory manipulation, all except Royal, I guess, and I don't know much about him except he seems pretty strong too."

"We're not talking about speed and strength here," Delphine argued. "We're talking about engineering ability and carpentry skills and experience and decent judgment, which none of you is old enough to have. You're just kids!"

"You already said that," Ananda answered. "Maybe one of the things you forgot to mention is courage. Corgan and I have that; I don't know about Royal."

Delphine jumped up. "I don't want you taking Royal on such a foolhardy venture!"

What Sharla had said seemed right on target—Delphine felt like Royal's mother. Keeping himself out of the discussion, Corgan began to think about boats. During his earlier stay on Nuku Hiva he'd explored every section of the island and every meter of its coastline, and there were no boats rotting in the sun or decomposing on the shore. Not even pieces of one. They'd have to make one from scratch. Corgan felt sure Mendor would have the necessary instructions somewhere in his/her computer data storage system.

They'd need wood and nails. Royal had built the table where they dined outside under the palms, so maybe he had enough leftover nails for a boat. Trees were plentiful; they could be cut down and sliced. All this was going to take time.

He thought about manpower—or womanpower. Cyborg had been injured because of the crash into the Atlantic, but he was fine now that he'd been Lockered; he could help with the work. Corgan couldn't picture Sharla with a hammer in her hand, but maybe she'd surprise him. And Delphine—if she realized they were serious about this, she'd have to quit arguing against it. Or maybe not.

"Okay," he said as he stood up to leave the lab. "I'm going to run this through Mendor's database to get some information."

As he hurried from the lab, Ananda and Delphine were still arguing, Delphine's voice rising in opposition as Ananda's lowered obstinately. He was so caught up in the possibilities that he hardly noticed where he was going until he nearly ran into Sharla. Kneeling a dozen meters away inside the shelter of the trees, she was pounding something with a rock.

"You look like you're killing it, whatever it is," he called to her. "What are you doing?"

"Making a dress like Delphine's."

"By beating it to death?"

"Sort of."

For a moment Corgan forgot that he was on his way to quiz Mendor, because finding Sharla alone was a luxury. She didn't have to explain why she was pounding; Corgan recognized the process of making tapa cloth out of the bark of the breadfruit tree. He'd watched Delphine do it when he lived on the island earlier. Dropping to his knees beside Sharla, he asked, "Need some help?"

"Sure. You can thump it for a while 'cause my arm's getting tired. I'll strip some more bark from the branches."

"Why are you doing this?" he asked as he lifted the mango-size rock from her hand. "It takes a long time to turn this stuff into cloth—you have to strip it, pound it, soak it, paste it, dry it out—"

She interrupted, "Because I don't have anything to wear except this one LiteSuit, which really belongs to you, and it's too big for me." She ran her fingers down the front of the gold LiteSuit, making the fabric shimmer in reflected sunlight. With her hair matching the LiteSuit, she looked like a priceless gold figurine. He kept pounding, but he kept glancing sideways at her too.

After the bark had softened enough, he rose to his feet and said, "Gotta go."

"Where?"

"To consult with Mendor."

"You're leaving me for Mendor?" She laughed a little as she said it.

"After I talk to Mendor, I'll be back to explain everything to you. But . . ." He paused, enjoying his dramatic moment. "In a couple of days I might be out of here."

He left her kneeling in front of the tapa cloth, looking surprised.

FIVE

"First," Mendor the father figure told Corgan, "you must find a tree with a trunk about thirty meters high and at least one meter thick. Then you cut it down and—"

"Thirty meters high! How am I supposed to cut down a tree that big?" Corgan demanded.

"That will be for you to decide, Corgan," Mendor answered, his eyes gleaming harshly in his dark gray digital image. "My computer database has instructions for a Polynesian dugout canoe that holds one hundred warriors, the kind that once crossed the Pacific Ocean. Unfortunately, I have no instructions for anything smaller than that."

"This is the second useless answer I've had from you

since I came back," Corgan complained. "What's with you, Mendor?"

Never before had he seen Mendor's face slide so rapidly from father to mother. Bright pink, Mendor cried, "You go away and leave me for four months, and then you come back here and I'm supposed to be as good as I was before!"

"Huh!" Corgan was dumbfounded.

"Sorry." The features slid again, still female, but darker. "Sorry, sorry. That outburst sounded like emotion, didn't it, and computer programs are not supposed to have emotions."

Was that a tear on Mendor's cheek? Something was definitely wrong. Corgan pulled aside the sheet that the Mendor images reflected from and stared down at the operations box behind it. The box lay open on the floor, spread wide, but that wasn't the problem—the operations box was versatile enough that it could be compacted to the dimensions of a deck of cards or expanded to suitcase size.

The real problem was obvious. A narrow beam of sunlight shone down from the roof onto the ramification gear inside the box. Corgan fingered the gear and found it hot to the touch.

"Ouch!" he heard Mendor say. "Please stop. That really hurts."

"Okay, I see what's wrong," he called to Mendor. "Some of the thatch must have blown off the roof, and it's letting hot sun hit your fibril connectors. I'll go fix it right now."

Climbing with hands and knees, he worked his way up the post that supported the roof, wondering as he scaled it who had actually built this barn. And who had built

Delphine's laboratory? Both buildings had been in place before Corgan landed on the island right after the Virtual War. When he reached the roof, he crawled to the spot above Mendor's box, and as he'd guessed, very little thatch remained on that section. He'd have to come back later with armloads of palm to cover the bare spots, but for now he could close up the hole that was causing the trouble.

When he began to scrape away some of the loose thatch, his hand touched metal. Cautiously he felt underneath and discovered . . . the knife!

For a long time Corgan sat holding it, staring at it. The knife edge, when he touched it, was still sharp, and the metal was so shiny he saw his eyes reflected in it. The blade, thirty-five centimeters long and five wide, broadened where it curved upward at the point. During his first stay on Nuku Hiva he'd used the knife often to clear jungle growth.

When was the last time he'd seen it? As he leaned back, brilliant sunlight penetrated his closed eyelids and he saw red, the color of blood. And he remembered. It was the day he'd nearly killed Brigand in battle, a twelve-year-old Brigand who'd attacked Corgan with this same knife. Corgan had fought back with a spear, and as he'd stood above Brigand, the spear poised over the boy's heart, he'd hesitated. Too long. He should have killed Brigand right then and there. How many innocent lives would have been spared if Corgan had plunged that spear into the young Brigand, the future assassin, who two months afterward would execute the entire Wyoming Supreme Council? By now Brigand had killed countless others, murdering anyone who opposed him.

Corgan's memory backtracked further. Two months before that nearly fatal battle with Brigand, when the clone-twins had been only eight years old—he shuddered as the grisly recollection tormented his mind's eye: Corgan carelessly leaving the knife beside the pool; little Cyborg crashing into the pool, where a rockslide trapped him beneath a boulder; Brigand taking the knife and . . . "Stop this!" Corgan hissed to himself, trying to force the images out of his mind. He felt invaded by the memory, as if the knife held a curse.

Or maybe he was imagining things. This knife was probably nothing more than a tool left behind years ago by one of the island natives and discovered by Corgan when he first came to Nuku Hiva. He couldn't even remember where he'd found it. But he couldn't *stop* remembering what it had done to Cyborg.

After he covered the hole in the roof with nearby thatch, Corgan climbed down, taking the knife with him. Royal stood waiting for him at the door of the barn, barefoot, wearing nothing but a ragged pair of pants cut off at the knees.

"Where'd you get that?" Royal asked.

"The knife? I found it on the roof."

"On the roof? Weird! Only it's not a knife," Royal said, pointing at it as he explained, "It's a machete. There's a difference between a knife and a machete. Who does it belong to?"

"I don't know. No one, I guess." Corgan wanted to change the subject. "So what are *you* doing up here?"

Royal gave a little shrug. "I just came to find out if you'd asked Mendor how to make a canoe."

"How did you know about that?" Corgan wondered. Not much more than half an hour had passed since the scene in the lab, and when Corgan left there, Ananda and Delphine had still been arguing.

"There's only six of us on this island, Corgan," Royal answered. "It's pretty hard to keep anything secret. So what did your . . . your . . . I don't know what to call your Mendor because I don't know what exactly it is. But it doesn't matter what Mendor said because I already know how to build a canoe."

"You do?"

"Yeah. My grandfather taught me—it's in our blood. I can make a real special canoe that three people can paddle all at the same time. You, me, and Ananda."

"What about Sharla and Cyborg? Maybe they'll want to go along."

"It'll be a three-person canoe, and we need the three strongest persons to paddle it. That's you, Ananda, and me."

Corgan said, "Yeah, Royal, if you can ever get yourself away from Delphine."

"Because of the cows? I'll just turn them out to pasture till we get back, and she can milk the ones that need milking. She doesn't mind that."

"No," Corgan answered, "because she wants to keep you here where she can watch over you."

Royal's dark brows lowered as he straightened his back and declared, "Hey, Corgan, I'm not Delphine's servant. I'm the boss of myself. I do what I want to do, and right now I want to make a dugout canoe, and that means we need a tree."

"All right!" They smacked fists and started down the hill toward the beach. Corgan glanced from side to side, checking every tree they passed until Royal told him, "Stop looking at trees that stand up. Look for ones that got blown over by cyclones."

"That'd be smarter," Corgan agreed.

"Look for a trunk we can trim to three meters long."

"Three meters long and how wide?" Corgan asked.

"Big enough to fit our butts. That's all."

Corgan took a quick check of Royal's butt, which was wider than his own but about the same size as Ananda's. "That'll work," he said. "Three butts in a boat."

Both of them laughed at that, but then, remembering Delphine's arguments, Corgan grew quiet, wondering if the dog hunt might turn out to be all for nothing. He was about to mention that when Royal announced, "Over there. That one."

The tree must have blown down some time ago because its branches were bare except for ground foliage creeping across them. A fat, scaly lizard sat on one of the branches, staring at them, insolent and unafraid. Corgan's eyes traveled from the ripped-out roots that pointed skyward to a usable section of trunk he figured could be trimmed to a length of three meters.

"Use that machete in your hand," Royal said. "We'll chop off the branches and slide the trunk down the hill, down to the beach. I have a hatchet, but it's back at the lab. I'll go get it. You wait here, Corgan."

After Royal left and the lizard skittered away, Corgan straddled the trunk of the fallen tree, picturing it as a canoe sturdy enough to sail the seas or at least the narrow passages from island to island. The trunk was about two thirds of a meter thick, wide enough to be hollowed into a thin-sided canoe. First they'd have to chop off the branches, as Royal had said. Corgan looked around and decided that moving the tree downhill wouldn't be easy because of all that thick growth they'd have to drag it through, the gnarled and twisted roots that snaked everywhere. They'd probably need to carry it on their shoulders most of the way to the beach, where they'd have room to work. He wondered how much the log would weigh after it got trimmed.

When Royal returned, Ananda and Cyborg were with him. "Royal told us what you're doing," Cyborg said. "We were trying to figure how we could help when there are only two chopping tools. Then I had this idea."

"Cyborg's so smart," Ananda said for what must have been the thousandth time in the past two months.

"Here's what I thought," Cyborg continued. "Sixty years ago or so people lived on this island, before plague wiped them out. They probably had houses with sheet-metal roofs and lots of other things made of metal. I bet some of it is still on the island, buried under the sand or covered by all this vegetation."

"So?" Corgan queried, getting up off the log.

"So if I trek around the island with the magnetism turned on in my artificial hand—I mean, turned to the highest strength—pieces of metal will get magnetized and pop up out of the sand. Or out of the leaves. We'll recover whatever's useful, just like the Hydrobots do back in the Flor-DC."

Slipping her arm through Cyborg's, Ananda added, "I'll bend the salvage into scraping tools to dig out the wood from inside the trunk. Maybe into cutting tools too."

That made a lot of sense. "We could use a fire to shape the tools," Corgan said.

"Not 'we,'" Ananda told him. "You already have the machete to work with, and Royal has a hatchet. This project is for Cyborg and me." She tightened her arm in his.

"So let's get started," Royal said.

"I'll clear away the vines," Corgan offered as he grabbed the machete—he had to remember to call it that—by the blade, feeling its sharp edge once again against his skin. Suddenly he felt a pull on his palm. Within microseconds it grew stronger and hotter, until the machete got ripped out of his fist. "Hey!" he yelled. "What happened?"

And then he knew. Cyborg had switched on his arm's magnetic force, setting up a vibration that made the machete's metal blade leap across space and stick fast to Cyborg's magnetized titanium palm.

"Whoo! You better be careful doing that," Corgan shouted. "You could have cut me!"

"Yeah. I could have. That would have been ironic—isn't this the knife Brigand used to slice off my right hand?"

It was the scene Corgan had tried to block from his memory—little Cyborg lying nearly drowned on the bank of the pool, bleeding from his right wrist, which no longer had a hand attached to it; Brigand crying that the only way he could save Cyborg from the boulder that trapped him underwater was to cut off his hand; Corgan furious because he knew that was a lie.

"Don't look so freaked out," Cyborg was telling him now. "It was just a demonstration of how metal will react to my artificial hand." He wiggled the titanium fingers, saying, "This baby comes in handy—hey, did you get that? Handy?"

"Funny," Royal responded, not smiling.

Cyborg shrugged, then said, "Come on, Ananda, let's go." He threw the machete into the ground, point first, handle up, embedding it deeply in the dirt.

After they left, crossing at an angle through the trees, Corgan picked up the knife and held it between his forefinger and thumb. If he hadn't needed it to build a canoe, he'd have run down to the shore and heaved it into the ocean. Nuku Hiva, though beautiful, seemed to be having a strange effect not just on Corgan, but on everyone.

Reading Corgan's thoughts, Royal said, "Ghosts."

"Huh?"

"I believe in ghosts. Many people died here from plague before the devastation."

"Yeah. I saw somebody die here too," Corgan said, "but not from plague. Grimber, Delphine's partner. He had a heart attack and fell down dead right in front of me and Delphine. She wasn't even sorry 'cause Grimber was such a mean scum."

"You buried his body in the sand, right? Delphine told me," Royal answered. "Bad ghosts like that don't go away, they just go into hiding."

If there were ghosts, this brooding tropical island would be the place to find them. It was here the spirit of a cannibal chief had entered Brigand, or so he claimed, right before he cut off Cyborg's hand. Ghosts didn't seem to worry Royal, though. In this dark, damp forest where moisture dripped from the leaves onto Royal's cheeks like tears, he hummed as he hacked away at the branches. Suddenly he gave a yell in Samoan.

"What?" Corgan asked, but Royal just pointed. The hatchet had uncovered . . . bones! Two bones, one long and one broken. "Human?" Corgan asked.

Royal nodded. "Leg bone."

Corgan peered closer at the bleached bones. He noticed faint notches on one and a slice mark on the other, maybe from a knife blade. "Look at that! This guy might have been murdered," he said. "Mendor told me the people who lived here were cannibals who ate their enemies."

Royal frowned, his eyes narrowing. "That was hundreds of years ago. Anyway, don't believe everything you hear about Pacific Islanders. A lot of it is just made-up stuff." He picked up one of the bones, then threw it almost savagely into the underbrush, saying, "Those marks were made from animals chewing on them. Probably wild boars. I'm gonna go find another tree."

Had Corgan said something offensive? Were Samoans cannibals too, hundreds of years ago? Should he apologize or just shut up? He chose the latter and hurried to catch up to Royal, who was stalking down the hill.

It was going well. Corgan used the machete to shape the bow, while Royal roughed out the canoe body with the hatchet. Cyborg, Sharla, and Ananda hollowed the softer insides of the trunk using tools they'd made from the salvaged scrap metal.

"Let's move it, you guys," Corgan called out. "We haven't even started to trim the float for the outrigger, and then Royal has to show us how to attach it."

Royal kept chipping wood to shape the stern, again humming a tune under his breath as he worked. "What's that song, Royal?" Sharla asked. "Sing it for us."

"Ah, you don't want to hear that."

"Why not?"

"Because I'm a terrible singer."

"Oh, come on, Royal," Ananda joined in. "You sounded pretty good just then. Sing it out loud."

"Okay." Royal set down the hatchet, grinning as he gave a little bow, then began:

"Fonuea, Fonuea, Laulau mai se Manamea,
O sa ai e i luga nei? O sa Letuli e i luga nei.
A ua ina, a la ina, O le a solo mata'iga,
Laulau tu la le i'a, Ususu!"

"What does it mean?" Sharla asked.

"Mmmm . . . it means, if I get it right . . ." Royal waved his fingers as though trying to pluck the words and music out of the air. "It means, 'Bring to me this lovely pair/Who are they that linger there?'"

"Uh-*huh*! He's singing about Ananda and Sharla," Cyborg declared. "'This lovely pair.'"

Royal laughed so hard he almost doubled over. When he caught his breath, he said, "The lovely pair are a turtle and a shark. So which one of these girls is a turtle and which is a shark? Ananda, who are you?"

"I'll be the shark," she answered. "I'll take a bite out of your neck and spit you into the ocean."

"That means Sharla is a turtle," Corgan yelled.

"Oh, great! So I'm slow and toothless." As Corgan started to run, Sharla threw a seashell at him that hit him square in the back. He yelled, but it hadn't hurt. They'd been working so hard they needed a break. It was fun to play for a while, tossing a coconut back and forth as in a game of Go-Ball, kicking up sand as they ran, hooting when Cyborg dropped the toss. Fun until Delphine appeared, looking stern.

They abruptly stopped their clowning and stood still, ill at ease.

"So, you're really going ahead with this?" Delphine asked, standing before them with her feet planted firmly in the sand, her hands behind her back.

"Looks like it, Delphine," Corgan answered.

"You know that I am adamantly against this venture."

All of them nodded and murmured, "We know."

"You made it clear enough," Ananda said.

"Well, since nothing I say seems to dissuade you, I want you to know that I've been reading Grimber's logbook. He kept records of the weather. If the atmosphere is really clear, according to his journal, you may actually be able to see the different islands in the distance."

"See them? You mean real sightings?" Corgan exclaimed.

"On the clearest days, from right here on Nuku Hiva, you can see as far as eighty kilometers out to sea, Grimber wrote. That could help you—although I will continue to hope and pray that you forget this ridiculous idea, which is totally without merit." She looked from one to the other, but none of them moved or answered.

"And so," she continued, "if you are lucky, you might be able to sight a destination quickly."

"Right." They were already lucky in one way—it wasn't cyclone season, so they shouldn't be blown all the way to . . . to wherever cyclones blew canoes in this part of the Pacific.

Delphine went on, "I've made the three of you new shirts out of tapa cloth so you won't get too sunburned." She suddenly brought her arms forward and held the shirts out to them. "I didn't have time to decorate the cloth very much," she said, "but you'll notice each one has a figure on it of a little dog. I painted them with kava juice."

That Delphine—what a class act! Corgan thought. He and Royal and Ananda crowded around her, thanking her enthusiastically as they accepted the shirts and pulled them over their heads, Ananda squirming into hers even though she had to slide it over her LiteSuit. Delphine accepted their thanks graciously but with enough reserve to let them know that nothing could make her approve of this crazy venture they insisted upon.

The next day the canoe began to take shape almost before their eyes. And Royal gave it a name: *Tuli.*

The seabird.

SIX

"One, two, three—launch!" Corgan yelled.

With Royal in front, Ananda in the middle, and Corgan last, they shoved the *Tuli* across sand into shallow water. *Let it float, let it float,* Corgan pleaded silently as the heavy dugout canoe slid into water, which got deeper and deeper, and then, "It floats!" all three of them shouted. They scrambled inside and grabbed the paddles. This test drive was mainly to find out if the *Tuli* would stay on top of the water and not sink like a stone.

On the shore the other three islanders stood watching—Sharla waving, Cyborg a little farther away with an expression of doubt on his sunburned face, Delphine looking scared.

"Start paddling," Royal ordered from his seat in the front.

Gripping the top of the paddle with his left hand, Corgan slid his right hand to about fifteen centimeters above the blade. The shaft felt smooth; Sharla had polished it with crushed coral. He dipped the blade into the gentle waves to the right of him and pulled back against the water's resistance. That wasn't so hard. Ahead of him Royal did the same, while Ananda, between them, paddled on the left, inside the outrigger.

"Are we trying to circle around?" Corgan asked, because the canoe was turning back toward shore.

"No! You need to paddle on the other side," Royal answered.

"The outrigger side?"

"Yeah. Behind the outrigger."

"Oh." Something wasn't working. No matter how hard Corgan pulled on the paddle, the *Tuli* made zero progress in the placid bay. He stroked from front to back but noticed Royal sometimes paddling from back to front— shouldn't they be doing the same thing? When the *Tuli* started rocking in the water, Ananda yelled, "Hey, you guys! Coordinate!"

"You steer, Royal, and I'll row," Corgan called as the canoe turned completely around, facing the shore, where Sharla held her hands over her mouth because she was laughing and pretending not to. Delphine held her own hands over her eyes, unable to watch.

"No, the guy in the back is supposed to steer," Royal yelled.

Corgan tightened his fists on the paddle. What was

wrong here? He'd flown the *Prometheus*, the most advanced spacecraft ever designed, flown it up above Earth's atmosphere without a single flight error. And here he was in this ancient form of transportation, used thousands of years ago by primitive aborigines, and he was floundering in the waves like an upside-down turtle. Ears burning with humiliation, he muttered, "We're gonna stay out here till we get this stupid thing to work."

"Let's change seats," Ananda said.

"No!" Corgan could just picture what would happen if they tried to change positions out there on the water—the boat would capsize, all three of them would end up in the drink, and Sharla would collapse onto the sand giggling.

"Have you ever paddled a canoe before?" Royal asked Corgan.

"No. You?"

"No."

"Both of you, turn off the testosterone and use your brains," Ananda told them. "Right now we're all working *against* one another. We have to work together. Lift your paddles out of the water while we figure this out."

Corgan wished Cyborg could be with them. Corgan and Ananda were strong and powerful, and Royal's muscles bulged even without the coconut oil, but Cyborg had the smarts they needed, the sharp intuition that keyed to the core of unfamiliar situations. After fifteen minutes of floating around, experimenting and splashing so much they were all soaked, Royal said, "Let's go back. I need to get some advice."

They managed to turn the canoe and head toward

shore, where tall palms stood like sentinels guarding the lush greenery. After they had shoved the *Tuli* onto the beach, Cyborg told them, "Looks like you guys used four times as much effort to get half as far as you wanted to go. We need to figure out the mechanics of three people paddling at the same time."

"No problem," Royal panted, brushing sand from his feet. "I'm gonna ask my grandfather how to do it."

The silence that followed was broken when Sharla said cautiously, "Your *grandfather*?"

"Yeah. He's been giving me all the instructions for building the *Tuli*. I just did what he told me."

"Uh . . . when did he give you those instructions?" Corgan inquired. "A long time ago?"

"No. Every night while we were working on the *Tuli*, my grandfather would come into my dreams and tell me what to do."

The silence lasted longer this time, until Ananda stammered, "I—I can understand that, maybe. It's sort of like that psychic connection between Brigand and Cyborg. Isn't it?"

Shaking his head, Royal told them, "Not exactly. My grandfather died before I was born."

"Uh, then you never knew him," Corgan stated, trying hard to make sense out of this.

"Sure I know him. I told you, he comes to me in dreams and tells me how to do things, how to be a man. See, before the devastation, missionaries brought my family to Utah. After the nuclear blast my grandfather sealed all the family into a trailer and drove to the Wyoming domed city, because it wasn't very far from Utah to Wyoming. The family survived because they were sealed so tight in the trailer that radiation couldn't get to them, but my grandfather didn't have any protection 'cause he was driving. He died a little later of radiation poisoning. He was a great man. I want to be just like him."

Looking almost ready to faint, Delphine gasped, "And this is why you decided you could build a seaworthy canoe, because you dream of your grandfather?"

Royal looked from one to the other. "What's the problem?" he asked.

As they glanced anxiously at one another, Corgan said, "I think we need to have a meeting."

Grimly Delphine answered, "Gather around the table. I'll put out food."

The discussion heated up as everyone added fuel to their arguments—Ananda saying that she couldn't see a lot of difference between the Brigand-Cyborg connection and Royal's visits from his grandfather; Cyborg answering that yes it was different, because he and his clone-twin were both alive and Royal's grandfather was dead. Corgan said that it didn't matter how they had gotten the instructions because the *Tuli* seemed to be seaworthy, and if Royal's grandfather could just teach them how to paddle, they ought to be able to manage just fine.

Delphine's arguments were the most vehement. She'd objected to the whole idea right from the beginning, she reminded them, and she didn't believe in visits from the dead or channeling or whatever else it was called. She was a scientist. Scientists didn't go off on harebrained adventures using questionable or inferior apparatus. Even though the dugout canoe had *appeared* to be seaworthy, they'd tested it only on placid seas, and who knew what would happen in a storm? Scientists would demand much more proof, and so should they. "You kids, your heads are just too far away from reality!" she cried.

Throughout it all Royal sat silent, looking a little hurt. Finally Sharla announced, "This is going nowhere. Only three people are involved in this expedition, and they'll have to decide for themselves. The rest of us should stay out of it."

Royal, Ananda, and Corgan exchanged looks. Finally Ananda reached out to cover Royal's hand with her own and said, "I'm in."

"Me too," Corgan declared, making it a three-person handgrip.

"So it's settled. Let's have a farewell around the fire," Sharla suggested. "All of us. You too, Delphine."

Reluctantly Delphine rose to her feet. Nodding stiffly, she said, "All of you may live to regret this. That is, I *hope* you live. There's nothing more I can say, so go ahead and get the fire started. I'll bring the mango juice."

After an hour of sitting quietly near the campfire, the six of them began to drift into pairs. Sharla and Corgan found a sheltered spot where waves crashed against a pile of rocks. Ananda and Cyborg disappeared somewhere, while Delphine and Royal stayed next to the fire, with Delphine leaning forward arguing fervently, apparently still trying to talk Royal out of making the trip. All six were aware that the next morning three of them would stay behind on Nuku Hiva while Corgan, Ananda, and Royal left the island on a mission that could end in failure. Or worse.

The moon had shrunk by nearly half, but it still cast enough light that Corgan could see Sharla in shadow. He reached out to brush her cheek with his fingertips, and as she turned toward him, his lips moved close to hers.

"Are you sure you want to do this?" she asked.

"Uh . . . kiss you?"

"Not that," she said, laughing a little and moving away. "I know you want to do that. I mean tomorrow—are you absolutely sure you want to take that clumsy dugout canoe out into the ocean just to search for a dog? It doesn't seem like a good enough reason. What if you don't come back?"

"Would you be sorry if I didn't come back?"

"You know I would. You're the only one who can pilot the *Prometheus*. If anything happened to you, I'd be stuck on this island forever. I mean, it's a nice enough island, but I want to go back to Florida. Eventually."

Go back to Brigand—that's what she really meant, Corgan thought. *That's all she ever cared about. Brigand.* If Corgan did drown in the Pacific, trapping Sharla forever on Nuku Hiva, it would serve her right. He moved away from her.

"Oh, Corgan, I'm sorry," she said as she reached out to him. "I was genetically engineered to be a code breaker, not a strategist like Cyborg, and I say dumb things sometimes. Of course I'd be sorry if you didn't come back. We have a history, you and I. And right now if you still want to kiss me, then . . . it's okay."

Did he still want to? Not as much as before, but he leaned closer to her, waiting for his feelings to tell him where to go next.

"Time to shove off," Corgan was about to shout, but then he remembered that Royal had declared himself captain. The *Tuli* had been packed with basics, as many as they could jam beneath the three rough-hewn crossways seats. At the bottom lay the machete, Royal's hatchet, and a cattle prod that arced sparks, useful for scaring wild animals and for starting fires. A cowhide container that Delphine had stitched held water, but probably not enough for three persons on a strenuous day. As for food, they had a few coconuts, bananas, and breadfruit. They figured they'd easily find food on whatever islands they reached, the same fruits and fish that were so abundant on Nuku Hiva.

"The sun's up, the wind's down, and once you get into the *Tuli*, I'll teach you how my grandfather said to paddle," Royal announced.

Sharla, Delphine, and Cyborg stood on the beach to see them off, Delphine looking afraid that the *Tuli* might not make it past the first breakers. After the three sailors had pushed the *Tuli* into the water and climbed in, Royal cried out, "Listen good," and he began to relay instructions from his grandfather, or so he claimed. Royal should paddle on the right side. Ananda, in the middle position, would paddle on the left, inside the outrigger. It would be tricky for her to keep from hitting the bamboo rods that held the float in place—she'd have to be careful, or she could knock the outrigger apart. Seated in the stern, Corgan was supposed

to steer. Royal told him that a paddle stroke that moved the
bow to the left would move the stern to the right and rotate
the canoe. When finally the three of them managed to stroke
with the same rhythm, the *Tuli* shot ahead nice and straight,
while Corgan turned quickly to wave good-bye. Royal's
grandfather's lesson seemed to be working.

They were heading out to sea with no compass, no
charts, nothing to let them know where they were going
except the position of the rising sun. By luck, the sea
looked flat and the sky was so clear they could see for
a distance of about thirty kilometers. All three of them
paddled in smooth rhythm, gaining far more speed than
Corgan expected; in fact, they were traveling amazingly
fast. *Muscle power,* Corgan thought. Two genetically
designed superpeople and one Samoan prince were making the seabird fly.

"I'll be the lookout," Ananda announced. "My vision is
better than normal."

"You do that." Corgan concentrated, trying to remember every detail of the map Mendor had found for him.
The biggest island in the chain, other than Nuku Hiva,
was called Hiva Oa, and it lay to the southeast. That was
the one they should logically visit first, since its size might
mean it had more flora and fauna than the others. But they
seemed to be heading due south, although Corgan couldn't
be sure. He'd spent so much of his life underneath a dome
that he had no experience using the sun to figure out
directions.

They hadn't gone all that far when Ananda cried,
"There! I see it! I see an island."

"It can't be Hiva Oa," Corgan answered. "We haven't traveled far enough. Hiva Oa's supposed to be a hundred twenty kilometers from Nuku Hiva."

"Who cares if it's Hiva Oa?" she called back. "Any island in the chain might have dogs, and at least we can see where we're going if we row to this one first."

"I agree," Royal said. "One island is as good as another."

Maybe it would be easier on their first day out to head for a landfall they could actually see, even though now it was no more than a slight gray-brown swelling on the horizon. Once again he pictured Mendor's chart and then announced, "I guess that one's Ua Pou. It's pretty close, so we should be able to reach it. We can search the whole island if we get there before sunset, and then shove off for Hiva Oa tomorrow."

"Exactly how far is it to Ua Pou?" Ananda asked.

"I think Mendor told me it's about forty kilometers from Nuku Hiva, and we've already gone around five. We should get there in a few more hours if no storms blow up."

Letting his brain go numb, Corgan turned his arms into mechanical levers that pumped at a steady, unchanging beat: dip the paddle forward, pull it back, swing it forward again, repeat the motion nonstop without trying to count the strokes. Just grip it and rip it. Every now and then he'd call out to Royal or Ananda to switch sides, and they would react instantly, swinging their paddles from the right side to the left side or the other way around. Once they got the hang of it, it was amazing how much speed they picked up, skimming faster and faster over the surface of the sea. They made a powerful, synchronized team.

In spite of the boring, repetitive motion Corgan's mind wouldn't stay still. He kept reliving last night, when he'd sat next to Sharla in the darkness of the bay. How he wished he could force his fingers inside her skull to pull out every last fragment of Brigand that lurked there, poisoning her. Sure, she'd let Corgan kiss her, and she'd seemed to like it, but he knew he never had all of her, all her attention or warmth or caring or involvement. Last night Corgan had been the one who pulled away, wondering if she was comparing him with Brigand.

"I'm getting thirsty," Ananda announced. Using the machete, she split the tops off three coconuts so they could drink the juice. Then they ate bananas, one person at a time while the other two paddled. Then the breadfruit. Hours went by as the strange island—probably Ua Pou—kept growing taller and wider ahead of them, its peaks thrusting upward from the ocean like spear points, with puffy clouds hovering over the tips.

Corgan wondered where they'd be able to land, because the tall cliffs seemed to drop straight down into the sea—they were solid rock, with no soil or green growth on them. He could see no beaches where they could pull the *Tuli* ashore. And now, still far from shore, the waves were starting to get choppy.

"We'll have to circle the island until we find a good place," Royal said, turning his head so Ananda could hear him and then pass the message back to Corgan.

"There! Look over there!" Ananda shouted. "Behind that curving jut of rock or coral or whatever it is. Looks like it's a lagoon. If we can steer around the arm of rock, we can pull up onshore. At least it seems low and level there."

Going straight ahead was one thing—the three of them had worked that out amazingly well. Trying to spiral the *Tuli* around a long, circling arm of rock was riskier. The *Tuli* kept revolving aimlessly until Corgan jumped into the water and pushed it from behind, guiding it toward the pebble-covered beach.

seven

Corgan said, "We'll divide the work. Royal, go catch some fish."

"You're giving orders now?" Royal protested. "I thought I was supposed to be captain."

"Yeah, you are—on the sea. I get to be captain on land."

"What about me?" Ananda asked. "What do I get to be captain of? The sky?"

Corgan thought fast and came back with, "You'll be the goddess of fire, Ananda. Wherever we go, you'll make fire."

She tilted her head to consider that. "Okay, I accept. I'll be the fire builder. Just don't think that makes me the cook, too. I don't like cooking."

"I'll cook," Royal volunteered.

"Agreed. While you two are busy, I'm gonna climb to high ground and try to locate Hiva Oa from here," Corgan told them. "It'll help if we know which direction to take tomorrow. On my way back I'll bring some fruit and water." Though Ua Pou's spires were bare rock, the hills between them grew thick with vines, tree roots, and foliage, the same as in the jungles of Nuku Hiva. Finding fruit would be easy. Grapefruit, mangoes, bananas—he'd pick twice as much as they could eat tonight, because if they didn't find any dogs on this island, tomorrow's voyage to Hiva Oa would be a long one. They'd need food.

Taking the water bag Delphine had given them, Corgan hiked to a high pass, enjoying the feel of ground beneath his feet after all those hours on water. Sweating from the steep climb, he stopped between two towering rock spires. The sun was setting—that was west. Hiva Oa would be south and east, more east than south, but he couldn't see very far. Giving up, he trekked down the hill and through the jungle again, pausing often to listen for the sound of splashing water. From time to time he heard another sound, a faint one. Maybe an animal sound! Dogs? Would they get lucky and find wild dogs right here, on their first try? But the noises he heard were too indistinct to recognize.

A waterfall noise, though, kept getting louder. Breaking through the thickly vined trees, he found it—a cascade thirty meters high, splashing into a pool at the bottom, sparkling in the low rays of the evening sun. It looked so inviting that he dived into the pool for a swim, washing off all the salt that had stuck to his skin from the sea. He gulped the fresh water and then filled the water bag, but when the sun started dipping lower, he knew he'd better get back to the others.

Picking his way through the tropical rain forest that was even more tangled than the one on Nuku Hiva, he suddenly stopped short. He'd almost tripped over something.

A dead animal. A wild boar. Female and not full grown, with its hind hoof stuck in a crevice in the rock. It must not have been able to free itself and died of thirst. Most likely it hadn't been dead very long, because it didn't smell bad. Maybe those animal sounds he'd heard were the last faint, dying squeals of the boar. Corgan considered dragging it back to the fire for the three of them to eat but decided against it since he couldn't be entirely sure how long it had been dead. Flies buzzed all around the boar's body, swarming especially over the eyes.

Grabbing fruit from the trees as he went, he wound his way through the thinning rain forest until he caught sight of Ananda's fire. There was Royal, holding two sticks with fish on them over the flames, while Ananda swung the machete, chopping breadfruit into pieces.

"I saw a dead boar back there," Corgan announced as he set down the water bag.

"How long was it dead?" Royal asked, reaching for a drink.

"I don't know. Couldn't be too long. In this climate things rot pretty fast."

"Want to show me?" Royal asked, getting up and handing the water bag to Ananda. "I could probably tell when it died."

"Not now. It's too dark inside the trees. I'll show you in the morning."

"You know, that presents an excellent possibility, Corgan," Ananda declared. "A dead boar, I mean. If there are wild dogs on this island, they'll follow the scent and start feasting on it tonight. Tomorrow morning if there are tooth marks on the bones, we'll know there are dogs here. And if there aren't . . ."

"Smart girl," Royal said. "Good thinking."

Fish, fruit, and fresh water made a satisfying meal. Royal had chopped piles of banana leaves for them to sit on, and later to lie on, because the beach was made of oddly marked pebbles not nearly as comfortable as sand.

Corgan quietly watched the others, noticing how firelight reflected on their faces and bodies. All three of them, he realized, had similar coloring. Royal's skin had the ruddiness of dark bronze, and when he smiled, his teeth shone white against his brown face. Although his hair was thick and black like Corgan's, it had curls sleek from coconut oil.

Long ago Ananda's grandparents had been software engineers from a country called India, Corgan knew. Before the devastation they'd come to what was then the United States to take classes. Her other grandparents were American Indians from a tribe called Lakota. From one or two or all of those grandparents she'd inherited skin more dusky than bronze. Her eyes were so dark that the pupils seemed to melt into the irises, and her glossy black hair hung straight down, except when she walked—then it swung rhythmically around her shoulders. Corgan had always known Ananda was pretty; now, seeing her with flame flickering in her eyes and with her lips slightly parted, he realized just how beautiful she was.

Royal's coloring came from Samoa, and Ananda's from her mixed ancestry, but Corgan had no idea where his own brown eyes and black hair had originated—except in a test tube. What kind of genetic legacy did he have? None. No ancestors had come before him. His life started from that first moment in the laboratory when random cells were fused to create him.

His musing ended abruptly when Ananda threw more sticks onto the fire and said, "I wish I knew what Cyborg was doing now."

"Probably the same thing we're doing," Corgan answered.

"Sitting beside a fire and watching sparks fly into the night," Ananda said.

"Did you ever have any boyfriends before Cyborg, Ananda?" Royal asked.

She stirred the fire before she answered, "Well, I was sort of interested in Corgan, but only when we met in virtual reality while he was still in Wyoming."

"And then you met the real Corgan and that finished it, right?" Royal laughed at his own joke, slapping his thick thigh in mirth.

Ananda smiled a little at that but said, "No, it was just . . . Cyborg told me that Corgan was hopelessly in love with Sharla, so I didn't think I had a chance. Besides, Cyborg was so . . . so . . ."

"So so what? What does Cyborg have that I don't?" Corgan asked, only half in jest.

"Mmmm, he just knows how to say things to make me feel good."

"Didn't Corgan say nice things to you?" Royal asked.

This time Ananda laughed out loud. "Corgan once complimented me because I didn't sweat too much for an athlete. That's the best he could do."

Royal chuckled, but then he admitted, "Sounds like something I'd say. I'm pretty dumb around girls too."

"Hey, speak for yourself, I wouldn't say I'm dumb exactly," Corgan objected. "I just haven't had much experience. Until two years ago I'd never met a real, live girl. Only virtual ones."

Looking dreamy as the firelight's shadows moved across her face, Ananda said, "Cyborg is not only sweet, he's intellectual."

"Hmp!" Royal countered. "I'd have thought a girl like you would want a guy who's big and strong in the body, not just in the brain."

"Why? Do you think I'm weak in the brain? Just because I'm the strongest female alive doesn't mean I'm mentally impaired. And Cyborg is no weakling in body either."

"No, no, I didn't mean anything like that!"

Corgan was enjoying this, watching Ananda get indignant while Royal squirmed.

Ananda went on, "I met Cyborg and I loved him right away, but he kept growing older because he was designed to mature rapidly—you know, two years older every month. And then he got Lockered and that stopped his premature aging, but now I'm growing up and he'll stay

sixteen forever. Which . . . might . . . become a problem,"
she finished weakly.

"It won't, Ananda, because we have the Locker," Corgan
assured her. "Whenever you decide you want to spend the
rest of your life at a certain age, we'll Locker you. I know
you probably have bad feelings about the Locker because I
traded Demi for it, but it can help you if you let it."

"I'm . . . reconciling to that," she answered. "The part
about Demi."

As the fire burned lower, the three lay on the beach far
enough apart that they wouldn't accidentally touch one
another in their sleep. Judging by the sound of his breathing,
Royal must have fallen asleep in minutes. Corgan lay awake,
listening to the waves. They rolled in rhythmically, slapping
at the shore, and then rolled back out again. He heard other
sounds he couldn't recognize, but they didn't seem to be
animal sounds—more like the calls of seabirds. He'd noticed
terns flying low over the waves, darting down to catch fish in
their beaks. Terns didn't caw or cry; they squeaked to communicate, not loud enough to keep him awake.

And then he heard Ananda softly murmur, "I'm sorry
for everything I said to you, Corgan, when you left Demi
on the space station."

"Forget it." It was over, and they needed to put it
behind them.

"No, I've been thinking about it, and I really did act like
a witch after I lost Demi. But now you're trying to make
that up to me, so I owe you."

"You don't owe me anything, Ananda," he told her. If
they could find a dog and clone Demi, that might distract

him from brooding over Sharla—he'd come to Nuku Hiva to reunite the bond they'd once shared, but it wasn't working. The problem was inside himself, he realized. Every time he and Sharla nearly connected, painful memories crept back to obsess him, so that he was the one who pulled back.

"Yes, I do owe you. I owe you the truth," Ananda said. She came closer to him, leaning over him to announce, "We haven't been honest with you—Cyborg, Sharla, or I."

"Not honest? What are you talking about?"

"Uh . . ." She paused, then in a low voice admitted, "We didn't tell you this, but Cyborg has been in touch with Brigand, doing that psychic connection thing they have where they can read each other's thoughts."

Corgan bolted upright to face her in the flickering firelight. "Are you serious! Why didn't *Cyborg* tell me?" he demanded, feeling the heat of betrayal rise through his core. "Why's he doing that thing with Brigand?"

Defensively Ananda answered, "Don't be mad, Corgan. It's not like he can turn the connection on and off—he can't control it if Brigand wants to telepath him. Anyway, Cyborg always feels like he's pulled between you and Brigand in a tug-of-war. You're his best friend, but Brigand is his clone-twin." She hurried on, "And he says he doesn't want to influence your choices about staying on Nuku Hiva. He says he . . . he's . . . *beholden* to you because you took him to the space station and made a deal to have him Lockered, and that's what saved his life."

Corgan cried, "You better tell me what's going on between Brigand and Cyborg!"

"Turn it down a notch, Corgan," she hissed. "We don't want to wake Royal. He doesn't know any of this."

"Tell me right now," Corgan threatened, "or I'll yell so loud they'll hear me on Nuku Hiva."

Hesitant, Ananda settled a few more sticks on the fire, making it blaze briefly. Then she said in a rush, "Here's the story. Brigand is forcing Thebos to build another anti-gravity spaceship exactly like the *Prometheus*. He plans to bring it to Nuku Hiva, then after he destroys you, he'll take Sharla and Cyborg back to Florida."

Corgan almost laughed, but it turned into a snort of derision. "What a joke! Brigand couldn't even fly the Harrier jet without crashing it through the dome. He'd *really* wreck a spacecraft like the *Prometheus*."

"He doesn't plan to pilot it," Ananda said. "He's going to make Thebos both build it and pilot it here."

"Thebos fly a spacecraft!" Corgan stared at her in astonishment. "Thebos is ancient! He couldn't even climb inside the *Prometheus* back in the Flor-DC—I had to install the monitors myself. No, this is just too lunatic. If Brigand forced him to do that, it could kill Thebos!"

"Calm down," Ananda said, putting her hand on his mouth. "This whole thing might not be real. Cyborg says maybe it's just a threat—just Brigand's strategy to get you back to Florida."

"But what if it *is* real? I can't let that happen! Thebos is my . . ." He searched for the right word—*teacher, surrogate grandfather, mentor*—"My friend!" he said. "I have to get back to the Flor-DC to see if he needs help."

Ananda's voice rose, but not enough to wake Royal.

"Hey, you're going too fast here! You said we'd hunt for a dog to clone Demi. You promised."

"Yeah." Corgan crossed his arms over his chest and bit his lip, his thoughts whirling. "You're right. I promised." That was supposed to be his good deed to atone for leaving Demi on the space station. Trying to sort it out, he said, "How about here's a deal—we'll hunt for dogs on this island tomorrow, and if we don't find any, we'll go back to Nuku Hiva."

Immediately she shot back, "Here's *my* deal. If we don't find any dogs tomorrow, we try one more island, and if we can't find any there, *then* we'll go back."

Corgan thought it over for six and nine-tenths seconds and then said, "Done." They touched fists. "Now go to sleep."

Maybe she did, maybe she didn't, but at least she moved away. Corgan stayed awake for a long time, worrying. Could Brigand be serious about the threat to fly to Nuku Hiva? Or maybe, as Cyborg suspected—or at least Ananda said he suspected—it was only a tactic to make Corgan return to the Flor-DC, where Brigand could waste him. Both clone-twins had been created as strategists, so they were way better than Corgan at playing mind games. But he couldn't take any chances. If there was a possibility the threat was a real one, he'd have to save Thebos from Brigand's insanity.

What bothered him especially was the secrecy. The three people he valued most had shut him out of the loop. Cyborg he could almost understand—Brigand was his clone-twin. And Ananda always sided with Cyborg. But Sharla!

Sharla's silence felt like just one more betrayal.

EIGHT

Morning came, amazingly beautiful. The clouds in the eastern sky changed from the hue of cherries to oranges to lemons as Ua Pou's high peaks caught the rising sun. A calm breeze flowed over Corgan's bare chest and dried his hair, damp from humidity. For a little while he lay unmoving, not wanting to get up and leave this sense of comfort that wrapped him.

When he finally turned to see if the others were awake, he found Royal crouched above the nearly dead fire, stirring the ashes with a stick. Royal was frowning, his dark brows lowered over narrowed eyes.

Rising, Corgan asked him, "What's wrong?"

"A dream," Royal answered. "My grandfather told me there's trouble ahead."

Although Corgan didn't altogether believe in these dreams, he felt his skin jump. "What kind of trouble?"

"He didn't explain. He just said there's too many ghosts on this island."

"Then, we should get out of here," Corgan said. "Get moving, Ananda. We need to load the *Tuli* and take off."

"Not till after we hunt for dogs," Ananda reminded him. "First we'll check the dead boar."

"Oh, yeah. I hope I can find it. It was getting dark last night when I saw the body, and I'm not sure how to get back there now."

"Maybe you left footprints," Royal said.

As they climbed across jungle foliage and swept through vines, Royal spotted signs that Corgan would totally have missed—not just footprints, but broken twigs and small depressions left in the dirt where Corgan had kicked rocks out of the way. Far in the distance they could hear, faintly, the waterfall. But there were other noises too, the ones Corgan had noticed the evening before but couldn't identify, and those were the sounds that grew louder—an odd kind of chirping, or squeaking, high and shrill, like an unoiled hinge. The farther they went, the clearer the sounds became, with enough tiny variations in pitch to hint that there had to be more than one whatever-it-was making the noise.

Then they broke through to the boar's body, or what was left of it.

"Oooh! It's awful!" Ananda cried out, turning away.

Only the boar's head was visible, chewed down to the skull, with the eyes and jowls and hide all gone. What was left was covered with mounds of undulating, heaving pink flesh. At Ananda's cry, heads flew up and dozens of pairs of glimmering eyes stared at them.

"Rats!" Royal stated, backing up.

"They can't be rats," Corgan argued. "They're too big. They're as big as cats, and they're naked. No hair at all. They're . . ." And then it hit him, and he knew what he was seeing, knew how this ugly mass of alien membrane had happened. "They're mutations!"

"I don't care what they are," Ananda quavered, "they're horrible!"

A few of the rats turned toward them, forming a row, rising up on their hind legs, their front legs waving. Others did the same, reminding Corgan of the New Rebel Troops that had guarded Brigand back in the Flor-DC, but these vermin were not guarding a leader, they were guarding their meal. Their heads moved from side to side, their mouths uttered a strange chittering sound, and their eyes shone a peculiar green as they peered at the three humans who had disturbed them. Some of the rats still chewed, their mouths moving rapidly up and down, and their long front teeth protruding over narrow jaws. But what made them look so obscene, so alien, was the hairless skin, soft and pink and supple and . . . almost human, covering their swollen bodies.

"The plague that wiped out the people on this island must have spread to the rats," Corgan said. "Instead of dying, the rats mutated."

"Maybe they grew so big because they ate all the people who died of the plague," Ananda said, shuddering.

"Maybe that's why they mutated. If there were any wild dogs here, the rats probably ate them, too. Let's get out of here before they decide we're food and come after us."

"They can't run as fast as we can," Royal said.

"How do you know that?" Corgan countered. "Even ordinary rats run pretty fast, and when these ones mutated, they might have turned extra swift."

Royal considered that and nodded. "Then, let's just start backing off. Nice and slow. Keep staring them in the eye."

"Which eye? There're about a thousand eyes," Ananda gasped as the chittering grew louder.

"No, only about a hundred eyes. You move, I'll stare," Royal told her. "Get behind me and back up a step at a time."

For one whole minute and forty and a half seconds it became a staring contest, Corgan and Royal in front, Ananda behind them, as the rat chorus rose in volume. Suddenly the first rat darted forward, followed by another, then half a dozen, then—

"Run!" Royal yelled.

The three of them raced through the jungle, barely ahead of the rat pack. When they reached the beach, Corgan shouted, "Load the boat. I'll hold them off."

Luckily the fire still had a few live coals. Corgan grabbed two sticks from the cinders, hoping the ends would keep burning, and began swinging them in an arc in front of the rats as they poured through the trees onto the beach. "Hurry up!" he yelled. "Get the canoe into the water!"

One of the rats rushed forward to lunge at Corgan's leg.

He kicked it and sent it flying across the beach, where it smashed against a rock. Immediately a group of other rats ran toward their fallen comrade and began eating it.

Another rat leaped for Corgan's face, but he dodged it. When the rat flew past his shoulder, he whirled and stomped on it, cracking its skull beneath his foot. More and more rats crept forward, some cautious, others darting at him. Thanks to the fast reflexes he'd been bred with, he managed to kick them out of the way as if this were a deadly game of Go-Ball, but the hordes seemed to increase in number. Their jibbering rose to squeals so loud Corgan almost missed Royal's command, "Get in the boat!"

"Fast!" Ananda screamed.

He turned and raced toward the waves. As he splashed through the water, he remembered having heard somewhere that rats could swim, but when he turned to look, he saw that the mutant rats were still onshore, feasting on their dying and dead mates that littered the beach.

Waves kept pulling the *Tuli* away from shore as Corgan struggled to swim toward the canoe. When he finally got close enough, Royal reached out with the paddle. Corgan grabbed it and Royal dragged him in.

"The water bag!" Corgan gasped, heaving himself over the side of the boat. "I never refilled the water bag."

"Don't worry. We have the coconuts and fruit," Ananda told him. "We won't dehydrate."

Corgan wasn't sure. "It depends on how far we have to go and how much we sweat," he argued.

"Well, I'd rather be thirsty than become rat food," Ananda shot back. "They were the most hideous things

I've ever seen in my life! Just be thankful they didn't eat us while we were on the beach last night."

"At least it's over," Royal said, "the trouble my grandfather warned me about."

Corgan hoped that was right, but trouble seemed to be surrounding him. "Check the sun," he said. "That's east. We're supposed to be going southeast to Hiva Oa." Shaken by the rat invasion, they were paddling out of sync, plus the wind had risen and the seas were choppy enough to push them off course. He had a feeling that more trouble might lie ahead.

They had to paddle twice as hard as they had on the first leg of their mission, and Ananda frequently stopped paddling to bail. The trip to Ua Pou had been helped by clear weather that let them see the island as they pulled toward it, but today the skies were cloudy. No matter how hard Corgan peered in what he thought was the right direction, he saw no sign of a land mass.

So deal with it, he told himself. *Think! Figure things out!* They'd better manage to reach Hiva Oa in ten hours or less. If they didn't, they'd be floundering around in darkness, and that would mean very big trouble. They were heading southeast, but southeast covered a lot of territory. Though Hiva Oa was supposed to be the biggest island in the chain, compared with the vastness of the Pacific Ocean it was no bigger than a single seashell on a wide beach.

The sun stayed mostly behind the clouds but slid out often enough as the day wore on that Corgan could count off the hours fairly accurately. With each passing hour his back hurt more, and the muscles in his arms started to burn. Most of all he felt thirsty, and they had no fresh water.

"Here," Ananda said, turning around to hand him a grapefruit. "Suck the juice out of it. That'll help with the thirst. Then eat the rest of it. We have plenty of coconuts, too, so we should be fine. Maybe."

"Maybe," Corgan echoed.

More hours passed and the seas got even choppier. Corgan's throat felt chokingly dry, and his arms were so numb he had to stop paddling, if only for a minute. He tried to hide it from Ananda, who seemed as energized as ever, but when she turned and saw him resting his paddle crosswise on the *Tuli*, she told him, "Go ahead, take a break." Before he could argue, she turned back and began to churn the water like a propeller.

One more hour went by. The three of them were paddling more vigorously now because they knew they needed to reach land before dark. Suddenly Ananda shouted, "Look over there! I see it! It's the island! We're gonna make it! Woo-hoo!"

"We're not there yet," Royal said grimly. "And we're taking in a lot more water than we ought to. These waves keep getting higher."

"Okay, you guys paddle and I'll bail again," Ananda decided, and started scooping water out of the canoe so fast the fish must have thought a squall had hit them.

Seeing their destination should have made paddling easier, since it let them know where they were heading. Yet the swelling tide built the surf higher and swifter, and as the sun dropped nearer to the horizon, the island didn't seem to get any closer. Soon they'd need to pick out a landing spot. "Do you want me to bail for a while?" Corgan asked Ananda.

"No, I'm fine, I bail and then I paddle." She'd turned toward him, and maybe that's why neither of them saw what was coming.

Royal did. He yelled out in fear just as the big wave hit.

nine

The wall of water wrapped around the three of them like the palm of a giant hand, lifting the *Tuli* until it overturned and tossed them into the roiling waters. The force of the rogue wave thrust Corgan so deep he scraped his chest on the sea bottom. He fought upward, rising toward the dark shape floating above his head—that had to be the *Tuli*. When he broke through the surface, he found Ananda clinging to the upside-down canoe, her wet hair pasted across her face, her eyes wide with fright. "Where's Royal?" she gasped.

Fighting for breath, Corgan hung on to the canoe with one arm while he turned around to search . . . and search . . . scanning 360 degrees of sea surface . . . and then doing it over again. There was no sign of Royal.

Ananda cried, "Find him, Corgan!"

Before she'd finished speaking, Corgan plunged into the sea, circling underwater with his eyes wide open even though the salt stung them, swimming through hordes of small silvery fish, hunting for any sign of movement. He burst upward for air and dived again, panic rising in him because twice before he'd done this very same thing, tried desperately to rescue a drowning friend—Cyborg.

His mind filled with an image of Delphine's accusing face. *Don't let her be right!* he prayed. *I can't lose Royal!* Holding his breath until his lungs grew tortured, he glided deep across the dimly lit ocean bottom. The waves that crashed toward shore rolled backward again, trying to suck him out to sea, but he fought the undertow until he saw a shadowy figure suspended above him. Face down, arms outstretched, hanging there motionless except for the swaying of the current—*Was he dead?*

Corgan shot upward to wrap his arms around the body, then hauled Royal through the waves to the *Tuli*. "Pull him across the hull of the boat," he panted to Ananda. "Lay him crosswise. Facedown. No! Keep his face out of the water—if he's not dead, he's got to puke up the seawater he swallowed."

As Ananda jerked Royal's head up by the hair, Corgan saw a cut across his forehead where the canoe must have hit him when it flipped; blood ran down Royal's cheek and into the waves. *If he's bleeding, he must be alive,* Corgan hoped as he reached across Royal's inert body, pumping hard against his broad, unmoving back—two, three, four times, a dozen times—until, "He's puking," Ananda shouted, and then, "He's breathing."

Corgan allowed himself eight and a half seconds to feel huge relief before he was forced to focus on the next target: the shore. How far was it, and how much longer could they count on the faint daylight? Only then did he notice for the first time that the outrigger was gone. "What happened to the outrigger?" he called to Ananda.

"I think it broke off and floated away."

The outrigger was the pole that kept the canoe balanced. Without it they could never make it all the way back to Nuku Hiva.

"Keep holding Royal, Ananda," he told her, "and keep his head up out of water. I'm going down again."

"Why?"

"Everything we had is gone—the food, the tools, the outrigger. I'll try to find the tools—we'll need them to make a new outrigger. And paddles." They could survive without the fishing nets and water bag if they had to, but with no tools they might never get off Hiva Oa.

On his first dive he found the machete. If it turned out to be the only tool he found, it would at least let him repair the boat. When he rose empty-handed from his second dive, he noticed that Royal was awake but groggy. Royal managed to say, "You saved me."

Corgan shook his head. "You can thank me later."

"We're drifting toward shore," Ananda said. "Should we try to turn over the canoe and get Royal inside?"

"No! Just leave it capsized and hang on to it the way it

is. And hang on to that machete, too, Ananda. I'm going back down."

"Don't take too long! We need to get Royal to dry land!"

He barely heard her last words before he dived again. The tools should have sunk right beneath the spot where the canoe capsized. By great good fortune both the hatchet and the cattle prod lay on the ocean bottom less than two meters apart. "Done!" he said when he reached the surface again, holding the tools in one hand. "Let's go!" He was winded enough that it would have felt good just to hang on to the overturned *Tuli* as it rocked in the waves, but there was no time to rest. He and Ananda started kicking the canoe toward shore.

Royal was dead weight, but the inrushing tide gave them an advantage. *Don't let us crash, don't let us crash,* Corgan kept praying. Clinging to the canoe, they rose and fell with the ocean swells, carried forward by a momentum so powerful that Corgan felt as helpless as Royal. He watched in fear as the waves in front of him broke into a spray of white foam against rocks that lined the beach. Each curling wave seemed to have a life of its own, as individual and distinct as the mountain spires on Ua Pou, but unlike the unmoving spires, the waves moved unpredictably. All Corgan could do was grasp the upside-down *Tuli* with one hand and try to keep hold of the tools with the other hand, hoping that Ananda had a good grip on both the canoe and Royal.

In the fading light he could see a flat beach ahead between mounds of rock, but the waves seemed to be carrying them more toward the rocks than the beach. "Kick harder!" he yelled to Ananda. "Go to the right! There's sand over there."

That Ananda! Her strength and instincts were amazing. Corgan couldn't have done it alone, but the two of them working together maneuvered the canoe toward the beach. Suddenly the waves became smaller and gentler, lapping at the beach instead of crashing. "You take Royal, I'll get the canoe," Corgan told Ananda as their feet touched bottom. At that moment sheets of rain began to blow across them, the drops hitting so hard they pockmarked the water's surface.

Ananda lifted Royal and carried him, his legs dragging, while Corgan shoved the *Tuli* from behind, leaving grooves in the sand as he pushed it high enough that the waves wouldn't pull it back. Then the real squall hit, dumping a deluge onto the shore.

Corgan took twenty-three and a fraction seconds to flip the boat right side up, wanting to catch rainwater inside it so they'd have something to drink, since the darkness was now nearly complete. The rain hit so hard it stung his skin, and it felt good, that rain. He stood with his arms hanging at his sides and with his face upturned to it, letting it wash away the sea that still clung to his body.

"You're safe now," Ananda told Royal as she held him in her arms, trying to support him upright. "We need a fire, Corgan. Royal feels so cold!"

"A fire? How am I supposed to build a fire in this storm?" Corgan started to tell Ananda she should be glad Royal was alive and not demand impossible things, but then he saw how bedraggled she looked. Her green

LiteSuit hung torn and sagging, her knuckles had been scraped raw, and seaweed stuck to her long, straggling hair. She must be exhausted after their ordeal, yet she kept trying to help Royal.

He picked up the machete and said, "I'll get some fruit we can eat."

"Don't go too far," she warned. "It's getting dark, and I don't want you to get lost. We need you, Corgan."

"I'll be back soon," he told her.

In spite of the pouring rain and the near darkness, picking fruit was as easy on Hiva Oa as it had been on Ua Pou or Nuku Hiva. All the Isles of Hiva grew lush and heavy with tropical fruit. Finding driftwood that had washed high on the beach was easy too. When the rain stopped, he'd maybe try to build a fire, although he wasn't too hopeful it would work.

After an hour the rain did stop. By then the driftwood he'd gathered was completely soaked. "It won't work," he told Ananda. "The spark from the cattle prod isn't like a flame—it's just an electric jolt. I can light things with it only if there's something dry and fuzzy to catch the sparks."

"Isn't there any other way to build a fire?" Ananda asked, worried.

"Not here. Not now. Not without lighters or hot coals, but even if we had those, we don't have any dry wood. At least we don't need a fire for cooking—we have bananas and mangoes."

"It isn't food I'm worrying about," Ananda said. "It's Royal."

He could see what she meant. Royal was sitting up, hunched over and shivering. "Maybe if he ate . . . ," Corgan suggested, but Royal answered, "Don't want to eat."

There was nothing to cover him with to keep him warm, nothing but seaweed to press against his bleeding forehead. Their clothes were wet—Corgan's jeans and tapa cloth shirt, Ananda's LiteSuit, Royal's shirt and cutoff pants. Corgan's shoes were so soaked that they squished when he walked, but luckily all three of them still had their shoes.

"I'm gonna cut some palm fronds so at least we'll have something to lie on," Corgan told them. "Best thing we can do is get some sleep, and when we get up in the daylight, we'll try to figure out how bad off we are. It's too dark to tell anything right now."

"Grandfather warned me," Royal muttered.

Corgan had gone only a few meters when he heard footsteps as Ananda caught up to him. "Listen," she said, "I think Royal's pretty sick. Remember, he's just an ordinary guy. He's strong, but he's not genetically enhanced like you and me. It's up to us to take care of him."

"Okay. But I don't know what else to do."

"I'll let you know." And then she was gone, hurrying back to Royal.

After Corgan had chopped palm fronds and arranged them under the trees, he called out, "We'll sleep up here where the waves won't reach us."

"I'm coming." Ananda lifted Royal to his feet and half led, half carried him to where Corgan waited. Still shivering, Royal sat on the fronds in the same crouching position. "Why is it so cold?" he asked. Corgan and Ananda exchanged glances. The night was wet but not really cold, maybe seventy-five or seventy-eight degrees Fahrenheit.

"Lie down, Royal," Ananda told him. "I'll lie next to you to keep you warm."

Standing silently, Corgan watched Ananda arrange Royal on the ground. Then she stretched out beside him, curling up to him with her arm across his chest. She glanced up at Corgan and said, "You too. Lie down on his other side."

"Me?"

"Do you see anyone else around here?" she asked. "Don't just stand there. Get down beside us."

Awkwardly Corgan settled himself onto the fronds. "Closer," Ananda told him. "We have to use our own body heat to keep Royal warm. Closer! Put your arm across him."

Corgan sucked in his breath. This was really weird.

Still shivering, Royal groaned softly, and Ananda wiggled even nearer to him. Corgan lay on his back with his right arm across Royal's chest, but that felt awkward. Fighting the urge to get up and move away, he turned on his side to face Royal and put his left arm across him, surprised at how much Royal was shaking with cold. Corgan lay stiffly, totally uncomfortable—not because he was lying on the ground, but because he was lying so close to another human being, and it was a male.

The only other person Corgan had been this physically close to, ever, was Sharla. She was the first person he'd ever touched, back in the Wyo-DC, two years ago, just before the start of the Virtual War, and the only person he'd ever touched body to body, although never very often or very entirely—no, wait! That wasn't true. There was one other person.

Corgan's wrestling match with Brigand in that final fight in the Flor-DC had to be considered close physical contact—Brigand with his oiled, bare torso, his powerful arms, his head butting Corgan under the chin. That was human contact, but it had been fueled by rage.

Now, though, lying uncomfortably beside the shivering Royal, Corgan had to fight the impulse to move away. He forced himself to stay still, to fill his thoughts with overwhelming gratitude that Royal had lived and not drowned. Delphine would go totally mental if anything happened to Royal. Or to any of them.

As the minutes passed, Corgan became aware of the night sounds. Some of them were the same as on Ua Pou—the squeaking noises made by the seabirds, the terns. He strained his ears to hear if there were any other squeaks that might be coming from mutant rats, but heard nothing like that. Yet there was another sound, a different sound. Wide awake now, he tried to identify it.

An animal sound, he was pretty sure. A howl—but different from the midnight yowling of the few feral cats on Nuku Hiva. This was far away, rising and falling, too faint to recognize. Whatever was making the sound wasn't close enough to be a threat.

His right arm curled under his head, Corgan tried to stay awake to figure out what he might be listening to, but sleep once again captured him, and he heard only the sound of his dreams.

TEN

The first words Royal spoke when he woke up were, "My grandfather came to me again last night."

"Wait, how are you feeling?" Ananda asked. Although Royal's forehead was swollen, his cut had stopped bleeding, and he sat up straight, not slumped over.

"I'm feeling good. Don't you want to hear what my grandfather said?"

"Yeah. Sure we do." So many things had come true, like yesterday's disasters, that Corgan found himself intensely curious about any new predictions. "Tell us."

"Grandfather said . . ." Royal paused, glancing at both of them, building suspense. "He said everything will be tranquil when two Royals take me where my heart will lie."

"Two Royals?" Ananda questioned. "What does that mean?"

"I don't know. He didn't explain."

Take me where my heart will lie. Could that mean a grave? A watery grave? It made Corgan a little uneasy, but no matter how much they quizzed Royal, he just shrugged his broad shoulders and said they'd have to wait and see.

They didn't have long to wait. While they ate pineapple for breakfast, things began to wash up onto the shore. First, all three paddles swept up onto widely separate sections of the beach, and Corgan ran from one to the other picking them up. Then came the bag Sharla had woven from rope to hold the dog if they caught one; it landed almost at their feet. After that the tapa cloth shirt Delphine had sewn for Ananda and then the water bag—they swept in and out on the waves until Ananda waded in and grabbed them.

"Do you see the outrigger?" Corgan wanted to know.

"No."

"Not to worry," Royal told them. "We can make another outrigger. There's plenty of wood."

"Right. We've got about everything we need now," Corgan said, "except fresh water—there's hardly any water left in the canoe. Will you be okay, Royal, if Ananda and I look for some?"

Royal nodded. "Maybe I'll take a nap and get an update from my grandfather." He grinned to let them know he was joking, then gave them a small wave of his hand.

As they explored the landscape, Ananda and Corgan saw that Hiva Oa had the same rugged volcanic peaks as Ua Pou and Nuku Hiva, with a wall of high rock surrounding the shores that circled the bay. "Best thing to do is get to some high ground where we can look around for a stream," Corgan told her. She followed him up a hill that wasn't much of a climb compared with the peaks farther away. Near the top of the hill they noticed several stone blocks fitted together into a low mound, with mortar between the blocks, holding them together. Corgan had seen something sort of like it on Nuku Hiva—the tomb of a long-dead cannibal chief. Would this turn out to be another chief's tomb?

When they reached it, they discovered a large, round boulder embedded in front between two of the square blocks that made up the structure. "There's writing on the boulder," Ananda said. She traced her finger along the grooves of letters someone had carved into the boulder, letters about twelve millimeters deep and nine centimeters wide. "*P . . . A . . . U . . . L*," she read. Another line of letters curved beneath the "Paul." "*G . . .*" Ananda's finger stopped as she said, "I can't tell whether this next one is an *A* or a four."

"If it's a name, it's gotta be an *A*," Corgan told her. "*A . . . U . . . G . . . U . . . I . . . N*. Gauguin. That's a strange name. Wait a minute! I remember that name." He frowned in concentration. "I think . . . Sharla told me, the first time we were on the Isles of Hiva, that some famous artist lived right here on Hiva Oa a long time ago. That was his name. Paul Gauguin. Here's a date under the name, 1903. So okay, so hi, Paul, if you're buried under here, nice meeting you, but we need to find water, then go back to fix the canoe."

"Aren't we searching for dogs? Isn't that why we're

here?" Ananda flashed him a sharp look to make sure he wasn't backing out.

"Sounds like you want to search," he responded, "even after all the bad things that happened yesterday with the mutated rats and the canoe capsizing. You know, we could have all been killed. Like Delphine said."

"But you promised to search for a dog! And we're here! So we should at least *try* to find one."

Corgan knew it would be smart to pack up and leave before something even more dangerous happened. This venture was too risky, and Corgan was plagued by his need to get back to Florida and save Thebos—if Thebos needed saving.

But Ananda's dark eyes kept searching his face, waiting for his answer. "Look," she said, "if we can't see any dogs on this island, then we'll forget the search and go back to Nuku Hiva. That was the deal. But you have to give it your best try."

"Okay, here's what I think," he told her. "It'll take me at least a day to make a new outrigger for the *Tuli*, or maybe less than that if Royal feels well enough to help me."

She waited expectantly. "I'm listening."

"So how 'bout if Royal and I work on the boat, and you can go on a dog hunt?"

"By myself? What if I find a dog? How can I catch it without any help?"

"With that bag Sharla wove out of rope. That's what it's for, to hold a dog."

"And you expect me to do that by myself—are you serious?" Ananda's stare was disbelieving. "No, you're not.

You've got to be joking. If there's a whole pack of dogs, they might attack me. I'll need help. That's not negotiable."

He shrugged, picked up a stone, and threw it toward the bay. "Okay. I respect that. You need my brains and brawn. We'll do it your way."

"Oh, give it a rest about the brains and brawn. I just need another pair of hands," Ananda told him, but she was smiling because she'd won.

After that it didn't take them long to locate a stream, where they rinsed out the water bag and filled it with fresh, clear water. Since there was no waterfall, Ananda knelt beside the stream and bent over it to wash her long hair, while Corgan pretended not to watch her. Though her strength was amazing, she was also graceful, and he had to admit she made a dazzling picture there beside the stream. When she glanced up at him, he looked away quickly, as though he'd been focusing on something else.

That's when he saw it. "Ananda, come look at this," he told her. "Not right here, but downstream a little farther."

She got to her feet, swinging her hair around so the drops flew out in a thin sheet. "What'd you find?"

"Something metal—it looks like a pole."

She reached it before he did, and when she picked it up, she said, "I think it's hollow. It's sealed at both ends." She handed the tube to Corgan. "You open it. There might be something alive in there."

"Oh, come on!" He took it from her, wondering how long the tube had been lying there near the stream. Probably since the inhabitants of Hiva Oa had died off, and that was decades ago. It must have been drenched by the rain that fell almost daily on these islands, and that was why Corgan was having so much trouble prying off either end of the tube: Corrosion had sealed the caps tightly. He picked up a rock and knocked it hard against one of the ends until finally he could unscrew the top.

"What's inside?" Ananda asked. "Anything?"

"Ooh, it's alive, it's a snake!" he teased. "I'm joking." He reached in and pulled out a rolled-up cloth as long as the tube. Tapa cloth? It felt different. "Here, take one side," he told Ananda. "Let's unroll it."

It was rolled from top to bottom—the top was a meter and a half wide—and as they unfurled the cloth, it became longer than it was wide, about two meters in length. "It's a painting!" Ananda exclaimed, and then both of them fell silent.

The picture showed a young man, or he might have been an almost grown-up boy, standing next to a canoe, a dugout canoe with three crosswise boards as seats. In the bay before him rose the tall, wide mound of rock, the same mound the *Tuli* had avoided crashing into the night before. The man-boy looked muscular across the shoulders, and his left arm, too, was well muscled as he raised a coconut shell toward his lips as if to drink from it. He wore nothing but knee-length pants. His skin glowed dark bronze, and his black hair had been cropped close to his head.

"Do you see it?" Ananda breathed.

"Yeah," Corgan answered, nodding. "I see it. Weird."

Except for the short hair, the painting looked exactly like Royal. Exactly!

"Two Royals!" Ananda said softly. "His grandfather

said two Royals." For a full minute they stared, unspeaking, as the breeze rattled the painting a bit. The amazing likeness unsettled Corgan, as if his world had tilted ever so slightly. But a new, more important idea hit him, one that dealt with the world the way he liked it—solid and real. Excited, Corgan declared, "This is a major find. Major! Do you realize what we've got here?"

"Art?" she asked.

Corgan half laughed, half scoffed. "Think, Ananda! It's a sail. We just lucked out—we found a sail and the outrigger both at the same time. This tube can be the outrigger."

"You're going to use this beautiful picture as a sail?" Ananda looked incredulous.

"Yeah, why not? What do we need with a painting?"

"It might be by that artist, that Gauguin."

"He died a long time ago. What we could really use is a sail, and this ought to work great."

Corgan began to roll it up again, but Ananda cried, "Wait! Look—there's a dog in the right corner of the picture." It was a smooth-haired, yellow-colored dog, short legged, with a long tail. "Dogs must have lived on this island when the picture was painted. Maybe they're still here!"

They hurried back to the beach, and even before they reached it, Ananda shouted to Royal, "We found Royal Two. Hurry up, Corgan. Show him his double."

After they had unrolled the canvas, Royal stood with his hands on his hips, studying it. "Do I really look like that?" he asked.

"Well . . . yeah!" Corgan exclaimed.

"Only exactly," Ananda confirmed. "It's like you posed for the painting, except it might be more than a hundred years old. It's Royal Two, definitely."

"And not only that, we found this tube we can turn into an outrigger," Corgan told him. "If you're up for it, Royal, we'll attach this to the *Tuli* and then make a mast for the sail."

"What sail, Corgan?" Royal asked, puzzled.

"You're looking at it. The painting will be a great sail. Do you think you can figure out how to make a mast?"

Royal just smiled. "Watch me!"

eleven

By moonrise the *Tuli* stood ready on the beach, a carefully refurbished craft. Royal had carved a hole in the bottom of the canoe, then inserted a long, thin pole and sealed it with resin from a breadfruit tree. Corgan tied spars across the mast to support the sail, and when the sail was furled in place, they packed all their supplies except for the cowhide water bag and the rope sack.

Ananda leaned over the fire she'd built, cooking a fish Corgan had speared. Raising her eyes, she asked, "I was wondering—did your grandfather say anything about a dog, Royal? It's like everything he tells you comes true. I thought maybe . . ."

"No, Grandfather didn't mention a dog," Royal

answered, "but the next dream is only a couple hours away."

In the morning, though, Royal reported that his sleep had been dream-free during the night. "No visits from my grandfather. I guess he already said everything he wanted to say."

All three of them had heard howls during the night, and they discussed which direction the howls had come from. "To the west," Royal said. "You have good eyes, Ananda, but I have good ears." He seemed to have recovered completely from his near drowning. The swelling on his forehead now showed just a bruise, and the cut had scabbed and was healing. Judging from the size of the breakfast he'd eaten that morning, his stomach hadn't suffered any from the ordeal. "Take the cattle prod," he reminded Corgan. "Just in case. I'll carry the rope sack."

"Are you sure you want to come along on this dog hunt?" Corgan asked him.

"I'm sure. I feel good, and there's nothing left for me to do here on the beach."

"You already caught a lot of fish—I'm using some of it for dog bait," Ananda told Royal. "And I've got the machete for a weapon, 'just in case,' like you said."

As they climbed a steep rise, the hot, humid air hung around them like an oven. Sweat dripped from Corgan's hair onto his forehead and into his eyes, making them sting. Mosquitoes swarmed around their heads. "I'm so soaked," Corgan said, "these bugs ought to drown when they bite me."

"You know what I really miss more than anything

else?" Ananda asked. "Soap. Back in the Flor-DC I had all these different kinds of soap. They smelled so good . . ."

"Take a sniff of the flowers around here," Corgan suggested. "They smell good too, and if you inhale them, maybe you won't notice my armpits."

"I'll notice. I'm already noticing."

They trekked uphill for another half an hour to the height where foliage started to thin and patches of bare rock showed. Suddenly Ananda exclaimed, "There we go."

"Go where?" Corgan wasn't sure what she meant, since she was pointing at the ground.

"I mean, look down there. See that? It's dog poop. Do you know what this means? There really are dogs here!"

Doubtful, Royal looked from the ground to Ananda and asked, "How can you tell this stuff is from dogs?"

"Royal, I had a dog for four years. I saw dog poop every day—I had to clean it up off the strip of grass Demi was allowed to use for her personal bathroom. Believe me, I know what dog poop looks like. Start checking around."

They didn't hear anything, but they did start to notice other clues—more droppings and a few short, yellowish tufts of hair caught on bushes not more than two feet off the ground. If the hair had come from dogs, the dogs must not be too tall. Maybe they looked like the dog in the painting.

"Stop!" Royal held up his hand. "I heard something in the bushes."

Ananda cautioned, "No, don't stop, keep going. If they're dogs, they'll be running away from us, and we don't want to lose them."

It was hard to hurry because they had to fight the vegetation. Ananda, full of energy, swatted at it with the machete to slice ropelike vines. When at last they broke through the final bit of foliage on the slope, she gasped, "Holy Shiva! Come and see."

On a ledge near the top of the rocky outcrop stood three snarling yellow dogs. They were not really yellow, but a mixture of gold and tan and paler colors all blended together, with darker hair on their snouts around their black noses. As they yipped and growled and snarled all at once, the hair on the backs of their necks rose straight up.

"Female?" Ananda asked. "Can you tell?"

"One of them's male," Corgan said. "I can't get a good look at the others. Got the rope sack ready, Royal?"

"Ready. Go real slow." The three of them crept forward, Royal holding the sack high in both hands while Corgan aimed the cattle prod. Ananda laid down the machete and cautiously reached out toward the three threatened and threatening animals, holding a piece of fish in her hand.

"It's okay, babies," she crooned. "We don't want to hurt you. We're your friends."

The dogs were not large, less than half a meter high at the shoulder, but their teeth looked as if they could tear a nasty chunk out of a person's leg or arm or neck. Recklessly Ananda kept advancing as the dogs backed up, their snarls getting louder, their lips curling back farther, and their jaws opening wider as they tried to intimidate this unknown species coming toward them. In the same soft voice Ananda coaxed them, "Here, look! Here's something nice to eat." She threw a little piece of fish toward them, but the dogs leaped out of the way and began to bark even more furiously.

"We have them trapped," Corgan said. "They can't back up any farther." The ledge the dogs crouched on was no more than two meters square, with a sheer drop on three sides and the slab of wall in back. Not good for the dogs, but not good for Corgan and Ananda and Royal, either. The ledge was a perfect height for canines to launch themselves toward human throats.

"Nice doggies," Ananda murmured. "Want more fish?" When she attempted to throw another piece of fish, two of the dogs leaped off the ledge, hurtling straight at her and knocking her down. As one lunged for her face, Ananda screamed, and Corgan zapped the dog with a charge from the cattle prod while Royal kicked the other one in its belly. Yelping, it sprang past them and ran into the jungle. Both Royal and Corgan wrestled the stunned dog and tied it with rope as Ananda scrambled to get up.

"Are you hurt?" Corgan asked her.

"I'm fine." Crawling to her feet, she cried, "The one you caught in the net . . . male or female?"

"Male," Royal answered.

"Then let him go."

Cautiously Royal began to loosen the rope from around the male dog, which slavered and snarled the whole time. "Move back," he told Corgan and Ananda. When he heaved the dog into the bushes, it ran away howling.

That left just one dog, still on the ledge and crouching forward in a threatening posture, teeth bared, jaws wide, ready to leap. Corgan said, "Go slow. It can't escape."

But he was wrong. With a squeal of fright that sounded almost like a human scream, the dog jumped off the ledge and fell to another far beneath, shrieking in pain as it landed. Ananda shouted, "It's hurt!" Picking her way along a series of narrow ridges that led down the escarpment, she scrambled with both hands and both feet to where the yelping dog lay.

Corgan and Royal followed her down the layered volcanic rock in time to hear her say, "It's female." Though the dog lay writhing on the ledge, it tried to lunge at them, teeth bared, its growls mixed with yelps and whimpers.

"Her back leg is broken. She's biting her own leg," Ananda said. "She doesn't understand why it hurts her so much. And she's terrified. We'll wrap her in the sack to carry her back to the beach."

Luckily the dog was too hurt to move much. They had to dodge her teeth as they threw the sack over her, and she kept fighting, biting through the rope, tangling her teeth and claws as she writhed and kicked her good back leg. Ananda murmured, "I feel terrible. I never meant for the poor thing to get hurt."

"So we should just leave it here," Royal answered. "Why take it with you if it's damaged?"

"Her leg's broken! That doesn't mean she can't be a surrogate mother," Ananda said. "A broken leg doesn't destroy her womb."

"And she's helpless now," Corgan added. "If she can't defend herself, she could get eaten by predators. I'm not gonna leave her here to be some other animal's meal."

It was not exactly a triumphal procession that wound

its way through the jungle to the beach, but it was better than being chased by mutant rats.

"I think we should keep her wrapped up," Ananda said. "She's less likely to damage herself that way. I'll tie her into the shirt Delphine made me."

"Use mine," Royal said, pulling it off. "I really don't like wearing a shirt."

As night fell and Ananda held the whimpering dog, by the light of the fire Corgan noticed how worried she looked. "What's wrong?" he asked, dropping to the sand beside her.

"I don't know. I—this is all my fault. Royal nearly drowning, this dog getting hurt." She searched his face with her eyes. "Am I selfish, Corgan? Because right now that's all I've been thinking. If it weren't for me . . ."

He answered, "Not selfish, it's just that you're passionate about things, Ananda. You love really hard. But I know how you feel—I make a lot of decisions that I think are the right ones, and then something goes real wrong." Wryly he added, "And nobody ever lets me forget my mistakes. But you ought to get some sleep—we'll be doing a lot of paddling tomorrow."

"Even with the sail?"

"If we sail and paddle at the same time, we'll get there faster."

The dog whimpered all night long, but Corgan managed to sleep in spite of it. Before dawn he was up, hiking back to the stream to fill the water bag. After they'd loaded the little bit of remaining gear into the *Tuli*, Ananda climbed in and placed the dog between her feet, then Corgan and

Royal ran alongside, shoving the craft off the beach and into the waves. They managed to clamber onboard without tipping the canoe or kicking off the new outrigger. As they paddled out past the breakers to calmer waters, and the breeze picked up and filled the sail, Corgan couldn't stop looking at the painting on the canvas. It unsettled him a little, and not in a bad way, it was just sort of . . . mystic.

There were the two Royals. The real Royal leaned to the left and then swung around to lean to the right, maneuvering the spar to guide the sail as the wind blew, and the wind kept blowing exactly where they needed it to. As the sail stirred, the youth in the painting seemed to come alive, to face them with his coconut shell held to his lips as if in a toast to them all. The double image was almost a hallucination—Royal manning the sail, his broad, naked shoulders at the same angle as the shoulders of the look-alike in the painting, and the painted youth bending familiarly toward Royal, then straightening upright as the wind shifted inside the painted sail, ruffling it. *Clones,* Corgan kept thinking. *It's like they're clones. The two Royals.*

TWELVE

As they sailed the *Tuli* through the last few waves to reach Nuku Hiva, Corgan felt triumphant. On the shore Cyborg, Sharla, and Delphine stood waiting for them, waving and cheering, and after the *Tuli* landed, Sharla broke away and ran toward Corgan, shouting, "Welcome back!"

Delphine wept as she embraced Royal. Then her expression changed to shock as she cried, "You what! Nearly drowned? Oh, my God! And look at that cut on your head!"

Sharla echoed, "Is that true? Royal nearly *drowned*?"

Corgan felt some of the glory slipping away. "No one drowned," he said defensively. "You can see we're all here and alive."

Not far from them, Cyborg and Ananda were locked in

each other's arms, with Ananda whimpering, "I missed you so much!" From the bottom of the canoe the dog howled and barked and yipped, and even the seabirds joined in the general clamor, squalling and squawking overhead.

"Well! You children must be famished," Delphine exclaimed.

"Water first," Corgan told her. "Some of your nice, pure distilled water from the lab would taste like—"

"Like ambrosia," Ananda finished.

"Come on, all of you, into the lab," Delphine urged them.

"I can't wait to hear about your adventures. But my heart's still in a state of shock over Royal nearly drowning! It's what I worried about every moment you were gone."

It was a small procession—the three stay-at-homes dressed in clean clothes, their hair combed and their skin fresh, while the three voyagers straggled behind with their torn, dirty, salt-stained remnants hanging from them, their hair snarled and their bodies full of bruises and scratches and grime. With her usual tact Sharla told Corgan, "You look awful! You must have had a really rough time."

"Thanks."

"We'll slay another fatted calf!" Delphine announced. "We'll roast it over a fire on the beach, and tonight we'll dance in joyful gratitude that all of you are still alive!"

The last thing Corgan wanted was to dance on the beach. But that's what happened hours later, after the travelers were clean and had been fed as much beef and tofu as they could hold. "Sorry. No dancing for me," Corgan told Sharla.

"You're not a lot of fun, Corgan," she answered. "You never learned how to play."

"Sure. I played games all the time. Golden Bees, Go-Ball—"

"Those weren't games, they were training sessions to sharpen your skills. Come on. Dance with me tonight."

"I'll look stupid."

"Who cares? We won't be telecast to a worldwide audience like in the Virtual War. This is just about us. And our friends," she added.

The music wasn't much more than repetitious drumbeats with voices squawking words Corgan could barely understand against a background of instruments he didn't recognize, coming from an audio player like nothing he'd ever seen before.

"It's old," Delphine admitted, "and the music is old too. It's what I grew up with." Surprisingly, Delphine looked lithe and rhythmic as she twisted her hips and waved her arms to the music. The others followed her motions, circling the fire in time to the beat, swaying and weaving. Ananda wore the tapa cloth shirt Delphine had made her and a swath of tapa cloth around her waist, tucked to make a skirt. It was the first time Corgan had seen her amazing legs. Royal had something similar wrapped around his waist, but he informed them loudly and repeatedly that this was definitely not a skirt, it was what Samoan men wore when they danced, especially during a war dance, when they were about to run out and club their enemies.

"Should I be scared?" Cyborg asked, grinning.

"You're not my enemy," Royal answered. "If you were, you'd be scared spitless."

Sharla had on a tapa cloth dress too, short enough to show that her legs rivaled Ananda's. As she danced closer to Corgan, she murmured, "I can tell you're not enjoying this."

"The dancing, no." Looking at the girls, yes.

"It's okay," she said. "Let's go sit on the beach." Moving away quietly so the others wouldn't ask where they were going, they searched out the same spot where they'd talked the night before the *Tuli* voyage. "Are you sore from all that paddling?" Sharla asked Corgan. "Lean back and I'll give you a back rub."

The fire burned high, and Sharla's fingers on Corgan's back excited him more than soothed him. "So what's next?" she was asking him.

"Maybe I should ask you that, since you know more than you're telling," he answered her. "Ananda said Cyborg and Brigand have been in psychic contact, and she told me what it was about. Why didn't *you* tell me, Sharla? I don't feel good about that. Actually, I'm kinda pissed over it."

Sharla was silent, but her fingers dug a little more deeply into his back. After seven seconds she answered softly, "Ananda wasn't supposed to say anything. You know, Cyborg doesn't start this messaging, Brigand does. He keeps blasting Cyborg's brain with images and thoughts."

"Does Cyborg try to stop him?"

"Yes. No. I don't know. They're clone-twins. Cyborg feels guilty for the way Brigand turned out. I keep trying to tell him it isn't his fault, but he has this guilt. All of us do—we all feel guilty about one thing or another, and it wastes us."

Her fingers dug even deeper into Corgan's back when he said, "You mean all of us except Brigand. I don't think Brigand understands guilt. That whole idea about Thebos building another zero-gravity spacecraft and flying it here—that would kill the old man."

Quietly Sharla said, "It's hard to realize what people can force themselves to do when they're being threatened. And Brigand can be pretty threatening."

"Threaten? Is he *threatening* Thebos?"

"I don't know. If he is, it's probably just a maneuver to bring you back to Florida."

Corgan tried to relax because he didn't want the back rub to end, but he had to wonder how much Ananda had told Sharla about his plans. After a pause he asked, "Did Ananda mention—"

"That you're all hot to go back? Yes. I heard. And before you ask, the news did not make me happy. Brigand says he wants to kill you. Why go to Florida and give him the chance?"

The answer was so obvious that he was surprised she had to ask. "For Thebos," he repeated. "I already told you—I have to save Thebos."

"I'd rather you saved Corgan," Sharla said, coming around to face him. "Thebos is an old man. You still have your whole life to live. Why do you have to act like a hero?"

He couldn't believe she'd ask that. "Because that's what I was made to be," he declared. "And I haven't been doing so great at it lately. Anyway, this is nonnegotiable. If Brigand's threatening Thebos, I'll have to take my chances with Brigand. It's time we had a showdown anyway. I can't keep running from him."

"Corgan! You can't win against Brigand!" Sharla cried out. "This is a colossally bad idea." She pulled away from him and crouched on the sand facing him. It was dark enough that he could barely see her face, which might have been a good thing because it helped him to remain determined.

"Stay on Nuku Hiva," she begged him. "For a while at least. We'll be together, and you can make some reasonable plans before you go back to Florida. Cyborg will help you plan—he's a strategist."

So tempting! But, "You think Cyborg's going to help me defeat his clone-twin? Sharla—get real. He didn't even tell me he was in touch with Brigand! No, as soon as the Demi clones get implanted, we're out of here."

"I can't change your mind? No matter what *I* want?"

"Afraid not."

This time it was Sharla who walked away, not saying good night, disappearing into the darkness. Why was it that something always happened to spoil things between them? He took a different route and headed for the barn, where he could be alone to think. Alone felt good. He didn't even tell Mendor he was back.

The next day in the lab the dog—Ananda had decided to call her Diva—lay safely confined inside one of the metal cages Delphine had used when she tested newborn calves for transgenic traits. With Ananda holding the dog's mouth tightly closed, Delphine needed only about three minutes to set Diva's leg, splint it, and wrap it tightly with a strip of tapa cloth. "She'll be fine," Delphine assured Corgan as Diva wolfed down the meat Ananda fed her and lapped up a quarter liter of water.

Sharla had come too; she and Delphine hovered over the animal cage talking about cell transfer and DNA and zygotes, things Corgan knew a little about, since he'd helped Delphine and Grimber during all those months when they'd implanted blastocysts into cows to create transgenic calves.

"Do you think it will work?" Sharla asked. Corgan noticed Sharla spoke only to Delphine, ignoring him.

Delphine smiled. "We'll give it a try. It depends on how viable the Demi cells still are. Cloning is tricky business, as you well know, Sharla." Delphine turned away from the cage to ask Corgan, "Is your time-splitting ability still as good as it used to be? It'll be important to implant the cloned cells at exactly the right stage of division."

"I think so." He nodded, and then he brought up something that had been on his mind all during the sail home. "Clones," he began, "they're supposed to be physically identical, right? I know their personalities are different, because everyone keeps reminding me how different Cyborg and Brigand act. But . . . how is it possible for two people to look exactly alike when they aren't related and didn't even live at the same time?"

Delphine gestured to where the painting hung on a wall. "You're talking about that, I assume. About the way it resembles Royal."

"Yes, the painting," Ananda chimed in. "It's like it's Royal's clone."

"The painting is nothing more than a look-alike," Delphine told them. "The odds that the youth in that painting had any genetic connection to Royal are about a trillion to one. Although, actually, at about those odds every human being is genetically related to every other one."

Sharla had gone to stand in front of the painting, examining it closely. "You still haven't given us a guess about why this looks so much like Royal."

"Obviously because Gauguin painted Polynesians," Delphine answered, "although I suspect that this is not an original Gauguin, just a copy. And Royal is a Polynesian, more specifically a Samoan. There's nothing magic or miraculous or ghostly about it. And speaking of ghostly, all these things I've been hearing that Royal says his grandfather told him—pure coincidence."

Raising her voice into lecture mode, she went on, "Life is full of coincidence, kids. Coincidence and chance. You stumbled upon a painting that looks like Royal. That's coincidence. But by chance this same painting that you found worked as a sail and may have saved your life. A lot of people believed, and still believe, that every surprising or unexplained event is determined by God. I don't believe that. I'm a skeptic because I watched the world being destroyed by armies that kept fighting about which god was the right one."

"My grandparents believed in Lord Vishnu," Ananda murmured softly.

"One of many," Delphine said. "But God, in whatever form he or she takes, didn't cause the devastation. People did. Throughout history. A hundred years before this last devastation a tyrant in Europe tried to exterminate all my people for their religious beliefs."

They were very quiet until Sharla asked softly, "Your people, Delphine? Who were your people?"

Delphine sighed and pushed back her thick, curly hair, which tended to creep forward across her cheeks when she wasn't wearing a headband. She didn't really answer Sharla, but said instead, "We've been talking about coincidence and chance. By chance my great-grandparents were helped by some decent people who put themselves at risk. By chance they were hidden on a ship, and they escaped to a country named Brazil. Again by chance, two generations later, my mother survived the devastation and brought me as a baby to the only domed city on the South American continent, and once again by chance I was chosen by the Western Hemisphere Federation to come here to Nuku Hiva to work on the transgenic cattle."

"That last part wasn't chance," Sharla said. "You were chosen because you're brilliant."

Delphine shrugged. "Coincidence and chance. They rule our lives. In the country my great-grandparents escaped from, the word for chance is *przypadek*. It also translates as 'fortuity, accident, or fortune.'"

All of them had been listening intently to Delphine, trying to understand what she meant. Ananda stood next to the cage, staring down at the dog, perhaps wondering whether chance would favor the birth of a clone of Demi.

Sharla moved hesitantly, pulling her thoughts together. Then she said, "But Corgan and I weren't created by chance, Delphine. We were genetically engineered."

Nodding, Delphine answered, "That's true. You were created to be excellent at certain skills, but that's not all you've done in your lives. Coincidence, chance, and choice—they're very different, and there's only one of the three you get to control. Choice. Many good things happen by choice, like Corgan saving Royal from drowning, which was a brave and heroic rescue. But as Corgan can tell you too, sometimes bad things happen by chance, like Cyborg's hand—if by chance Corgan hadn't left the machete at the side of the pool—"

Corgan felt the hot blood rising to his cheeks. "Don't go there! Please!" he warned her, wanting her to stop. Wouldn't he ever be allowed to forget his careless action that made Cyborg lose his hand? Feeling accused, he hurried out of the lab and by chance nearly ran into Cyborg, who was pushing the levers that controlled his artificial hand.

"This thing isn't working exactly right," Cyborg complained, but Corgan burst out with, "Why didn't you tell me you were in communication with Brigand? I had to find out from Ananda!"

"Whoa, whoa, whoa! What's gnawing on *your* insides?" Cyborg held up both his hands as if to stop Corgan's rush of words. "Okay," Cyborg went on, a flush creeping onto his sun-reddened cheeks, "Ananda told me that she told you, and I guess I should have mentioned it to you before she did. But you know how Brigand is—talk, talk, talk, and half the time I try to tune him out. Anyway, Thebos is so old there's not a chance Brigand can make it happen, not a chance he can bring another spacecraft here."

"Chance! I don't want to hear any more about chance," Corgan cried. "Chance and coincidence—I want some good hard science and mathematics and engineering to get these Demi puppies cloned, and then I plan to fly the *Prometheus* back to Florida and beat the crap out of Brigand once and for all."

"Hey, give it a rest, Corgan. There's no reason for hostility between you and me."

Corgan blurted out, "Yes, there is! Don't you keep me out of the loop ever again! I want to know what's happening. I'm the commander of the *Prometheus*."

"Yeah, Corgan, you talk a good game."

Standing stock-still, Corgan asked coldly, "What does that mean?"

"Nothing. Let's play Go-Ball or something. You'll beat Royal and me because that's what you were made for—to win at games."

"Made to win! Yeah! I think I'm starting to figure where you're coming from." They stared at each other, neither of them moving until Corgan said, "What you mean is that I didn't win the Virtual War. Right? Is that what you mean? That I actually lost the war, but Sharla saved me by cheating? That's why Ananda was trained to fight a new war. And everybody knows it by now. Brigand has probably announced to the whole world that Corgan, who was supposed to be a hero, is nothing but a fraud!"

"Slow down! Take it easy," Cyborg said. "Nobody knows that except us. Brigand didn't tell anybody."

"He didn't?" That was a surprise.

"He'll never tell. Brigand wants people to think you're a reasonably good fighter because that makes him look all the stronger, since he's already chased you out of two domed cities. If everyone thought you were a loser, it wouldn't be much of a victory for Brigand, so he doesn't want people to think—"

"That I'm a *loser*?"

"Wait! No. I didn't say that right. I mean . . . I don't know what I mean."

Corgan stood stiffly, his jaw and his fists clenched. Was that what everyone thought of him—that he was "reasonably good" but ran away from a real battle? A loser who could fight with virtual images but who couldn't stand up to actual flesh-and-blood combat with a live tyrant?

"Hey, Corgan, don't obsess over—," Cyborg began, placing his hand on Corgan's shoulder.

"Stop touching me with that hand or I'll scorch your circuitry," Corgan growled.

"*What?* What the devil's wrong with you?" Cyborg demanded, stepping backward, glaring at him.

"Yeah, the devil. You got it. The devil's what's wrong with me. And the devil's name is Brigand."

Cyborg said quietly, "I know how much you hate him, but Brigand saved my life, Corgan."

"But that was *my* job," Corgan yelled. "*I* should have saved your life. I was in charge of you. If only Brigand had told me where you were trapped, I could have freed you."

"Brigand said time was running out, Corgan. I was drowning."

"Time! Nobody knows more about time than I do. No, he just wanted to be the dominant clone—the *hero*. But it was my fault because I should have . . . should have . . ." Corgan slumped and turned away, saying, "Never mind. Tell everyone I'm out of here for a few days." As he walked past the table where the six of them had breakfasted only an hour earlier, he reached for the machete he'd left on the bench. That cursed machete!

THIRTEEN

The clean sand, the clear sky, the caressing beach, the foam-capped waves rushing onto the shore, these had been Corgan's idea of paradise—once. But paradise was no longer rewarding or even bearable, not on this day. He ran into the dark, somber, dripping jungle until he could no longer run because roots and vines and branches tripped him. The farther he went, the darker the jungle became, matching his mood.

The jungle had grown so thick since he was there more than four months earlier that a trail was no longer visible. It didn't matter—Corgan knew where he was heading. Moving more slowly, he sidestepped obstacles instead of slicing the thick vines and roots. Soon he heard it: A waterfall always announced its presence before it became visible. He broke through to the clearing and there it was: the high, narrow veil of white water splashing from black volcanic rock forty meters above his head. Once, he'd thought it beautiful; now it seemed sinister. This was where the misfortune had happened.

Holding the machete flat on both his outstretched hands, as if making an offering, he lowered it to the side of the pool at the precise spot where he'd left it on that terrible day. He wished a rockslide would crash down and bury it.

He wanted to be alone, at least for a while, away from Cyborg and Delphine and Sharla, his supposed friends who'd kept pulling against him, arguing with him, accusing him. For hours he sat unmoving on a boulder at the side of the pool, trying to purge his mind and think of nothing, of no one. But disturbing thoughts kept rolling around inside his head, and he couldn't scour them away.

Would anyone miss him if he stayed here until he got his issues sorted out? Back at the lab Delphine and Sharla would be planning the Demi cloning, yet they could manage without him. He had one talent that might have helped them a bit, his time-splitting ability, but it wasn't crucial to the experiment. As the sun slid down toward the tops of the trees, Ananda and Cyborg were probably sitting together on the sand, touching. Royal would be fishing or cooking or building something for Delphine. Only Corgan was alone.

And this was a perfect place to be alone. Fish swam in

the pool—lots of fish. Fruit fell to the ground and grew into more trees that bore even more fruit. Better not wish for a rockslide to bury the machete, though—if he stayed here long, he'd need the machete to gut the fish and shoot sparks from stones to light fires.

Night fell. Hours passed. The sun rose on another day. No one came to look for him. He ate, swam, caught fish, and brooded for one more night, going over all the things that had happened in the past month, the past year, trying to mentally document his slide from hero to zero. Another day and night went by, and then, unexpectedly, on the third day Sharla appeared, picking her way through the growth.

"Why are you doing this?" she asked. Not *Hello* or *We're worried about you* or *We miss you.*

"You noticed that I was gone?"

She sat beside him, curling her legs beneath her. "Feeling a little sorry for ourselves, are we?"

"It's not just that I'm feeling sorry for myself. It's more than that."

"Want to talk?" she asked. "If you do, I'm here."

He hadn't expected sympathy or caring, and he couldn't think how to answer. His mood lightened just a bit. Sharla waited for him to speak, and when he didn't, she said, "Delphine implanted four blastocysts into the dog. She's hoping at least one of them will develop."

"How long before she knows?" he asked.

"A week, maybe less. She's an amazing woman, Corgan. I learned a lot from her, and not just about implantation. She's had a lot of rough spots in her life, but she just kept picking up the pieces and moving on. More than anything she wanted a baby of her own. Radiation poisoning in a nuclear accident not only left her sterile, it caused a tumor that had to be removed, so she couldn't even be implanted with someone else's child. I guess that's why she keeps trying to mother all of us. And she has a lot of wisdom to pass along."

"So does Thebos," Corgan answered.

Ignoring that, Sharla continued, "It would make Delphine ecstatically happy if we all stayed here forever on Nuku Hiva."

Corgan shook his head. "This whole island is haunted by bad memories. Don't you feel it?"

Sharla scoffed, "No, I don't feel it, and neither does anyone else. It's you who's haunted, Corgan. I mean, what made you come right here, to this particular pool where Cyborg lost his hand?" She glanced at the pool, glanced back at him.

"Because I know this is where the really bad stuff in my life first began," he answered. "With my big mistake. You heard what Delphine said—'if by chance Corgan hadn't left the machete at the side of the pool'—"

Sharla interrupted with, "Wrong! You misinterpreted because you never let Delphine finish. She was actually going to say that if you hadn't, by chance, left the machete where you did, Cyborg might have drowned. Meaning it was a lucky thing, a good thing, that you dropped it where Brigand could find it."

"That's what she really meant?"

"Yes! And she was right. Think about it!" More quietly

Sharla said, "I was here, Corgan, remember? I saw it all. Brigand cut Cyborg loose from the boulder, but that was only the first part. It's you, Corgan, who saved Cyborg's life. You're the one who forced the water out of his lungs, you're the one who ran, carrying him in your arms, all the way back to the lab, where Delphine kept him from bleeding to death. You were his savior."

Savior. How could she call him a savior? "He was my responsibility, and I failed him."

"Wrong again!" After a breath Sharla went on, "You obsess over Cyborg's lost hand way more than he does. As if it were a colossal mistake you made. You need to reevaluate, Corgan. You've got to see that you played the part of the hero in that rescue."

His spirits began to rise. She'd almost persuaded him, and she might have if she'd stopped right there, but then she had to add, "And you've done a lot of other really great things too. Like, you won the Virtual War!"

His sense of redemption sank as if shot by an arrow. Climbing to his feet, he cried, "You know that's not true, Sharla. Back in the Wyoming DC, right before Brigand's revolt, you admitted that you cheated in the Virtual War to make it look like I won. I didn't want that to happen," he insisted, pounding his thigh with a fist. "Before I met you, I never did anything wrong in my whole life. Then after we met, you broke the code and got me out of my virtual Box, and I lied about that to Mendor, and that's when everything started to go wrong, and after that things just kept getting worse."

"So it's all my fault?" she asked hotly. "Everything is?"

He sank back onto the ground and told her, "No, it's not your fault. I wanted those things to happen. I wanted to be free and to be with you. I liked being a hero, only I wasn't a real hero."

"And that's what you want to be. A real hero."

"Right. A real one. Not a fake."

"Then, start with this," she said, coming close to him. "Listen to what I'm saying. Back in the Wyo-DC you were rushing to escape from Brigand's rebels, and I didn't have time to tell you the whole truth about the war. You heard only about the cheating. There's more to the story."

Corgan waited, holding his breath, half afraid of what was coming.

"When we were fighting the Virtual War," Sharla continued, "the two other federation teams broke a lot of rules. I saw what they were doing, but I kept ahead of them—mostly." With vehemence she added, "If they'd played honestly, by the rules, you would have won, hands down. When it came close to the end, the guys from the Eurasian Alliance pulled a quick fake maneuver that I didn't catch in time, so I recoded the clock. I added a hundredth of a second. That's how you won—we said they didn't get their troops to the top of the hill at exactly the right split second."

Corgan couldn't believe it. He gasped, "You mean *everybody* cheated?"

"A whole lot more than I did." She nodded, looking directly at him. "I swear on my life that what I just told you is the truth. So you're going to ask me why I didn't report what happened. I didn't because there'd have been a big blowup and a rematch right away, and poor little Brig just couldn't take that. He was half dead by the time the war was over. I had to protect him."

Sharla moved even closer, and this time she reached out to Corgan. With her hand on his cheek she said, "And you . . . you told me before the war that you wanted so much to come here to Nuku Hiva—what good would it have done if I'd started all that trouble? The more I analyzed it, the more I believed that if the war had been totally honest, you'd have won big-time. And I blamed myself—if I'd been smarter and faster, I could have knocked those other punks right on their butts. But mostly, what I did was because of Brig."

"Wow!" Corgan moved to sit with his back against the tree, and Sharla slid down beside him, her shoulder next to his. Her hair smelled good, like the frangipani blossoms. He tried to absorb not just the scent of her, but all that she'd told him. Did it change things? Yes. It brought him up one rung on the hero ladder, but he still had a lot of rungs to climb.

"I've been doing some thinking these past few days," he told her. "About good choices getting screwed up by bad chance, like Delphine said. It's what keeps happening to me."

"Welcome to the world, Corgan. That's what life is like. Real life, not virtual reality." Leaning closer, she said, "But you have so much to be proud of. You left Demi on the station to save both me from brain damage and Cyborg from premature aging and death—so that means you've saved Cyborg's life twice. And you really did win the war.

Corgan, I believe in you. You're good, you're strong, you're decent. Why don't you believe in yourself?"

Humbly he answered, "I'm working on it. I just can't seem to get it all together. What makes you so wise, Sharla? We were both born in the same lab on the same day."

Her smile looked a little off center, tinged with irony. "Because I was a naughty kid and I broke out of my virtual-reality Box when I was seven. I met real people, in secret, and I saw them labor and sweat and die. You stayed protected in your own little Box till two years ago. For all those years you were clueless, and you're still clueless a lot. But that's just you, Corgan."

"No, it isn't. Not for long," he promised her. "I'm ready to take charge. I know what I need to do."

Maybe she believed him, maybe not. When he asked, "Will you stay here tonight?" she began, "I really should go back to the lab and check on . . . ," but after his arm tightened around her, she decided, speaking slowly, "I guess Delphine doesn't really need me. Yes, I'll stay."

Later, as the stars brightened, Corgan knew what he was *not* going to do. Sharla might have let him, but this wasn't the right time. Too many elements of their lives remained unresolved. Were her feelings for him friendly, romantic, or just tolerant? And how did he feel about her? He loved her and he always had, but it was an insecure love without enough trust. He suspected she might fly straight into Brigand's arms as soon as she saw him again.

And then there was the age thing. So complicated! Sharla was now sixteen for eternity. Brigand kept aging two years every month, which should make him about twenty-two right now; twenty-two and counting. Corgan was sixteen but would mature normally, eventually reaching middle age and beyond while Sharla stayed at sixteen. Maybe he ought to forget all those mathematics and just love her in this moment, here, now, in the warmth of the night. Love her with his heart and arms and mouth . . . and that's all, he decided. He wouldn't attempt anything more than that.

Sharla slept, but Corgan stayed alert, planning his next moves. The night was long and lonely, even though she lay there beside the pool with her head on his lap, her golden hair spread across her cheek. At dawn, when she awoke, her blue eyes reflecting the perfect sky, Corgan said reluctantly, "We need to go back."

"To Florida? I can't talk you out of it?"

"No."

"It scares me," she murmured. "I couldn't bear it if I lost you."

"It's like Delphine was saying," he told her, "about choice and chance. I've chosen this duty to make sure Thebos stays safe, and I'll have to take my chances."

There was one last act he had to perform before they left this waterfall. He picked up the machete and flung it high into the air, where it arced, spun, and then fell precisely into the center of the pool, splashing as it hit. That gesture might not wash away all the bad memories, but it was a start.

As he pushed through the jungle once again, Sharla stayed behind him, stepping carefully across the gnarled roots of trees that must have been standing there before all the islanders died of plague. They arrived at the beach just as the sun cleared the horizon. "We'll stop here," Corgan said, pointing to the lab. "I'll tell Delphine first."

They found her peering into the cage where the dog, Diva, lay. "She's getting tamer," Delphine said before she even said hello. "She seems to know we don't want to hurt her. Last night she ate out of my hand." Smiling as she turned toward them, she asked, "And where were you two last night?"

"In the middle of a long conversation," Sharla answered. "And now Corgan has some news for you."

After he told her, Delphine reacted the way Sharla had predicted: Her eyes swam with tears and she cried, "But we've been so happy here, all of us, all together! Do you really have to go, Corgan? Sharla and Cyborg and Ananda, too?"

"That'll be up to them," he answered. "But you and Royal can come with us if you want to. There's room. . . ."

Even before he'd finished, Delphine started to shake her head. "Royal loves it here. He says that Nuku Hiva is the home he was destined for. He feels it's part of his heritage."

This was no surprise—Corgan had figured as much. All night long he'd tried to think about what would be best for all of them, especially Delphine, and he'd come up with a possibility that he was now ready to offer. "I owe you, Delphine," he began. "For a lot of things. And I have this idea—uh, maybe you ought to sit down."

"Goodness!" She laughed a little, without mirth. "That sounds mysterious." But she moved to the chair Royal had built for her; it looked something like a throne.

Corgan pulled up a stool in front of her and leaned forward to look into her eyes. "What would you think about being Lockered, Delphine?"

"You mean, be young again?" Her eyes widened as her hands clutched each other.

"Any age you want," he told her. "You can be the same age as Royal, and I can Locker Royal so he won't ever get any older, just like Sharla and Cyborg are frozen at the ages they are now. You just figure out the date you want to go back to, and you get inside and I turn on the power and—"

"That would be incredible!" Delphine breathed. "Unbelievable! But I don't know . . . what if I . . . ? You mean, any age at all?"

Sharla nodded but warned, "It gets really complicated. It stops your life at a certain age and you stay there forever. There are things I'm still not sure about, like will I keep learning more and more and start to think like a mature person, or will I always think like a sixteen-year-old?"

"Yes, that's pretty scary," Delphine agreed, but then she grabbed Sharla's arm and apologized, "You're extremely mature for a sixteen-year-old, Sharla. It's just . . . yes, I'd like to be Lockered, and I'm really grateful that you'd let me, Corgan, but I'll have to do an awful lot of thinking before I can decide what age I want to be permanently. How long do I have before I make my decision?"

"By tomorrow," Corgan answered. "I want to leave here tomorrow."

Delphine gasped, "So soon! And so much to think about! What about Diva? What about the dog? I don't even know yet if the implanted embryos will mature."

"I don't see that it's a real problem," Sharla assured her. "Diva's either going to be pregnant or she isn't. You can teach me how to take care of her when she goes with us. If she's going to bear a Demi clone, she needs to be where Ananda is, and I'm pretty sure Ananda'll want to go back to Florida. Corgan told me Ananda is treated like a princess in the Flor-DC."

"Yeah, Ananda's their hero," Corgan agreed. "Okay, I've got a lot to do, so I need to start." On his way through the door he called back, "You and Royal think about it, Delphine, and tell me what you decide by tomorrow morning. Come on, Sharla. Let's go talk to Ananda and Cyborg."

FOURTEEN

The reaction was not what Corgan had expected. While Ananda looked unsure, Cyborg said he wanted to stay on Nuku Hiva.

"And not go back to Florida?" Corgan asked him, astonished.

"I don't mean exactly that . . . it's more like I don't want *you* to go back," Cyborg answered. "Not if it turns into a death match between you and Brigand."

Corgan swung his leg across a fallen tree trunk and sat there as he demanded, "Which is it, Cyborg? You're afraid *I'm* going to die or you're afraid *he's* going to die?"

"Corgan, I don't want anybody to die. If you say we

have to go back, let me try to negotiate a peace between you and Brigand. I'm a strategist, remember?"

"Yeah, I remember. And I remember that Brigand is also a strategist. You can negotiate as much as you want—his strategy will be to agree to anything you say. Then he'll probably stab me in the back, but I have to take my chances. Because of Thebos."

Trying to remain reasonable, Cyborg said, "You need to consider all the possibilities. What Brigand channeled to me about forcing Thebos to build another *Prometheus* and then fly it here—that could be a big lie."

"I understand that," Corgan said. "But I just can't take a chance, because it might be true, which means I have to protect Thebos. So I need to hear from both you and Ananda, are you coming with me tomorrow?"

"The answer should be obvious," Cyborg told him. "Haven't I always been with you? Leaving the Wyo-DC, leaving the Flor-DC, I was your man then and I'm your man now."

"And where Cyborg goes, I go," Ananda added. "We're with you."

"Great! There's still one more person I'd better go and tell. Well, not really a person. I have to talk to Mendor."

As Corgan hurried up the hill, his mind was full of details that needed attending to in order to prepare for tomorrow's flight. Inside the barn, when he pushed open the LiteSuit material that marked off the makeshift Box, he heard a voice that was neither male nor female say, "I could sense your agitation the second you appeared. Tell me what's happening, Corgan. Do you need my help?"

"I don't think so, Mendor. It's just that I have a lot to do. We're leaving here tomorrow. I have to go back to Florida and deal with Brigand."

Was it illusion, or did Mendor's green eyes grow larger, rounder, becoming more appealing, like a baby's? "Take me with you," Mendor said softly.

"Huh?"

"I can assist you. I can provide useful information. I wouldn't be difficult to transport, Corgan—you can compress me into a package no bigger than the palm of your hand."

This was unexpected. "Why would you want to come with me?"

"Because when you're not here, I die. After little Cyborg left, I was programmed to work only with you, Corgan." The voice, usually so placid, rose in intensity. "When you're with me, I come alive. Now you may be about to battle for your life. Let me help you to defeat Brigand. I know I can help."

Why not? Corgan shrugged. "Sure, Mendor. I'll ask Sharla to pack you. She'll know how to disconnect and compress you."

Spherical waves of pleasure seemed to radiate out of Mendor's image as the face changed from gold to warm flesh tones. "Thank you," he/she breathed. "I won't fail you."

Corgan left Mendor and stepped into the darkened barn. He saw his blue LiteSuit lying across the bunk, clean and unwrinkled, and wondered who'd laundered it—Sharla? Not likely. Delphine? Probably. Whoever had done it, he was grateful, because as the commander of the *Prometheus*, he needed to look good. Still, he would hate to say good-bye to his old jeans.

Hurrying down the hill, he called loudly, "Sharla, do you hear me?"

A flash of sunlight on golden hair moving through the trees showed that she'd heard and she was heading toward him. "Is something wrong?" she cried when she was still eight meters away. "What do you need?"

"You. I need you." As they came together, he grasped her hands and asked, "Would you please give me a haircut?"

"A haircut?" This time when she laughed at him, he didn't mind. It felt good to hear her laughter, strong and full and genuine. "I guess I can manage that."

He sat on a log while she began combing and snipping his hair with scissors she borrowed from Delphine. "You have great hair," she told him. "On top of your head, I mean. I'm not such a big fan of your facial hair. You need a shave."

"Right." He didn't have a razor, but he knew Royal had one. Although Royal was younger than Corgan, he had a pretty thick line of black hairs on his upper lip, probably even more than on Corgan's, but hey—it wasn't a contest. "Don't stop," he pleaded when Sharla put down the scissors.

"But it'll get too short," she told him. "Your hair looks fine now."

"Thanks, but—could you keep combing for a while longer?" Her fingers in his hair soothed him, let him relax enough that he'd be able to deal with leaving this island, which had once again begun to feel like paradise. Maybe Sharla was right—the haunted feelings had all been inside Corgan.

Sharla mentioned, "Delphine wants to make a farewell dinner for us tonight and then have one more dance around the fire. She says nothing will ever be as good again as this time we've had together. She wants tonight, our last night, to be special."

"I can deal with that. I'll even dance, if you promise to wear that dress again."

That evening, as the sun drew closer to the horizon, Corgan and Sharla walked down the hill together. He still had on his jeans, and Sharla, as she'd promised, wore her tapa cloth dress for this one last time on Nuku Hiva, and maybe the last time ever. Delphine stood in front of the table, her arms outstretched to welcome them. Cyborg and Ananda were already seated; Royal came forward from the barbecue pit bearing a wooden tray with a steaming rib roast of beef and two huge lobsters. As he set it on the table, Delphine said, "Raise your glasses, everyone."

They weren't really glasses, just laboratory beakers full of mango juice, but everyone did as she asked. "Here's to the finest young people on the face of the earth," Delphine toasted them. "To Corgan, may you find success. To Sharla, who will forever be a beautiful sixteen-year-old. To Ananda, who will have two new copies of her beloved Demi—yes, I confirmed that today; they're growing. To Cyborg, destined to advise Earth's rulers with his wise and decent judgments. And . . ." Delphine's voice grew softer, "To Royal, a prince in every way."

Corgan wondered if he was supposed to say something in response, but Cyborg spoke first. "To Delphine, whose brilliant mind is matched only by her boundless heart."

That did it for Delphine; she couldn't hold back the tears any longer. Ananda and Sharla hurried to comfort her, one on each side, their arms around her, their hair—Sharla's pale gold and Ananda's ebony—sweeping across Delphine's face as they bent over her. The three males—Royal, Corgan, and Cyborg—sat there awkwardly, not knowing what to do when a grown woman cried.

It wasn't until after they'd eaten their feast, as the last edge of the visible sun gleamed like a ruby on the crown of the waves, not until they'd built their fire—bigger than usual—and danced around it, sweating from the movement and the heat, that Corgan sought to win the most important commitment. He took Sharla's hand and led her into the trees as the music still drummed in the background. The heat of the night and the jungle's dampness made the scent of flowers almost dizzying. Putting his arms around her, he asked, "Sharla, will you be coming with me tomorrow?"

"I will. Because I want to be there for you. You saved me when I needed you most. You risked everything to take me to the space station, and the Locker fixed me. I'll never desert you, Corgan."

Joy filled him, and he wanted to stay and savor the moment, but there was one more thing he needed to do. "Let's go," he told her.

"Where?"

"To the *Prometheus*. If we're Lockering Delphine tomorrow morning, I want to be sure everything's working right. I haven't checked inside the *Prometheus* since we got home from the dog hunt."

Ananda and Cyborg had disappeared somewhere together. Tiptoeing past Delphine and Royal, Corgan overheard enough fragments of conversation to know they were talking about Lockering. "Wait, I want to take off my shoes," Sharla said, pulling back. "This might be my last chance to walk in the sand. I'll probably never get to come back here again."

Corgan took off his shoes too, and the two of them ran into the edges of the waves and then back to the beach. Sand stuck to their wet feet and wedged between their toes. Each time they went into the waves to wash off the sand, it covered them again on the beach, making them laugh like two little kids. "Maybe we shouldn't leave," Sharla said. "Maybe we should stay here forever."

"Maybe we *can* come back one day," Corgan told her. "Once I take care of what needs to be done, I'll be free. If I'm still alive."

"Don't say that!"

They reached the *Prometheus*. Though there was no moon, enough light came from the stars to let Corgan again admire the craft, a sphere flattened both top and bottom. He offered his cupped hands to support Sharla's foot to give her a boost up the side so she could reach the entrance. To minimize air friction, Thebos had installed only one handhold, near the top. After Sharla opened the hatch and slid down into the *Prometheus*, Corgan followed her.

Sharla mentioned, "We brought sand in on our feet. Is that a problem?"

"I'll sweep it up tomorrow before we launch," he told her.

He touched the control panel, lighting it. He didn't need to turn on the power to read that the fuel cells were full—more than a week's worth of sunlight streaming onto the solar panels had recharged everything. "I installed these monitors myself," he told Sharla. "Thebos told me how to do it. You don't remember anything about Thebos, do you?"

"No." She frowned. "I don't remember anything that happened between crashing through the dome and then climbing out of the Locker in the space station, when I'd become sixteen forever. I keep thinking about Delphine. Do you wonder what age she'll choose?"

"Not really, but I am thinking about age. Someone else's. Before Cyborg got Lockered, Brigand kept channeling pain into Cyborg's head and blitzing him with psychic commands to come back to Florida. Then, after the Lockering, all that stopped. Cyborg said he could tell that Brigand was happy for him."

In the darkness they couldn't see each other too well, but Corgan sensed that Sharla knew exactly where he was going with this. He said, "Could that charge from the Locker have reached all the way through Cyborg and entered Brigand, ten thousand kilometers away? And if that happened, is Brigand now permanently sixteen just like Cyborg, and neither of them will die of premature aging?"

"Corgan, I don't have a clue. I don't know whether something like that is even possible," Sharla told him. "I created both of them, but I still haven't figured out how that psychic connection works. Brigand's a lot better at it than Cyborg. He controls it, turning it on and off when he doesn't want Cyborg to know something."

"So Cyborg isn't sure whether Brigand got Lockered by remote channeling? Or did you even ask him."

"No. I mean yes, I asked him, but he doesn't know. We won't find out till we're back in the Flor-DC."

Would it make any difference? Corgan wondered. If they got into a battle, would age play a part? It probably would. If Brigand was now six years older than Corgan, he'd be bigger, stronger, faster. And maybe . . . smarter.

Corgan shivered, and not because the *Prometheus* felt cooler than the weather outside.

FIFTEEN

Corgan couldn't sleep. All night long his brain throbbed with plans, tactics, calculations, and lists of essentials. Before the first glow of dawn he rolled off the bunk and went to a nearby stream, where he knelt naked in the cold water, washing every centimeter of himself. Then he took Royal's razor from the shelf in the barn; without asking permission, he used it to shave his face clean. Last, he pulled on his LiteSuit and picked up Mendor—Sharla had compacted the program the night before.

The sun had barely risen as he strode down the hill, but he figured everyone would be awake on this important day. He was right; Delphine had food ready and insisted that all of them eat. As they sat around the table—for the last time—Corgan asked her, "Have you decided, Delphine?"

She folded her napkin, creasing it carefully. "Yes. But you can ask Royal first."

Royal sat on the edge of the bench, hunched over with his hands dangling between his knees. "I don't want to be Lockered," he said, his voice low. "I want to grow up to be a man. Like my father. And then I want to be an old man. Like my grandfather." Royal looked from one to the other and explained, "And I want to stay on Nuku Hiva. I could never live under a dome, because I love the sea and the rain forest too much."

"Did your grandfather tell you that's what you're supposed to do?" Ananda wondered.

"No. It's my own decision," he assured her. "But Ananda, remember what my grandfather said on Hiva Oa? He told me that everything will be tranquil when two Royals take me where my heart will lie. Well, this is where my heart lies."

In the silence that followed, one by one each of them turned expectantly toward Delphine. "My turn?" she asked. "Well, after a great deal of thought I've chosen to be Lockered. I want to become twenty-eight years old."

"Really?" Ananda came right out and asked her, "Why twenty-eight, Delphine? Is it because you want to be young and strong again? Then, why not twenty or twenty-one?"

Delphine smiled a little. "The answer to your first question is yes, I want to be young and strong again. As for the second question—why twenty-eight? Because there's such a lack of data about Lockering."

"Huh? I don't get the connection between answers one and two," Cyborg stated.

As they all looked at Delphine quizzically, she began to explain, "You see, kids, I'd received all my university degrees by the time I was twenty-four, and then I spent the next four years doing original research on genetics. I want to retain all that knowledge. If I were to go back to twenty years old, would I lose all memory of those eight years of learning and experimentation? Would they be erased? I can't tell."

She glanced from one to the other. When she saw they still didn't comprehend, she continued, "We have only two samples of Lockering that I could possibly research—Cyborg and Sharla. Cyborg has told me he remembers everything that happened between his two dates—the date of his Lockering and the date of the age he was returned to. He remembers, but Sharla doesn't recall anything between *her* two dates. Of course, Sharla was brain-damaged, so that's a mitigating factor. Anyway, a mere two cases are not a large enough sampling for any scientist to create reliable data. I'd need at least a hundred research subjects who'd been Lockered, and that number doesn't exist. So I'll return myself to age twenty-eight, to the time when I'd done most of my major work, just so I can feel certain that all that input will stay in my brain. Understand?"

"I . . . guess so," Cyborg answered. "Maybe we could discuss it more."

Because the clock in his head kept ticking toward the departure time, Corgan said, "Not now. We need to get moving. Sharla, you take Delphine to the *Prometheus*. The rest of you can wait here. We won't be long."

Corgan hurried toward the spaceship to arrive ahead of Sharla and Delphine. He leaped up and grabbed the hand-hold, then opened the hatch to swing himself through it. There was now enough daylight inside to illuminate the whole deck. Quickly he swept the sand from the night before into an empty metal box and climbed through the hatch to throw the sand over the side. Holding the box, he jumped to the ground just as Delphine and Sharla reached him.

"Sharla first," he said. He felt a bit disappointed because instead of a dress Sharla was again wearing the LiteSuit, the gold-colored one she'd borrowed from Corgan. Since it was too large, she'd cinched the waist with a strip of tapa cloth. After Sharla had entered the ship, Corgan said, "Now you, Delphine," but even standing on the box Delphine couldn't stretch quite high enough. With a lot of pushing by Corgan and pulling by Sharla they got her inside the *Prometheus*.

Immediately Corgan turned on the power to the Locker, listening closely as the motor started up. It sounded right, and when he laid his hands on the outside to feel the vibrations, they seemed to be throbbing at the correct microspeed. Next he opened the Locker and asked Delphine, "Want to take a look inside? This is your last chance to change your mind. After you enter, you'll be strapped in and I'll close the door. You don't have claustro-phobia or anything, do you?"

"No, I'm fine." Still, she appeared a little apprehensive

about the makeshift construction of the Locker. Taking a deep breath, she told him, "The date I'd like to return to is September 20, 2060. Can you do that, Corgan?"

"Any special reason for that date, Delphine?" Sharla asked her.

"It's right before I began my relationship with Grimber. I'm actually hoping Lockering will erase *that* part of my memory."

Since Corgan remembered what a disagreeable man Grimber had been, he could totally sympathize with Delphine's choice. But maybe memory erasing wouldn't happen. As Delphine had said, they had no real data. "Okay, I'm setting the dials now," he said. "Sharla, help her into the Locker. Is she going to fit?"

"She fits fine. This is exactly how they did it with me, Delphine," Sharla commented as she settled a thin metal helmet onto Delphine's head. "These metal cuffs go around your arms. It might seem kind of scary, but—"

"I'm not scared. I'm excited. I can't wait for it to start."

Sharla closed the door, Corgan threw the switch, and the whine of machinery built up to a crescendo. He stared intently at the whirring dials as they spun backward by minutes, hours, days, years, all the way to 2060— December, November, October. . . . At September 20 he smacked the red button that stopped the power, and the whine of the motor wound down to a low buzz, then died.

"I'll open it," Sharla said, glancing at Corgan. Both of them knew this was the moment for worry. If anything had gone wrong, they were about to find out.

Sharla unsealed the door and out stepped Delphine.

Becoming young hadn't turned her into a raving beauty, but her flesh was firm and she was a lot thinner—the tapa cloth dress hung on her in folds. Her lips were full, her hair was as wild as ever but without any gray, and her eyes shone with joy. "How do I look?" she asked.

"You look wonderful!" Sharla exclaimed.

This time Delphine had no problem sliding down from the hatch of the *Prometheus*; she even jumped the last meter and landed firmly on her feet. "I feel so young! I *am* young!" she cried, almost singing it as she headed back toward the lab. "Does anyone have a mirror?"

Standing in the shadow of the trees, half hidden, Royal was waiting. He must have liked the way Delphine turned out, because when he saw her, he stepped forward quickly, smiling and saying, "Greetings, Miss Delphine. I'm here to escort you back to the lab. I thought you might feel a little shaky after being Lockered."

"I feel great!" she exclaimed. "But thanks for coming. I'll race you back." Delphine started to run, with Royal sprinting after her to catch up.

"Hey, Royal," Corgan shouted after them. "Tell Cyborg and Ananda to come here right now. We need to get everything control-tested so we can take off. We're losing time."

When they arrived, the four of them loaded their gear first, stowing it so it wouldn't float around when the *Prometheus* shed gravity. Then Cyborg brought water to fill the containers. Sharla found a safe place to secure Mendor—she'd condensed the program to its smallest size. Ananda secured Diva's cage to the inside deck so the dog wouldn't float around in zero gravity, and she murmured softly to Diva, trying to calm her. "This must be so frightening for her," she said. "But I think she's bonding to me. She's been licking my hand when I feed her."

Or maybe it was Ananda who was bonding to Diva. In spite of all the protests she'd made that no dog would ever be able to take Demi's place, she was paying a lot of attention to this wild yellow dog who whimpered for Ananda to pick her up and hold her.

Corgan supervised the inspection of every instrument in the *Prometheus*, making sure nothing essential to flight could be overlooked. He issued orders and the others obeyed, knowing that only Corgan understood the operations of the spaceship. By the time the sun reached its zenith, they were ready to take off. Outside, Delphine and Royal stood on the concrete pad, waiting to watch the launch. While Corgan adjusted the touch-screen monitors, his three passengers grinned with anticipation because they knew what would happen when the *Prometheus* took off.

"Here we go," Corgan said, but Cyborg yelled, "Wait! Stop! Something's happening!"

Through the port they could see Royal take a running leap up the side of the *Prometheus*. He must have grabbed the outside handle to hold on, because he started pounding on the hatch.

"He's changed his mind and wants to go with us!" Ananda cried. "Quick, open the hatch."

While the pounding continued, Corgan quickly turned off the spacecraft's thrusters, then touched the button that unlocked the hatch. Cyborg yanked it open, shouting, "Get inside," as he reached for Royal.

"No, I'm fine, I'm not coming in," Royal answered. He held on to the edge, resting his shoulders and arms on the inner ledge of the hatch. Visible only from the chest up while the rest of him hung outside the spacecraft, he said, "I need to tell Corgan something."

Corgan, startled, asked him, "What?"

Royal spoke as casually as if they were having a conversation at the picnic table. "My grandfather gave me a message in a dream. It was for you, Corgan."

"Me?"

"Yes. He came to me in the dream the first night you went out there in the jungle by yourself, and then after you got back, I kind of forgot about it. I'm glad I remembered before you left here."

"What . . . uh, what did your grandfather say?" Corgan asked him.

"He said, 'Tell this to Corgan: If you don't lose your head, you'll win.'"

Taken aback, Corgan repeated, "If I don't lose my head, I'll win?"

"You got it," Royal said, nodding as if the message weren't particularly astonishing.

"Did you ask him to explain that?" Corgan wanted to know, but this time Royal answered with a head shake.

"I don't talk in these dreams, I just listen to my grandfather. So that's it. At least I got to tell you before you left. Have a safe trip." And with that Royal let go and slid down the hull to the ground, where Delphine waited.

"Weird!" Ananda breathed.

"Really weird," Sharla agreed. "But . . . is it supposed to be a warning?"

"I can't worry about it now," Corgan answered, although he was more than a little perplexed. "Lock the hatch, Cyborg. Everybody hold on to something. We're taking off."

The *Prometheus* slowly lifted itself from the ground while Sharla and Ananda waved wildly at Delphine and Royal beneath them. Each girl gripped a bar with one hand and waved with the other, but when weightlessness hit, their bodies rose horizontally behind them as though they were stretched out facedown on an invisible bed. Kicking her feet in empty air, Ananda cried, "I *love* antigravity propulsion! Let's dance, Cyborg."

Cyborg, usually so serious, fell under the spell of weightlessness too and turned somersaults in the air, looping around Ananda, laughing and reaching out to give her little pinches as she squealed and tried to grab him. Sharla sailed to Corgan and spun around him until they bumped into Ananda and Cyborg, sending all four of them flying in different directions. It was fun, but, "I gotta watch what I'm doing," Corgan said. He needed to confirm that their ascent over Nuku Hiva was vertically accurate.

From six hundred meters high the lush green growth, blue waters, and white-capped waves sent a pang of regret through Corgan because he was once again leaving this Eden. At two kilometers the shape of the mountain ridges revealed how volcanoes had created the island and how erosion had sculpted the valleys. At four kilometers the whole island was visible, with fringes of land reaching out into the sea like tentacles, and by eight Corgan began to see the entire chain of the Isles of Hiva.

No more time for sightseeing, and no more time to play games in weightlessness. "Sit down and strap in," he told them. "I'm ready to generate the gravitational field."

With a thud, gravity returned and their bodies felt normal again. Corgan set the course for east-northeast at an altitude of eight kilometers. Until they got close to Florida, he wouldn't need to pay much attention to navigation. But other matters required a lot of attention.

"Cyborg," he began, "I'm going to need your cooperation."

"I thought I'd already been cooperating," he answered. "What else?"

"I can't let you know where I plan to land. If I do, Brigand will siphon the information out of your brain and he'll be waiting with his New Rebel Troops when we get there. He already knows we're on our way, I guess."

Cyborg nodded apologetically. "I guess. I'm sorry. I can't help it."

"I know you can't. So I'm asking you to stay separated from the rest of us. Go down into the galley. Go into one of the closets so you won't hear anything we say here on the deck, and stay there. When we get close to where we'll land, I'll come and get you. Then I'll have to blindfold you."

Frowning, Cyborg clenched and unclenched his real hand for a long minute, then answered, "I understand the logic. I'll do what you say."

"Cyborg . . ." Ananda reached out to him.

420

"It's okay," he said. "See you all later. Somewhere."

"That's kind of cruel," Ananda murmured after he'd gone. "But he's being great about it, isn't he? So, where are we going to land?"

"Come over here," Corgan told Ananda and Sharla, "and I'll show you." He touched the monitor screen to create a three-dimensional hologram of Earth. "Wait, let me ratchet it up," he said, making the hologram loom larger and spin slowly. "Here's where we are," pointing to the central Pacific. "Here's where we're going." He showed them Florida. "We're traveling pretty slow because flying through Earth's atmosphere takes longer than flying above it in Earth orbit like we did before. But slow is good because I want it to be dark when we get there. There's no moon tonight."

As he turned from the hologram, Corgan explained, "When we left the Flor-DC, we flew up through the hole in the dome that Brigand smashed when he crashed the Harrier, which you don't remember, Sharla, because you were brain-injured then. Well, we can't get back into the city the same way we flew out, because the dome has been fixed. Cyborg told me that—he got it from Brigand, and I believe it because they were working on the dome when we left. With the hole sealed up again, there's no entrance."

"Then, how will you . . . ," Ananda began.

During those restless hours of the long, sleepless night Corgan had worked it all out. "We'll have to land without any light at all," he told them. "Even a small or dim light would be visible from the Flor-DC, and Brigand's going to be watching for us. Ananda, I'll need your sharp eyes to help me see in the dark. Sharla, I'll need your sharp mind to calculate the distances I give you down to single meters. It doesn't matter that you can't remember Florida, Sharla, because even Ananda doesn't know exactly where we're going to land. Only I do."

"Tell us!" Ananda urged.

Looking down through the port in front of him, Corgan saw islands beneath them. He checked the hologram of the slowly rotating Earth and saw that the islands were named Hawaii. They were on course. It would be a while before they reached darkness, before they reached their destination, enough time to rehearse his plan thoroughly, to go over every detail with Sharla and Ananda.

"We'll be landing inside a bomb crater," he told them.

SIXTEEN

Time was one thing the devastation hadn't altered. Even though Earth was mostly destroyed on its surface, it still rotated at the same pace; it still orbited the sun.

"There's six hours' time difference between Florida and where we are now," Corgan told them. "I don't want to get to Florida until dark, so we're gonna take a detour and fly low over the Wyo-DC and do reconnaissance. Mendor can probably catch some sound waves that leak through the dome."

"If the Wyo rebels see us," Sharla objected, "they'll message Brigand through the fiber-optic cable."

"They won't see us. Look at the Earth hologram—it shows the weather all over the planet. There's plenty of cloud cover above Wyoming to hide us even if the rebels were looking for us, which they won't be. While Mendor's checking for sound waves, we can scope the dome through the infrared instruments to see if anything looks different. We'll just circle above Wyo and try to pick up information."

"Why do you want to do that?" Ananda asked.

It took him a moment to answer, "Call it long-range planning."

Sharla became alert at that. "You're making plans about the Wyo-DC?" she asked.

He stalled. "Let's say I'm trying to consider future options. If I *have* a future, if Brigand doesn't kill me as soon as we get to the Flor-DC." He gave a short laugh, but Ananda and Sharla glared at him, letting him know this was not something to joke about.

Ananda said, "Since we have extra time, I'd like to go down to the galley and wait with Cyborg. I won't say anything to him about where we'll be landing."

"Bad idea," he told her. "No way, Ananda. You might accidentally let something slip."

"I wouldn't leak anything. Trust me."

"It's not that I don't trust you, but you get carried away sometimes when you're around Cyborg, and I'd rather not take a chance."

"I said I wouldn't!" Ananda insisted, her voice escalating. "I'm a responsible human being, Corgan. Sometimes you treat me like a baby."

He half rose in his chair. "I know you wouldn't mean to spill anything, Ananda, but *do not go to Cyborg*! If you try to, I'll wrestle you to the deck. You're strong and I'm strong, and it would probably be an even match and we'd both get hammered, and then Cyborg would zap me with his bionic hand for messing with his girl, so I'd be double trashed. And where would that leave you, since I'm the only one who can fly the *Prometheus*?"

As if testing him, Ananda started to move toward the stairs, but Corgan got there first, blocking the passage.

"Oh, all right!" Ananda yielded irritably. "Although I could probably take down both you and Sharla at the same time without even half trying."

"How about just one of us? Would you like to try that?" Sharla asked, rising to the challenge. "Corgan, turn off the gravity."

Corgan hooted. "I'm staying out of this one. I want to watch the two of you duke it out in zero gravity." He touched the switch to disconnect the energized gravitational field, and in a split second weightlessness struck. Right away Ananda launched herself at Sharla but flew past her and bounced off a wall. Sharla started to giggle as Ananda swung a fist, which did nothing except propel both of them backward. With their hair unleashed by zero gravity to spread around their heads in clouds—one gold, one raven—they looked like sea goddesses battling underwater.

Sharla, always graceful, maneuvered herself across the cockpit, diving down and then floating upward, frustrating Ananda, who couldn't catch her. By then Corgan was laughing riotously as he hovered around the periphery of the deck. Quickly Ananda twisted her body to change direction and go after him. She landed a fist on top of his head, which made him bounce off the deck and rebound up through the Earth hologram, emerging at the North Pole. He dived for Ananda and caught her around the knees. Then Sharla caught Corgan around the knees, and the three of them rotated lengthwise like a lumpy sea serpent. Even Ananda laughed so hard she got the hiccups.

"We'll declare a truce," Sharla offered. "Shake hands on it."

When Ananda reached to clasp Sharla's hand, the two of them began to spin around each other faster and faster, twirling like two dolls caught in a whirlpool, squealing with glee. "It's impossible to fight in zero gravity!" Ananda shrieked. "That's why Corgan wouldn't fight me, because he knew he couldn't win."

"Try it this way," Corgan told them, and grinning, he turned on the gravity. They fell to the deck at once, arms and legs tangled and heads bumping.

"That was bratty!" Sharla shouted, and to Ananda, "Let's get Corgan." The two girls jumped on him and began pummeling him, four fists swinging nonstop against his head, neck, and arms. This time there was no zero gravity to protect him.

"I give up! I give up!" he yelled. "Two against one. No fair! Call a cease-fire!"

Cyborg's face surfaced suddenly in the stairwell from the galley. "What's happening up here?" he demanded. "I keep hearing all this thumping. Did something break?"

"Just Corgan's head," Ananda answered.

"We were having a weighty discussion," Sharla told him. "Or maybe it was weightless."

"Is everyone okay?" Cyborg asked.

"Oh, yes," both Ananda and Sharla answered. "Corgan may be a bit brain-damaged," Sharla added, "but it's hard to tell because he always acts that way."

"Hah! It's only when two women come after me at once," Corgan told him. "Happens all the time. Bye-bye, Cyborg. See you in Florida."

Ananda waved him good-bye, and Cyborg, with a last look of uncertainty, disappeared.

Corgan was glad that Delphine had fed them a big meal that morning—the spaceship's food was stored below in the galley, where Cyborg waited. Ananda seemed resigned to staying on deck now, so maybe in a couple of hours Corgan could go down and get them something to eat.

Having nothing to do but look out the port at the changing surface of Earth eventually grew tiresome for the girls. Ananda took Diva out of the cage and held her while Sharla cautiously petted the dog. "I think pregnancy is good for her," Ananda was saying. "She seems much calmer, even though her leg must still hurt."

"If she has two Demi clones, will you keep both of them?" Sharla asked.

"I haven't decided. Why? Would you want one of them?"

Sharla shook her head. "I couldn't be responsible for any living creature. Not now. I just don't know where my life is heading, or where I'll be."

So Sharla felt as uncertain about the future as Corgan

427

did. At least that meant she wasn't totally committed to Brigand. "Hey, look down there now," he said. "That's the coastline of what used to be called California. Remember it, Sharla? We saw it before, when we flew to Nuku Hiva in the Harrier jet right after the Virtual War."

They were cruising low enough that the devastation was visible all up and down the coast. Huge, gaping holes pockmarked the landscape. Broken dams had flooded kilometers of bottomlands, turning the water green with tons of slime. Empty shells of what had once been buildings raised shattered walls. "I read that there used to be huge cities down there," Ananda said. "One of them was called Lost Angels or something like that."

"Lost Angels!" Corgan chuckled. "You're not so good at remembering city names, Ananda. A couple of months ago you told me the destroyed city closest to the Flor-DC was called Carnival. That was wrong. It was really Cape Canaveral." Right away he was sorry he'd said that—he didn't want to clue her into their destination. Not yet.

Quickly changing the subject, he asked Sharla, "Will you restore Mendor now so I can consult the program? Then come over here and figure out how to work this infrared scope. When we get close to the Wyo-DC, I'll have to start navigating full-time. You can do the infrared imaging, okay? Ananda, you watch the compass to keep me on course, and the altimeter to make sure I don't sink down through the cloud cover."

"Say 'please,'" Sharla told him.

Ananda echoed, "Yeah, say 'please.'"

Palms together in front of his face, he bowed and said,

"Please." Trying to keep two girls happy was a bigger job than sailing the *Tuli* into a headwind.

In less than an hour they'd reached the airspace above the Wyoming domed city. The Earth hologram had been right; he couldn't see through the cloud cover, but he was intensely curious about the Wyo-DC's dome. Had it been sealed once both Harrier jets had flown away from the city? That's what he'd try to find out. Yet it wasn't the only reason he wanted to hover over the Wyo-DC. He had a sense of attachment to the place: It was where he'd been conceived in a test tube, gestated in a laboratory, and raised in a virtual-reality Box. Maybe he wanted to see his roots once more, even from eight kilometers high.

"Why are we doing this?" Sharla asked again.

"I'll tell you sometime," Corgan answered. "Not just now."

Ananda complained, "You're keeping Cyborg prisoner for this extra time, and you won't even give us an explanation."

"I am the commander of the *Prometheus*, and I'm not required to explain my flight plan to the crew," Corgan said with authority, or at least he hoped he sounded authoritative. "I give the orders. But I will tell you one thing—I want to gather possible evidence of what the Wyo-DC is like now that Brigand is gone." What Corgan really wanted to know was whether the rebels were in charge and running things—ruining things? Or were the citizens ready to rebel against the rebels? He hoped Mendor could pick up some sound from the dome. Mendor's instrumentation was so sensitive that he/she had once caught the rumble of a volcano erupting on an island called Japan.

As Sharla set up Mendor, Corgan marveled all over again at how the program could expand from palm size all the way to room size. But rooms were solid and real, while Mendor was mostly shimmering illusion. "You'll have to check it," Sharla said. "It's coded so it won't respond to anyone but you, Corgan. It's that iris identification thing."

Corgan stepped in front of the wavering curtains of light—they looked almost like the aurora borealis they'd passed through on their way to the space station. "Mendor, turn on," he instructed. He stood still so Mendor could check the pattern of the iris in his right eye—that took only forty-seven hundredths of a second.

"I'm here, Corgan," Mendor announced. "Thank you for taking me with you."

"No problem," Corgan said. "We're flying over the Wyo-DC right now. . . ."

"My old home," Mendor said.

"Mine too. But I don't have visual contact because of the cloud cover. I'd like you to pick up whatever sound you can, Mendor, and record it in your memory banks for analysis."

"I can do that," Mendor answered, with a face halfway between mother figure and father figure. "But may I ask why?"

Corgan sighed. "Not you too, Mendor. Just do it, okay?"

Intensely curious and standing only a few meters from him, Sharla and Ananda had been able to hear everything Corgan said, but they couldn't see Mendor or hear Mendor's words because those were beamed to a frequency wired into Corgan at birth. "Are you checking the compass?" he asked Ananda. "Look, you can enlarge the Earth hologram to monitor where we're flying. That little gold pinpoint of light shows our flight path. I want to keep circling for a while. Sharla, start focusing the infrared scope. Uh . . . please! First get some distant images, then close-ups."

"Just what in particular are you looking for?" Sharla asked.

"Whether the retractable doors in the Wyo-DC dome are operational."

"Is this part of that future planning you were talking about?"

"Possibly."

Mendor announced, "I have a fix on the domed city. Some sounds seem no different from before Brigand's revolt. I'm recording the noise of the machinery in the food factory. Also the gear shifts of the hovercar transport system. But . . . there are also screams. I hear people screaming."

That sent a jolt through Corgan. Screams could mean the rebels were torturing citizens again, the way they'd done during the revolt. "Analyze whatever you can," he told Mendor, "and record it."

Maneuvering away from the Wyo-DC, he tried to get the screams and what they implied out of his mind because he had to concentrate on navigation—he'd have time later to worry about them. He set the flight speed on slow, wanting to arrive over Florida around ten at night, when darkness would be complete.

"Let's eat," Ananda suggested. "I'll run down to the galley and get some packs of food."

"I think I better do it," he told her, and amazingly Ananda didn't argue.

Below deck he found Cyborg asleep and nudged him with a toe. "Help me grab some food packs," he told him.

Cyborg scrambled to his feet and pulled open the galley door. "You'll need water, too," he said, "to mix them with."

"There's water on deck. Listen, Cyborg," he said, whispering, hoping Brigand wasn't tuned in to Cyborg's thoughts at that precise moment, "when we land, I have to blindfold you. You can't know anything about . . . anything." Better not say more.

"I understand." Cyborg shrugged as though it didn't bother him, at least not too much. "If Ananda objects, you can tell her it's fine with me."

"Thanks, friend. I can always count on you. And . . ." Corgan shifted from foot to foot before he managed to continue. "Listen, I want to apologize for what I said that day, about scorching your circuitry—"

"Forget it," Cyborg interrupted. He gave Corgan a little punch in the shoulder that almost made him drop the food packets.

"No, I can't forget it. I had a meltdown and I acted like an ass. You gotta know, Cyborg, that no matter what happens—"

"Let it go, Corgan. We're good. You better take that food up to the girls."

Hesitating, Corgan stood before his one real friend,

wanting to articulate his feelings, to tell Cyborg how grateful he was for that friendship, but Corgan hadn't been engineered to express his thoughts easily. "Right, I'm on my way," he said, and hurried up the stairs to the deck, where he found Sharla and Ananda hovering over the dog.

"Did you bring something for Diva?" Ananda asked. "I think she's starved."

"Yes, I remembered. You ought to eat too, both of you, and then get some sleep."

For once they listened to him without arguing. Maybe because he was sounding more like a commander or maybe just because they were tired, they did what he suggested for once. After they'd eaten their rations and fed the dog, they went to sleep.

Another hour passed, and Mendor suggested, "You should rest too, Corgan."

"I can't, Mendor. I have to check too many things. If I'm off by a hundredth of a degree, it'll be total disaster."

"Shall I relax you?" Mendor asked. "With soothing music?"

"I don't want to be relaxed. I need to be energized."

"I could play Delphine's favorite music from the 2060s."

"Anything but that!" Corgan cried. "I just want to talk to you."

"About?"

There was no stool for Corgan to sit on, so he stood facing the cloth that held the attentive expression Mendor wore now. He began, "Royal's grandfather talks to him in dreams, and he gave Royal a message for me. This was the message: 'If you don't lose your head, you'll win.'"

"Interesting," Mendor said, his/her pale green face rippling. "But nothing remarkable. I assume you want my interpretation."

"Yes."

"First, forecasts made in dreams are not scientific. However, I would interpret Royal's message as a general rule for life, not a specific warning. It just means that one should always remain calm and think about things logically to achieve the best results."

"What about the winning part?" Corgan wanted to know.

"Be in control and you're sure to win success."

"That's it? I thought it might be about a showdown between me and Brigand, because everyone keeps telling me how much he wants to kill me." With a shiver he remembered those screams coming from the Wyo-DC. "And I so much want to see him squirm and suffer for all the terrible things he's done to people, in both Wyoming and Florida."

Mendor suggested, "Shall I bring up your old skill-building games—Golden Bees, and Precision and Sensitivity Training? You can sharpen your war skills."

Those were the games that had helped him train for a war fought virtually with hand-size digital images of enemy soldiers. They wouldn't be much help in hand-to-hand combat with a brutal Brigand, if that's what lay ahead.

But why not? "Sure, Mendor," he said. "Bring on the Golden Bees."

SEVENTEEN

Corgan leaned over Ananda and placed his fingertips on her lips to awaken her. When her eyes flew open, he whispered, "Shhhh," and she stayed silent. Gesturing for her to follow him, he led her halfway around the circular deck of the *Prometheus*, as far away as he could get from where Sharla sat asleep in her chair, her head resting on crossed arms. He didn't want Sharla to hear any of what he was going to say.

Ananda waited, her dark eyebrows raised inquiringly as Corgan murmured, "We're getting close to Florida. I need to give you the details of the plan, but you have to promise that you won't repeat any of this to Sharla or Cyborg."

"You're going to tell me and not Sharla?" Maybe it was the intensity of his eyes and voice that made Ananda quickly agree, "Okay, I promise."

"Here's the deal, Ananda. I never told you or anyone about this, but Thebos's old laboratory, where he worked at Cape Canaveral, is connected by a two-mile tunnel to the underground chamber of the Flor-DC."

"*The* tunnel," Ananda said, nodding.

"Yeah. You saw the door to the tunnel the day we were in the underground chamber—"

"I remember. When you opened the door, Demi sneezed, so we thought there was contamination inside and we didn't go in."

"Right. Well, that's where we're going to land," he told her.

"In the tunnel?"

"Ananda, get real! I couldn't park this big spaceship inside a tunnel. Look, I'll explain, but I have to talk fast. Thebos built the *Prometheus* in his laboratory at Cape Canaveral. Then after the devastation he dug that tunnel from his lab to the Florida domed city—it took him seven years. When it was finished, he dismantled the *Prometheus* and carried it piece by piece through the tunnel into that concealed upper floor inside the Flor-DC. That's where he put the spaceship back together."

"In that secret room we flew out of?"

"Correct. Okay, here's the important part: A little while later the roof of his entire laboratory back at Cape Canaveral collapsed, because it was weak from the nuclear attack maybe, so now there's nothing there but a big crater."

"The bomb crater you were talking about. I'm getting the picture."

"Uh-huh. So we'll land in the crater, and we'll go through the tunnel to the Flor-DC."

"Brilliant!" She smiled. "And Brigand doesn't know about the tunnel?"

"I'm . . . pretty sure he doesn't." Staring straight into Ananda's eyes, he put his hands on her shoulders and said, "You absolutely must not even hint at any of this to Cyborg, because he's sharp and he'll figure it out if you breathe a word, and then it goes straight to Brigand's foul brain."

"My lips are sealed," she promised.

"And Cyborg has to be blindfolded while Sharla leads him through the tunnel. The whole time."

Nodding, Ananda said, "So that's why you didn't want Sharla to hear all this, because you don't want her to spill any hints to Cyborg. Okay. What's my job?"

"You'll help me carry the Locker through the tunnel. I don't want to leave it in the *Prometheus* because . . . I'll tell you why later."

Corgan hadn't mentioned all the things that could go wrong. The most serious one: He'd have to navigate toward a landing in total darkness because from as far away as twenty kilometers any lights on the *Prometheus* could be spotted from the Florida dome. Brigand would already know, from reading Cyborg's mind, that the *Prometheus* was on its way, and he'd have lookouts posted around every section of the dome. But the one thing Brigand didn't know about—Corgan fervently hoped!—was the existence of the tunnel.

After Sharla woke up, Corgan asked her to repack Mendor. Like Ananda, Sharla seemed to sense the seriousness of their situation, and without question she hurried to follow orders. All of them were tense as the *Prometheus* descended through the thick, humid Florida atmosphere. "We gotta turn out the spacecraft lights now," Corgan announced. "In about thirteen minutes we'll be close enough that they'd see our interior lights if we left them on."

The night had never seemed so black, with barely enough ambient starlight to make out shapes on the ground. Corgan had no trouble observing the lighted Florida dome, but the crater where Thebos's laboratory had once existed was totally invisible. As the *Prometheus* drifted forward like a ghost ship, with no illumination except the very dim numbers that barely showed up on the monitors, Corgan wished he had levers or toggle switches instead of touch screens to control flight. If he could grip something, it might ease his tension.

The crater where he wanted to land was located two miles—3.2 kilometers—from the dome, the exact length of the tunnel that connected the two points. Where the roof of the laboratory had collapsed inward there should be no trees growing, no growth of any kind, just rubble. "Ananda," he said, "look down. Can you see any trees?"

"I can hardly see anything. Trees? Mmm, maybe."

He told her, "Look for a place that *doesn't* have trees."

"It's pretty hard to see in the dark . . ."

"I know."

"But I think over there . . ." She pointed.

Ananda was right, there were no trees, but there was a pond instead. Corgan managed to gain altitude just before he would have landed belly-down in the water. "We'll search again," he said through clenched teeth.

They hovered, almost unmoving, until Ananda said, "Down there. No trees, and I see some shapes like broken walls."

Corgan gave thanks that Thebos had engineered the *Prometheus* so flawlessly it didn't stall out when it barely moved. "We're just two meters aboveground," Sharla called out.

With the *Prometheus* suspended beneath the rim that surrounded the pit, Corgan turned on landing lights, but on only the bottom of the craft. He kept them dim, just bright enough to confirm that they'd found the crater. After the spacecraft had settled gently onto the ground, Corgan cut the motor and dropped his face forehead-down onto the control panel, his arms hanging lifeless, his breathing shallow. Total relief. He'd made it.

"Well done," Sharla murmured, hugging him.

Then they heard Cyborg say, "I can tell we landed. Can I come up now?"

"Yes, but you don't know where we are," Corgan told him for Brigand's benefit.

Although Corgan was aware they needed to move ahead with the next step, he could hardly force himself to stand up. He was drained, not by failure, but by success. Cyborg and Ananda waited silently while Sharla rubbed Corgan's shoulders. "You were totally amazing," she told him.

"Thanks," he said weakly. "We should start out now."

With effort he got to his feet and said, "Ananda, we'll carry Diva's cage on top of the Locker. Sharla, you lead Cyborg." And to Cyborg, "Sorry, friend," as he untied the strip of tapa cloth from around Sharla's waist and wound it across Cyborg's eyes, making sure he couldn't see a thing. "I'm taking two portable lights from the *Prometheus*," he told them, "one for me and one for you, Sharla, so we can tell where we're going. But Cyborg stays blindfolded, and you can't say a word to Cyborg about what you're seeing, Sharla. Got that?"

"I understand," she said. "Maybe I'll recite poetry to him."

"Just keep quiet," Corgan ordered. "Don't talk at all. It's safer that way. Cyborg, try to keep your mind blank. Don't even connect to any messages from your feet about what's underneath your steps. Okay, Sharla, help Cyborg . . ." He was about to say "help Cyborg get out of the *Prometheus* and climb down to the ground," but even that simple comment could channel information to Brigand. Instead Corgan gestured, not using words.

After they'd all disembarked, Corgan and Ananda unloaded the Locker and the dog cage. Standing silently in the rubble-filled pit, Corgan swung his light around, remembering how he'd found the monitors here in boxes half covered with dirt. The crater's crumbled walls reached several meters higher than the top of the spaceship, and now, for the first time in decades, the *Prometheus* stood once again in the place where it had been created, back in those pre-devastation years, when this was a real laboratory and not a bombed-out hole.

Quickly Corgan shone the light on the door to the

tunnel. He wanted to get his group out of there before they inhaled too much contaminated air. A person could breathe a certain amount of dangerous pollution without immediate ill effects, but this deep pit might have collected additional particles from nuclear fallout.

He pried open the door that led to the tunnel, then gestured for Sharla and Cyborg to go first. Because of the blindfold Cyborg stumbled a bit, but Sharla supported him by holding his arm. Once inside the tunnel Corgan began to worry because whatever happened next could be out of his control, determined by chance, that favorite concept of Delphine's. "Fall back a little bit," he muttered to Ananda, shifting his hand to relieve the pressure from the Locker they were carrying. "I want to tell you the rest of what you have to do, and I don't want them to hear."

After she'd slowed down, he told her, "Here's the deal. When we get to the end of the tunnel, you'll go through the door and seal it with mud so it looks undisturbed. Then you sneak up to the main level—I mean really sneak, like, being as invisible as you can. Try to reach Thebos. Tell him we're here, and tell him we need a way to get to the medical center or wherever he wants us to hide."

The greatest uncertainty was whether Ananda would be able to find Thebos—would he still live in his chambers in the center? "If it turns out Thebos is in danger from Brigand," Corgan whispered, "bring him back to this tunnel, and we'll rush him to the *Prometheus* and take off for Wyoming. That's why I checked out the Wyo-DC on the way here."

"Then, why are we bothering to carry the Locker all the

way through the tunnel now?" Ananda asked softly.

"Because Thebos might refuse to go to Wyoming. If he does, we can Locker him right here."

"What if he doesn't want to be Lockered?" Ananda asked.

That stopped Corgan so abruptly he almost lost his grip on the Locker. He'd never even considered that Thebos wouldn't want to be Lockered. Royal hadn't wanted to, but Royal was only fifteen. Thebos was ninety-one! Full of aches and pains and brittle bones, and short of breath and forgetful, he claimed, although Corgan thought that last part was only an act.

"Nah," Corgan disagreed, "there's no way he won't want to."

"Then, I'll do everything you've told me," Ananda said, "as long as I don't run into trouble with the guards. If that happens, I'll knock some heads."

"Just don't let Brigand know where we are!" Corgan warned.

Using his extraordinary ability to calculate time, Corgan could predict precisely when they'd reach the tunnel door—2:40 A.M. At 2:38, after setting down the Locker, he stopped Sharla and gestured to let her know that she and Cyborg should wait where they were.

Corgan moved to the tunnel door, with Ananda following right behind him. As he reached for the handle, her hand shot out to grab his, and she whispered, "Wait!"

"What? We have to hurry."

"I think there's a big flaw in your plan," she murmured softly. "I don't think it's possible for me to get all the way to the medical center without a single person noticing me—the city is never totally empty at any time. I mean, they have street cleaners and other workers out at night, and every single person in the Flor-DC recognizes me. I'm a celebrity here. They'll know I've been missing for a few weeks, and if they spot me, they'll get excited and tell the newspeople right away, and Brigand will find out."

His hand froze on the door handle. What Ananda had said was true. Everyone knew her, and for her to move through the underground chamber, up the elevator, and through the streets to the medical center without being seen was chancy at best.

"You're right," Corgan told her. "Change of plans—you stay here with Sharla and Cyborg, but don't say anything Cyborg can hear. I'll go and get Thebos myself."

"Just be careful," Ananda warned.

Corgan opened the door a crack to peer through it. The underground chamber was dark and seemed empty, so he opened the door wider. After he'd slipped through and Ananda had pulled the door shut behind him, he stood in total darkness for a few seconds, wondering if he should turn on the handheld light but deciding against it. Fumbling in the dark, he felt the outline of the door and began to scoop up dirt to fill the cracks so they wouldn't be visible.

The light, when it blazed, blinded him. As he whirled around, all he could see was a fist holding a thick club that came smashing down on him. Then . . . nothing.

EIGHTEEN

"If you don't lose your head, you'll win." Royal's voice echoed in Corgan's not quite conscious mind. Corgan knew he hadn't lost his head because it hurt so much. As his eyes slowly opened, he tried to reconstruct what had happened, and when. He remembered a sudden bright light and a club streaking down. . . . From the way his head hurt, he must have been bashed pretty hard. He wondered if his skull was cracked.

Where was he now? He saw only four gray walls surrounding a floor smaller than his old virtual-reality Box back in Wyoming.

Where were Sharla, Ananda, and Cyborg? Were they still in the tunnel, or had they been found and pulled out and beaten too? Surely Brigand wouldn't have let his guards hurt them—he had no quarrel with anyone but Corgan. Most likely they hadn't killed Corgan right away because Brigand was saving that pleasure for himself.

He couldn't tell how much time had passed since he got whacked. Crawling on his knees, he reached a wall and sat against it, rubbing his head where it throbbed. As his brain cleared a bit, he looked around again. Bare walls, floor, and ceiling, no glimmer from a light source, and yet he was able to see. But there was nothing to look at. Never in his life had he been so totally without sensory information of any kind. Here there was nothing visual, nothing audible, or even olfactory, like the smell of a jungle. He could feel the floor and the walls, but they communicated nothing, not the slightest vibration that might indicate something was moving outside. No door, no window, just blankness. This was total emptiness.

At first he thought he might be hallucinating, but a tray full of food seemed to glide slowly through one of the walls, becoming visible a centimeter at a time, like a virtual image. When he crawled over to the tray, he found that it was real and that the wall behind it, when he touched it, felt solid. How the devil had the tray moved through that impenetrable wall?

He poked at the food, fake food made from soybeans mostly, but that was what he'd grown up on, and he ate it because there was nothing better to do except count the minutes and seconds, waiting for something to happen. Apparently his time-splitting ability hadn't been erased by the blow to his head, but he still didn't know the actual hour of day.

Three hours and nineteen minutes after he'd started counting, Sharla and Ananda suddenly appeared through the same wall, and again their entrance port vanished instantly. As they rushed to him and hugged him, he asked, confused, "Are you in jail too? Is your cell on the other side of mine?"

"No, we're not locked up," Sharla answered, looking worried about his condition. "Are you all right? Let me see your head. You're not bleeding, but there's a big lump."

"I'm so terribly terribly sorry," Ananda cried. "I swear we didn't speak a word inside the tunnel, and I don't know how the guards caught you, but somehow they must have known you were there. I guess they could see the outline of the tunnel door 'cause you didn't have time to hide it, so they pried it open and pulled us out."

All that planning, all that caution, all for nothing. Discouraged, Corgan leaned back against the wall and asked, "If you two aren't locked up, where did Brigand put you?"

"We're sharing Ananda's rooms in the city," Sharla answered.

Ananda added, "Everything there is just the way I left it. Nothing has been touched, not my clothes or my shoes. . . ." Choking up a little, she added, "Even Demi's dog dish is still there, in the same place it always was."

"And Cyborg's in the apartment on the other side," Sharla was saying. "You're the only one in jail, Corgan, and we all feel horrible about it."

Not as horrible as Corgan felt. "What about Thebos?" he asked. "Is he all right?"

"Yes. He'll come to see you as soon as he can sneak in here," Sharla answered in a rush. "Thebos is just amazing. We were terrified when Brigand declared you an enemy of the revolt and ordered you executed, but Thebos came up with this great idea to stage a face-off battle between you and Brigand. It'll be a spectator sport, Corgan against Brigand, with all the citizens invited."

"But not a fight to the death," Ananda said, "thanks to Thebos. He convinced Brigand."

It was hard to take in all this news, especially with his head throbbing. "You've seen Brigand, Sharla?"

Nodding, she said, "And he isn't sixteen, he's grown up. He did not get Lockered long distance by telepathy, like we thought he might have. He's about twenty-two now, and he's big and brawny and strong, so it's a huge relief that Thebos talked him out of a fight to the death with you."

Corgan's pride withered a little because he'd always believed he could defeat Brigand in a fair fight. But he knew he should be grateful. Since he still felt dizzy from the blow to his head, he stayed sitting on the floor, and the girls sat beside him, cross-legged, one on each side.

One more question swept into Corgan's consciousness. "The Locker! Did Brigand get the Locker?"

Sharla answered, "Like I said, that Thebos is an amazing guy. He was right there when the New Rebel Troopers brought the Locker up from the tunnel, and he managed to slip a dual-core processor out of the mechanism. Then he told Brigand that it must have been damaged during the flight, and he'd have to fix it later. Oh, there's so much to tell you, so much going on out there!"

"But Brigand doesn't know we're visiting you," Ananda reported. "We're being super careful so he won't find out, but he's so busy trying to run the world he doesn't have much time for anything else right now, and that includes Sharla. He got rid of the Supreme Councils, both here and in Wyoming, and no members of the New Rebel Troops know anything about governing. So everything's a mess out there. Things are breaking down everywhere."

Corgan took a deep breath. "So, what's next? What am I supposed to do now? How long is Brigand going to keep me in this cell?"

Ananda and Sharla both looked concerned. "We don't know," Sharla said.

"We're just lucky we got in here to talk to you. We're not supposed to be here—we had to bribe the guard to get in," Ananda added.

"There's a guard outside?"

"Yeah," Sharla answered. "Big, rough-looking guy."

"With shoulders like boulders," Ananda added. "Which matches his head, because he has about as much brains as a rock."

At that the two girls laughed a little, smacking each other's palms.

"How'd you bribe him?" Corgan wanted to know.

Casually, as if the topic weren't too important, Ananda answered, "I told you I'm a celebrity in the Flor-DC. I promised to give him an autographed holographic image of me."

Months ago Corgan had seen how much the Flor-DC

citizens loved Ananda. They not only admired her as the strongest, most athletic woman anywhere, they felt protective of her because they knew about the tragedy that had killed her parents when she was only two.

Sharla told him, "Try to get over that lump on the head and let us figure things out, Corgan. We've got the best minds in the world working for you—Cyborg and Thebos. That's what's giving us hope. We'd better leave now before Cyborg starts wondering where we are and Brigand channels him, and you know how that goes. Good-bye, Corgan. Please do everything to stay safe. I promise you we're doing all we can to keep you alive."

"Wait! Before you go, can you tell me the actual time? What time is it now, and how long have I been in here?" He needed a set point to get his timing ability in sync again.

"You've been here thirteen hours, seven minutes, and twenty-seven seconds," Ananda answered. "Remember, I'm a time-splitter too. And right now it's four thirty-nine P.M. plus some inconsequential seconds."

When they disappeared, Corgan leaped at the wall and tried to figure out how it could vaporize like that to allow things through it and then turn rock solid again in microseconds. He ran his hands over the whole surface and felt nothing. The wall seemed as impenetrable as steel. Feeling weak again, he sank to his knees.

And then the awareness slowly swept over him. Sharla had come to see *him*. She'd connected with Brigand, but she'd managed to get away from him to come to Corgan. And she'd conspired with Cyborg and Thebos to help

Corgan. Sharla was on his side—against Brigand!

He stretched on the floor with his arms over his head, letting it sink in and trying to evaluate. Was he right? Had she really chosen him over Brigand?

Then he rose to his feet. If his friends were trying to set up a fair, impartial, aboveboard match to keep him alive, he'd better do his part. The dizziness was still there. With one hand against the wall he walked the periphery of the cell, staggering a little at first, but concentrating to keep his balance. Then he walked it again without holding on, again and again, going faster each time, until he could stay balanced even with his eyes closed.

After precisely one hour he lay on the floor to sleep. In this confined cell there was no way to tell day from night, no brightening or dimming of the light, so he set up an hourly training schedule to make himself strong. It came into his mind that if his jailers watched him training, they might try to sabotage him by not letting him sleep, but that didn't happen. No lights shone in his eyes, no loud noises bombarded his ears, and the floor, although hard, didn't get cold.

When he awoke in the morning, his breakfast was already there, sitting in the corner, bland but wholesome. Even better, he found a wet cloth he could wash himself with and a bottle of Nutri-Build, the same drink Mendor had given him when he was preparing for the Virtual War. Who was putting these things into his cell?

Another day went by, and he could feel himself grow stronger. Where was Thebos? There was nothing in his cell to distract him, so Corgan's entire attention centered on his body, his reflexes, his speed. And beyond that—his tactics.

Brigand must have an artificial knee. Most likely Thebos had built one for him after Brigand's knee got shot off in their last battle. How could Corgan take advantage of that? He practiced kicking at the height of Brigand's knees until he got so fast he couldn't see his own foot swing, just a blur.

During the breaks he allowed himself he sat on the floor and stared at the wall in front of him, trying to figure out how it dissolved and instantly reformed when something came through it. His jailers were smart—they never sent the food tray through the same spot or at precisely the same hour. Corgan could sit there concentrating on a section of the wall, waiting to pounce, and the food tray would slip through at the other end of the wall before he could reach it, with the wall solidifying behind it fast enough that even Corgan's time-splitting ability couldn't get a grip on it. Only once did he almost make it. When he saw the edge of the tray skim inside, he shot out his arm and hit the mark so quickly that his fingers penetrated two centimeters before the wall hardened, sending such a jolt of pain through his fingertips that he decided he wouldn't try that again.

The next day Thebos arrived suddenly, his pale, sunken eyes brightening with affection as his shaky fingers grasped Corgan's shoulders. Corgan had to remind himself not to squeeze too hard when they hugged each other, but he was overjoyed to see the old man.

"Dear boy," Thebos murmured. "I am so relieved that

you returned safely. And I am so deeply touched that you came back to this city because you were worried about me."

As Thebos's eyes filled with tears, Corgan felt his own eyes stinging. "Are you well? Are you okay?" Corgan asked. "I was afraid Brigand would work you to death."

"Oh . . . Brigand," Thebos answered scornfully with a wave of his hand. "I've been putting on my doddering-old-fool act for Brigand so he doesn't expect much of me. I use a cane, I shuffle, I speak slowly and forget what I'm saying halfway through—it works." As Thebos related that, a chair slipped through the wall for him. Corgan wanted to ask how it was done, that in-and-out-of-the-wall technique, but he might not have much time with Thebos. When the old man sank into the chair, Corgan slid to his knees in front of him, like a penitent asking for a blessing.

"What about the Locker?" Corgan asked. "Will you use it to get young again? Sharla said you disabled it, but you could fix it, and Cyborg could take you back to whatever age you want."

Thebos arranged himself more comfortably in the chair. "Later perhaps. I don't want to fix the Locker now because Brigand would demand to be Lockered, and I don't want him to live forever. He's completely immoral—he should not become immortal."

"Maybe I'll take care of that," Corgan said.

As though he hadn't heard, Thebos continued to speak, drumming his gnarled fingers on the chair arm. "The match between you two will be a great spectacle for the crowds to watch. Since Brigand seized power and things started falling apart, he's been keeping the masses entertained by spectacles—the old bread-and-circuses concept. That was a ploy of the ancient Roman emperors."

Corgan, as so often happened, had trouble following Thebos's meaning.

"Your dual combat," Thebos went on, "your conflict, battle, match, whatever you want to call it—Brigand is now hell-bent on staging it. He desires it to be a public performance with the largest possible audience. And whatever Brigand wants, Brigand gets. For the moment."

Corgan considered that. It would be weird to fight in front of a crowd, but it seemed he didn't have a choice. "Just make sure he doesn't oil his body this time. The last time we fought he was so greased up I couldn't get a good hold on him."

Before he'd finished saying that, Thebos started to shake his head. "No, no, no," he protested. "It's not going to be that way at all. No physical contact. It will all be virtual reality. A new kind of Virtual War."

"What?"

"We devised this so cleverly," Thebos congratulated himself. "Cyborg and I. I know engineering and Cyborg knows his clone-twin better than anyone else does. So we're creating these huge virtual images of you and Brigand, about nine feet tall. There will be a line drawn between the two images that neither of them can step across. You and Brigand will be strapped into wired chairs facing each other, but you'll be seated behind your virtual avatars—"

"Virtual!" Corgan gasped.

453

"Let me finish! You will control the movement of your avatars entirely through your thoughts, because you will be unable to move in the chairs. Think of it, Corgan! A battle controlled only by brain waves. Each of the large images of you and Brigand will be mathematically divided into one hundred sections. As one avatar hits the other, it will take out one section at a time. One hundred blows to destroy an avatar completely, or fewer if you strike a strategic area like the eyes or brain or heart, which will stop your opponent cold."

Corgan could hardly comprehend. "You mean we'll be strapped into chairs and have to move these big images of ourselves *mentally*?"

"Exactly."

"What about the fight-to-the-death part?"

"We've worked it out this way: The winner," Thebos announced, "will decide the fate of the loser. That creates endless possibilities for a thrilling finale."

"I don't like this idea!" Corgan cried, clenching his fists. "Brigand will find some way to make it look like he won."

"Calm down, Corgan! Cyborg and I will watch every move like hawks. We've been brainstorming this ever since you got back. This is by far the safest scenario for you. If you enter into physical combat, you'll lose, because Brigand is a full-grown man now and you're still a youth. Brigand is taller than you and he outweighs you. Give us credit for thinking up this ingenious scheme to offer you a chance!"

"No!" Corgan argued. "I can take him. I've been training."

Thebos gave a little snort, but not of laughter. "Don't

delude yourself, Corgan. You haven't seen Brigand lately. He's bulked up like Goliath. And you're just a David. But you don't understand that reference either, do you? Don't you see? We're trying to save your life."

Raising his head, Corgan declared, "If I die in a real fight, at least I'll die with honor."

"Spoken like a teenage idiot," Thebos scoffed. "The whole idea is for you *not* to die at all." Thebos leaned forward, his watery gray eyes staring straight into Corgan's. "Listen to me, Corgan. You have to wonder why Brigand would even agree to a contest where so much is at stake for him. The answer is that he's supremely confident he'll win. He's an adult now, with a mature brain, and he's a strategist. We've assured him that the contest will be scrupulously fair, and he believes that because his clone-twin is part of the team, so he can check up on Cyborg mentally whenever he wants. What does he have to fear? Nothing! At least as he sees it."

Corgan felt a chill in his chest as Thebos's words sank in.

"On the other hand," Thebos went on, "you spent the first fourteen years of your life training for a virtual war. Some of your skills may have become a bit rusty, but those skills can resurface, I'm confident of that. They're an intricate part of you. They're in your genes. But . . . regardless of the outcome, you don't need to worry. If Brigand defeats you, I'm working on a plan that will whisk you away so you'll be safe from harm."

Corgan rose to his feet, trying to untangle his thoughts. He knew his friends were attempting to save his life, but he didn't want to come off as a coward. "I'm not happy about this, Thebos. It's just another way for me to run away from Brigand again."

Thebos stood up too, shakily. "Once you think things through, you'll realize that this solution is an excellent one. But now I must go, before I'm missed."

Thebos turned and shuffled—the shuffling was real, not pretense, Corgan noticed. When the wall atomized to let him through, Corgan moved so fast he pushed Thebos and himself into it simultaneously, managing to catch Thebos upright on the other side and set him on his feet. "What are you doing?" Thebos cried.

"I'm breaking out," Corgan yelled, throwing his fist into the guard's throat.

Thebos pleaded, "Corgan, wait!" but Corgan was running and the guard was sinking to the ground, clutching his throat.

Corgan recognized instantly where he was—he was familiar with the entire layout of the Flor-DC. He'd had plenty of time to explore it when he'd taken Ananda's dog for walks. Finding his way easily now, he raced toward the center of the city, noticing as he ran that the streets were littered with trash and that people stood around talking when they should have been at their jobs.

He reached the building where the Supreme Council had met, but the elevator didn't operate, so he ran up the stairs three at a time. If Brigand had executed the whole Council, their empty quarters might be a place Corgan could hide while he sorted out what was happening and planned his next move. But the door to the room was locked.

Frustrated, he ran back down into the street. He'd try

to make it to Ananda's rooms and stay there until nightfall, when he could sneak into the medical center with Thebos. He ran toward the moving walkway and leaped over its wall. The second he cleared it he realized the walkway wasn't working, even though he could hear the motor running. The impact sent a jolt of electricity through him, stunning him, and before he could get up again, a dozen New Rebel Troopers surrounded him.

"The shortest escape in history," one of the troopers sneered.

NINETEEN

"Make sure all this is recorded," Brigand was saying to someone near him. "I want it to be broadcast, but not until after I edit it."

The words didn't register with Corgan, who was struggling against the New Rebel Troopers, three on each side of him. At first he'd barely noticed where he was, but when he finally quit struggling, he looked up to see Brigand seated on what looked like a throne—large and gilded with carvings of the same sharks' teeth, sunbursts, snakes, scorpions, and death heads that he had tattooed all over his torso. His chest tattoos were visible, too; he wore a shirt of shimmering transparent cloth that let all his grotesque markings show through.

The tattoo on the left side of his face, from the middle of his forehead down the center of his nose to his chin, looked a little different now because Brigand's face had broadened at the forehead and the jawline. His chin was firmer, his cheekbones more visible, his red eyebrows were thicker, and his eyes seemed set slightly deeper, but the most startling thing about his new appearance was his size.

"Bulked up" was what Thebos had said about Brigand. Big was what Corgan noticed—in height, in the wide shoulders, the arms with bulging muscles, and the deep chest. Corgan couldn't help thinking about sixteen-year-old Cyborg and comparing him with this grown-up version of him. Was this the body Cyborg would have grown into if he hadn't been Lockered? How did Cyborg feel when he saw this adult Brigand; what was it like knowing he'd never be as brawny as this, or as strong as this, no matter how long he lived?

They stared at each other, Corgan defiant, Brigand with an expression of scornful amusement. "So, you came back," Brigand finally said. "You must have missed me a lot."

"It was the bullet that missed you, unfortunately," Corgan said. "Too bad it shot off your knee instead of your head."

One of the New Rebel Troopers looked ready to gut-punch Corgan for that taunt, but Brigand raised his hand. "No, don't crush the little worm. We'll keep him intact for the skirmish."

As Brigand spoke, he didn't quite meet Corgan's eyes; his face turned just slightly to the left. Corgan glanced in that direction and saw the wide lens of a visualizer trained

on the scene. It seemed Brigand wanted this whole preliminary encounter recorded, probably so he could drum up
enthusiasm for the coming match.

"You're not very smart, you know," Brigand told him.
"We discovered that tunnel entrance weeks ago. We kept
it guarded so none of our political prisoners could escape
through it, but mainly because we figured you'd come
back." Brigand waved toward the visualizer lens and
said, "Strike out that last line, men. I don't want it on the
broadcast."

"Why can't we fight right now?" Corgan demanded.
"We're both here in the same space—let's get it over
with. I don't need any fancy virtual games to dress up
our battle so the citizens can have fun watching. This is
between you and me, not between you and me and the
whole world."

"Listen to the little man," Brigand sneered, getting up
from his throne and casually descending the three steps
to the floor. Corgan noticed the slight limp, and also that
Brigand's pants were *not* transparent and were tucked
inside his boots. "You're trying to aggravate me so I'll
destroy you right now," Brigand said. As he came closer,
Corgan saw that Brigand now stood a whole head taller.
"But no, I won't deprive the citizens of their coming entertainment, Corgan. In fact, because I want our match to be
free of any taint of dishonesty or discrimination, I'm going
to send you back to your comfortable lockup and supply
you with the best food in the Flor-DC, with an airbed for
comfortable sleep, and with a woman if you want one. . . ."

"Don't be obscene."

Brigand carried a small whip with a fringed end; as the New Rebel Troopers held Corgan tight, Brigand swept the fringe across Corgan's face, tickling him on the lips. Corgan jerked back and spit, but Brigand quickly moved out of the way. "Such disgusting manners," Brigand said, turning toward the visualizer lens. "And troopers, make sure you put some kind of body-cleansing mechanism in his cell. He smells bad."

At that moment Cyborg rushed into the room, panting. "Hey, Brigand, do you need a negotiator here? The rules for the face-off say there shouldn't be any preliminary harassment."

"Tell that to your undisciplined little friend," Brigand answered as he turned and headed toward the steps of his throne. "He tried to spit at me."

"Hey, undisciplined little friend," Cyborg said, coming close to Corgan and grabbing him around the back of the neck with the artificial hand. "Don't go spoiling everything." As Cyborg pulled Corgan closer and gave him a light punch in the ribs with his real hand, Corgan felt something being slipped inside his LiteSuit.

"How 'bout if I take Corgan back to his cell?" Cyborg asked Brigand. "I mean, I'll accompany his guards while they escort Corgan, and we'll get him tucked in for the night. He needs his sleep and so do you, Brigand. The great face-off is less than twenty-four hours away."

Brigand stared hard at Cyborg. It was strange to observe the two of them, so identical with that flaming red hair, but now separated by an age span of six years. "You claim to be neutral, clone-twin," Brigand said. "Should I trust you?"

"Sure. I don't have to go with Corgan, I can stay here with you. It's your call."

"I think that would be a good call," Brigand said. "Let's invite Ananda and Sharla to join us for a little late-night supper, with lights turned low and soft music. I'll send a couple of New Rebel Troopers to bring the girls."

Corgan's muscles tensed, making the troopers tighten their hold on him. If he could have broken free, he'd have charged at Brigand right there and then, but the troopers holding him were big men, and strong. They dragged him away and back to his cell, but this time when he was shoved toward it, he could see how the entrance and exit worked. An outside switch vaporized the wall to let any object or person be propelled inside without a millimeter to spare and without a microsecond wasted before the wall turned solid again.

There really was an airbed on the floor—when did that arrive? Instead of lying on it, Corgan kicked it in frustration. Then he remembered that Cyborg had slipped something through the neck of his LiteSuit. When Corgan pulled it out, his spirits lifted. It was Mendor, compressed into a little square box. Silently he sent thanks to Cyborg.

He'd never before tried to reconstitute Mendor. Sharla had always condensed the program and later opened it up again. Puzzled, he held the small package in his hand and shook it a little, and as he stared at it, it began to expand. "Hey, great!" he cried, but not too loudly because he didn't want to be heard. "Turn on, Mendor."

In seventeen hundredths of a second the full-blown Mendor images filled the cell, just as they had back in the

Wyo-DC when Corgan thought the whole world existed only in his virtual-reality Box. Mendor's aura was now a shimmering mixture of blues and greens, the mother/father face filling one whole wall of the cell, the other walls pulsating with muted abstract designs.

"This is so much better than on Nuku Hiva," Mendor enthused, "where I had only those flimsy curtains of LiteSuit cloth to project against. Four walls are what I was designed for. How are you, Corgan?"

"Not good. But glad to see you."

Settling more into the mother image, Mendor said, "Oh, I've been having quite the adventure since you and I last spoke in the *Prometheus*. First Sharla opened me, and then she created the iris identification program for Thebos so he could communicate with me."

"With Thebos? Did you communicate with Cyborg, too?" That could have been a bad idea.

"No. It wasn't necessary. I just interfaced with Thebos. And when Thebos and I had finished—with input from Sharla and Cyborg conveyed through Thebos—Sharla reconnected the ID to your own iris pattern, Corgan, so you and I could interface again. Smart girl." A little rose-colored glow crept into Mendor's image, which always happened when Mendor was pleased about something. "Mmm, I'm really enjoying this nice virtual-reality Box," he/she murmured as colors expanded in a rainbow of waves across all four walls.

"It's not a virtual-reality Box, Mendor," Corgan contradicted. "It's a jail cell. And I know I can't get out because New Rebel Troopers are standing guard outside."

"Jail cell or not, it works fine for me. Look, there's your dinner tray." Mendor's face slid back into the nurturing-mother persona. "I want you to eat all of it, Corgan, because it's nourishing and you'll need all your strength."

"Why? I won't even be able to land a punch on that son of a—"

"You'll need your mental strength. Now, start eating and I'll explain what has been happening."

Some of it Corgan already knew, or had figured out. It was Thebos who'd thought up the virtual-war concept, quickly approved by Brigand because he knew it would appeal to the citizens.

"It shouldn't be called a virtual war, Mendor," Corgan broke in. "It's not between the three worldwide federations, it's just a fight between two people, me and Brigand."

"Brigand wants to call it that. You were the hero of the first Virtual War, Corgan; he wants to be the hero of the second. Let him have his little ego trip."

"Little! I don't consider that little."

"Brigand's in charge here in the Flor-DC. He's the ultimate authority. Nothing happens unless he approves it. Your confrontation will be a public challenge. He loves crowds," Mendor went on, "and feeds on their adulation. I'm told he makes speeches where he throws out prizes just to hear people cheer. And that, dear Corgan, will be a problem. Have you thought . . ."

At this Mendor's image began to change into the stern father, the colors darker and more somber. "Have you thought how distracting that will be for you? All that cheering and applause? You will be trying to focus your mental energy on your avatar's movements. A shrieking crowd will break your concentration. Brigand's used to crowd noises, but you're not."

Corgan paused in his eating, although he was enjoying the food, which was real and delicious. "Mendor, you're not remembering the first Virtual War. I was bombarded with sounds—people screaming when they got blown up, land mines exploding, aircraft roaring right over my head—and I didn't lose my concentration."

Mendor's color grayed a little more, a sign that he didn't like to be argued with. "That first Virtual War seemed entirely real, but subconsciously you knew that every sound and image was nothing more than an electronic creation. During this new virtual war real people will surround you, stomping and cheering and booing and, who knows, maybe throwing things at you. This will be distracting, to say the least."

"So what are you saying, Mendor? That I can't do it?"

"No. I'm saying we have about twenty-two hours to work on your powers of concentration. You do have one advantage. Brigand has never developed the kind of self-discipline you had when you trained for the first Virtual War. But Brigand has the genes of a supreme strategist, so he has that particular advantage over you."

Corgan had finished eating, and he shoved the tray against the wall, not caring anymore about the mechanism through which the tray disappeared. "Mendor, I don't understand something," he said.

"What is that?"

"You said Thebos and Cyborg put together the rules

and everything about the contest, and Sharla and Thebos designed the program."

"That is correct." Mendor's color brightened a little, out of interest in where this might be heading.

"So if everyone's so crazy determined to keep me alive, why didn't they just tip the program so I could win?"

Mendor seemed to withdraw, his face becoming larger, sterner, and darker. "You surprise me, Corgan. In fact, I'm quite shocked. What you just asked would be . . . *dishonorable*."

Corgan felt the blood rise to his cheeks. "I'm sorry, Mendor. My brain must have flipped. Maybe it was that whack on the head."

"You were raised to respect virtue, integrity, decency, morality—"

"Mendor, please stop! I do respect them, and I said I was sorry." Corgan didn't know whether to get down on his knees to apologize or just turn off Mendor's program. "It was a stupid thing for me to say, and you've ragged on me enough, so give it a rest, Mendor."

"Remember the oath you spoke every day when you were training for the first Virtual War?"

"Sure, I remember it."

"Recite it now," Mendor demanded.

Corgan stood up straight and raised his right hand. "'I pledge to wage the War with courage, dedication, and honor.' You really think Brigand is going to play by those rules, Mendor?"

"We can't do anything about Brigand, who is entirely *dis*honorable," Mendor answered. "We can keep *your* honor intact. And don't forget for a second that honor matters more than life."

Once, Corgan had believed that. Did he still? Maybe, but lately there was a lot more he wanted to live for. He now belonged to a group of friends who really cared about him: Cyborg, Ananda, Thebos—and Sharla. Especially Sharla. His confidence in Sharla kept growing.

"Stop your dreaming!" Mendor ordered. "It's time to practice." Following Mendor's directions, Corgan took a spoon from the dinner tray and placed it two meters in front of him. Then, as instructed, he stood with his back against the wall.

"This is what you must do," Mendor told him. "We don't have your virtual avatar to practice on, but if you can manage to move this spoon using only your thought waves, you'll be able to control the avatar. Concentrate!"

Corgan stared at the spoon, blocking out everything else in his line of vision. Once, he'd been able to move digital figures without touching them by bringing his hand to within two hundred microns of an image and using his own electromagnetic energy as a force for motion. But those were digital images. This was an actual object, made of photons and electrons but having mass and occupying space. "Focus," Mendor whispered. "Focus, Corgan. Converge your brain waves into a band of pure mental energy. The narrower the better."

Corgan tried. He shut his mind to everything except Mendor's words. "The energy band is two centimeters wide," Mendor murmured. "That's too much! Compress it more. That's better. You must narrow it to one centimeter."

Corgan felt pressure build inside his skull. He became aware of the nerves that connected his eyes to his brain; he could actually see those nerves, colored blindingly bright. The sound of blood pounding in his head grew louder and louder, until he thought it would explode out of his ears. "You're getting closer," Mendor encouraged. "Focus! Try harder."

Corgan pulled the energy from every single neuron in his body, forcing it to fuse into a single luminous thought wave. Then—did he imagine it?—the spoon moved. It clattered on the floor as Corgan sank against the wall, utterly drained.

Mendor looked triumphant. "I'll bet all the electronics in my storage unit that Brigand can't do *that*!" he/she stated, morphing back to the dual-gender image because pride in a prodigy's performance was both a mother thing and a father thing. "Corgan, I am so immensely proud of you. Take a big swallow of Nutri-Build and try it again. See if you can move the spoon farther the next time."

The next time, and the next time, and the next, Corgan managed to move the spoon. Mendor was a relentless taskmaster. Or mistress. But he/she stopped the practice session right before Corgan was ready to abandon the whole contest and concede everything to Brigand.

"No, you will not surrender," Mendor ordered. "If you surrender, or if Brigand wins, he has the right to choose your fate. Do you want to let him make that choice?"

Corgan mentally ran over all the tortures Brigand might choose to exterminate him with. Death by being thrown into the toxic waters of the Atlantic, an ocean full of monstrous mutations that would love to shred a human and eat him. Or death by being stripped naked, hung upside down in the city center, and stoned by the citizens. Or death by having his body parts chopped off one by one. Whatever death Brigand chose for Corgan, it would be brutal and spectacular so the masses could watch and be entertained, unless they couldn't stop puking.

TWENTY

With Mendor surrounding him on all four walls, Corgan got prodded to practice, to eat properly, to sleep enough, and to focus, focus, focus, until he got so tired of the word *focus* he started reversing the letters in his mind to *suc-off*.

One hour before the battle was scheduled to start, his brain felt like a jangling mass of biological neurons tangled with invasive electronic filaments. At that moment a brand-new LiteSuit of translucent material appeared in his cell.

"It's blue!" Mendor exclaimed. "Your favorite color. You can put it on right now, because while you slept, I cleansed you all over, but gently, so you wouldn't wake up."

Corgan hoped it was Mendor the Father who'd cleansed him, not Mendor the Mother. When he lived in his old virtual-reality Box in the Wyo-DC, he wouldn't have worried about such things, but now he was older and more squeamish.

After he got dressed, Mendor bombarded him with last-chance instructions for thirty-seven minutes and fourteen hundredths of a second, then stopped. "Your muscles are awfully tense," he/she said.

"What did you expect? I might be going to my death."

"Corgan!" Mendor protested. "All your friends are trying to prevent that." In the next breath Mendor murmured soothingly, "Let me massage those knots out of your muscles." Because Mendor was the most advanced program in the world, he/she managed to knead every muscle in Corgan's body all at the same time. It definitely helped. He felt better until four New Rebel Troopers appeared, entering through the wall.

"Time to go," one of them said. "You must be mental. We heard you talking to yourself for the last twenty-four hours."

"Wouldn't you be mental if you had to fight Brigand?" another trooper asked. "'Cause this kid's gonna lose, and we know what Brigand's Instrument of Fate is." He started to laugh.

"What are you talking about?" Corgan demanded. "What Instrument of Fate?"

"It's what Brigand's gonna use on you when he wins," the fourth trooper explained, "because the rules say the winner gets to decide the fate of the loser."

Growing alarmed, Corgan asked, "What's my Instrument of Fate for Brigand if I win?"

"How should we know?" The trooper shrugged. "If you didn't already get one, I guess you don't have any. But you really don't need one, because you're gonna lose. Come on, now. Move!" They grabbed him so roughly he didn't have a chance to say good-bye to Mendor, who was invisible and inaudible to the New Rebel Troopers.

Thousands of people were jammed into the city center, and another hundred thousand would be watching the challenge broadcast to all parts of the city through the visualizer. As Corgan arrived, he heard the crowds cheering, whether for Brigand or Corgan or just because of the free entertainment, there was no way to tell.

One of the guards pointed and said, "Over there is Brigand's Instrument of Fate." It stood next to the painted boundaries of the battle area. Although draped by cloth from top to bottom, it looked menacing. Nearly three meters tall, its shape was wide, bulky, and angular. Could it be a torture rack? A gallows? The troopers kept holding Corgan so tightly he wondered if he'd have to fight the war that way, with four burly punks hanging on to him.

Where was Thebos? Corgan scanned the crowd as much as possible, turning only his head because the rest of him was held immobile. He couldn't catch sight of Thebos. Maybe getting jostled in a crowd this size would have been too difficult for him, so he'd decided to watch the match on the telescreen in the medical center.

Corgan noticed Sharla and Cyborg standing on the

line that divided the battle area into two halves. It didn't bother him, at least not too much, that they'd been positioned in the center between Brigand's and Corgan's positions—it made them appear neutral, he supposed. *Were* they neutral? Both of them had strong ties to both Brigand and Corgan. Yet when Sharla looked at Corgan, he could tell from her eyes that she was scared for him, that she was silently sending him her support. Cyborg, though, stared straight ahead.

To the left of Corgan hung a score panel showing black-and-white outlines of two figures he guessed were meant to be the avatars. Each of the drawings had been sectioned into a grid of one hundred blocks—those must be the areas he'd have to hit, one after the other, on the actual avatar warrior figure. Above the drawings a sign posted the scores, now showing zero and zero, with BRIGAND lettered on one side and CORGAN on the other. He wondered if the Flor-DC citizens were betting on the final score. Or maybe the citizens of all three federations were watching from all over the world, via fiber-optic cable.

There was a sudden disturbance across the square. The crowd surged apart as though cleaved by a knife, backing up in waves as the noise level rose. Brigand had arrived, and not just arrived, he'd made a grand entrance. Only when he came close to the cleared battle area did Corgan get a look at him. He had on a *cape*, for crud's sake! It swept from his shoulders almost to the floor, a gold cape decorated with stars and moons and galaxies. Who was he supposed to be—Mr. Andromeda? When he stopped, he raised his arms, pumped his fists, and turned around in a quick circle, causing the cape to swirl out around him. People cheered. Corgan felt like heaving.

Next, two heavy armchairs were carried in and set down on each end of the arena, one of them only a meter in front of Corgan. It was then that Cyborg stepped forward, and the crowd grew hushed.

"People of the Florida domed city," Cyborg began, his voice amplified so loudly it echoed three or four times. "We are here to witness a contest between Corgan, the hero of the first Virtual War, and Brigand, the ruler of the Flor-DC, with the winner to decide the fate of the loser."

Cheers erupted. These people seemed to cheer over anything, Corgan thought.

"I'm going to state the rules of the battle," Cyborg continued. "Each contestant will be strapped to a chair, unable to move. Each will be represented by an avatar—you people out there will be able to see both avatars, but Brigand will see only Corgan's, and Corgan will see only Brigand's. The two contestants will control their avatars entirely by brain waves, not by touch."

Cyborg paused, waiting for quiet. "Each avatar is two hundred forty centimeters tall, and the surfaces of both avatars have been divided evenly into one hundred sections, from head to toe and from the left side to the right side. Each division is a square that measures twelve centimeters on all four sides. When one opponent strikes another opponent, the section where the blow lands will disappear. You can follow this," Cyborg said, "by looking at the score panel up there, because when a section gets knocked out, its position on the grid will turn black."

Corgan turned to study the grids. They'd been laid out with such precision it had to be the work of Thebos. Since he didn't know whether the grid lines would be visible on the actual avatars, he tried to memorize the sections' positions—over the heart, over the eyes, and there was one over the knee he might try to hit. No, he told himself, that would be stupid. He'd be fighting a digital avatar, not the real Brigand. Brigand had a bad knee, but the avatar wouldn't. *Think logically,* he commanded himself.

Cyborg was continuing, "If a contestant knocks out all one hundred grid sections, he'll win, obviously. But he can also win if he obliterates all the vital organs of the opponent's avatar so it can't fight any longer."

That's the clue, Corgan told himself. *Go for the vital organs.* How could he tell where they were, though, if he could see only the front surface of the avatar? The eyes would be obvious, but where was the heart located? Somewhere in the chest, but according to the grid on the diagram, the left side of the chest where the heart ought to be was divided into four square sections. The heart might be behind any of them; Corgan didn't know much about anatomy. And the avatar would be moving the whole time, making it hard to zero in on any one area.

"Now the opponents will go to their chairs."

Brigand strode over to his chair. He looked commanding as he turned and smiled toward the visualizer lens.

Corgan was shoved to his chair by four New Rebel Troopers, who immediately strapped him into it. Metal bands coiled around his wrists, elbows, and biceps. Other bands bound his thighs, knees, and ankles. A softer band of some other material circled his forehead—that's where the electronics were located. If he sat perfectly still, the bands didn't hurt. That was good. It would remind him to forget his body and concentrate on his brain waves.

Cyborg was still speaking. "The battle will last as long as it takes for one avatar to be destroyed. As soon as the battle ends, the winner will announce the fate of the loser. You can see over there"—he pointed—"that Brigand's Instrument of Fate is already in place. I mean, you can't see it because it's covered up, but that's where it is."

Cyborg had started to sweat. "Uh, one more thing. We gave names to the avatars so you could keep them straight. We . . . abbreviated . . . 'Corgan's avatar' and 'Brigand's avatar.' Corgan's will be called Cavatar, and Brigand's will be called Brave."

Oh, great! Corgan thought. Brave and Cavatar? Who came up with that? It sounded like Brigand's was a warrior and Corgan's was tooth decay.

"So," Cyborg cried out, his voice cracking, "let the games begin."

Four and three-quarters seconds rushed by before Corgan comprehended the mechanics of this battle. He was looking through the eyes of his own avatar at Brigand's, Brave, which lurched toward the center line that divided the battlefield. Brave was so grotesque that Corgan had to fight his shock at Brave's appearance. His body was half as wide as it was tall, naked except for a narrow loincloth that barely covered what it was supposed to cover. His bulging thighs looked like moldy barrels, and across his chest sinews stretched as thick as cables over blood red skin that resembled slabs of raw beef.

Worst of all was the head. Brave's forehead bulged like a gorilla's. His yellow hair hung down over his eyes like snakes, and the eyes burned like coals. Ugliest was the raging open mouth that showed pointy black teeth and a monstrous, meaty tongue. Corgan had to take in all this in a fraction of a second because Brave stood at the line, goading Corgan with roars of "Approach me, you coward!"

Concentrating his brain energy, Corgan moved Cavatar to the line. Brave's first blow hit Cavatar in the chest. When Corgan glanced at the scoreboard to see just where he'd been struck, Cavatar got hit again. That was a lesson quickly learned: Don't look at the scoreboard. He focused his energy force on a point in Brave's throat, wanting to stop the roars, but before he could strike, Brave hit Cavatar in the groin.

The crowd yelled and screamed at that, but Corgan knew he had to block out the noise and make some hits, or this battle would be over before he'd landed a single blow. Looking through Cavatar's eyes, he sent his avatar's fists swinging out—one, two, three, four hits against Brave. But then the voice of an invisible referee rang out, "Not valid. Cavatar crossed the line."

Corgan groaned inwardly. He desperately wanted to look at the scoreboard again to see if he had any points at all, so he thrust both of Cavatar's fists forward and in a fraction of a second managed to take a quick glance. Brigand seven; Corgan one. Frustrated, he groaned out loud and heard the groan come out of his own Cavatar, magnified enough to sound fearsome.

And then, like a bolt of lightning, the prophecy tore into his consciousness as powerfully as though Royal and his grandfather were standing next to him. *"If you don't lose your head, you'll win."*

That was it! He had to protect Cavatar's head. And the opposite—*destroy Brave's head*! Electrified, Corgan let out another roar, which slowed Brave for seven tenths of a second, enough for Cavatar to land two more hits, one to Brave's cheek and the other to his forehead. The crowd yelled. This was more like it. Corgan was just about to hit him again when Brave's hoarse, gravelly voice yelled, "Watch your eyes."

Instinctively Corgan raised Cavatar's hands in front of his eyes to protect them, but instead of going for the eyes, Brave hit Cavatar in the chest. Corgan had been suckered! *Never react to what Brave yells,* he ordered himself. Had Cavatar's heart been knocked out? No, he seemed to be moving well enough. Once again Corgan tried to go after Brave's head, and this time the hit scored big. He took out one of Brave's eyes, and the monstrous Brave couldn't scream because a second punch tore out his throat.

Now Corgan blocked out everything except the need to fight. He didn't feel the bands that strapped him to his chair, didn't hear the yells of the crowd, didn't care about checking the scoreboard. He could feel his blood pumping with the desire to destroy Brave, could feel the neurons in his brain throb with impulses he channeled into waves so strong Cavatar surged forward, his fists pounding. And after eight and a half minutes Brave was beginning to fumble. His blows still landed, but Cavatar was making more hits.

Then Corgan misjudged and Brave knocked off one of Cavatar's hands. Corgan wasn't too worried; Cavatar could hit with his other hand, which he did, blinding Brave in his remaining eye. But Brave still didn't quit. He stood toe-ing the line, swinging wild punches so fast that Cavatar had trouble getting past those massive arms. Corgan wanted to get to the brain, to wipe out every section of Brave's skull the brain might lurk behind. When Corgan's Cavatar lost both feet, he balanced on the stumps of his ankles and swung upward from beneath Brave's pivoting arms. Luckily, Corgan couldn't feel his avatar's pain.

Next Brave gave a kick and sheared off the top of Cavatar's head. Corgan panicked! *"If you don't lose your head . . ."* Another split-second glance at the scoreboard showed that Cavatar had lost only one part of the left lobe of his brain. Could Cavatar still fight? He had three quarters of his brain left and an eye that could see Brave's ravaged face. He landed four more punches to Brave's head. That did it. Brave fell to the floor, where Cavatar pounded him again and again with his one remaining fist until only a few random pieces of Brave were left—one hand, one thigh, an elbow, and a piece of his heart. Brave was dead.

Instantly the chair straps sprang open. Corgan could stand. Bewildered by the roar of the crowd—were they cheering for *him*?—he just stood there. Suddenly a man rushed forward and grabbed him, pulling him to the center of the arena, where he raised Corgan's hand high. The cheers grew louder.

"Who are you?" Corgan asked the man.

"It's me, Thebos," he answered. "I got Lockered so I could get you out of here fast if you lost. I'll explain later."

So many shocks, one after the other! Corgan would never have recognized Thebos. He had a full head of curly brown hair and eyes that gleamed with energy. His skin was as taut as his muscles.

"How old are you?" Corgan asked in awe.

"Thirty. But look at the crowd, Corgan! They're cheering for you. You won!" Lofting Corgan's wrist, Thebos cried, "Folks, let's show our appreciation for Corgan here. The hero of the first Virtual War is once again a hero—of our own virtual war."

This time the roar was deafening.

Brigand would have slumped in defeat, except that his head was still strapped to the back of his chair. His face showed fury and hatred as Sharla, Cyborg, and Ananda rushed to Corgan, hugging him, slapping his back, congratulating him. Corgan's brain was still spinning when Thebos nudged him and told him, "You need to say something to these people. They want to hear your voice, Corgan."

As the visualizer lens trained on Corgan, the crowd's noise tapered off in anticipation. "I just want to say . . . ," Corgan began. "I mean . . . maybe now the Flor-DC can be returned to the citizens," he shouted. "There's a brilliant man here who can clean up the city and make your lives better again. He's right here—Mr. P. T. Thebos." This time it was Corgan who raised Thebos's arm in triumph, and the cheers doubled in volume. "And Ananda is your star, citizens," Corgan shouted. "Welcome her home to the Flor-DC."

Ananda pumped her own fists in a gesture of celebration, turning from side to side, nodding and smiling like the champion she was. Not wanting to intrude on Ananda's moment, Sharla and Cyborg stepped back, but Corgan couldn't keep his eyes off Thebos. He'd seen Sharla Lockered, and Cyborg and Delphine, but the transformation of that ninety-one-year-old elder into this young, supple, quick-moving, quick-talking man was phenomenal.

"*Nan*-da, *Nan*-da, *Nan*-da," the crowd kept chanting, but Ananda said, "Corgan, this is your party, not mine." When she raised her hands for quiet, the chanting died down, except for one high, shrill female voice that rang out from the crowd.

"What's your Instrument of Fate, Corgan? What'll you do to Brigand?"

"I don't—," Corgan started to say, but Thebos muttered, "Stop! Don't try to answer."

"Uh . . . I'll be choosing that tonight," Corgan told the crowd.

Then another loud voice shouted, "Show us Brigand's Instrument of Fate. What was he going to do to you?"

Corgan looked around at his friends, then told Ananda, "You go ahead," and she strode across the square to the tall, shrouded object. When she took the cloth in her hand, the crowd grew so hushed Corgan could hear a baby whimpering. With a somber expression Ananda pulled off the cloth to reveal . . . a guillotine!

"He was going to cut off my head!" Corgan gasped as, behind him, Sharla let out a cry of horror. *The dream!* Once again Royal's grandfather's words rang in Corgan's head, this time in a different pattern. *If you* don't *win, you'll lose your head.*

Corgan felt an icy shock creep up his spine, and in that second he became a believer.

TWENTY-ONE

Sharla was crying, her arms wrapped tightly around Corgan's neck. "Brigand really planned to kill you!" she wept. "I thought he was just messing with your mind, messing with all of us, but he meant it. You were right . . . and Thebos was right. . . ."

Though he tried to comfort her, Corgan felt pretty shaken too. "Can we end this now?" he asked Thebos and Cyborg. He wasn't used to standing up before throngs of people and trying to think of what to say, and he wanted to be alone with Sharla.

"It's up to you," Thebos answered.

Cyborg said, "You're the winner, Corgan. You get to make the rules, at least for today." Cyborg seemed as unnerved as the rest of them by the grisly instrument of death that stood nearby, seeming to loom more massive than it actually was.

"What do you want to do with Brigand?" Thebos asked. "Should we put him in the cell where you were?"

"Yes, but be sure to disconnect the mechanism that lets the cell's wall dissolve. I don't want Brigand to get out," Corgan said.

At Corgan's signal troopers released Brigand from the heavy chair. Brigand stood and straightened himself to his full height, then raised his chin and stomped through the square as if he were leading the troopers rather than being led, as though he were the victor rather than the defeated. "Don't let him get away," Corgan shouted. "Hold him! Tie his hands." Brigand threw a look not just of contempt, but of pure hatred toward Corgan and the friends around him.

Some of the citizens started to leave the city square, until Corgan said, "Let's go, Sharla," and took her hand to lead her away.

Then, in a rush, a few dozen people surged forward. In the same way they'd chanted for Ananda they began to yell, "*Cor*-gan, *Cor*-gan, *Cor*-gan," wanting to reach out and touch the new celebrity.

"Run!" Corgan yelled to Sharla, and they did, all the way to the medical center, where Corgan slapped his palm into the DNA identifier to force open the door. They barely got in before the herd of admirers stampeded outside the center, pounding on the door. "That was close," Corgan gasped. "I don't like this hero stuff."

Inside, Corgan and Sharla were surrounded again, this time by the members of the Robotic Nurse Corps. "We watched everything!" Nurse Eleven proclaimed in a voice that bubbled with enthusiasm, totally unlike the bland, controlled tone the robotic nurses usually used. "Congratulations, Corgan!" And then Eleven proudly added, "*I* was the one who took care of Corgan after his drowning when he first came to the Flor-DC."

"That's right, Eleven. You're the one who zapped me with an arc gun when I tried to get out." Eleven's human-like face blushed a pale pink until Corgan said, "But I forgive you, Eleven. I deserved it."

Right then the door swung open and slammed shut immediately as Thebos ducked inside—the new Thebos, whose appearance was still so startling that Corgan's brain needed a quarter of a second longer than normal to process it.

"Wow!" Thebos exclaimed. "People are so celebrity obsessed! Maybe you should hide out here in the center for a couple of days till the furor dies down."

"Yeah, maybe, but listen, Thebos," Corgan began, "we hardly had a chance to talk out there, and I really want to hear about your Lockering. When did you do it, why did you do it, why did you choose thirty years old—the whole story."

"You mean right now?" Thebos asked. "With all your fans battering the door?"

"Yeah, sure, we can talk now, you and me and Sharla, too. Eleven, can you give us an empty room? And keep it private?"

"Gladly." Spinning on her wheels, Eleven rolled along the hall to the room where Cyborg had recuperated from the crash into the Atlantic. She opened the door and said, "I'll allow no one else to come in. If anyone tries to, I'll zap them with that same arc gun." Was that a little robotic humor? Corgan chuckled.

As Corgan and Sharla sat on the edge of the hospital bed and Thebos pulled up a stool to face them, Corgan's eyes scanned this room he remembered so well—the stark whiteness of the walls, the intercom voices that had seemed to come out of nowhere, the feeling of isolation.

"So!" Thebos began. "You want the whole story? Here it is. About two hours ago I found out that Brigand planned to guillotine you if he won the face-off. One of the troopers, who is a decent guy, slipped the information to me. Right away I tried to figure out my options. Dismantle the guillotine? Couldn't do that because it was guarded by half a dozen troopers."

Thebos ran a hand through that thick, curly brown hair that Corgan wasn't used to—and neither was Thebos, perhaps, because he kept touching it. "The smartest option would have been to get you out of your cell and manage an escape," he said. "But I made a stupid mistake. I mentioned that to Cyborg, forgetting that Brigand clues in to everything Cyborg hears. The next thing I knew, seven hulky troopers burst into my quarters and told me I was under arrest."

Sharla broke in, "I was there in the room when the troopers came and so was Cyborg. Three of the thugs made us leave and marched us over to the arena. They told us we had to stand on that white line till the face-off started. But . . . tell me what happened to you after we left, Thebos."

"Well, fortunately the troopers hadn't tied me up," Thebos continued. "They just locked me in and left me there. I was all alone in my quarters—with the Locker! And of course the troopers had no clue what the Locker was, if they'd even noticed it when they were there. It took me less than a minute to get it in working shape again. I'm an engineer extraordinaire, remember?"

"I remember." Corgan had once studied the blueprints for the *Prometheus*, the most amazingly designed flying vehicle ever built. Thebos was a creative genius, for sure, maybe the greatest that had ever lived.

Looking intently at Corgan, Thebos told him, "I knew I had to save you if you lost the challenge. But how? There I was, a doddering ninety-one-year-old, too feeble to knock down the door and fight the guards. And even if I did escape, I'd be noticed right away because everyone in the city would recognize me. Unless I became invisible . . ."

"Invisible!" Corgan gasped.

Thebos had begun to grin. "So then I thought, what better way to become invisible here in the Flor-DC than to shave sixty years off my appearance? Nobody would recognize me. I'd already figured out the way the Locker worked and that I could trigger it from inside."

"You Lockered *yourself*?"

"How am I going to tell this story if you guys keep interrupting?" But Thebos was laughing now. "So I went into the Locker as an old fool, and I came out as a . . .

well, what you see here. Next I pulled the pillow-covered-by-a-blanket trick to make it look like I was in bed. Then I pounded on the door and told the guards that they'd locked me in the room by mistake, along with the old man, and I pointed to the bed. Of course the guards didn't recognize the new young Thebos, so they let me out." Thebos laughed even harder. "And then . . . they apologized for locking me in!"

"Holy . . . !" Corgan blurted out. "I can hardly believe it."

"Pretty amazing, huh?" Thebos agreed.

"But," Sharla began, "Corgan won the fight, so he didn't need you to rescue him after all. It was a matter of chance, wasn't it? Delphine talked about chance; she said other words for it were 'fortuity,' 'accident,' and 'fortune.'"

The amusement faded from Thebos's face. "You're right," he murmured, serious now. "I took a chance because I wanted to rescue Corgan, but that turned out to be unnecessary. And here I am young again, without a reason for being that way. I guess I'll have to find a new purpose for my life." In the quiet moment that followed, the three of them looked at one another, their expressions showing relief that things had turned out so well, but uncertainty about this pivotal point in their lives. Thebos stood up then and said, "I should go find Cyborg and Ananda and tell them how this all happened too. They didn't get a chance to hear the whole story. Do you two want to come with me? Or . . ."

"No," Corgan and Sharla both replied in the same breath. "We'll stay here for a while," Corgan added.

After the door had closed behind Thebos, Corgan

asked, "Can you believe it? What a guy! Do you think he's sorry he's young now?"

"Why would he be? He's going to live forever," Sharla answered.

Corgan nodded. "And so are you, Sharla. But once, in this very room where we are now, I thought you weren't going to live at all. This is where they brought you after the Harrier crashed," he told her. "They put you onto this bed right here. You were all pale and bloody, and the robotic nurses said you might die. I was so scared!"

Sharla took his hand and said, "When I saw that guillotine today, I was terrified that you could have died too, Corgan. I don't ever want to lose you."

For a moment he was silent. Then, pressing her hand, he asked, "Does that mean it's you and me now? No more Brigand?"

As Sharla moved closer to him, she raised her face, her blue eyes steady on his. "Brigand lost me a long time ago, back in the Wyo-DC when he executed the members of the Wyo Supreme Council. He said They were bad people, but that wasn't true. You and I knew Them, Corgan—maybe They didn't care enough about the citizens, but They weren't cruel. Just thoughtless."

"Wait. Back up. To the first part of that, the part about Brigand losing you a long time ago." All those months Corgan had been longing for Sharla, believing she was committed to Brigand—but she really wasn't? "Why didn't you tell me?"

Seeing the uncertainty on his face, she answered, "I just . . . wasn't ready. Right from the beginning I've known you're going to be a great leader. Maybe I've been afraid that if I got too close to you, I'd lose my identity. I want to be my own person, Corgan. I've always made my own choices and I always will. You're strong and you're growing stronger, and now you're a hero again. It's just . . . I don't want to fade into the shadows if I stand beside you. I guess that sounds selfish—"

"No, it doesn't, and you won't fade. How could you? You're pure gold," he said, holding her tightly.

"Pure." She smiled at him. "You were always worried about that, too, but it's true. And I know now that we'll be good together, because with you I can be stronger than I am if I'm alone." Her face was so close that the kiss was only millimeters away.

"Hold that thought," he said, pulling back just a little. "Eleven!" he shouted to the ceiling. "Turn off every monitoring device in this room, hear? Both visual and audio. I don't want anyone spying on us, no robots and no humans. And turn off all the lights in here—we don't need them."

The room became dim, then dark, then totally black. "Okay, now!" Corgan said.

He was the world's greatest controller of time, able to divide it into microseconds, but for the next while, time stopped as he shared with Sharla all his hopes and ambitions for their lives, now that he still had a life. When at last he opened the door to peer into the hall, the light blinded him a bit. Taking Sharla's hand, he said, "Let's go to Thebos's quarters. Everyone ought to be there by now. I think they'll be glad to see us."

TWENTY-TWO

Corgan and Sharla heard music. The closer they got, the louder the music boomed, and when they threw open the door, they found a party in full swing, literally, with Thebos, Ananda, and Cyborg dancing around the room. "Like this!" Thebos was shouting as, with arms straight out, he bounced on one foot and pivoted around, holding his other leg hip-high. Where once his clothes had hung loose on his frail body, they now strained tightly across his shoulders, chest, and thighs.

"Here are the young lovers," Thebos shouted out.

"We were just talking, that's all," Corgan said, smiling. "You know, like conversation."

"Yeah. Sure." Thebos chuckled.

But it was true. In the darkness of that medical room Corgan and Sharla had talked and planned and decided what should be done, where they should go, what they could contribute to their world. Without a pause in his wild twirling Thebos cried, "Corgan and Sharla, come over here and form a circle with us. I'm teaching everyone to dance Greek."

They clasped hands with the others and scrambled to follow Thebos's instructions. "The music sounds a little bit like music from India," Ananda mentioned, laughing. "My grandma called it *bhangra*."

"This is pure Greek," Thebos assured her, panting a little. "All together now—boy, girl, boy, girl. Stay in a circle and watch my feet—step, step, step, skip a little, take another step forward, step back, hold one another's hands and hold them up high. It's how we used to dance at Greek weddings. I haven't danced in fifty years—it feels so good! *Hopa!*"

Even Corgan, who didn't much like dancing, got caught up in the joy of the moment. It had been a wild day: whipping Brigand at the challenge, seeing the guillotine that Brigand had had in store for him, but most important, knowing at last that Sharla loved him. So he stomped and kicked and yelled "*Hopa!*" every time Thebos did, even though he had no idea what *hopa* meant. Except that it must be Greek. Like Thebos.

When at last they were all winded, Thebos turned off the Greek music and they sank to the floor, still in a circle. Smiling, they congratulated one another, because each one of them had played a big part in the day's success. "Hey, I never knew," Corgan asked, "what did Cavatar look like?"

"I'll show you." With a wave of his hand Thebos illuminated the walls, those same walls that had once been covered with equations about thrust and propellant and zero gravity. And there, looming over all of them, was Cavatar.

Corgan studied his alter ego. Cavatar was nowhere near as ugly as Brave had been. He looked just as big, but the hair on his head was short and black, and his skin was tan, not meat colored. "Who designed him?" Corgan asked.

"I did," Sharla answered, settling against his chest. "Thebos designed Brave."

"Well," Thebos began, "take a look at us now. Here we are, all together, and Brigand is in the cooler. I think it's time for you to tell us, Corgan, what his fate will be."

Corgan gazed around at the circle of his friends, the best and only friends he'd ever had in his whole life. But he shook his head. "You'll find out in the morning, which is now about nine hours, thirteen minutes, and twenty-seven and three hundredths of a second in the future, or at least it was when I started this sentence. Let's talk about anything else."

After an awkward silence Ananda suggested, "Like our plans. We'll talk about our plans and tell what we're going to do now." She linked her fingers into Cyborg's, smiling up at him.

"Well, first," Cyborg announced, smiling back at her, "Ananda's going to be a mother."

"What!" Corgan straightened up so fast he made Sharla's head bounce.

Ananda giggled. "He's talking about the puppies. In a few weeks Diva will have Demi's puppies, or clones, I should call them. And I decided I'm not going to get Lockered until I'm at least eighteen so I can try to catch up a little bit to Cyborg's mental acuity. There! Did I use that word right? *Acuity*?" she asked Cyborg.

"You're learning." He pulled her against him.

It was a loving circle: Cyborg and Ananda, Corgan and Sharla; only Thebos sat alone, probably thinking about Jane Driscoll up there in the space station with her husband and son. "What about you, Thebos?" Cyborg asked.

"Personally?" Thebos shrugged. "I haven't had a personal life for so long I'll have to ease into it. But other things first," he answered. "If I'm going to live forever, I'll have a long time to work on Earth's problems. I'd like to restore radio communication so we don't have to rely on fiber-optic cables, which break down too often. Then I'd like to work on cleaning the atmosphere so people don't have to be confined to domed cities. I mean, look at Nuku Hiva. Why is the air breathable there but nowhere else? I'd like to go there and find out."

Corgan got an image in his mind of Thebos meeting Delphine. What an interesting possibility that could turn into—Delphine and Thebos, those two brilliant scientists staying young forever, while Royal grew old by choice.

"But even before that," Thebos continued, "we have to restore reasonable governance to this city. Who's with me on that?"

"Ananda and I are," Cyborg answered. "We'll work with you."

494

"Excellent. And also I want to build that new zero-gravity spaceship. *Prometheus Two*. If the three of us—Cyborg and Ananda and I—gain enough influence in the new Flor-DC government, we'll persuade the citizens to make retractable doors in the dome, like in the Wyo-DC. That way I can launch *Prometheus Two*."

A second spaceship? "Why do you need another *Prometheus*?" Corgan asked, his hopes rising. "The first one still flies."

"Let me answer that with another question," Thebos said. "What are your plans, Corgan? And I assume they include Sharla."

Everyone turned toward them, waiting for their answer. Corgan inhaled, then said softly, "We'd like to go back to the Wyo-DC. That was our home. The New Rebel Troops have probably wrecked things there by now. Maybe if we go back, we can help put the place together again."

Before Corgan had finished, Thebos began to nod. "Somehow I figured that was what you'd want. That's why I plan to build *Prometheus Two*, so you can have *Prometheus One*. It's yours, Corgan. Yours and Sharla's. You can fly it back to Wyoming any time you want."

Elated, Corgan and Sharla hugged each other, and after that there was a lot of group hugging. Then Corgan suggested that everyone get some sleep, because tomorrow would be a mind-busting day. Instead of moving into separate rooms, they all arranged themselves on the floor of Thebos's quarters. Blankets weren't necessary; they kept one another warm.

Corgan actually slept. Maybe it was sensing Sharla near

him, maybe it was knowing she would go with him to the Wyo-DC, maybe it was feeling like a hero again. For the first time in many nights his sleep was dreamless. And then, before he was ready, morning arrived.

"Time to proceed with Brigand's fate?" Thebos asked, glancing around the room. All of them sat up quickly, rubbing sleep from their eyes but very alert.

"Where is . . . ?" Corgan asked.

Thebos seemed to know what he meant. "I had it moved into one of the medical rooms."

"Right. First, have the guards bring Brigand here to your quarters, Thebos. If Brigand has anything to say before I create his fate, I want everyone to hear it."

Corgan didn't feel too nervous, which made him think that what he was planning was the right thing to do. The others stayed very quiet, especially Cyborg, who looked pale and tousled. Ananda reached up to smooth his wild red hair.

Not long afterward the door flew open and Brigand filled the doorframe. From behind, two unfamiliar guards pushed Brigand into the room so hard he stumbled, falling onto one knee right in front of Corgan. Glaring up, he snarled, "I'm not down here begging for mercy. This stupid artificial knee gave out. It's a piece of crap, just like Thebos is a piece of crap. Where is that freaky old geek? Did he die finally?"

"Oh, he's probably around somewhere," Thebos answered. Since Brigand didn't recognize him, the irony was wasted.

"Wait outside the door," Corgan told the guards, and

closed it in their faces. "Brigand," he said, looking down at him, "you should say good-bye to all these good people because you won't have another chance to."

"You're going to kill me?" he sneered. "Corgan the avenger is going to destroy Brigand?"

Corgan answered sharply, "I just want you to say your good-byes while you can."

Brigand stared around him, hostility on his face. "There's no one in this room I give a crap about," he declared. "Do your dirty deed, Corgan, whatever it is. You're a sniveling little failure. You won that face-off only because I let you."

"As if I believe that," Corgan answered.

Brigand taunted, "It's nice you decided not to kill me until this morning. I've had a whole night to mess with your mama."

"I don't have a mama," Corgan told him, anxious to end this waste of time.

Still on his knees, Brigand looked amused as he said, "Sure you do. The mama who raised you, the one that turned from a mama into a papa when you were bad. Mama, papa—who knows what gender Mendor is, but whatever, I played with it."

Even kneeling in defeat Brigand managed to arouse anger in Corgan, who felt ready to lash out and hit him. But Cyborg broke in, "If you want to look at it that way, then Mendor is my mama too, Brigand. Mendor raised me when I was a little kid back on Nuku Hiva."

"Right, bro. That's how I managed to crash into the program. Your iris identification is still in Mendor's memory, and my iris ID is identical to yours." Brigand laughed, defying them all.

It wouldn't matter if Brigand had disabled Mendor's program, Corgan thought. The Mendor in the cell was just a copycat program of the original Mendor still in Corgan's old virtual-reality Box in the Wyo-DC. But Brigand went on, "So revenge will be mine—as someone said somewhere, sometime. Just wait!"

Empty threats. Brigand was powerless. "Come on, it's time to go," Corgan told him. He yanked Brigand to his feet, announcing, "I'm doing this alone. Just me and Brigand." Shoving him to the door, he turned to say, "The rest of you, please wait here and I'll call you when it's over." He left them standing wide-eyed and apprehensive in Thebos's quarters.

Four more New Rebel Troopers were waiting in the hall. Though yesterday they'd seemed loyal to Brigand, now they started pushing him around. "Stop that," Corgan ordered. "Just bring him into this room."

Inside, the troopers looked with interest at the object braced upright in the center of the room, but Brigand was busy announcing, "I suppose this is when I dispose of all my worldly goods. Ha! I don't have any worldly goods. Except this." He pulled off his shirt, probably because he wanted to show off his cannibal tattoos one last time. After rolling up the shirt, he handed it to one of the troopers, saying, "You can give this little memento to my trusted lieutenant. You know which one."

"Enough talk. Put him in here," Corgan said, indicating the Locker, "but keep holding him." After they'd forced

Brigand inside, Corgan fastened the arm straps and then the metal helmet onto Brigand's head. "Now close the lid," he told the troopers.

"What is this thing?" one of them asked. "Are you going to electrocute him?"

"Just go," Corgan told them. "Shut the door on your way out."

Brigand must have heard the door slam shut. From inside the Locker his muffled voice rang out, "Screw you, Corgan!"

Funny, Corgan thought as he turned on the power. *That's what I said to him once.*

He'd worked out the dates in his head as closely as he could. As the whine of the motor crescendoed, he narrowed his eyes to stare at the dials. Then he threw the switch that turned on the program. The dates whizzed backward almost blindingly fast, just as they'd done for Delphine, for Sharla, for Cyborg, and presumably for Thebos. When the numbers on the dial spun to the date Corgan had chosen, he hit the red button.

Ignoring the screams that came from inside the Locker, he went to Thebos's quarters. "It's done," he told all of them. "You can come in now if you want."

In total silence they followed him to the room, where the screams had diminished to whimpers. "The Locker?" Sharla cried. "He's in the Locker?"

"You Lockered him?" Cyborg asked. "That means he's going to live forever!"

"Right." With hesitation Corgan touched the handle that opened the Locker. What would they think when they saw what he'd done to Brigand? He pulled open the door.

Ananda was the first to react. "Where is he?" she wanted to know, staring at eye level into the Locker. "He's not here!"

"Yes he is. Look down," Corgan answered.

The red-haired baby lay kicking and squirming at the bottom of the Locker, his face contorted with fury as he began to scream again.

"Is that Brigand?" Sharla gasped. "Yes, I can see . . . I remember how he looked when he . . . how old is he?"

"Six months. He'll live forever, but he'll never grow any older," Corgan told them as Cyborg dropped to his knees, staring speechless at his clone-twin, the infant Brigand.

"Why did you make him six months old, Corgan?" Thebos asked quietly.

"Because as an infant he can never hurt anyone again. He's trapped in a body that can't walk or talk."

They seemed stunned as they stared at the red-faced, screaming infant. "Even as a baby he was difficult," Sharla murmured uncertainly. "He demanded attention every minute."

No one looked happy. Maybe what Corgan had chosen for Brigand was too harsh, but it was all over now. His voice strained, he said, "Ananda, would you please call the robotic nurses to come and get this baby? He'll need to be taken care of—for the next hundred years and for eternity."

TWENTY-THREE

Weeks later Ananda sat on the floor cuddling the two Demi clones. Just eight days earlier Sharla and Corgan, Ananda and Cyborg, had stood near the same spot, silent and attentive, distancing themselves a meter and a half from the surrogate mother, Diva, as she gave birth.

For Corgan it had been a miraculous moment. This was how ordinary life began in the real world of people and animals, so much more inspiring than the world Corgan had been born into, where babies got designed inside a test tube and were engineered for desired traits. That unnatural conception was how four of them had started out—Corgan, Sharla, Cyborg, and Brigand. And Brig, too, poor little brilliant Brig, whose flawed genetic engineering had condemned him to a short and painful life. The only one conceived and born naturally was Ananda.

These newborn puppies had been replicated—Delphine had cloned them from Demi—but they hadn't been altered at all from Demi, and the birth was real, two tiny bodies coming out of a living mother. As Diva licked the babies clean, rolling them around on their backs, their tiny squeals sparked emotions Corgan hadn't known he possessed: awe and respect for the beauty of life, along with wonder at the marvel of birth. Even though the newborns' wet coats lay flat against their tiny bodies, he could recognize Demi's markings: black hair all over except for white chests, white legs, and a band of white around their necks. Their muzzles were soft and pink almost all the way to the eyes. They reached out with stiff little legs, stretching their toes as though trying to touch this strange new world that they couldn't yet fathom because their eyes were still shut.

Now, eight days later, they lay nestled in Ananda's arms, still unable to see, but dry and soft and pretty. Diva watched from a box nearby, alert for any sounds or movement from the pups. She allowed no one but Ananda to touch them. As one of the pups yawned, curling its pink tongue, Corgan asked, "So, was it worth it, Ananda—all the trouble we went through to find Diva so she could have Demi's clones for you?"

Hesitant, Ananda answered, "I . . . can't tell for certain. I mean, I feel guilty for loving these precious little puppies as much as I do, because I think of my poor Demi up there in the space station with that weird Nathan, and I wonder if she misses me as much as I miss her. I don't want her to miss me—I want her to be happy, but . . . I'm mixed up about how I feel! Because these cloned puppies really are Demi. Aren't they?"

It was Sharla who went over and gave Ananda a hug, telling her, "It's all right to love the puppies. They're Demi clones, but they're themselves, and each one's a little different." And then, more softly, "It's possible to lose someone you loved, Ananda, and discover that you love someone else even more."

Those words sank into Corgan's consciousness like warm rain onto parched earth. He felt gratified because he knew the words were about him, and he wanted so much to accept them all the way. Maybe he would never be completely sure of Sharla, just as Ananda might always feel a bit of doubt about her love for the new dogs. Still, each of them had to be grateful for what was given to them, and build on it.

Cyborg turned from what he was doing to tell them, "I've sorted through Brigand's things, and take a look at what I found. He was keeping a Chronolog."

They gathered around the screen, with Ananda still holding the puppies. The lines on the screen read:

VIRTUAL WAR CHRONOLOG

The first terrorist attacks	Year 2001
The first plagues	2012
Eleven nuclear accidents	2012–2035
Nuclear wars begin	2038
Worldwide contamination; devastation complete	
Domed cities built to protect survivors	2038–2058

"I never knew he was doing this," Cyborg said. "I wonder when he started writing it."

"I wonder when he finished it," Ananda said. "Look at the next entry, Corgan. It says '2066, Corgan and Sharla are born.'"

The entries continued with a history of Brig's birth, their victory in the Virtual War, Corgan and Sharla's months on Nuku Hiva, and then it read:

> 2081 Sharla clones Brigand and Cyborg in her laboratory. She takes baby Cyborg to Nuku Hiva for Corgan to raise. Four months later, when the clone-twins are about eight years old, Cyborg nearly drowns, but Brigand rescues him by cutting off Cyborg's hand, which was trapped beneath a boulder. *And that is the truth, I swear it! I swear!*

"So that *was* the way it happened, Corgan," Cyborg stated.

His cheeks burning, Corgan answered, "At least Brigand thought so." Had Corgan been wrong all along about the mutilation? He felt a sharp stab of uncertainty. If Brigand, for the noblest of reasons, had actually done what he said in the Chronolog—would it have changed anything? Not for Corgan. He and Brigand would have hated each other just as much, because both of them loved Sharla. But Corgan detested Brigand even more because he was evil incarnate, a treacherous bully who destroyed anyone that stood in his way.

The remainder of the Chronolog was about things that everyone knew: the Wyo-DC revolt, Corgan's escape in the Harrier, Brigand's crash through the dome, Sharla's brain injury. Brigand had even written about the voyage of the

Prometheus to the space station, information he'd somehow managed to gather out of Cyborg's head while Cyborg was orbiting Earth.

They scanned the lines down to the last one. Brigand's final entry read, "Tomorrow I will execute Corgan."

That was it. No more. That final entry made Corgan feel justified that he'd Lockered Brigand—it was self-defense. At least Corgan hadn't murdered him. He never wanted to kill anyone, not ever, no matter what happened. He'd experienced war, and even though it was only a virtual war, the sights and sounds of suffering had cut into his conscience like exploding shrapnel.

It was Cyborg who brought up the question, one that had disturbed Corgan during several restless nights. "Thebos, can I ask you something?" Cyborg began. "When we were on Nuku Hiva, Delphine said she wasn't sure whether the Locker would wipe out a person's memories of things that had happened in their life before they got Lockered. Can you tell us? After you went back to thirty years old, did you forget what you learned between, say, age sixty and age ninety-one?"

Sharla added, "I've been wondering that too. I think all of us have."

"Mmm, it's hard for me to give you a definite answer," Thebos told them, speaking slowly as he glanced from one to the other. "Memory is so inexact, especially among old people. I'm not sure what was in my memory at different stages of my life, but I *have* noticed that I'm starting to remember things I haven't thought of for seventy years or more. Like songs lyrics from when I was in middle school."

Middle school? What was that? Corgan wondered. Before he could ask, Sharla raised a different question. "Thebos, please, can you tell us . . . what about Brigand? He's six months old now, but is it possible he remembers everything that happened in his whole life?"

Cyborg broke in, "Because that would be brutal. To have everything he ever learned and experienced stuck in his mind when he can't walk or talk or anything—that's cruel and unusual punishment! If his brain is still storing all of it, it'll be hell for him, because as a baby, he can't do anything. He's trapped! Helpless!" Cyborg shot a glance at Corgan, the person responsible for Brigand's fate.

"Wait now, wait!" Thebos raised his hand. "We need to think about physiology and neurology. I can't specu-late about Brigand, but I can tell you about my own reactions," he said as he slid quickly into lecture mode. "An old person's brain starts to get holes in it—I don't mean actual holes; I mean that the branches that are sup-posed to come out of the brain cells just aren't there any more. Aging had definitely impaired my ninety-one-year-old brain to a certain extent. Now I've gone back to a younger, more vibrant brain that lets me remember a lot more things, even if they're dumb things like song lyrics and dance steps from my teens. So what it comes down to is that I now have a more operable brain. As to how much I remember from before I was Lockered, I haven't figured that out yet."

Corgan's attention was riveted because he'd been trying to deal with some doubts of his own. Had his punishment for Brigand been—could it have been—too merciless?

"There's a huge difference between a baby's brain and an adult's brain," Thebos went on. "In brain size alone a baby obviously can't store as much information as an adult. So I really doubt that Brigand remembers his life before he was Lockered."

Corgan's sigh of relief was so audible that Sharla squeezed his hand.

"But . . . ," Cyborg stammered, "you're not sure."

"Can't be sure of anything, Cyborg," Thebos told him. "We just don't have enough data to come to any scientific conclusions." He paused, glanced down as though considering something, then told them, "I'm going to share with all of you what I've been tossing around in my own mind since I Lockered myself."

"Hold on just a minute." Ananda returned the puppies to their mother and then joined the rest of them in the circle on the floor. They'd been spending a lot of time together in Thebos's quarters, learning from him while they enjoyed one another's company. It had become a habit for them to arrange themselves in the identical circle: Corgan, then Sharla next to Ananda, then Cyborg, and at the focal point of the perimeter, Thebos.

"Okay, here's what I've been considering," Thebos told them. "After we get the Flor-DC straightened out and running again, I'd like to do some reverse engineering on the Locker and find out if I can change its operation. The way it works now, when you're Lockered, you get frozen into one age forever. Maybe I can rework it so that after you get Lockered, you can go forward again if you want to and mature naturally from that age on."

Cyborg brightened. "Then Brigand could grow up to be a normal kid!"

No way on Earth, Corgan wanted to yell. It didn't matter what age Brigand might grow to, he'd always be a savage ready to annihilate anyone who opposed him. Corgan was about to say that when he looked up and saw the hope in Cyborg's eyes.

The words of protest died on Corgan's tongue. If Cyborg wanted to pretend that his clone-twin was redeemable, Corgan would not destroy the illusion. Instead he gave a little half nod in Cyborg's direction.

Turning away, he told himself that it was time to forget Brigand and concentrate on his own future. His and Sharla's.

He crossed the room to pick up the i-pen beside the screen, where Brigand's Chronolog still glowed. "August 15, 2082," he wrote. "Corgan and Sharla will fly the *Prometheus* to the Wyoming domed city."

Sharla smiled at him. Tugging at his fingers, she took the i-pen, leaned over the screen, and added, "Where they will remain happily ever after, except for a few tours through the universe."

That was it. The Virtual War Chronologs had ended. Now all of them would begin the task of rebuilding Earth, trying to help the human race grow strong again.

"Save this Chronolog," Corgan said to his friends. "The world needs to remember."

THE END

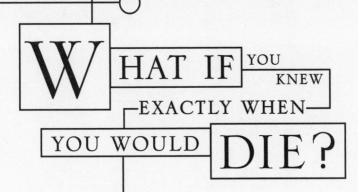
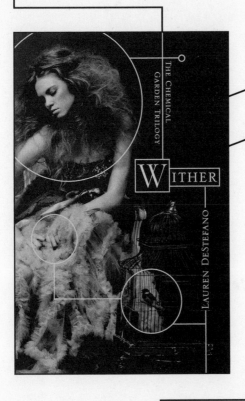

An unlikely romance.

A terrifying dream world.

One final chance for survival.

Nevermore

KELLY CREAGH

EBOOK EDITION ALSO AVAILABLE

From Atheneum Books for Young Readers

TEEN.SimonandSchuster.com

Ancient secrets. Deadly danger.

Dark Reflections

THE WATER MIRROR ✦ THE STONE LIGHT ✦ THE GLASS WORD

KAI MEYER

FROM MARGARET K. McELDERRY BOOKS
TEEN.SimonandSchuster.com

A THRILLING FANTASY TRILOGY OF DANGER AND ADVENTURE FROM THREE-TIME NEWBERY HONOR WINNER NANCY FARMER!

★ "A tale of high adventure and exploration that reads with unexpected sensitivity, warmth, and humor."
—*Bulletin of the Center for Children's Books* on *The Sea of Trolls*, STARRED REVIEW

★ "[Draws] readers into this complex world and [leaves] them looking forward to more."
—*School Library Journal* on *The Land of the Silver Apples*, STARRED REVIEW

★ "Farmer's richly imagined saga is filled with danger, action, [and] delightful comedy."
—*Booklist* on *The Islands of the Blessed*, STARRED REVIEW